KU-189-373

JOAN EADITH OMNIBUS

Hospital Girls
A Very Loud Voice

JOAN EADITH

timewarner
paperbacks

A *Time Warner* Paperback

This omnibus edition first published in Great Britain by
Time Warner Paperbacks in 2006
Joan Eadith Omnibus Copyright © Joan Eadith 2005

Previously published separately:
Hospital Girls first published in Great Britain in 1995
by Little, Brown and Company
Published in 1996 by Warner Books
Reprinted 1997
Copyright © Joan Eadington 1995

A Very Loud Voice first published in Great Britain in 1997
by Little, Brown and Company
Published by Warner Books in 1998
Copyright © Joan Eadington 1997

The moral right of the author has been asserted.

A CIP catalogue record for this book
is available from the British Library.

ISBN-13: 978-0-7515-3777-2
ISBN-10: 0-7515-3777-2

Printed and bound in Great Britain by
Clays Ltd, St Ives plc

Time Warner Paperbacks
An imprint of
Time Warner Book Group UK
Brettenham House
Lancaster Place
London WC2E 7EN

www.twbg.co.uk

Hospital Girls

To my agent Robert Tauber for all his continuing sound advice and cheerful kindness. He helped me on to the very first rung of this literary ladder to reach this fifth book.

JOAN EADITH

CONTENTS

I

LEAVING HOME

Never was there such a change as that which took over Manchester when the Second World War began. Schoolgirl trips to the upstairs dining-room in Hill's Tripe Shop to gobble up a tempting three course meal for one shilling and sixpence, followed by a mooch round Lewis's department store to stare at all the glitter, were suddenly buried. Buried, not by bombs but by a change in the population. Manchester was no longer a lady-shoppers' paradise. It was bulging with uniforms from every armed service: Britain, Australia, New Zealand, Poland, France and the United States of America.

The password was 'NAAFI Canteen'. Military police in their flat, red-topped hats, white blancoed cross-webbing and white belts, marched sturdily round the city in case a soldier suddenly went berserk in a pub and began hurling beer glasses. It was a time when young women, genuinely waiting to meet their great grandmothers outside London Road Railway Station, were regularly insulted by suggestions that they might have been waiting for something entirely different, and were asked to show their identity cards by women inspectors. The whole civilian population was kept on the move; except in Piccadilly Gardens where the old Royal Infirmary had once been. Here life had come to a complete standstill as bodies of fighting men and their girlfriends lay locked together on the grass in view to all.

May Greenrigg was making herself a hat for the hospital interview. She had cut the brim off a bottle green one of her mother's and had stitched some brown hen feathers in a small border all round the crown. It looked awful, but it also looked patriotic – a sign of wartime, make-do and mend. She also wore her mother's imitation black astrakhan coat and her aunt's old shoes. She felt on top of the world. Her face glowed from washing with Pears Soap. Her chestnut hair shone courtesy of a threepenny packet of Glamour Girl Shampoo. She even wore cream cotton gloves and salmon-pink, artificial silk stockings. She was delighted to have been accepted to train as a nurse. Having never been ill in her life, and never been a patient in hospital, she wondered what she would do if she ever had to see a man without clothes; white marble statues of men wearing fig leaves were the only kind of naked men she had seen. Her mother was a widow.

She arrived at St Alphonso's in Bell Lane on time and with five minutes to spare.

'A hospital,' said a tall angular matron named Throstle in her purple, long-sleeved frock with white muslin collar and cuffs, 'a hospital is a *special* world. A hospital knows no ordinary boundaries, or prejudices. A hospital cares for all human beings regardless of creed or colour. Hospitals are places where everyone's job is geared to preserving and repairing human life.'

There were ten females in front of the Matron. They were sitting there like hypnotised rabbits, on bleak wooden chairs, dressed by permission of clothing coupons and ingenuity. All except two elderly nuns of about twenty-seven. They were already attired like nurses, in navy blue coats. Their dark serge caps revealed straight hair sawn off half-way across their ears – uglier than any man could manage. They wore heavy flat-soled shoes accompanied by thick grey stockings. One had a very cheerful, smiling but bony face. The other had smaller, rather prim features and appeared calm and aloof.

May was quite intrigued. She had never seen nuns out of their black and white robes before. Fancy them being here at Saint Alphonso's , she thought. It heralded a certain respectability before they'd even started.

She stared across at another girl who was dressed like the Queen, in a crimson felt hat with a large heavy halo. The girl was small and plump and dark with bright eyes. She clutched the handle of a bulky handbag like some ancient grandmother but was no more than eighteen. Of the others two were Irish, and the other five, including May herself, were from the environs of Manchester.

St Alphonso's, commonly known as Bell Lane, was one of the largest hospitals on the west side of the city. A

3

bomb had already resulted in the death of one of its well-loved and respected doctors. From the outside it was a dreadful looking three-storeyed, soot-stained, red-brick monolith. Its sister building, just across the road, was attached to it like an umbilical cord. This was the Workhouse, where the poor, destitute and old still worked their hours away – care of Manchester Corporation.

The only saving grace of both places was a municipal pride in well-planned patches of garden. Along the front entrance roads the grass at Bell Lane was as smooth as a billiard table. The flowers in regimental rows of bright blues, reds and yellows, bordered with evergreen shrubs, were never to be picked or even smelt. Even so they gave a sense of pattern, and well-tended security.

In spite of the external gloom of all the buildings (eleven terrible blocks, with awful back yards revealing iron fire escapes to each floor, grim as prisons) Bell Lane had in its extensive grounds a brand new training school for nurses, converted from an older building. Along the main inner road close to the mortuary, the laundry and the Hospital Chapel, it was called the PTS which stood for Preliminary Training School. Inside, it shone with modernism.

Inside the building was painted in shining shades of pale green. Apart from the actual rooms termed the Training School, other space was designed as a new Nurses' Home, complete with kitchens and ironing boards.

The nursing profession was entering uneasy times. Florence Nightingale and her team of helpers from wealthy families who had often been aided by ladies with self-supporting incomes had disappeared, nearly 80 years ago. Nursing was now tottering between the old and the new. But the old days of gentility still held sway, in terms of financial power. Some hospitals in Manchester still charged the nurses money to train, and parents had to pay for their uniforms. Parents were glad to do it as it signified their own respectability and a good personal income. Their girls would be mixing with the right people, in a teaching hospital full of handsome, well-educated medical students, and every mother still lived in hope.

Almost all nurses lived in the hospital; they spent nearly all their lives there. They worked from half-past seven in the morning until half-past eight at night, with a three hour break. There was one day off and one half day a week. They were watched from on high with eagle-like precision. Lights went out at half-past ten and all women were supposed to be inside, locked up, and in their own single beds.

Once you entered the place all fripperies of an idly spent youth vanished. Adventures of rather spoilt fifteen-year-old girls missing the last bus home from dances and having no money for taxis, whilst they rang kind fathers to come with a car to fetch them home were nothing but a rash dream.

Even the Matron and the Hospital Medical Super-intendent, Dr Frome, had private living quarters within this closed society. But their rooms and those of the other doctors were secret places to the humble nursing staff. Any nurse entering this territory was immediately expelled in permanent disgrace before they could reveal anything.

Once, when some American Army Doctors were staying at the hospital for a few days, and had been invited to a social where ordinary nurses were present, two of the girls were invited to a reciprocal gathering by two of the American doctors to this territory. The nurses were never nurses again. It was whispered there had been an on the spot dismissal the following morning. Rumours that they had been raped or even murdered were scotched when one was seen working in the aircraft department at Metrovicks. She revealed that they had been frozen out the moment they passed the threshold. The other one had gone to work in her father's clothing factory on Work Of National Importance.

The heavy double door with its two grey stone steps, which those two innocents had dared to challenge, leading to this unknown sanctuary of virtue or vice, was set half way along the main ground floor corridor, on the opposite side to every other door and opening. No one knew where it actually led or how it was planned, but all the time they wondered. Did the great ones have plain, box-like dressing tables, beds with standard black tubular steel frames and thin, washed-out looking flock mattresses? Were they, in The Territory, allowed to have pictures and pin-ups on their walls? The nursing staff in the rest of the hospital, in the old and new Nurses' Homes, certainly were not!

It was not until the following November that the girls in May Greenrigg's group were to find out the awful truth about this hidden world.

There were four fresh batches of would-be student nurses each year. But there was a heavy drop-out rate.

Many dedicated and enthusiastic, starry-eyed creatures, who felt they had been specially called to the profession, had second thoughts, often within the first three months before the written examination took place. Examinations were high on the hospital list. There was also one at the end of the second year. It was essential to pass each exam in order to go ahead for the third year finals of both Hospital and General Nursing Council. All studying had to be done in a nurse's frugal spare time. There were no 'terms' for nurses bolstered by months or weeks of freedom in between.

The exam at the end of the first three months was to make sure all the girls knew the parts of the human body and where they were located, starting with the bones. They also studied First Aid with the help of a jaundiced-looking dummy. They learned how to do complicated bandaging for all occasions, and they were shown how to make all manner of special beds with specific pillow arrangements and blanket requirements according to different illnesses. Such things as learning how to dust and sweep the wards and clean the bathrooms, lavatories and sluices were learnt on the wards, along with emptying and disinfecting spittoons, bottles and bedpans.

The girls were led to the sewing rooms to be measured for their uniforms. Then they were allowed to go home and wait until the following week when their uniforms would be ready and they would be starting their careers. But first, before they left, they had just been given a cup of weak tea and a digestive biscuit.

The two nuns spoke little except to Sister Sorenson, the Sister Tutor who wore a starched, ribboned bonnet with a bow under the chin and a scarlet petersham belt with an ornate silver clasp at the front. Her Bell Lane Hospital training badge was displayed on her bosom. All trained nurses had two badges: their silver and blue State Registered Nurse badge with the name and date of qualifying on the back, and their hospital badge which varied in style according to where they had trained. This hospital badge was a record of having passed all the hospital examinations.

The nuns were known only as Downs and Nulty. Downs, the cheerful one, came from County Armagh and turned out to be popular and quite humorous. But Nulty was very cool and starchy. No one ever knew their first names. This was typical since as soon as nurses began training they too became surnames only. Liz, Shirley, Queenie, May, Dizzy, Ada, Dorothea and Karina were soon supplanted by Frankel, O'Malley, Marney, Greenrigg, Oaklands, Sawbridge, Philips and Stewart.

The rest of the girls in the room hovered about, keeping well out of earshot of the sister. The two Irish ones, Shirley O'Malley and Queenie Marney, talked between themselves. The girl in the crimson halo, whose name was Frankel, was hovering uncertainly on her own in the background nibbling a biscuit. The others chattered at random to anyone who would join in. Someone who said her name was Dizzy Oaklands soon became the life and soul of the party, even though she was apt to sniff and cough and wipe her nose on her sleeve because she had lost her handkerchief.

'It was stuffed up my knicker leg but it's completely vanished. I was nearly late,' she snorted in a loud voice. 'Just imagine being late in this place. They'd probably get the handcuffs out.' After this she accidentally crushed a digestive biscuit underfoot and caught the sharp gaze of Sister Sorenson as she tried to scoop it up. Sister Sorenson turned away with a sad inward sigh. Mentally she gave Miss Oaklands a mere week to last out.

Another girl, Ada Sawbridge, who had brightly-painted red fingernails, was nearly going to smoke a cigarette but put it back hastily in her mother-of-pearl cigarette case when she found there were no ashtrays. She was already waning. She had left a good job working at the District Bank in Manchester because she felt she wanted to help people more. But it did all seem as if it was going to be *very* restrictive.

May Greenrigg was glad to leave it all and get home again. She had two single-decker, red and cream buses to catch to carry her back to Croftsbank Road where she lived. Her home was the top half of a shabby mansion which was divided into two flats. The owner, forty-five-year-old Mr Rooks, whose wife had died long ago, lived in the bottom half.

May, and her younger sister Coral, who was still at school, lived with their widowed mother. Their mother had worked for Mr Rooks as his typist for years. He had a small factory which produced liquid washing soap.

Barry Rooks had been attracted to Lotty Greenrigg the moment she came enquiring about the flat, with her two very young daughters by her side. His quick mind had quickly summed up the potential of an attractive woman who readily paid him in advance for the flat.

Within three months of her arrival he had asked her to marry him. But this was not before she had been duped into doing all his washing under the pretext of testing the soap. Then this extended to carrying heavy zinc buckets of water about to test-wash the floors, the bannister rails, the doors and kitchen walls.

'The two of us, with you as my chief tester when you marry me,' pleaded Barry, 'the two of us could be worth a million in a couple of years' time.'

Lotty Greenrigg had never taken up his tempting offer. Her lips remained firmly closed to kisses. She suggested he got all his washing sent to the laundry and saw how *their* cleaning agents worked. She told him to keep on with his regular charlady but had shrewdly suggested she might be available to do some typing for him for a decent price, and a reduction of rent. And that was how it had always stayed.

Liz Frankel went into Manchester and caught the train back to Little Ditchfield. She had come to England as a schoolgirl refugee just before the war, and was placed with a very rigid couple who already had some children of their own. They meant well but preached hell-fire sermons: it was agony for a young girl bereft of family who had suffered a real hell already. The one advantage of being with them was that she now spoke excellent English, with perfect grammar and a mild accent.

She gave thanks, now, for being able to leave the rigid family, for now at least she would be a person in her own right. This loneliness was far better than the last sort.

As she sat there in the jolting railway carriage, the haunting vision of her own parents and her own young sister came into her mind. That terrifying evening in her own country when they had been interrogated by a sheepish official who was listing all the people in the town who were Jews. Embedded in her mind was the scene of their comfortable sitting-room in an ordinary house. Her ten-year-old sister Mima. Her darling mother and her solemn-faced but kindly father. They knew the man who was compiling the list; he was one of their neighbours. He was terribly ashamed and apologetic and said to her father: 'I will mark only you down as Jewish, Nathan, and no one else. Your wife Ruth is not a proper Jew. I will not list her.'

The two men looked hard at each other.

Nathan Frankel knew the man was doing his best to try to save his wife and children. He half nodded his head. But in seconds his wife was standing beside him holding his hand. 'I *am* a Jew!' she cried. How can you pretend, when you know us so well? When we have been friends and neighbours and your children and our children have played together. When our children have been in the same school with Adolf Hitler staring down from the same classroom wall. How can you deny me my roots? What is happening to this country we were all born in?'

Shortly afterwards Liz had been sent off alone to an organisation which helped refugees. At first she had cried and refused to go, but her mother had implored her – her own face swollen with tiredness and weeping. 'At least you will survive, my cherished daughter. You are fortunate in being able to speak some English. At least there may be *one* of us. Perhaps if we get through this terrible war we might all meet again in happiness. There is only this one chance left to us at present, my child. Not money.

Nothing except our love and your own intelligence and determination. Our only property is this house we live in. And what will happen to that in these days, even if it survives the bombing?'

The very next day Liz was sent away on the road of escape. But within a few days news came through to her that her mother and father and young sister had been rounded up with others in the town square, ready to be moved like cattle to Auschwitz concentration camp.

Meanwhile she was shipped to England by the organisation who helped refugees. It was they who had dressed her up in the crimson-haloed hat and provided her with the handbag. 'This is what the right people wear,' someone said.

Many of the group May was in had lost parents. Dorothea (Dotsy Philips) was another one. She had been brought up in India, and been sent over to England to a boarding school. After this, she had lived with an aunt and uncle in Sale and was now nursing. Her father, an army officer, had died of cancer in India; her mother had stayed out there. She had been looked after by her ayah who was her nanny when she was young. Her ayah was now middle aged and still lived in India with Dotsy's mother.

There was also Ada Sawbridge who was an only child and an orphan. She was at least twenty-two and had a rich boy-friend. With Karina Stewart it was the loss of a mother. Her mother had died of tuberculosis in the Bell Hospital after a life on the stage as a dancer. But it was not all sadness; both Shirley O'Malley and Queenie Marney came from large boisterous families, as did Dizzy Oaklands from

Gatley who had five sisters and an older brother who was in a Reserved Occupation as a research chemist.

The following week, when the girls all met again to start their training, they were arrayed in their blue cotton, short-sleeved hospital frocks with a three tucks border round their skirts for shortening or lengthening. No skirt was allowed to be less than twelve inches from the floor.

'We have short sleeves all the time, because we're up to our elbows in the muckiest work,' said Dizzy Oaklands one day. 'Just you notice how the Staff Nurses all have special removable lengths so that they can either have long sleeves when standing in for Sister, or short sleeves when they are busy scrubbing up and doing the dressings on the ward.'

The girls were also given a scarlet wool hospital cape and a supply of white caps. After surviving the first three months, every person had one white horizontal tape mark on their sleeves – near their shoulder to show they were now first year student nurses. Second years had two marks, and third years three.

All the nurses flocked off duty in groups. The Sister, the fully qualified Staff Nurse, the third year Nurse, the second year Nurse and the first year Nurse. There were also state enrolled nurses and nursing auxiliaries. Movement at the end of the day in the gathering dusk at Bell Lane was of small red, white, and blue processions, often led by a fragile, elderly nursing sister in a starched white apron, a white crest of a head-dress, a navy blue cotton frock with long sleeves, stiff white cuffs and narrow-buttoned, shiny starched dog-collar.

The following week the girls were unpacking their

suitcases in the bedrooms allocated. The rooms were close together on the first floor at the top of a flight of ancient stone stairs. The stairs were modernised with a bronze-coloured steel bannister.

May and Liz were in the corner room 10, just at the top. Ada, Dotsy and Dizzy were opposite in number 15, close to a small kitchen-cum-ironing room. Karina, Shirley and Queenie were a few yards along the corridor, near the bathroom, in room 21.

May and Liz hesitated as they stood in their room. It had a very high ceiling. They each had a wooden locker, a single wardrobe and the usual tubular iron bedstead. A utility chest of drawers was near the window, and there was a washbasin with a small mirror above it, along with a wooden chair each.

'Which bed do you want?' said May.

'Ooh . . . I don't mind.' Liz smiled and was silent.

'I'll have the one nearest the door then,' said May.

'Are you sure? Would you not like the one closest to the window?' Liz said hesitantly.

'No. It's an advantage in a way to be nearer the door. It'll probably get me up earlier when we're called in the mornings. Or if I wanted to get in the bathroom before anyone else. Or getting in to bed quickly at night.'

They both nodded to each other.

'Dizzy Oaklands has already tried to work out a plan for getting into the hospital without being seen if she happens to be late,' laughed May. 'If the Night Sister finds out you get reported to Matron. Sometimes people get kicked out. Ada Sawbridge is already saying she doesn't know whether she'll be able to stick it.'

Liz nodded. 'I will just have to stick it.' Then she said: 'I will have the bottom drawer of the dressing table and you can have the top one. Would you mind if I put a family photograph on top of the dressing table?' Slowly she drew a silver-framed photograph out of her bulky leather handbag. 'It's of my father and mother and me and my sister in Germany when we were once on holiday.' She stared at the photograph for a few seconds then placed it methodically to one side on the top of the dressing table. 'It's terrible to think I shall never see them again.' She muttered the words half to herself.

May watched her fleetingly. She nearly said: 'Oh – you'll be sure to see them again . . .' then stopped in her tracks. She knew it was a shallow thing to say. The war was doing horrific things to people. Instead she said cheerfully: 'Put up as many photos as you want. I don't mind at all. I haven't brought much. I don't live far away. I thought I'd see what sort of a room it was first. I expect I can cram most things in the wardrobe, though I might bring a pair of bookends from home to put along the window ledge, if it's allowed.'

The two girls settled in without much trouble. Liz stayed in the room and looked through the work they had to study, and at their timetables for meals, and the list of hospital rules.

May wandered along to see what Dizzy Oaklands, Ada Sawbridge and Dotsy, were doing. She found they were all parading round the bedroom laughing, with their capes on. Open suitcases were scattered about, there were clothes and books all over the place. Dizzy had put her hood over her head and had stuck some cotton wool round her chin like Father Christmas. She turned towards May. 'And what would *you* like for Christmas, my dear?'

'Err . . .' May was taken aback. She lived quite a quiet life with her young sister and widowed mother. She would not have dared to stick cotton wool on her chin the minute she arrived.

'Sit down on that bed and take no notice of her,' said Dotsy Philips laughing. 'Would you like some coffee?' She found a cup with a green and gold border and a chip in it. 'I didn't bring any really good ones. My aunt and uncle would have had a fit. Decent cups are scarce these days.' She found some coffee which was bottled in the same way as brown sauce. It was really coffee and chicory, but it was much cheaper than pure coffee. Then she went into the kitchen and filled up the cup with boiling water from her own small metal teapot which she had filled from the geyser. There were three hospital tin-openers in the kitchen drawer so she was able to open one of the six small tins of condensed milk she had brought with her.

The laughter rising into the corridor from room 15 was getting louder and louder. Then just as Dotsy was carrying back the cup of coffee and the condensed milk there was a sudden silence. A grey-garbed home sister was standing there stiffly in the doorway of the bedroom. It was Home Sister Axton, chief sister of the three who supervised the nursing staff. She stared at Dizzy Oakland's cotton wool beard.

'Nurse!' she said in a voice chilled like the North Pole. 'Get that rubbish off your face at once!'

There was a silence. Everyone was transfixed.

'All I can say is, I sincerely hope all that cotton wool is your own property. If I thought for one moment it came from this hospital, you would go to Matron and be dismissed immediately!' Then she turned away, her face as grim as a hatchet, and marched off.

After an uneasy silence Ada Sawbridge said: 'She must be joking – surely? We're not just little kids.'

'But that's just the point, Ada,' said Dotsy Philips. 'She thinks we are, because of us all acting the goat.'

'Surely we can have a bit of fun in our own bedroom?'

'Not with cotton wool we can't,' said Dizzy, slowly removing it. 'She's just trying to get at us. I'll bet they use loads of hospital cotton wool at Christmas. It was just that we were a bit early with it.'

By this time Queenie, Shirley and Karina had arrived from room 21 to crowd in with the others and find out what was going on. Soon the whole place was bubbling up again and the noise became uproarious as arguments about cotton wool were bellowed across the bedroom . . .

'Put it on again Diz, just to show the others. She put it on with soap. Stick it back on, Dizzy.'

Dizzy put the beard back on again and every one collapsed about in laughter.

But not for long, as the door knob rattled and this time not one home sister but two grey-clad women stood there. One was Sister Axton again and the other was Miss Grange the Assistant Matron, a thin person of few words.

Immediately Dizzy dropped like a stone between two of the beds, rolled underneath and began to scratch off the cotton wool. The other girls lined up hastily in front of the beds in a neat row with expressionless faces, and Queenie

Marney hastily wiped tears of laughter from her eyes with the back of her hand.'

Miss Grange surveyed the scene with quiet dignity. She had a very precise, unemotional way of speaking. Her face was like an oil painting. The pink colour and the expression never varied. No one could ever have imagined her as a normal person in ordinary clothes.

All she said was: 'There is far too much noise coming from this room. You must always remember the other nurses. There are senior nurses in this block who are on night duty. One day you will be in their position.' She left the room without another word, followed by Sister Axton.

In subdued fashion everyone went back to their own rooms, leaving Ada, Dotsy and Dizzy to continue sorting out their suitcases.

When May got back to her own room Liz was sitting upright on her bed with her back resting on two pillows against the iron tubular frame. She was reading *Anatomy and Physiology*. She looked up, smiled and said: 'Have they all got settled in?'

'Didn't you hear all the noise?' May said with amazement.

'No?'

May began to describe it all, and Liz's face lit up into a smile. She got off the bed and put her books away. 'Shall we go for a walk round the hospital grounds?'

May nodded. Suddenly she was glad they had Dizzy Oaklands in their lot. At least it would never be all work and gloom and war with her about.

2

THE FIRST DIP

'Fancy us being the only group this year who've kept together without anyone leaving,' murmured May to Liz as they queued up in the dining-room for their early morning breakfasts.

The porridge being dished out was the sort commonly described as 'lining your guts'. It had been boiled for hours and was flecked with tough, scratchy husks and brown speckles. It was served with a ladle from a steel drum by one of the night sisters who dolloped it onto thick plates. On each of the long, heavy deal tables there were large white enamel jugs with dark blue edges full of thin, pale watery milk. The tables had bulging brown-painted wooden legs and were littered with jam jars and small, open tins. Each tin or jar had the name of the owner on it. They were sugar rations. Everyone got a weekly loose sugar ration to use for food or drinks. Some people saved it. Others finished it off too soon. Others carried saccharine tablets about as artificial sweeteners. (They were minute white tablets which dissolved immediately with a slight frothy residue. They were said to be a by-product of coal.)

Liz had transferred some of her sugar to a small brown paper bag with her own spoon inside, and she measured it out methodically and carefully, but May never used any and left hers to accumulate. Every so often she took what she saved back home to her mother. All the girls had started their first three months on the wards. May and Liz were on what was known as the Chronic Block.

'It's to start you off in a safe place where you can't do too much damage,' said Dizzy Oaklands, cheekily.

'Talk about the kettle calling the pan!' gasped May. 'Where have they dared to send you then?'

'Male Surgical,' said Dizzy proudly. 'With Dotsy Philips and Ada Sawbridge.'

There were four chronic wards: two male and two female in the oldest part of the hospital, set away from the busy 'acute' blocks. The mens' wards had a sprinkling of elderly male nursing attendants besides the female nurses. These were to help with heavy weights and men's ailments and urinary conditions.

Some patients on both male and female chronic blocks had been there for years and had survived because of very good and conscientious nursing care. But some of the medical conditions were very sad.

May and Liz were put on 12MLS which stood for Male Long-Stay. Most of the patients had no other home, and needed nursing care even though they were capable of moving about.

Mr Lively, the State Registered Nurse in charge, was lively in name and nature. He was a married man with two children and lived away from the hospital, which was a rarity. Before the soldiers arrived, it was the only ward in the whole of the hospital which was not governed by old-fashioned starchiness.

The moment the two girls arrived they felt at ease.

His first words were: 'You two can go into the day room and help Paul here, to make some cards for every one to play housy housy, this afternoon.' Paul was a boy who had been on the ward for years. He was small and tubby and good natured with dark hair, rather pop-eyes, a snub nose and steel-rimmed glasses. Eagerly Paul led them to the day room, where the bingo cards were being prepared. Each card had to have the name of the patient on it. It was a very good way of finding out the names of everyone and where their beds were. (People were in small rooms containing four to ten beds.)

By the end of their first day with Mr Lively Liz and May had got to know the run of the whole of 12MLS and where everything was. They had helped with the medicine list, helped with some baths and they had dusted and tidied lockers. They had also played a game of housy housy.

'On *my* ward, the care, comfort and happiness of the patient comes before making the corners of every counterpane exactly ninety degrees for the matron's round,' stressed Mr Lively. 'Many of the people here have no other place to go. Some have come over from the Workhouse.'

Later that evening, when all the girls were back in the

nurses' home talking about the day, May and Liz realised how lucky they'd been to start off in the happy atmosphere of Mr Lively's ward.

'How did all you others get on?' laughed May.

Dizzy gave a great groan of despair: 'I'm dreading going back to Male Surgical with Sister Mackonicky tomorrow. The minute we walked on the ward she was like a jailer. She gave us instructions and warnings about our work with never a glimmer of kindness in her face.' Dizzy looked at Dorothea: 'Isn't that right, Dotsy? To put it crudely she was bloody hell.' Dizzy stared up at the ceiling with a bleak expression. Dotsy Philips and Ada Sawbridge nodded their heads in agreement.

'And she isn't even old!' said Dizzy. 'Anyone can see she's a real little self-centred dictator. She's just mad with power. And the Staff Nurse was even worse – wasn't she Ada?'

Twenty-two-year-old Ada nodded again and opened a packet of Craven A cigarettes with slim shapely fingers. She had rather a husky voice and always seemed quietly sophisticated. 'Mackonicky's very small and Staff Nurse Trencher's like a tall telegraph pole. They were as thick as thieves together.' She offered the cigarettes round but no one else smoked. In any case there was a secret unspoken feeling that smoking was completely banned there – for girls under twenty-one.

They all watched her with slight awe. She owned a beaver lamb fur coat, and her man-friend still managed to drive a large black Humber in spite of petrol rationing, when most people had put their cars in cold storage until the war ended.

'Are you sure no one wants a ciggy?' Ada took a deep luxurious breath, then coughed. 'Even our ratty old bank manager at the District Bank was more polite than those two on that ward.'

Dizzy Oakland's face was still a picture of misery. 'I shall never last out with them. She made me re-dust every single locker and bed rail, then told me off because my cap went askew. But as soon as that Doctor Livingstone arrived into the duty room, she and Trencher were in there with the door shut drinking tea, eating biscuits and cackling like a pair of geese.'

'Dizzy's quite right,' said Dotsy with a sigh as she manicured her neat finger nails. 'I happened to tap at the closed duty room door to ask Staff Nurse Trencher where the thermometer tray was, and if looks could kill I'd be a gonner right now. They were eating Marie biscuits as if it was the end of the world and grinning like Cheshire cats. They couldn't close the door on me quick enough. I hope I never grow like that.'

'Don't you worry, Diz,' said Dotsy. 'The only good thing is it's not just you she picks on. She gave me a look as cold as icicles in the sluice when I accidentally opened the shanks at the wrong time and all water sprayed out from round the bed pan.'

Karina Stewart just sat there quietly and smiled. She thanked her stars that she'd been on Female Medical with Sister Kinnon and Staff Nurse Dawson. They were absolute darlings. Sister Kinnon was plump with a fresh pink and white face and metal grey hair. She had a soft soothing Celtic accent and a deep sense of humour born of wisdom. She looked after her young student nurses like a kind mother hen – just as she did with her patients.

Shirley O'Malley and Queenie Marney had been on Female Gynaecology. 'We never even had time to breath,' said Shirley. 'It's the land of douches and no mistake. But Sister was all right, wasn't she Queenie?'

Queenie nodded. Secretly it had come as a great shock to her to see so many women suffering from miscarriages and illnesses connected with their reproductive systems; and to hear from talk on the ward that the other half of the world was composed of rotters who were men. Her own mother and father seemed to get on quite well, in spite of her mother looking after a big family. And Queenie loved her father. It all depended on where you were seeing it from. She frowned slightly. Was she or wasn't she going to be able to survive it all as a nurse?

Shirley was made of sterner stuff. Hers was not to reason why. She listened and saw and was always in the group, but much of the time she kept her own council. On the wards she moved round with brisk, stern good sense. She was never a gossip. The barbs from people like Sister Mackonicky rolled off her like water off a duck's back. Never once did she doubt that with God's care she would become a fully-fledged State Registered Nurse – and perhaps one day – even be the Matron of her own private nursing home. But she did not waste too much time with idle dreams, she just got on with it.

The soldiers had arrived, almost by stealth.

Convoys of wounded had come in throughout the night like silent marauders. The whole pattern of the hospital was changed in a few hours. It was as if a magic wand had been waved. No longer was it a heavily-weighted female domain still tied to out-dated Victorian severity.

To May Greenrigg it was a strange situation. Part of another spinning world was touching the surface of the old hospital like the rasp of coarse sandpaper. Everywhere you went soldiers were wandering in and out through the lodge gates, some in ordinary khaki, others in bright blue, armed forces sick bay suits and white cotton shirts and red ties.

Men on crutches were now a common sight in the hospital corridors. Men with limbs in plaster, men with aeroplane splints for fractured collar bones, which meant that an arm was fixed like a bent wing at shoulder level; soldiers with bandages being wheeled to X-ray, others being pushed on stretchers by nurses and male orderlies to the operating theatre.

Soon all the girls were moved to different wards again as part of their training. This time it included the nursing of the war wounded soldiers, and night duty.

May Greenrigg had already faced the shock of seeing her first male private parts, on a male medical ward as she handed a man a urine bottle to use. It came as quite a shock to her to see the dark hairy undergrowth of his pubic regions. Especially as in normal circumstances the human body (of both sexes) was discretely covered up so that only the portion relevant to an injury or complaint was showing. This gave greater dignity to both the nursing staff and the patient. Even someone having their bottom rubbed to prevent bed-sores would have the sheets draped carefully round the place, so that all areas were as depersonalised as a piece of jigsaw puzzle.

This first man who casually gave the game away to eighteen-year-old May was tall, dark and handsome with a lovely smile. Until one day he lifted his smile from his mouth and let it rest in a tooth mug. It was the complete initiation ceremony.

3

THE BED SOCK

Greenrigg and Frankel had lost their first names. It was a sign of being truly in the throes of nursing. From now on the whole group hardly met each other during working hours as they were moved to different wards. One might be on Casualty whilst another was on Female Medical, or even in some entirely different hospital. During their training, the girls spent three months at Booth Hall Children's Hospital on the other side of the city. On night duty too – which was another three month period when they were split up. In this way they met many more nurses from other groups – some who became lifelong friends. Nevertheless, once they were off duty they still remained together at lectures, exams, and in the nurses' home.

There were distinct advantages to never working with your best friends. May Greenrigg soon found that some people were completely different characters in private life to the way they were within the restrictive discipline of the wards. Often, she thought, the ward work brought out their worst points as far as intermingling with their friends went.

May felt completely alone when the soldiers suddenly arrived. There was only one shining star – the young and highly competent Sister Millston.

It was strange to come on duty in the gloom of early morning to find the ward full of quietness and injured men. A glass trolley stood covered in sterile cotton towels. In any other setting it could have been a tea trolley laden with anything from knives and forks to cakes containing artificial cream. But on a hospital ward, at this particular moment, it signified something entirely new.

The towels which covered the trolley were like small oblong tea towels threaded with a check line of pink thread. Every towel had to stand the test of being relaundered and packed into specially designed metal boxes with handles. These boxes were, along with other metal drums full of dressings and swabs, placed daily in a huge steel oven of gigantic size in the Autoclave Department which was full of pipes and clock-faced temperature gauges. The drums and their contents were then sterilised at very high temperatures.

Sister Millston took some Cheetal forceps which were standing in a stainless steel holder full of Dettol on the lower glass shelf of the trolley and lifted the covering cotton towels away. The top tier revealed some steel trays set with sterile syringes and needles, with some small bowls of cotton wool swabs and some empty stainless steel, kidney-shaped receivers. There were also two or three small, dark brown glass containers about three inches high. They were topped with flat, screw-type black lids. Under the lids was a covering of brown rubber bordered with light aluminium alloy. Each bottle was just over half full with strong looking deep yellow liquid.

'This is the new drug: Penicillin,' said Sister Millston in undertones. 'It has to be given by intramuscular injection. It's the first time it has been used here and is only for the soldiers at present.'

Later in the morning Sister Millston took May with her, whilst she and Staff Nurse Royston went round with the dressings' trolley. They always started in the main ward with the most serious and needed dressings first. May was asked to put the screens round the bed of a young paratrooper named Croxton. He was lying there, his young round face as white as a ghost. His mouth was trying to muster a casual smile across his firm jaw and white teeth. He was nineteen.

The three nursing staff stood by the trolley.

'Paratrooper Croxton is an amputation case,' murmured the Sister.

May and the Staff Nurse turned back the bedclothes whilst the Sister was scrubbing her hands and wrists at the washbasin in the ward. The basins had long, arm-like levers on the taps so that you could work them with your elbows, to avoid having to touch the taps.

Carefully the bandaged stump of what had once been Croxton's left leg was uncovered. Its crude end was fastened up like a small flour sack, with large black stitches and clips.

He had been in a parachute drop with the Airborne Division when they landed at Arnhem. Croxton had lost a leg and some of the toes of his foot on the other leg. He came from Durham, and had belonged to the local operatic society. On his locker was a card decorated with lipstick kisses from his girl-friends, along with some small paperback copies of Shakespeare's plays. He lay there in a drugged haze. 'My leg is still very painful. It's agony – all along it. Right from my big toe.' He spoke evenly.

The area he described was a complete blank. Only the drawsheet with its rubber undersheet was there. His leg had vanished for ever but the pain was real.

'It's referred pain from the lost limb,' explained Sister Millston to May.

Later that day Croxton's parents arrived to visit him. His younger schoolboy brother, his mother with a small white handkerchief clutched tightly in her hand and his solemn, sad father. They were all dressed in heavy navy blue coats; their general demeanour was of strained, heart-breaking self-control. For at least the boy was still alive.

Liz Frankel was being initiated in a similar way on another military ward. She was standing in a side ward where Sister Stevens and Staff Nurse Longsight were removing the dressings from Leonard Crawford's burnt body. He was from the Tank Corps. There was a small photograph of him on the locker: handsome and fair-haired in a neat suit with collar and tie. But now his face was entirely covered in bandages of Vaseline-gauze, his face thinned down to skeletal proportions, along with parts of his arms and legs. His face was unrecognisable and he swore with agony the moment any dressing was touched. Later he was to have plastic surgery carried out by a famous Australian surgeon.

Dizzy Oaklands had been let into the soldier section more gently. She was in the small convalescent home within the grounds known jokingly as 'Bed and Breakfast' (B and B). Its official title was Male Military CH. The men there were on the road to recovery and were allowed out of the hospital in their blue uniforms. Many of them suffered from depression and boredom – commonly called being 'browned off'. But browned off was a superficial term for many as they lay on their beds in moods of deep hopelessness and desperation. Their ability to move about, and even leave the hospital grounds, was not coupled with many efforts to cheer them up. They had no shoulders to cry on. Even Dizzy Oaklands was consumed with grief for them.

'Armstrong's lying there in that stupor because he's just had a letter saying his wife's expecting a baby from someone else,' said Corporal Garry Sanders staring at his pal lying on top of the next bed. Armstrong was a picture of genuine and pathetic misery. Sanders, who reckoned his own wife had already left him, was bright and cynical and was just going out.

Dizzy Oaklands was strongly attracted to Sanders. He was tall and long-legged with brown wavy hair and quizzical dark eyes shaded by heavy eyebrows. Recovering from a fractured hip, some bullets had been removed from his pelvis. Was he really so hard and cynical as he made himself out to be? Dizzy gave him a fleeting look. Lots of people were interesting but it didn't mean you could fall for them.

Sister Flufton, who ran the ward, was teetering on the edge of retirement. She treated the men like five-year-olds. 'Those naughty, *naughty* boys, Staff Nurse. They've gone out again to a Dominoes Drive. Make a list of their names as soon as they get back and smell their breath.'

Sister Flufton also hoarded sauce bottles. She had a pantry full of them.

'Don't give Wilson, Campbell, Sanders, or Armstrong on table four any sauce with their meal today Staff Nurse. Check the list. They all came in through the window last night. It was well past nine o'clock.'

The end of November was turning out to be a cold, freezing month and there had already been a slight sprinkling of early snow. During the blacked-out nights nurses hurried along and kept to the main streets as much as possible in case of being molested. A rumour had gone round that the Matron herself had been caught on the pavement along Bell Lane by a man who had uttered in pressing tones: 'Can anyone come?'.

'Whatever did she say?' asked Karina Stewart with wide-eyed horror, as all the others began to giggle.

'She said: "Of course you can my man. Come with me." Then she deposited him at the hospital lodge and told them to take his name and address, but he ran off cursing.'

'And then I expect she disappeared very quickly into her private quarters,' said Ada. 'Do you know – I've *never* yet seen her outside the hospital?'

They all agreed.

'I just can't imagine what she would look like,' said May. 'Do you think she wears a fur coat?'

'Or purple bedsocks in bed and a nightdress case embroidered with the Manchester Corporation's coat of arms,' added Queenie Marney.

'Perhaps she's a man in disguise,' Shirley O'Malley said.

'There is one thing certain,' said Dotsy Philips as they sat around just before going to bed drinking very watery Horlicks, 'Even if she is we'll never be the ones to know.'

Then Dizzy suddenly startled them all. 'Don't speak too soon my dears. I've heard tell a special party's to take place in the Doctor's quarters and I might be going to it.'

At first the words didn't sink in and they all kept chattering about other things. Then Liz said: 'What was it you just said, Dizzy?'

'I said there's going to be a "do" on in their place. And I might be going.'

There was a shocked silence. Was she just swanking and making it all up to impress them?

'I'm not kidding if that's what you all think.' Dizzy's round face and mass of unruly hair glowed with assurance. 'It so happens that my brother, who's best friend Julian, who's a final year medical student at the Princess Infirmary, is going to it. Julian is taking his fiancée Estella, who is Professor Pontilengo's daughter, and our Alan asked me if I'd like to go with him as his guest.

'I know what you're all thinking. About how no one's allowed to go in the place, and how those nurses once got kicked out. But no one could possibly do the same to me if I'm with my brother as a proper guest at a private party.' Then she added with dash of devilment: 'Whilst I'm there I'll try and find out what Matron looks like when she's off duty, and any other interesting facts.'

True to her word, two weeks later, after the finish of day duty, at 9 pm at night, Dizzy Oaklands stood there in the nurses quarters. She was arrayed in a long frock made of parachute silk dyed orange, with her older sister Valda's sapphire necklace adorning her shapely neck. She also wore a deep blue velvet evening jacket with a stand-up collar. She bowed in regal triumph to those who stood round her, unaware of the harrowed expressions of anxiety on some of their faces.

'For goodness' sake watch your step, Dizzy. Don't do anything rash,' scowled Ada.

'Yes. And forget all that rubbish about Matron and what she looks like off duty,' pleaded Karina Stewart with a groan. 'None of us really cares a fig.'

'Don't forget your silver sequined party purse with the long chain handle. It's still lying on the bed,' said May. 'I feel really envious. The last real party I went to was when I was still at school.'

'It all depends who your friends are,' said Queenie. 'Sure the only proper parties I ever see are the ones at home in Ireland.'

'And us in the middle of all these soldiers,' added Shirley O'Malley. 'No one would believe what a quiet life we lead.'

'We aren't here for parties,' remarked Ada Sawbridge with sudden primness.

'Don't forget your party purse, Dizzy,' said Liz with a slight smile. Then with a motherly concern she hurriedly reached over and handed it to her, adding, 'Don't drink anything too strong.'

Dizzy checked inside her purse – small white handkerchief, hand embroidered in each corner with rose buds, shiny, imitation-gold powder compact, Outdoor Girl lipstick, a small blue bottle of Blue Moon Bourjois scent, half-a-crown in case of emergency, a small leather-backed address book and a pencil to match with a silk tassel on the end of it. Then, after displaying these contents to all, Dizzy carefully unfolded a piece of lined exercise book paper and said: 'And this recipe for home-made lemon cheese.'

They were all stunned.

'For heaven's sake, whatever do you need *that* for?'

'In case I'm stuck for conversation,' said Dizzy calmly. 'Me Ma once gave it me out of her handbag. You never know who you'll meet at parties.'

The rest of them stared at each other and tried to keep their faces straight. There was little chance of Delyth Georgina Oaklands being short of words, or anyone ever being introduced to the lemon cheese recipe.

That night as the other girls lay in their beds they wondered how she would be getting on. It was obvious that as far as the rest of the hospital was concerned not a word had been uttered about a private party in the hospital grounds. Although one nurse on Dotsy Philips's ward did mention that she had seen shining limousines driving along one of the side roads near the old Nurses' Home where the dining-room was situated.

'But she thought perhaps it was a funeral,' said Dotsy. 'She said a man got out of it wearing spats. With a rolled black umbrella.'

Dizzy had put on her scarlet hospital cloak to meet her brother at the lodge gates. The men in charge there were very friendly and knew all the nurses. They were the only ones aware of the party being held in the doctors' quarters.

'So you're going to it eh?' said Cyril Beccles the main gate keeper. 'It's not often you nurses gets a look in?'

'I'm going with my brother and his friends. They'll be arriving in a Humber.'

Cyril narrowed his eyes and stared at the bright orange skirt and the hospital cloak. 'I reckon Matron'll get a shock to see that colour scheme.' He cleared his throat apologetically. 'It's quite unusual. Will she be there?'

'I sincerely hope not,' she muttered. She shrugged her shoulders and smiled slightly. Maybe the least said was the safest policy.

Soon afterwards her brother Alan and the others arrived. 'You may as well jump in with us, kiddo – and we'll park further along.'

'We're meeting old Barny by the front door of the medic's quarters,' said Julian.

'Can I leave my nurses cape in the car?'

'Sure.'

'I don't really want to look like a nurse,' said Dizzy. 'I'd sooner just be mingled in with you, if you don't mind.' Dizzy looked puzzled. 'Who on earth is Barny?'

'Dr Blenkinsop-Barns. Surgical officer. Just arrived here.

You're sure to have seen him around. Very big. Bushy brown hair.'

Julian's girl-friend, Estella, was wrapped in a reversible velvet evening cloak. It was a soft jade green on one side and black on the other. Her smooth dark hair was parted in the middle. She wore an embossed, ivory satin dress, a double string of pearls and dangling earrings. She was as beautiful as Hedy Lamarr, the film star.

All the way down the corridor, with Barns leading the way, Dizzy was in a sweat of panic in case she was seen by a night sister. And by the time they reached the steps leading to the secret apartments she was trembling with terror. The other four were laughing and chattering as they rang a small brass encircled button.

Supposing the Matron herself greeted them? Dizzy felt like fading away. Her cheerful bravado had dropped to zero.

'It's terribly cold weather isn't it?' said Estella with kindly comfort as she saw Dizzy's teeth chattering slightly. 'The sooner we get inside and warmed up, the better.'

Alan looked at Dizzy. 'Cheer up Sis. You look like a wet week.'

The door was opened by a small maid dressed in a black frock. She was wearing a cotton apron and pleated white cap.

Barns handed her some coarse, wartime paper visiting notes typed with each of their names. The words INVITA-TION FROM DR BLENKINSOP-BARNS was printed thinly at the top.

Dizzy began to relax at last. At least it seemed official

and above board. They were in a drab, oblong vestibule, with six heavy mahogany doors. All of them were closed. A row of ancient monochrome medical officers of health looked at them from above a black, marble-topped table with brass-handled drawers. There was an ink stand on it, a large leather-bordered blotter with pink blotting paper and a maroon visitor's book.

The maid gestured towards the book and the four of them signed it. Dizzy put her name and ditto under her brother Alan's entry.

Then the maid led them up some steep secondary stairs to a narrow-bannistered landing where other passages led off. The ladies were led to a room marked LADIES CLOAKS on the right. The two men were guided further down a corridor to the left where every door had a person's name or instruction stuck in a brass card holder: Dr Rory Mackie, Dr B.L. Slater, Mr G.H.C. Pennylove, LINEN CUPBOARD, Dr H.R.C. Blenkinsop-Barns, BATHROOM, W.C., Dr Rose Stansfield. (It had always been a sore point with Doctor Rose Stansfield, Obstetrician, to have been fixed in all this maleness. Many other women might have welcomed being among their colleagues, but having to go backwards and forwards along the corridor to get to the other ladies' apartments, and to their bathroom and lavatory, was an imposition. Not that the washing facilities were supposed to be single sex at the doctors' end. It was more egalitarian than that, but there was always the chance of heavy thumping on the bathroom door. The moment she began to dust lavender talcum powder on herself with a powder-puff, expletives like 'Christ!' and 'Bloody Hell! – Is she going to

38

be there all bloody morning?' would be floating through the air.)

The party was chugging along downstairs. The room was big with a grand piano at one end. At least thirty people stood about eating potato crisps and drinking sherry. Dizzy found herself being addressed by her proper name, Delyth, the whole time.

A trio of violinists arrived and played some Schubert. It was a far cry from seeing what Matron's bedroom looked like. And as for Matron Throstle herself, there was no sign of her nor any other person connected with the nursing staff, except for the Hospital Medical Officer Dr Frome. With slim-rimmed glasses and black, brilliantined hair (a bald patch glimmered in the electric light), he stood there with a glass in his hand murmuring to an exceptionally weighty female.

Dizzy breathed with deep relief, and finished off her second glass of sherry as she talked to Julian. Julian was extremely annoyed at being stuck with Dizzy even though he was smiling and behaving like a perfect gentleman. His cup was running over with good luck at the moment. He was all set to start a career in gynaecology under the wing of Professor Pontilengo. He and Pontilengo's beautiful daughter Estella were all set to announce their engagement the moment he qualified. There was a certain amount of smugness in the air. He was six foot tall and always held his chin very high. At the moment he was holding it extra high and bouncing up and down slightly on the soles of his feet. He was trying to catch sight of Estella who was being far too flirtatious with Henry Barns. They sat on a small couch behind a potted palm. Julian could just see Estella's feet. She had kicked off her brocade court shoes. He sucked his teeth and set his lips together with mounting anger.

'It's very nice here isn't it?' said Dizzy, in a pleasantly warm haze.

'Mmmm. Very *nice*.' Julian tried to smile.

'The violinists are good,' said Dizzy.

'Mmmm. Very *good*.' Julian's chin turned away briefly from the direction of Estella as he heard a roar of laughter bellowing out from Barns. He tapped his foot slightly on the carpet. 'Er, look Delyth, I'm not the best companion at the moment. Old Fruity Sampson's sitting there on his own and all forlorn, why don't you go and cheer him up?'

Dizzy looked at Julian sharply as the warm haze evaporated. He was obviously trying to ditch her. 'Who's Fruity Sampson, Julian?'

'He's an anaesthetist. He's the sort that has to be molly-coddled along or he gets too gloomy and threatens to jump off bridges. It's all the carbon dioxide and nitrous oxide.' Without more ado Julian pushed her firmly towards Fruity Sampson, sat her down next to him, and brought them both a drink.

Fruity Sampson eyed Dizzy with gratitude. It wasn't often he got a decent looking female plonked almost on his lap, he thought. He knew this Delyth girl was being dumped. He had seen Estella with Barns, and realised fur and feathers might be flying. He was often at parties where fights broke out, but he always managed to move out of the firing range.

'Enjoying yourself, eh? Not a bad crowd here.'

Dizzy nodded politely as she sipped a Pimm's. It

wasn't a bit as she had imagined. She was quite relieved in a way.

'Do you come to these things often?' Fruity flicked her a lizard-like glance.

'It's the first one I've ever been to.' She didn't dare get too involved in conversation, in case she said too much about being a student nurse. Student nurses just were not part of this world.

'What's your poison then? Medicine? Dentistry? ENT?'

She was thankfully saved from the awful fate of having to reply as a woman walked over to them holding a champagne glass and smiling.

Fruity staggered gamely to his feet. 'Ah, Rose. Allow me to introduce you to Delyth.'

As Dizzy stood up he added, 'Delyth, this is Rose Stansfield. Obstetrics. Look. Why don't we all adjourn to that spot over there near the sideboard, where a few more decent chairs are empty, and you two ladies can have a natter?'

Dizzy's heart sank. A woman with eyes as sharp as this one would have a whole life history scraped out of her in ten seconds. She smiled valiantly and followed Fruity as he led the way.

As they drifted to the other chairs a thought struck her: perhaps this was the time to open her party bag and extricate the small, folded piece of paper with her mother's lemon cheese recipe written on it?

The first thing forty-year-old Rose Stansfield said, as soon as they sat down, was, 'Are you a nurse?'.

Dizzy Oaklands went tense with fear. The question was put so bluntly. She could hardly hand her the lemon cheese recipe to try and fob her off. Instead she summoned up a glazed smile, pretended-to be slightly deaf, and said: 'They aren't half belting out the music on that old gramophone. That record "Tangerine" seems to be all the rage these days.' Then she stared across to where a large, corpulent man in a bow tie was dancing stomach to stomach with an angular lady in a spinach-coloured, tubular dress. She resembled Popeye's Olive Oyl.

'Who ever are those two?' Dizzy said.

'Monty Middleton, a GP from near Edgely, and Elaine Driffield, a hospital almoner.' Rose stared long and hard at the woman in green as she spoke.

Dizzy realised that she had somehow said the right thing. Rose had transferred her gaze to Dizzy and was staring at her with pleading vulnerability as she sipped her champagne. 'Elaine is a wonderful, *wonderful* person. Yes, I know what people, and even you perhaps are probably thinking, she does look remarkably like Olive Oyl. But she's so kind, and caring, and hard-working.'

'So is Olive Oyl,' thought Dizzy to herself as she looked solemnly into Rose's face.

'She's one of my greatest friends,' said Rose getting more and more confidential. 'Can I get you another drink?'

'I'll have one of those fizzy fruit ones,' said Dizzy, deciding to play safe with something non-alcoholic, and realising that even a scrap of time separated from Rose meant less chance of revealing her background. But even so, she realised that now Rose saw her as a person to confide in, Doctor Rose Stansfield would be busy dwelling on her own life rather than winkling into Dizzy's. Dizzy sat back more comfortably on her chair and began to relax.

Hours later Dizzy was still sitting there. Her eyelids were almost closed. Rose's steady drone had taken over from the gramophone records. 'Tangerine' had finished long ago, along with 'Blue Birds Over The White Cliffs of Dover', 'Big Noise from Winnetka', Whispering Jack Smith, 'Tiger Rag', Fats Waller, Spike Jones and the City Slickers, and Gracie Fields.

'. . . So as I was saying, I really and truly feel that one woman stuck on her own along that corridor with all the men, and having to trail backwards and forwards every single day and night to get to the female side of things is asking a bit much. Naturally there are far better women I would like to be near rather than Lizzy Grange and Penny Axton. And as for the big white chief, Tessy Throstle . . . well, I realise she keeps herself to herself but it would be far better for me to be with the senior female nursing staff than be landed with all those men. Ideally of course, *if* I had the choice I'd like to be close to Elaine, but unfortunately she lives out and that awful Monty Middleton has his clutches on her. He's a widow, but he was never faithful to his wife for more than five minutes. Elaine of course has never married. My own husband was impossible to live with. He never grew up properly, and he always wore his socks in bed . . . Would you like me to show you round upstairs to try and explain what I mean? We could go to my room and walk up and down the corridor so that you'd get a better idea of it. I hope I'm not boring you.'

Dizzy woke up with a start. The whole evening had been exceedingly boring up to now. But perhaps the rest had done her good? Walking up and down the corridor upstairs sounded ideal to counteract it. Anything was preferable to the present situation and at least she would have something to relate to the rest of the girls about where Matron hung out.

'Yes, I'd like that Rose. Let's go now before anyone captures us for a dance or anything.'

'I hardly think our chances of a dance are as hopeful as that Delyth. No one's been anywhere near us the whole evening.'

Rose stood up tentatively and wobbled slightly then said: 'Follow me then.'

Dizzy followed her in nervous anticipation, determined to take in every detail of their short journey: the colour of the thick stair-carpet, the shape of thin, pink porcelain lampshades, the doors marked with doctor's names.

Rose reached her own door and got out the key. 'I hope you've noticed what I'm stuck between, Delyth.'

Dizzy nodded. Her mind ticked out the words: Blenkinsop-Barns. BATHROOM. W.C. Dr Rose Stansfield. BROOM CUPBOARD. At least Rose was next to the W.C. and Bathroom. As far as she was concerned, at this crucial moment, it didn't matter whether it was male dominated or not. She was dying to use the toilet, followed by a splash of water on her face to freshen herself up.

'You see what I mean?' said Rose, hovering there with the bedroom door open. '*Me*, between the W.C. and the wretched broom cupboard! And you should hear it when the chains are pulling, and the vacuum cleaners are going.'

'I think I'll just pop in the bathroom all the same, if you don't mind,' said Dizzy hastily before she became trapped in Rose's bedroom.

'Oh do. Of course. Afterwards I'll show you that tea-cosy Elaine knitted me, and then we'll go up to Tessy Throstle's end.'

Rose closed her door and Dizzy went into the bathroom. It was much worse than the new ones in the Nurses' Home. It was still Victorian. There was a tall casement window made of brown painted wood. A massive wooden towel rail with half-moon hooped ends offered both thick cotton 'Turkey' bath towels fit for a Roman orgy, and some of normal size. The bath stood alone next to cold, white wall tiles. Like a giant black bowler hat squashed oblong, it showed a startlingly rough, slightly browned, mildewed lining, which gradually paled to the colour of ground rice pudding at its top edges. There was a very worn, brass plug hole and greenish-brown water marks.

In a corner across a stretch of brown cork linoleum was a solitary lavatory with a folded, wooden-framed hospital screen beside it. The screen was the only cheerful thing in the place. It was covered in a dainty floral material – known as 'spun silk', a sort of rayon mixture – which was threaded with curtain wires. Dizzy went over.

As she sat there on the seat she suddenly heard the door rattle. A male voice said, 'Damn it! There's already some bloody fool in there. Try the single one next to Rose.' There was the sound of violent retching. And a rushing of feet.

Dizzy hovered there quietly waiting for peace to return. Then she had a wash and idled about in the room for a few moments. When she thought it was calm again she went to the door. But even now she could hear voices murmuring close by.

She opened the door and stepped out into the corridor. As she stood there the bedroom door next to the bathroom was flung wide open, and a sound of loud laughter filled the air. She could smell brandy.

Dr Barns appeared, then turned towards his bedroom. 'You'll all have to clear off. I'm on call don't forget, and I need to be in a fit state. Get Julian out as soon as he's recovered properly. He should never have mixed his drinks and wolfed down all those savoury ducks. I'm going to have a quick prowl to Night Sister's office to see if things are okay. Anyway it's been a good spree, in case I don't see you all again. But you'd better start cooling a bit. Leave the old Cadillac here 'til morn and get a taxi back.' He totally ignored Dizzy hardly aware he had even seen her. He was walking past Rose's room now.

Her door was slightly ajar. She was peering out. 'Barney? Can you spare a minute?'

He went in and the door closed.

From where she was Dizzy could just perceive in the room Barny had left, the legs of a girl sat in a chair in gold brocade court shoes and an embossed ivory satin frock. It was Estella 'Hedy Lamarr' Pontilengo, in his bedroom. Then she heard other voices. One was her brother Alan's. She looked in cautiously. There was a massive groan from Julian.

'Sis? Where've you sprung from?' said Alan querulously. He was sweating and white like someone on a rocky Channel crossing.

'Where've *you* sprung from you mean! I've been listening to that Rose person from Obstetrics all night. She's in the room just beyond this one. She's supposed to be showing me round.'

'Showing you round, my poppet?' It was a new voice with a familiar, slightly muddled slur to it. 'Why don't you let me show you round instead? What was it you wanted to see?'

Before she could reply Rose was standing beside her. 'Take no notice of this lot. The one lying there is a final year student.' She pointed to Alan. 'And that's a friend he brought with him.' Then ignoring Estella she said: 'And that one, who was just talking to you, is Bert Slater. Medical. And obviously pie-eyed.'

Dizzy nodded silently. She could see who Bert Slater was. He was one of the junior doctors on Acute Medical. Usually he looked as if he couldn't say boo to a mouse. But now he was sparkling with befuddled enthusiasm.

'I can show you round *everything*,' he said. 'Where would you like to start?'

'She's coming for a walk with me along this corridor to the *ladies quarters*,' said Rose icily. 'Come along Delyth. The least seen of them, and *him*, the better.'

'Eh. Hang on! I'm coming. Delyth? Haven't I seen you somewhere before?' Bert Slater was tottering after them, his crimson satin tie strung almost back to front round his neck.

'Take absolutely no notice of him, Delyth. As you can see it's quite a walk along all this lot. Just imagine how *I* have to go backwards and forwards morning and evening to get to civilisation. I'll take you into the bathroom at this female end. It's the one the Home Sisters use and you'll be able to smell the delightfully scented Lux toilet soap, and feel the gentle warmth of the heated radiator. As I was saying, the situation of course is to have a place of one's own, like Doctor Frome, and Matron.

'I once went to a small soirée in her apartment, in aid of The Florence Nightingale Nurses Benevolent Fund. We had the most marvellous scones, and her bathroom is a dream. It has lambskin rugs. And in her lavatory she has a wonderful crinoline lady with knitted frills who hides the toilet roll.'

Dizzy smiled at her with genuine love. At last she would have something to go back and tell the girls. Matron's very own crinoline lady . . .

'I say there, wait for me.'

Bert had disappeared, but he was back again.

Rose showed Dizzy every detail of the female quarters, including the small sitting-room for friends and visitors with its copies of *The Lady*, *The Nursing Mirror*, and a whole array of nursing books in a glass-fronted bookcase.

They were now outside Matron's closed front door. 'It's a pity I can't show you inside,' droned Rose. 'But if you give me your address, perhaps we can meet again, and if any other special get-togethers happen in her place I could invite you along? By the way, you never told me what *you* do? I expect it's my own fault for talking too much.'

Dizzy smiled politely, and left it at that. Suddenly, just as they were turning away and she was getting ready to go back to find Alan, to get him to walk with her to the Nurse's Home, Dr Bertram Slater slid elegantly to the floor, semi-conscious, right beside them.

The two females gazed at him with supreme shock. Rose knelt down beside him with a sigh and felt his pulse.

'It's very weak and thready. Ring Matron's bell immediately. If she's in, it'll be the quickest way to get help.' Rose regarded him mournfully. 'I always thought he was so strong.'

Dizzy rang the bell. She was starting to shiver. Trust it to be her luck to be involved in something so unforeseen as this.

A maid came to the door then went quickly to summon the Matron.

The Matron was in a dressing-gown and wearing hair curlers. 'I'll phone for some porters,' she said with cold calmness.

'I'll stay with him,' Rose said to Matron. Then she looked at Dizzy and said rather formally, 'Could my friend Delyth wait inside your place, Matron?'

Fortunately the Matron had not got her distance glasses on. To her Dizzy was nothing but Dr Stansfield's guest. 'Of course. Please – do step inside. Mary, my maid will show you into the sitting-room.'

Dizzy sat in the room like a frozen statue. Then as she began to thaw a bit she looked around. There was a heavy aroma of well-preserved, late Autumn apples from a nearby fruit bowl. How absolutely amazing to be here in these private rooms. She thought of the way she'd joked to the others, before she had come to the party. What a strange fate.

The room was like something from another age. The walls were shell pink and there were two sofas covered pale green. Dark green chenille curtains hid a black-out blind at the window and close by was a freestanding globe of the world pivoted on brass. Three black fretwork

Chinese Chippendale chairs with side arms stood on a carpet that had a diamond trellis pattern of fawn and crimson. A glass case on a bookcase, near a grandfather clock, contained stuffed birds.

Dizzy felt quite overwhelmed. Her heart began to thump. One thing was certain she must get out as soon as possible. Nothing would be worse than the sudden attention of Matron Throstle being focussed on her. In a mounting flood of panic she walked to the living-room door, opened it carefully and peered out. Her mind went blank. Like all the corridors and passages in the whole of these quarters, once all these heavy mahogany doors were shut it became nothing but a tomb-like maze.

She glanced about fearfully. Which way then? Which unrelenting door led you out? She could not even remember the path she had come in by! All that remained now was an image of Matron wearing a navy-blue quilted dressing-gown and wearing the sort of curlers you could buy at Woolworth's. She had followed that dressing-gown and those awful curlers unquestioningly.

She decided to go straight down the short passage to where there was a heavy-panelled door facing her, rather than try the opposite direction which meant turning a corner and perhaps being regarded with suspicion for prowling about. She was quite sure now that the door at the end was the one leading to the small hall and out to the main entrance. Her nervousness was soothed and she hurried forward. The door opened easily; always a good sign. She breathed at last with relief.

Then, in the next half second she turned to jelly in complete terror.

Matron Throstle was staring at her. She was gazing with all seeing eyes from a large photograph on the wall. Standing at attention, she was wearing full uniform, along with the Assistant Matron, three Home Sisters and the Sister Tutor. And on a dressing-table, next to a large modern bed was a picture of the Matron and a friend wearing peaked eye-shades and carrying tennis rackets.

Dizzy felt like swooning. She looked round in a numbed daze. Was she going to have to open every other door to find out where she was?

At that moment, like the last brick in a crumbling edifice about to bury her, she heard the Matron's voice round the corner at the other end of the passage.

'Yes. It was just as well you got him transferred to the side ward on M7, Rose. You never can quite tell in a case like that, especially if it's linked to a bit of jollification . . .'

Dizzy shut the door swiftly from the inside and went, as quietly as possible, under the bed. She was met by two leather suitcases. She curled up with thudding heart beside them.

'*Please*, oh please dear God, don't let me be found. Please let me get out safely. Out of this damned place for ever. Amen.' She was breathing with tiny, short breaths as the Matron's voice and footsteps drew nearer and nearer.

The Matron had come into the bedroom to put an expensive silk scarf, hand painted with a scene of young Mozart playing billiards, over her hair curlers. She hurried because Dr Rose Stansfield was in the sitting-room having a small night cap of sherry and the Matron now planned to hurry her up a bit then get back to sleep. She left her bedroom again within thirty seconds.

'I wonder what happened to Delyth?' said Rose a trifle blearily. 'By the way, I know it *is* rather a strange time to discuss it but whilst I'm here I really *must* mention the predicament I'm in – being stuck along that other part of the corridor with all the men . . .'

Tessy Throstle felt her heart hardening with cold anger as Rose meandered on, and on, and on . . . describing in detail the daily cycle of the doctors in the rooms close to her, and the torture of having the broom cupboard and the W.C. so close.

Matron Throstle's porcelain teeth were ground together with tightly clamped resolve, as her mind simmered with the thought that she was being denied the rightful amount of essential sleep required for her busy daily schedules. Her face was a white mask. Her eyes had narrowed to sleepy, hard slits. The moment Rose put her sherry glass down on the walnut occasional table, and even though there was still some sherry left in Rose's glass, she placed it firmly with her own on a small silver tray and stood up. 'I must get to bed now Rose. Thank you for being so helpful about Dr Slater. I –'

'Thank you, Tessy. So as I was saying, if you could just manage to put in a good word for me to be transferred to this end?'

Matron Throstle was honest enough not to nod her head one way or the other. As she showed Rose off her premises, she made a mental note to have a word with Dr Frome tomorrow about Dr Stansfield's predicament. Perhaps it would be better if Rose was encouraged to live across the road in the old Workhouse, thought matron icily. There were some very good quarters over there entirely unused. Matron began to feel better. Yes, that would be the perfect solution for her, she thought.

'Where on earth have you sprung from?' said Rose, seeing Delyth in the corridor as she made her way back to her room.

'I was wondering where you were? I'm on my way to find my brother Alan and then get –' She was going to say 'back to the nurses' home' but stopped just in time. She had managed to crawl from underneath Matron's bed and when she emerged had found a fluffy bed sock caught in the folds of her crumpled orange skirt. She was still clutching it in a soft pale blue ball in her hand.

'Where in hell's name have you been?' Alan was hovering outside Dr Blenkinsop-Barn's door. 'I've been searching the whole perishing place! Barny went to bed ages ago. Julian and Estella went off in a taxi.'

Rose waved goodbye and closed her bedroom door.

They walked swiftly from the Doctor's quarters and down the steps into the long, silent, stone corridor of Bell Lane Hospital. There was not a soul in sight. Dizzy led him through the early morning shadows towards the Nurses' Home to where the night light was shining. The lower door was open and there were voices talking.

She flitted like a shadow up the first flight of stone steps, past room ten at the top corner of the first floor, where Liz and May slept, and then with heart-thumping haste to her own room, number 15. With God given thanks she opened the door. The noise of it rattled in her ears like the sound of a thunderstorm. Everything echoed. She closed the door and gazed at Ada and Dorothea dead to the world, as she dragged off her finery quickly in case a night sister suddenly opened the door. She put on her winceyette pyjamas and pushed everything she had worn under her bed with her bare foot. Not a second too soon as she heard footsteps approaching outside and voices. The room was now snoozing in silence. Dizzy buried herself beneath the cold sheets. The footsteps and voices moved away. What a strange night. Suddenly she thought of the bed sock stuffed into her party purse. It would be something to show them all tomorrow. She smiled blissfully. In seconds she had drifted off into a full, satisfying sleep.

4

LIZ FRANKEL

The next morning Dizzy was far too bleary eyed to mention the bed sock, as they all staggered down to the dining-room to get their porridge and a thin spoonful of scrambled egg.

There had been a change over of wards and they were all due to go on night duty for three months, starting the following day. Work would finish at midday, and a free afternoon was allowed. The next day was ordained as their official day off for the week. Some of this had to be used to get some sleep, ready to go on duty at seven-thirty in the evening. They would be working until half-past seven the following morning with an hour's break for 'supper' in the middle of the night. They were to be night time 'runners'. All except Liz Frankel. Runners were student nurses who were sent to wards where extra help was needed.

After dinner that afternoon they stood there looking at the notice board to check the change over list. Being newcomers to working on nights they had all been given the same wards they were already working on during the day. These were their bases, unless they were required to act as 'runners' at any time during the night.

Feelings of relief rippled about. 'At least we'll know where we are, Liz,' May said to Liz smiling. 'Starting off on our old daytime wards means we'll know where everything is.'

Liz nodded, then said: 'Except that I can't see my own name on those lists, May. It's the only one missing.' She began to frown. Her rounded girlish cheeks were paler.

They both became silent.

'It must just be a mistake,' said May. She and Liz got on quite well. Liz was a good companion and conversationalist, in spite of the recent horror and turmoil of her life.

'I hope that's all it is.' Liz looked through the list again. Her dark brown eyes were filled with hurt below thick dark eyelashes. 'Perhaps they think I'm not good enough.' She whispered the words and tried to joke about it.

'Rubbish! You're a marvellous nurse. You're the best of all of us. And as for exams, you outshine everyone without even seeming to try. I'm not just *saying* it, Liz. We all think so.'

To most student nurses night duty was also looked on as a time to get some studying done for the forthcoming preliminary nursing examinations. These exams were at a crucial halfway point. If a nurse failed them she could not go on to the final General State Registration. She would have the choice of changing to another course, but the blow of failure often resulted in many deciding to opt out altogether and do some other type of work. Much of the work available was described as war work, usually in factories or agricultural. May had already planned to join the land army if she failed her prelims.

Liz stared and stared at the board. All the surnames were there except her own: Liz Frankel . Everyone was listed for the same ward they were now working on during day duty, except her.

May had been looking at other notices on the board. She came back to Liz and grabbed her arm. 'Your name's over here on an entirely different list.'

They both stared at the board with alarm. Liz was scheduled to spend night duty on a totally different ward, in a different part of the hospital. Liz re-read the words again and again, murmuring them with disbelief: Ward GPW1.

'German Prisoners of War!' gasped May. They both stared at each other.

Like the other armed forces, wounded German prisoners of war had suddenly arrived in a batch overnight. They were hardly ever mentioned. All that was known was that nursing staff working on the German Prisoners' Wards were not allowed to speak to them even in the course of carrying out nursing duties. Since most student nurses could not speak German, apart from one or two hospital staff who were refugees from the continent, this was no real hardship. This was a strict rule; girls breaking the 'no fraternisation' rule were sacked immediately.

Secretly, May Greenrigg was surprised that Liz was being sent to ward GPW1. How could any person in their right mind impose such a hardship on a girl who had already suffered so badly? she thought. Those terrible details Liz had described in her quiet, calm way – almost apologetically – about her own country, would stay with May for ever. On top of that, when Liz had arrived in England, she was placed with an extremely narrow-minded family who had treated her as if she was less than their own children. So much so, that she had been iso-lated from others who could have helped her. And now, once again some faceless authority was putting her in another place of isolation made even worse by wartime circumstances. May took a deep, sad breath. She knew that nursing stood apart from politics and wars, but how ever would Liz manage to cope with this final injustice?

'They've made an awful mistake!' said May at last.

Liz shrugged her shoulders slightly, and did not speak. Both of them knew they were powerless to do anything. The only power you had was to leave the hospital. Hospital life followed a plan arranged like every other part of life. The nursing of German prisoners of war demanded care that could not be deemed 'fraternising'. Nurses went about their duties in a civil manner but there was no actual normal communication. 'Fraternising' was a word signifying disapproval during the war. It was mainly aimed at women who were too friendly with any armed forces other than British. And in the case of Germans it reeked of being a traitor to one's country and a friend of the enemy. In that sort of climate, any under-ling who dared to query the hospital organisation was regarded as a traitor.

Liz tried to keep calm, but as the time for the now

dreaded night duty approached she became a bundle of nerves. However would she face them – the German soldiers lying in their beds? She arrived on the ward with a feeling of doom. It was one of the oldest and most old-fashioned in the hospital. The black, cast-iron radiators surrounded by thick wire mesh down the centre of the ward, reminded her of coffins. And then, as if fate had stepped in to save her from total misery, she found she was not going to be there entirely without her own group. There was another one there – it was one of the nuns.

Usually, the nuns were so much at a distance the nurses forgot they were part of the group. The only time they were seen was at meal times or on the wards, or hurrying backwards and forwards in their outdoor clothes when off duty.

Nurse Downs smiled at Liz from her well-scrubbed healthy-looking face with short, hacked-off hair. 'Heaven knows how we'll get on,' she said in undertones of brisk cheerfulness. 'Sure, an' I can't speak a word of German?'

Liz smiled faintly and nodded. 'I do. But it's not going to be much use.' She was in exactly the opposite position. German was her native language; but it would be the first time she had heard any of her own tongue since she had arrived in Manchester. Yet she would not be able to speak in any case.

'At least you'll be able to keep us on the right path as to what's going on,' said Downs. She had large smiling tombstone teeth that looked as if they could munch and grind through anything. Her hands were broad and plain. Her eyes were grey and perceptive looking. She walked everywhere with flat-footed deliberation.

Liz began to feel slightly better. It was like having a kindly aunt with her. In their own ways they were both square pegs in round holes.

The Day Sister showed them round the ward, before she and the day staff went off duty. Neither of them had seen Sister Starky before. The sisters lived and had their meals in completely different areas of the hospital. She was plump and middle aged. She explained that they had an army interpreter on hand during the day, and that one of the hospital night sisters spoke German. 'Not to mention Dr Steiner the Houseman, who is on call. So it's not quite as difficult as it seems.'

Most of the soldiers were in a very bad state, much the same as their British counterparts: limbs blown off, tank burns, shell shock, fractured pelvises and many terrible gunshot wounds.

The girls walked past bed after bed of thin, pale-faced men lying between white sheets. Many had a glucose-saline drip or plasma or blood bottle by the bedside on a metal stand. The metal stands were painted with dull silvery paint. A rubber tube slowly dripped the contents of the bottle into the patient's vein, in an arm or a leg, by way of a small metal cannula inserted into the vein and stitched into position. Names like Schmidt, Brugmann, Baer, Planck, Reis, and Zweig, floated through the air as the Sister reported on their injuries and general conditions.

When the round in the main ward was finished the Sister said: 'We have one more patient to see in the right-hand side ward: Ernst Jünger, aged eighteen. He is suffering from multiple gunshot wounds which are now healing satisfactorily, but his temperature has suddenly risen to a point of crisis and he is delirious. He has been put on penicillin.'

Liz, Nurse Downs and Sister Starky went into the side ward. There were two beds inside but one had no mattress and was unused. It smelt strongly of carbolic disinfectant; the black iron frame had just been thoroughly washed, after yet another spirit had floated from it.

The room had no redeeming features. Both beds had small grey metal bedside lockers. On the top of Jünger's locker there was a tipped up enamel jug with water all over the place, and a small enamel drinking mug.

Ernst Jünger was sitting sideways on the edge of his bed in a white hospital nightshirt. His thin legs were bandaged and his light brown hair was darkened with heavy sweat and clung to his scalp. He stared ahead gabbling in German; his eyes were wild and staring and his cheekbones were like rouged spots in a blotchy, feverish face.

'He is due his next intra-muscular injection of penicillin at 9 o'clock,' said Sister Starky, studying his charts which were clipped to the bed rail. 'His temperature has come down slightly already.'

She turned to Liz. 'Nurse Frankel, go and get a cloth to mop all this water up whilst Nurse Downs and I get him back to bed properly.'

Liz hurried away to the sluice. Jünger's voice and words were ringing in her ears, searing her brain. He was calling for his mother. He was asking if he was in hell. He was rambling. Talking to his father in desperate mutterings and sudden cries about the fighting and the war.

Calling for his mother. Talking to his father. Liz began to tremble violently as she found a cloth and a bowl to wipe up the water. She hardly dared to go back to the room where he was. She felt she might break down.

With all the strength she could muster and a terrible numbness taking over her thoughts she walked back to the side ward. The Sister and Nurse Downs had gone and Jünger was now sitting up in bed with the pillows arranged properly behind him. He was silent, and his eyes were closed. She began to mop up the water. Then, just as she was taking hold of the enamel jug to get it replenished from the kitchen he suddenly opened his eyes and looked at her. He seemed quite normal now, and asked her for a drink of water in German. Then he apologised for spilling it before.

Without thinking she replied to him, speaking quickly in low comforting tones: 'You have a very high temperature but it should be down in a few hours. You are not in hell. You are in hospital and people are doing their best to help you. I am just going to the kitchen to fill your jug again.'

He stared at her amazed. As if he could not believe it. He looked carefully at her round face with its beautiful dark, caring eyes, and the neatly modelled mouth speaking the words. He frowned slightly at the bluebell coloured frock and the starched white apron.

'Am I in Germany?'

She touched his hand slightly. 'We are both here. In England. I am one of the new Night Nurses.' She took the jug and left the side ward.

They were the last words she spoke to him for the

whole of that night. And when the Night Sister arrived it was Nurse Downs who attended to give him his next injection, whilst Frankel stayed in the main ward and looked after the needs of the other men, remembering now to answer them briefly only in English.

When she went down for second supper that night (there were always two sittings for meals), Dizzy was there and the place buzzed with an undercurrent of hilarity, as they all ploughed through shepherds pie and beetroot.

'Oh yes. It's all perfectly true,' said Dizzy in a loud triumphant voice. 'I've brought it with me.' She produced a crumpled, woollen bed sock. 'The men in the Military Convalescence Home thought it was an absolute hoot when I told them about it. They said they'd have a whip round and pay me five pounds if I could get the other one, and they'd get it framed. But, I said once is enough for me. And they all began to laugh. The trouble with working up there on B and B is that you've got to be *very* careful how you put things. Some of them always make it seem suggestive.'

'All men are like that,' said Nurse Titheridge, who was completely humourless and had already reported a soldier, who was almost immovable in a plaster-cast for exposing himself to her in the night. Even though the whole ward was then put in an uproar, as the rest of the men rushed indignantly to his defence and said she was off her head.

'You can't trust a single one of 'em as far as you can throw 'em. I was really glad to get back to Female Medical.' She looked at everyone with a hard challenging glare.

A more solemn atmosphere followed this as people began to wonder. Was she right or wasn't she? Then they all went to the Night Nurses' sitting-room and some of them, including Dizzy and Liz, managed to be first to the sofas and get in an hour's quick sleep.

5

DECEMBER

The wind was howling outside. There was sleet in the air, but inside Bell Lane all was warm and secure. No one had to worry about heating, or needed to queue up at local gas works with a pram for a bit of coke to keep a slow fire going, or even stoke up a small grate with some nutty slack then top it with damp brown, used tea leaves. The lives of ordinary people beyond the hospital gates were only met when you went home; if you had a home to go to.

May Greenrigg hugged her scarlet cloak close to herself. She left the wards and dashed thankfully through the outside to the Nurses' Home. Tomorrow was her day off at last.

Tomorrow if the weather improved she would get out her second-hand bike from the hospital bicycle shed. Her mother's friend had passed it on to her. She would be skirting Manchester and cycling back through Chorlton and Stretford to Urmston, with red raw cheeks and her nose practically frozen off in the sooty, misty air. But if the weather was really bad she would have to waste hours going the long way round standing endlessly at bus stops to catch connections for slow running buses. Then when she was back she would catch up on the local newspapers and listen to some radio programmes. There was never a moment of time to do such things at the hospital. And no one would have wanted to anyway. Life there was geared differently. Yet, as the words to some rather sentimental song said: *'You'll be so nice to come home to . . . So nice by the fire . . .'*

The weather the next morning was far worse than she had expected. It was freezing. She put on her old navy 'siren suit' which was an all-in-one trousers and top, made of cheap cotton mixture velour. It was fashionable; Winston Churchill wore a similar style in newspaper photographs, and was a popular choice for everyone. Then she put on her new green coat. This was made from a good quality woollen blanket, which Mr Rooks, in the bottom flat to theirs, had 'come across'. Coming across things in mysterious circumstances was very common. May had it dyed emerald green, and took it to a tailor to have made into a coat, which meant no clothing coupons had to be used.

The tailor had been recommended to her by one of the girls at the hospital. He was about forty. He was large, dark and virile. And when he measured her for the coat he asked her casually if she had a boy-friend. She was slightly taken aback. The measuring tape and the hands were very close to her body, in the cramped untidy room at the back of his shop.

'Oh yes. Yes.' She faced him with swift calmness as she thought of an ideal boy-friend to have. 'We're just about to get engaged. His ship's in dock at the moment. He's in the Merchant Navy.'

He nodded politely and his hands dropped away as he noted the measurements in a small notebook with a stubby pencil from behind his ear.

He made her a beautiful coat.

On the way back home on the crowded bus in the biting weather, May began to think about Liz on the German ward. Liz had not said much about it but it had led to her admitting how lonely she got.

'I expect it is to do with not being in contact with anyone who understands my background. Because I am a German Jew,' said Liz, with quiet and proud bluntness. 'There are probably lots of people close by I could go to for help or consolation, but it's hard to get in touch when we're all so tied to the hospital. Especially on night duty, and then lectures and studying in our off-duty periods. I don't feel now I would have the energy to go round as a stranger trying to introduce myself. Nor would I want to get involved in anything too religious.' She spoke in a matter of fact way. She always thought very deeply about everything, and suffered agonies over small things. Sometimes, in May's opinion, she magnified them out of all proportion.

As the bus trundled along towards Urmston May thought of the time recently when Liz had come off duty from the wards trying to hide her tears. 'One of the men was terribly abusive to me. And of course I understood him perfectly.' She looked at May bleakly. 'Among other things, he called me a fat little pig. He said it really viciously. Perhaps he was right.'

'Liz! How can you possibly say that? You're a normal feminine shape. You must *never* take any notice. You're getting too sensitive. He was just getting at you. Like they get at anybody. There are always one or two. Even Ada Sawbridge had trouble with a patient, the other day. He told her to "wipe that silly grin off her face." Just because she'd smiled. Shirley O'Malley was once told to get back to the bloody Irish bogs. Even Dotsy Philips was called a heartless, stuck-up bitch and she's the kindest girl in the world.'

Liz sighed. 'It was a bit more than that.' Then she said: 'I wish I had a proper, faithful boy-friend. Someone I could turn to. Whatever you say to comfort me, May, how could a man ever have called me such names if I was really thin?'

'Because he's just a nasty type,' said May consolingly. 'People like that thrive on going round insulting others. The world is full of them. And to put it bluntly – if you really want to find a decent boy-friend, the whole world is at your feet.'

May hurried along Croftsbank Road to the flat. It was like being released from prison to get away from the hospital for a day off.

When she arrived her mother Lotty was sitting there with the wireless on, making coloured paper chains at the square dining-room table. There were sheets of cheap, silky tissue paper coloured deep blue, canary yellow, a lovely salmon pink, and tomato red. There was a little white bowl next to her full of greyish flour and water paste, and a coarse, black-bristled paste brush.

May's young sister, Coral, who was still at the local grammar school was crouched on the floor with a small enamelled tin of Reeves water-colour paints. The top of the tin was shaped in a raised row of three hollows which served to mix the colours when you opened the lid. Good paints like these were expensive. In Woolworths and other places there were always the thin and flat jumbo-sized sort for young children. The cheap ones were the only kind she had ever had before; these were proper artists' colours.

Coral was painting a poster for school. Every year there was a poster competition for the best poster advertising Christmas Carol Evening and the posters were put up along all the school corridors. They were of a very high standard, and meticulously painted.

May handed her mother a bag of sugar she had saved from the hospital and kissed her. 'Thank goodness I'm home! Any news?' May always looked forward to catching up on local tit-bits. They did not have a telephone to keep in touch, but Mr Rooks had one downstairs.

'Barry is getting at me to marry him, again,' said Lotty to May when Coral had gone round to her friend's house. 'It's becoming very awkward. I'm happy to keep things just as they are, but I'm completely at his mercy. He could turf me and Coral out of this place any moment he chose. Yet if I agreed to marry him I'd literally be his slave for evermore. His constant nagging is getting me down.'

'But surely you'd have to be in *love* with him to marry him?' said May in wide-eyed shock.

'I'm not sure,' said her mother slowly. 'We get on very well together as separate people, but marriage can often change things entirely. He already has a lady-friend called Mrs Mossop who lives over your way at West Dodsbury but perhaps she's just an old family friend. I've no idea really. Men can be very devious.'

May's mother looked a mass of lines and tiredness in the dull electric light. Then she brightened up. 'Oh, and he wants us to go down and have a glass of sherry with him. He often asks how you're getting on at the hospital. I think he's got a Christmas present for you. We'll pop along and see him in about half an hour.'

Barry Rooks was in his black waistcoat without a tie when they got downstairs. He was smoking a curly briar pipe full of St Bruno Flake and wore what May had always thought of as wedding-cum-funeral trousers of a black- and grey-striped weave. He was a thin man with a pale, jowly face like an underfed hound. He could get very bad-tempered and irritable. But today he was at his best as he poured out the sherry.

'So how's life at that den of vice, then?' he said to May. 'Has Matron been doing the cancan again?'

May laughed and told him about Dizzy Oaklands and the blue bed socks. Then the three of them all drank each other's health.

'I've been asking your mother to consider marrying me.'

'And I keep telling him to wear a tie,' said Lotty, swiftly dampening the subject.

Barry walked over to a small leatherette settee which was no more than a dump for old newspapers and magazines. From behind the back of it he drew out a large, flat box which had been hastily wrapped in crumpled brown paper.

He handed it to May. 'Don't say I never give you anything and don't ask where it came from. What's inside ought to fit you because you're about the same size as your mother. Give or take a few inches.'

May opened the box with anticipation. Any thing to wear was the luck of the draw these days, she felt. She'd even heard of girls cadging long johns from the Americans. The wrapping inside was harsh, cardboardy, fawn paper. Perhaps it was something from a second-hand, ex-army surplus dump?

'You won't see many of what's in there about,' said Barry watching her closely. 'Not unless you're one of the "angels dining at the Ritz, with that nightingale singing in Berkeley Square".'

Slowly, May pulled away the crude brown wrapping. A gleam of miraculous material caught her eye. Her hands felt the delicate slither of cool and luxurious, genuine silk. Her fingertips caught gently at a heavy oyster pink, sleeveless satin gown. She gasped with amazed delight. It was decorated with deep flamingo-pink, ribbon rosettes and each one held a glittering diamante. Dotted all over the gown itself were random seed pearls. May and her mother stared at the dress – first in joy, then in alarm.

'Where on earth did it come from?' asked Lotty anxiously. They both knew that one of the most popular of the women stall-holders at Urmston market had already been sent to prison for selling dress material free of clothing coupons. Every innocent gift bore a background of suspicion.

'Ask no questions and you'll be told no lies,' said Barry Rooks with a slight smile on his face. 'Put it like this: some woman in Mayfair flogged it to a pal of mine for peanuts to raffle for the poor and needy. And when I told him about you hospital girls up here in the mucky north, he passed it over at a knock down price out of the goodness of his heart. Don't get me wrong. He did try to raffle it but the poor and needy were the ones who bought the tickets see? And every time they saw the prize they said: "I wouldn't even be seen dead in a thing like that! How could I wear that at the Co-op hall or the Church Assembly Rooms?" So it kept getting raffled and re-raffled until he got flaming well fed up with it.'

Then Barry looked at May and said: 'Maybe hospital girls'll have a bit more savvy?'

May nodded. She thought of Dizzy in her bright orange frock made of parachute silk. She thought of Liz without a decent dress to her name. She thought of all of them and how they often pooled their clothes, their coats and even their shoes. 'It's absolutely marvellous, Mr Rooks. It's a wonderful present. It will be well worn, believe me.'

'Go and try it on then. And stop calling me Mr Rooks. It's been Mr Rooks for years and years now. How about Barry for a change?'

May hesitated.

'Yes. Do what he says. Go and try it on,' urged her mother, smiling.

May went upstairs into her mother's dimly-lit bedroom,

took off the siren suit and stood there in her common interlock vest and knickers. Then stripping completely she went to the chest of drawers and found one of her mother's rayon underskirts, which had very cheap, thin ribbon straps and just about covered her bottom. She put it on. She was naturally prudish at the thought of standing in front of Mr Rooks all naked underneath. Yet her thick interlock knickers were far too bulky to wear with the delicate gown. She looked in the drawers again and found some French knickers of her mother's, which were pale green and had a thick border of coffee coloured lace round the wide legs, with the label SECONDS inside them. She slipped them on. She felt respectable at last.

They both stared at her in silent awe when she emerged in her finery. Barry Rooks nodded his head backwards and forwards so many times that Lotty said he was like the drunken duck on his own mantelpiece. (The drunken duck was a small, yellow mechanical bird perched over a glass of water which went backwards and forwards in almost perpetual motion.)

When May and her mother were back upstairs again in their own rooms, Lotty said: 'I'm glad you accepted that present.'

'I'll *say*,' May said, glancing towards the cardboard box. 'You only come across clothes like that once in a lifetime. Or never!'

'As a matter of fact, he offered the frock to me first. Me, at my age.'

'You aren't exactly old, mother. You could always have asked him to find you a mink stole to go with it.' May looked at her with humorous affection.

'The trouble is you have to have the right man to go with it, too,' murmured her mother sadly.

'Maybe just wearing it will produce one,' laughed May. 'I'll try and get Liz to wear it sometime. It might bring her luck.' She began to tell Lotty about Liz on the German ward, and about how lonely she was. 'If only she could make contact with someone close to the hospital, mother. Some homely place to be comfortable in, with people who know what she has suffered, but who won't make a meal of it.'

Later that night when both May and Coral had gone to bed, there was an air-raid warning, but neither of the girls would get up to go to the steel shelter in Mr Rook's dining-room. Urmston was just out of the main range of a blitz attack, and the bombs they had had were scanty, compared to Manchester blitzes, or people in the South of England with the terrible unmanned flying buzzbombs.

'It'll be a false alarm,' said May sleepily.

'The girls just refuse to move from their beds,' said Lotty fatalistically as she and Barry sat downstairs together waiting for the all clear. Then, to pass the time away, Lotty began to tell Barry all about Liz. 'She's the nurse who shares a room with May.'

'Tell May I'll have a word with my friend Mrs Mossop in West Dodsbury,' said Barry drowsily. 'It's right on their doorstep! She'll have her fixed up in no time.' Then he said: 'Why do we only share our lives in a steel air-raid shelter in this room, waiting for the all-clear?'

When Lotty was back upstairs, she lay in blessed solitude, and thought about her own husband who had died when the children were small. Tears welled up in her eyes. It still hurt to remember. They had been so young and enthusiastic. Such good pals, and so full of life. He'd been entirely different to Barry Rooks. She tried not to think about it too deeply. It was all past now and even she was a different person from twelve years ago.

Just before May went back to the hospital Barry jotted down Mrs Mossop's address at West Dodsbury. 'She'll be able to help your nurse friend if anyone can. She's lived there since the year dot, and knows every living person within ten square miles. I'll tell her you'll be popping in one day. She's a clerk in the Ministry of Food, at the Ration Books Office, next to the parish hall at Dodsbury Roundabout.'

May went back to the hospital by bus. The parcel was far too big and too precious to fix to the carrier of her bicycle.

True to his word, a few days later a note written in his scrawling hand (on a half page of exercise book paper) arrived. It was tucked in a home-produced Christmas card which Coral had made.

'. . . So I've had a word with Eileen Mossop, and she's found the very people, for your friend to visit. They have a huge furniture contract for providing the ministry of defence with metal filing cabinets, and they own offices in Manchester. They are anxious to help in any way possible.

Eileen often meets Mrs Meyer at the W.V.S. when she and Mrs Meyer are on hand in emergencies with the tea urn.

The Meyers' private address is Bretsom House,
The Green, South Dodsbury.'

May knew the area well. It was where all the ten foot ivy-covered brick walls were, with jagged broken bottle-glass cemented along the top, and where 'No Hawkers' or 'Circulars' were allowed and everyone had to 'Beware of the Dog' at wrought iron gates.

It went on:

'They have a twenty-two-year-old son in the air force
called Leo who's supposed to be a bit of a Brylcreem
boy . . .'

Two weeks before Christmas, Liz Frankel was sitting in Alvina Meyer's huge kitchen whilst Alvina checked the December puddings with the cook. Adaptability was Alvina's watchword. Rich lavishness belied her own skills. She made all her own soft furnishings, and tailored and restyled her own clothes out of old ones with such professional precision that they looked like new. She took pieces from the many worlds she had been born into.

The puddings were a special wartime recipe which included grated carrots, potato, prunes and coffee essence, laced heavily with baking powder. These were what she called 'Charitable Patriotic Puddings'. Meanwhile tucked away in muslin in the cold room were four proper December Family Puddings bulging with currants, raisins, spices, breadcrumbs, Demerara sugar, black treacle, eggs, and almonds.

She smiled at cook cheerfully. 'Those CPP's look delicious. Tell Esme to cut holly leaves from the old green baize billiard cloth. Use some of that bright red, unravelled jumper wool with the knots that look like red berries, and decorate the top of the wrappings with them. Then take them straight to the Merry December Distribution Centre for Mrs Pierce-Constantine to deal with.'

Liz sat meekly in a corner, smiling politely. Alvina was about the same age as her own mother, but entirely different. Alvina Meyer had the fairest, frizziest of hair, and startlingly white pearly teeth. Her nose was thin and elegant. Her high cheek bones were delicately made-up with a faint blush of Max Factor. There was a quirk of humour in the curves of her mouth.

In contrast Liz's mother had been small, dark, rather plain and had never worn make-up. She was rounded and more comfortable looking. Liz's own life in Germany had been solid and normal like a great many people in England had enjoyed. Her father had been an office worker and her mother a housewife. They had both been interested in music and had sung in a choir. Liz's earlier school education had been exactly the same as everyone else's in the place where she had been born.

Mrs Meyer seemed to walk above the clouds in a brisk and beautiful world, doing the most peculiar good deeds for all, Liz thought.

Alvina turned to her and said: 'Sorry to have to start at the kitchen end, my dear, but I just had to make sure everything was properly organised. We'll go into the sitting-room now.'

She nodded regally towards the cook saying: 'Ask

Pauline to send us up coffee and chocolate biscuits.'

When they were sat in the sumptuous sitting-room with two settees covered in golden brocade covers she said: 'What you need my dear is proper details of our local life. I will take you round myself and introduce you to our Rabbi. The Reform Synagogue, in Park Place, Cheetham Hill Road, was destroyed in the city blitz. But of course the Great Synagogue, built in 1858, the one with two domes, still stands. As soon as my son Solly is home on leave again from the Air Force, I will ask him to tell you about Manchester and how, in the past hundred and more years, refugees from violence and terror have settled here.'

Liz stared silently. What a difference from the home she had been placed in before nursing, where she had felt herself to be an outcast from the rest of the family. And how wonderful to be going to meet this boy Mr Rooks had described as a Brylcreem Boy in his note.

By the time the visit had ended Liz went back to Bell Lane feeling that a whole new vista of hope had opened out before her.

Two days before the end of December, and true to her word, Alvina Meyer introduced Liz to her son. He was on a forty-eight hours special leave and was now a bomber pilot.

As he stood before her smiling, Liz fell in love with him immediately. Tall and thin with dark curly hair, he stood in a blue-grey air force officer's uniform with its proud emblem of R.A.F. wings.

That memorable day, when he showed her all round Manchester and they held hands, their faces were full of laughter and happiness. It was like a homecoming for Liz. On their way back to Bretsom House at South Dodsbury there was a sudden silence between them as Solly said, 'We're living in terrible times. My family came here from Germany over a hundred years ago. We spent many holidays there when I was a small child. And yet here am I going out there to bomb them – because of Hitler. Before the whole world becomes a holocaust.' He said no more.

As they walked towards the green at West Dodsbury that day, they both sat down on a curved wrought-iron park seat under some bare lime trees. The pavements were damp and cold. It was three o'clock in the afternoon and almost dusk. But in wartime there was no lamplighter going round with a long pole, reaching into each street lamp to light it with a soft, heartening flame. Sometimes the moon and the stars were there. But today there was murky freezing mist.

'There is one other thing,' said Solly slowly. 'Everything's been so good with us . . . that I haven't had the courage to tell you.' He looked at her with passionate and loving intensity. His arm was round her shoulder in a wide, comforting embrace, but the other hand, resting on his knee, was clenched in desperation. 'It has been like love at first sight with us. But,' he muttered the words swiftly in a low voice, 'I'm already engaged.'

The words were like the bell of doom. She tried to remain calm, but she felt stone cold with sudden dread. One fleeting moment of happiness. One small green shoot of hope nipped before it had hardly begun. Was this to be the story of her life? Hastily she tried to blink back the tears.

'On my next forty-eight hours leave, I'm engaged to be married.'

They looked at each other in total quiet. Liz quivered like an aspen leaf and they buried their heads against each other, as if there was no tomorrow.

'At least, we've had this day,' thought Liz.

'At least we've met and known this one day,' said Solly as if reading her very thoughts. They smiled at each other and he kissed her on the cheek. Then they stood up with sad reluctance and made their way back to South Dodsbury.

Christmas for Liz on the German Prisoners' Ward was a time of mixed feelings. It was a comfort in some ways to see signs of festivity when she and Nulty arrived for night duty. Someone had painstakingly made a nativity scene entirely from wooden matchboxes, all cut and coloured and glued into a tableau. A small Christmas tree now graced a table in the ward. It was decorated with paper roses, and there were apples too. Small net bags of gold-papered chocolate coins hung from the tree along with crystallised sugar sweets. There were also toffee cigarettes and small circular wooden boxes of Turkish delight.

Someone had produced a concertina, and in the dimness of the night-lights the men joined in carols on Christmas Eve: 'Weihnachtslieder' and 'Nun Danket alle Gotte' (Now thank We All Our God.) Brahms's Lullabye was played, too. And one soldier who was very young, played Mendelssohn's melody from 'Fingal's Cave' on a flute.

Ernst Jünger, in the side ward, was much better and

joined in the singing. He greeted Liz with genuine cheerfulness.

They were like brother and sister as she stood there laughing and talking to him in German. He knew quite plainly now that she was Jewish. One evening she had even described how she had come over here as a schoolgirl refugee, but she had not mentioned the harsher facts. She could tell by the sudden tenseness in his face that he was aware of such things.

He had suddenly muttered to her in a low angry voice as if releasing feelings that he never normally showed: 'This war is madness. This Christmas message "Good will to All Men?" What does it mean any more when we all murder each other? When I was a boy I saw Hitler as a modern age of hope. I thought of him as a man who built broad new roads to freedom and joy. I looked through a child's unquestioning, innocent eyes.' He stared hard at her. 'We are both pawns in a game played by merciless fanatics.'

Liz turned and looked towards the blacked out window. She smiled slightly and in her usual calm, understated way she said: 'It was quite a shock for me to be sent to this ward to nurse people brought up to hate the Jews. Yet all the time we are all bound by conventions, like that one of nurses not being allowed to hate anyone and to treat all patients equally. It is always strange that men fight battles yet expect others to show no discrimination. When they are wounded they hope to be cared for and repaired to fight again to kill and torture more people.' She turned and looked back at him.

He looked at her pleadingly. 'But it isn't like that with us?'

She shook her head in uneasy silence, then brightened up and smiled. 'It's good to see you so much better. It's a reward. It's marvellous for us to sometimes be able to find the privacy to talk secretly. We have so much more in common than with Hitler. It will prove itself in the end. Let peace be with us both. They grabbed each other's hands and clung together in one fleeting seasonal grasp of goodwill.

Early in the new year Liz received a very good quality envelope. It was a deep creamy beige colour, and the handwriting was large and flowing. The postmark was local. Liz was puzzled at first; there were so few people who ever sent her a personal letter. Then she realised it was probably from Alvina. She put it in her uniform pocket, then when she got to her room, she opened it.

As she read the words her heart began to race and her face went pale.

> . . . And so it is with great sadness I have to tell you that our beloved son Solly has been lost in a bombing raid . . . He so enjoyed that day when you met.
>
> Please keep coming to see us.
> Alvina.

Liz stood like a statue. There were no tears now. Only an empty void. She placed the letter carefully back in the envelope, and put it with her small bundle of family photographs and treasured possessions. She told no one. Not even May. She stopped up the tears inside. Then one afternoon, she got up early from her day-time sleep before going on night duty, and she walked in the dusk to the seat they had sat on together and sobbed her heart out. Her young face was drenched with sadness and despair. Then she composed herself back to a terrible calmness and walked back to Bell Lane, ready for another night on the German Prisoners' Ward.

6

SHOCKS
AND
UNDERCURRENTS

All the girls were off duty sitting around in room 21. They were still on night duty, but it was nine in the morning now, and they had a lecture to go to before getting to bed.

Meanwhile, May's frock, christened Lucky Dip, was being tried on by Karina.

Karina Stewart and Ada Sawbridge were about to have the same day off together. Ada had invited Karina to make up a foursome with herself, Ada's rich boy-friend, Ronny Ronson, and a friend of Ronny's. Ronny Ronson belonged to the Worshipful Order of ELKS; the initials stood for Endleby Locomotive Kings, a highly prestigious society of industrialists. They were going to a very special private dinner-dance at the Grand Hotel where there would be formal evening dress. The Grand was not far from Piccadilly Square Gardens.

Ronny Ronson was a man of forty-five for ever

teetering on the edge of marriage, and Ada was the most permanent girl-friend to date.

His friend for the foursome was fellow ELK, Maudesly Cooper who was fifty-six and had been married for thirty years. Maudesly always kept business entirely separate from family matters and the Elks were considered business.

'Yes love,' he said soothingly to his wife.' I know it's at the Grand. But you know as well as I do that Elk dos are the most boring things on earth. It's all men's talk luvvy. Yes. I know women *are* allowed but believe me, my precious, they always hate it. Quite often they keel over with sheer fatigue after the tenth speech on rolling stock. I've never known the same woman to appear twice in a row at an annual get-together. It's just too much for them. Believe me, Bertha my little angel – you'll be far happier sitting here mottling your legs in front of the fire.'

Bertha, who was two inches taller and as wide in the belly as he was, stared at him hard but said nothing.

'That frock looks de . . . *vine*,' cooed Ada encouragingly as Karina wriggled into it. 'It's so tight you look just like a very slinky mermaid.'

Karina's face fell a mile. 'Don't say that, Ada. A slinky mermaid is the very last thing I'd want to look like.' Her dimpled cheeks went all solemn.

'In the very best sense of course, Karry,' said Ada hastily. 'It's terribly elegant, really. You'll give us both a bit of tone. No one could fail to bring the house down in it.'

'Bring the *house* down? I certainly don't want that!'

Karina began to struggle out of it again but everyone protested.

'It's fantastic – isn't it May?'

'She looks a million dollars, doesn't she Dotsy? Those pink ribbon rosettes on it with the seed pearls in them are somehow – just *her*.'

'Let's hope I look as good when I borrow it to go out with Herby Dawson.'

'Who in heaven's name is Herby Dawson then Shirley? I thought you said you had no boy-friends except Patrick O'Dwyer?'

'She looks beautiful in it. The colours are so good,' said Liz quietly.

'Stop trying to flannel her Liz. You know how vain she is.'

Karina laughed and looked round at them all. 'Maybe I will wear it after all.'

Everyone clapped. It would be the frock's first outing.

'Not even I have tried it out, yet,' said May with mock ruefulness.

That afternoon, before Karina went to bed, she swamped her face with Ponds cold cream. She left it on for about half an hour then wiped the residue off. She felt that it was a great triumph if what was wiped off looked grimy because this proved it was cleaning out the pores, reaching all the muck and grime of Manchester in places ordinary soap and water could not reach. She carefully bound her wavy fair hair into tortuous looking knots with pipe-cleaners and put a grey georgette turban round her head. Then she slept like a log for four hours, from two until six in the evening.

Karina still yearned for other things apart from nursing. Already she wondered whether she had taken the right step. Her mother, who had died in Bell Lane, had been part of show business. She missed her mother dreadfully, and kept a beautiful chocolate box with a tinted photograph of her glamorous, dark-haired, shadowy eyed mother on its cover, surrounded by tea roses. All the girls were amazed and impressed. Karina herself was small and fair with a beautiful natural pink and white complexion.

Once when Karina was on night duty with another nurse called Parkin, who had always yearned to go to Hollywood and had once been in 'Humpty-Dumpty' in a Christmas pantomime at school, they were both bemoaning their fate. Karina had spent part of the quiet hours writing to the Windmill Theatre in London, to see if they could both get jobs of some sort there. It was a very famous vaudeville place run by someone called Vivien Van-Dam.

'I'll offer our services and say we'd like to be in the chorus. I've got all my dancing certificates for ballet and tap. I'll tell them my mother was a dancer, and that you were once in a pantomime.'

About a week later she received a personal reply to her letter. It thanked her in glowing terms for her kind offer, but said that they would be doing the country a far greater service by remaining as nurses.

Karina had never been out before on a blind date with Ada. But Ada's slightly older poise, and her well-manicured fingernails with their carefully coated nail varnish spread a feeling of mature security amongst all the girls. Especially as she had once worked in the main district bank in Manchester, not to mention her kid leather court shoes (worth a fortune), and her mushroom-coloured, perfectly-tailored costume with its slight slits on either side of the pencil slim skirt.

Her hair too was a picture. She would shampoo it very carefully and set it into extravagant, soft brown waves kept in place with green setting lotion from a bottle on the dressing-table, which neither Dizzy or Dotsy Philips ever dared to borrow. And she always slept in a bright blue, silk hair net, changing during the day to an 'invisible' one. The invisible ones were as thin as spider's webs and could be bought in all shades of hair. They were always on display cards in chemists' shops and in hairdressers. Yes, Ada was very fond of nets. She had a smart biscuit-coloured felt hat too, which she sometimes wore with a purple snood at the back, with her costume. Snoods were as thick as deep sea fishing nets and seemed very sophisticated.

The meal at the Grand that night had been arranged by private and patriotic caterers. The menu included snook vol-au-vents. The wine was Cambrusia 43, a staggeringly bad grape year for Manchester glasshouse vineries. The toasts were brief and followed by gulps of water. And all that could be said of the roast venison was that it elasticated many a jaw and loosened a few dental fillings, as everyone got busy with toothpicks and said how good the rhubarb chutney was. One man took his dentures out completely and put them in a fingerbowl where he scraped them with a pastry fork. No one said a word, they just ignored him. He was a head of a powerful engineering firm, and had left his wife at home in favour of a young woman, who broke into helpless giggles the minute anyone spoke to her.

Karina sat there politely in her wonderful frock. She had dined on a few potted shrimps, mashed potato florettes and a bit of watercress, followed by raspberry junket. She and Ada decided to drink only ginger beer.

Ronny Ronson could not take his eyes off Karina. He was completely smitten. Meanwhile Ada in her plain but tasteful navy blue was being almost smothered by the attentions of Maudesly Cooper.

'By . . . tha's a grand lass Ada. Ronny's a lucky chap to have thee as his young lady. And a nurse an all. What a perfect combination. That's where my Bertha falls down really. She 'asn't that essence of caring what we men always desire. She lacks the ultimate sympathy. But to 'ave a nurse . . .' He gave a big snorting groan of desire.

Ada felt her temper rising as she stared across at Ronny who was whispering in Karina's ear. Karina was smiling at him and nodding. Surely she wasn't being taken in by *him*? Taken in by his thin gingery moustache and his earnest eyes?

Ada breathed with furious frustration. She knew he had certain charms or else why would she have remained his girl-friend for so long? It certainly wasn't just his Jaguar. But never would she have dreamed the tables could suddenly be turned in this way.

Everyone sat there waiting for another speech to be made. It was about aerodynamics, and was to be followed by a display of natural movements by three ladies in flowing wispy shifts bound round their busts with leather thongs, and dancing bare foot in the true footsteps of Isadora Duncan. This was much appreciated. It was followed by two musical duets with songs from the musical *The Whitehorse Inn*.

By the end of the evening Ada saw that Ronny's hand was slyly caressing Karina's shoulder. Her own fate was the story of the whole sad marriage history of Maudesly, who said his wife had never really understood him, and asked her if she would like to come and visit his factory.

It was a sad ending to the night. Everyone drove back with superficial politeness. But Ada knew full well she had lost Ronny Ronson for ever to Karina. Karina knew it too, but didn't know what to do about it. As for the two men, it was one of the best ELK dinners they had ever attended. Ronny Ronson felt completely rejuvenated as he dreamed of possible forthcoming pleasures with delightful Karina. He wasted no time in thinking about repercussions with Ada. He was confident he could wipe her from the slate in five minutes flat. He thanked God he had never tied himself up in a marriage yet.

Meanwhile Maudesly was very happy. He had thoroughly enjoyed dissecting Bertha's failings to a captive listener, and when he got home, Bertha had knitted him another half sleeve of cable-stitch for his pullover.

'I shall be coming with you next year,' she said coldly.

In spite of the Meyers' terrible loss of their own son Solly, Alvina still remembered her social duties. One of them was to introduce Liz to a suitable young man to keep her company sometimes. But the agony of losing her only child stayed with her like an eternal flame. It was fanned by a fateful hope that perhaps he had not been lost after all. There were so many men who had no real place of death except a short official notification on a scrap of paper. There was always a dreadful longing that somehow some of these young war heroes – the cream of a generation – might have survived in spite of it all, and come walking in the door one day. Many mothers were driven to spiritualism to try and get in touch with their lost ones. Others were beleaguered by nightmares for years.

A week or so after Karina and Ada's turntable night out, which had left them on non-speaking terms and had caused embarrassment among the rest of the girls, Liz received a short note from Alvina Meyer saying that she knew of a young man who would very much like to meet her.

. . . He is nineteen. His name is Belvedere Parish, and he works in one of the research laboratories at Manchester University. Both his parents are abroad. He lodges in a small flat in South Dodsbury over a newsagent's shop. I have given him your address and meanwhile here it is: B.C. Parish, 14 Lonbarrow Lane, South Dodsbury. I am sure he would be very glad of your company. He hasn't many friends of his own age.

All the best to you both . . . and kind regards,
Yours Sincerely,
Alvina Meyer.

Liz hesitated as she re-read the letter. She still felt the

awful loss of Solly. She began to think about her days off. She never did very much except study for exams, perhaps talk to the other girls, or go and have a look round Manchester. She never went out dancing or to the pictures. She sensed that if she wanted to keep Mrs Meyer as a focal point for help and friendship, she should show willing and get in touch with this young man. Perhaps the best thing to do was to wait a week to see if he got in touch with her first. Then if he did not she could at least tell Alvina she had tried to contact him, even if the whole idea of a liaison fell through.

The following day, early in the morning about nine o'clock, just when she had settled down in her room after night duty, a message came through that she was wanted on the telephone downstairs in the Nurses' Home.

'There's a man wanting to speak to you,' said Dizzy, who happened to have been walking past the phone when it was ringing. 'Someone called Mr Parish.'

Liz hurried down the steps with her heart thumping. The telephone was on the wall. She lifted the receiver awkwardly. Her voice cracked slightly with nervousness. 'Hello? This is Nurse Frankel speaking.'

The voice at the other end was calm and polite. 'My name is Belvedere Parish. I believe we have a mutual acquaintance: Mrs Meyer.'

'Y-yes . . . She got in touch with me. She gave me your address. She said you live in Lonbarrow Lane. It's not far away.'

There was a few seconds of awkward silence, then Belvedere said: 'I'm usually called Clive for short. It's my middle name. Clive Parish. Forget all that Belvedere stuff.

93

I expect Mrs Meyer told you I work at the university? I don't aim to stay there for ever. I'm in a reserved occupation at the moment but I aim to join up, in the army, as an officer.'

'Oh . . .'

'What I had in mind was . . . p'raps we could have a day out together? Sometime when you get a day off at the weekend. If the weather is good we could go out for a cycle ride. I have a push-bike, and Mrs Meyer could provide you with one. She will always pass the messages on to me as far as making arrangements are concerned. By the way, I'd better tell you here and now, I do have a rather special girl-friend who works with me in the lab, but I don't mind having a day out with you from time to time. And as you can see I believe in complete honesty. Mrs Meyer seemed to think it would be a good idea for us to meet. She knows my parents who are abroad.'

'Yes. Oh yes. Yes, I'd like to come out for a cycle ride. I had a bicycle when I was at home in –' She stopped suddenly. 'I'll let you know when my next day off at the weekend is properly arranged. Sometimes we get changed about.'

'That's fixed then. You can tell Mrs Meyer I phoned you, and ask her about the bike whilst you're at it. How many miles do you reckon you'll be able to do?'

'I'm not sure. I –'

'Anyway – never mind that just now. See you later.' He rang off quickly and Liz felt slightly dazed. She was a mass of mixed feelings and uncertainty. He already had a girl-friend. Was she fated to always meet men like that? And why tell her he was honest, when she had never thought otherwise? All the same it would be interesting to meet someone. Someone away from hospital life and entirely different.

That evening she studied the new off-duty list. In ten days time she would be having a Saturday off. The next day, she phoned Mrs Meyer to tell her and to ask her to let Clive know.

'I'm truly delighted my dear,' said Alvina Meyer. 'You can both meet here on the day. Perhaps eleven o'clock for morning coffee and biscuits would be a good time, and I'll have the bicycle ready. I don't know Belvedere *very* well – but I can assure you that his parents are charming. He's a very handsome young fellow. I'm sure you'll both get on wonderfully well.' By the end of the phone call Liz was full of happy confidence as she counted the nights and days towards the special Saturday.

It was the third weekend in January and there had been perpetual heavy rain, but Saturday saw a change on the barometer in the nurses home from RAIN, to just beyond 29 to CHANGEABLE in smaller letters.

Liz hurried along to Mrs Meyer's with growing pleasure. She had borrowed May's siren suit to wear, and a large baggy corduroy windcheater belonging to Queenie Marney, along with a pair of lined leather gloves from Karina. She looked like a small, well-padded dumpling. All the girls had assured her she would need to keep really warm in case the weather suddenly changed to snow.

'You always have to remember that when it comes to going out with a man who is a fanatical sports type,' said Dizzy, 'they sometimes forget all about *your* comforts entirely. They could well land you up shivering to death in the middle of nowhere and miles away from even a humble cafe or milk bar. Make sure you take a tin of Horlicks tablets with you in case of emergency, and have a good spoonful of that Radio Malt of Dotsy's before you start off.'

By the time Liz actually arrived at the walls of Bretsom House she felt as red as a boiled lobster. Surely she would not be able to cycle far in all this clothing? But there again, it was quite true the weather might suddenly change for the worst, and she had no idea where they would be going.

'Let me help you off with that jerkin for a few minutes dear,' said Alvina tactfully. 'Belvedere is already here. The bicycle has been checked over and oiled for you by Crispin. He's eighty-five now. His era was probably that of the penny farthing.' She smiled jokingly.

Liz felt nervous as she followed Alvina into the sitting-room. She wished she'd had something better on than May's old siren suit.

The man who rose to greet her was twice her height with clean-cut features and an aura of complete self-confidence. He gave her a slow quarter of a smile, which just showed the tips of his hard white teeth. He was wearing a black alpaca jacket, brown corduroy cycling shorts, ribbed, three-quarter, grey stockings with Saxe blue turn-down tops, and special cycling shoes with leather flaps.

'How do you do?' he said.

'Very well, thank you.' Liz sat down and Alvina offered them both the coffee and biscuits.

'Have you planned the route?' smiled Alvina.

Belvedere Clive Parish produced an Ordnance Survey map from the largest pocket of his jacket, and opened up part of it for Mrs Meyer to look at as he pointed with his finger to some minor byways leading towards Derbyshire and Sheffield.

'I'm not quite sure yet. It gets dark very quickly. But if we get some pedal power going, we'll soon eat up the miles.' He folded the map again briskly.

Alvina glanced quickly towards Liz. She was sitting there like an outsider. 'Do you think you'll be all right Liz? Don't go and try to do too much.'

Liz smiled. 'I shall be all right Mrs Meyer. I'm looking forward to it.' But her heart was sinking. She had an awful feeling that none of it was going to work.

Mrs Meyer waved them off. 'I'll see you when I'll see you then,' she said. 'But don't stay out too late in the blackout.'

Liz looked at their bicycle lamps. Both lamps had most of the light covered except for a small T shaped slit. She hoped they would be back long before having to switch the lamps on.

As they set off, Clive said bluntly: 'I was supposed to be going out with Cicely, my girl-friend today from the lab. But she understands about you.'

Liz felt awful. Obviously he didn't mean to be condescending. He rode by the side of her, but all the time he was setting the speed so that she felt bound to keep up with him, which took the pleasure out of the ride.

As they sped along he seemed obsessed by Cicely's virtues. 'She's exactly right for cycling. She's very slim. Very slim, indeed. She speeds along like a true little racer.'

Liz could feel herself getting more and more tired, as they rushed along country lanes in the cold wintry sunshine, with never a hint of resting. By now they had stopped riding side by side and Clive was leading the way. But where to?

A gap began to widen between them as he pressed on, up hill and down dale. They were in an entirely lonely, unknown area now. The trees were sparse and there was not even a cottage to be seen. The weather began to change to a misty grimness, as the road wound higher and higher in a hellish grind. Liz's eyes were stinging with alarm and misery. Surely he hadn't actually forgotten she was supposed to be having a normal, sociable cycle ride with him? Then to her disbelieving horror the worst happened. Her back tyre began to go flat. She felt it begin to thump and bump on the hard road and slur heavily as she slowed down.

She got off the bike, and leaned it against a stone wall. Then she took off her gloves and looked in the small black leather holder which was attached by straps through small slots to the back of the saddle. Inside was a yellow rusting tin. It was hard to open and her fingers soon became numb with cold. When she eventually managed to open it, all it held was a piece of grey french chalk.

She almost lay down with despair and fatigue, but the earth was wet with frost. She leaned against the wall. There was no sign of Clive. Surely he would realise in the end that something had happened? She began to blame herself. Maybe if she had been thinner, like his wonderful girl-friend, none of this would have happened. Perhaps she had tired quickly because of all the extra body weight she was carrying. She knew that the other girls insisted she was a normal size but maybe they were being too kind to her. On the other hand, a layer of reasonable fat was supposed to keep you warmer in wintry conditions. She felt in her pocket for a handkerchief to wipe her nose and felt the small flat tin of Horlicks tablets. It was easy to open and she took two out to suck. When she got back she would definitely take herself in hand, she thought, and try to lose at least a stone.

About twenty minutes later, as she paced up and down in shivering hopelessness, she saw the faint sign of Clive's bicycle lamp returning on the other side of the road towards her. He looked furious. His dark eyes flashed angrily as he crossed over to her.

'What the hell's going on? I thought you were behind me.'

She felt thoroughly ashamed. 'I had a puncture.'

'Well?' He glared at her. 'Didn't you mend it?'

'I couldn't – there wasn't –'

'You *couldn't*?' He eyed her with weary scorn. 'That's another thing about Cicely – she can *always* mend her own punctures. Where's the outfit?'

'That's the main trouble Clive. There's only a piece of french chalk there.' She knew it was only half the truth. She doubted that she would have even managed to use the tyre levers to get the tyre loosened in the circumstances.

'It wasn't until I'd had a cup of tea myself at a roadside café,' he said through tight lips, 'that I realised you must be stuck somewhere.' He talked on and on as he mended the puncture from his own repair kit. He talked more to himself and the bicycle than he had done to her in the whole ride.

Everything was back to normal in about seven minutes.

'I expect we'd better return then. No point in going on in this weather now.'

On the way back to Alvina's, Clive took a short cut through New Mills where they stopped at a small shop cum snack bar which had two glass-topped wicker tables. There was a Fougasse poster on the wall. They were everywhere these days, even on buses and had a clever, slightly comical tinge. It said: 'Walls have ears. Careless talk costs lives.'

They ate hot potato cakes with tomato sauce, and drank Camp coffee. He had mellowed slightly. 'Pity it turned out such awful weather. I expect you'll be back on the wards again tomorrow. What sort of place are you on?'

'I'm on nights on a German prisoners of war ward.'

He looked startled. '*Them*? I never knew we had them in Bell Lane!'

She began to feel nervous. She hoped she wasn't giving away official secrets.

'They don't deserve anything as good as that after what they're doing over there,' he said viciously. 'They should rot in eternity! It's a wonder you didn't refuse to work there. I'm absolutely amazed at someone with your own history.' He dried up suddenly.

She went very pale and silent and tried to sip her coffee. She felt hate rising within her. Not hate against her own predicament, but hate towards him for being so blind to all the terrible complications of it. The last thing on the earth she had wanted was to be put in a position where she had to nurse the men from Hitler's army. But nursing knew no discrimination, and nursing was what she had decided to do in this country.

When they got back to Bretsom House, Alvina was waiting for them anxiously. 'I began to think there must have been some sort of accident. It's so dark.'

Neither of them mentioned the puncture. They refused her kind offer of a meal. All Clive wanted was to get back to his own routine with Cicely. He regarded it as a wasted day, but prided himself that he had done his duty by helping Mrs Meyer to be kind to Liz. He secretly thought that Nurse Frankel was a bit strange to be on that ward without saying anything. The sooner he managed to get in the army himself as an officer, the better. It was his one glorious dream.

Liz didn't know what to make of the day. She had learned that Belvedere Clive Parish was not going to be the answer to her prayers. But at least she had responded to Mrs Meyer's friendly help. One result of the outing was a resolve to lose a stone in weight.

She was silent as Clive walked back with her to the hospital. Yes, losing an extra stone might make all the difference to her life. Especially with people like Cicely about.

They shook hands and said goodbye politely outside the hospital lodge. There was no suggestion of meeting again.

'Give my regards to Cicely,' she said.

A few weeks later, when some of the girls were having

mid-morning cocoa in the nurses' dining-room after a lecture, Dizzy said to May: 'I'm getting a bit worried about Liz, May. She seems to be getting terribly thin all of a sudden. Has she said anything to you about taking those wretched metabolism tablets? She reckons she takes a full half grain every day and they're working absolute wonders. She'll kill herself if she carries on like that.'

May gave a slight sigh, half of relief that Dizzy had broached the subject, which had been nagging at her for ages, and half of worried gloom. As they left the dining-room and walked back to the Nurses Home she said: 'I've known for ages. She makes no secret of it. But how can we do anything about it? We can't possibly mention it to anyone. We'd be traitors to her. It is her own life and she's free to do what she wants. She's always been a bit upset over being the slightest bit plump, after some awful patient was once rude to her on the wards. It's pure madness really. I expect all the terrible happenings in her life have made everything a negative picture including herself.'

'Do you still get on well together?' said Dizzy.

May nodded. 'You see she's so academic about it. She actually tells me what strength the tablets are and of course it isn't as if they're listed as DDA's or anything and are under lock and key. In fact she gets me to take her pulse sometimes to check it. She's meticulously thorough. She's delighted they are working so well. Obviously I warn her and tell her it's dangerous. But what else can you do?'

The two girls stared at each other gloomily, then changed the subject and began to talk about Karina and Ada.

The night before, on her night off, Karina had been caught coming in at two in the morning by Sister Ballantyne whose one mission in life was to get any nurse sacked not in before ten-thirty at night.

Ever since Karina had become involved with Ada's former boy-friend, Ronny Ronson, there had been trouble. First of all, she and Ada were no longer on speaking terms, and when one of them realised the other was sitting in the dining-room with the other girls, each would move to a far corner of the room and talk to someone else. Most people felt sorry for Karina because she was so nice, and they felt that she and Ronny Ronson would make a good pair. He was going to pay for her to get her voice trained so that she could be an opera singer, and he kept pleading with her to leave the hospital. She had refused because they were not actually engaged yet, and as she said to Shirley O'Malley, 'You never can *quite* tell with men. I wouldn't want to be left high and dry with my nursing prospects ruined because he'd dumped me or anything. Though I must say things aren't all that cheerful at the moment with Ada suddenly hating me so much.'

As for Ada – she had buried herself in her nursing career with a born again fanaticism. Her sophisticated shell became harder and harder. The only person she seemed to remain natural with was Dotsy Philips. She had put in a request to have a single room or if that was not possible to share with Dotsy.

'I can just see me landing up in another triple room with the nuns,' said Dizzy blankly.

'They'd never allow that!' said Queenie as they sat in the dining-room for dinner one day, where Queenie was busy eating peas off a very sharp knife. 'Nuns need religious sanctitude.' Then she put down the knife and groaned: 'I hope it never gets to the point where Karina leaves and they put you in with me and Shirley.'

By the following Wednesday, events had speeded up. Ronny Ronson had asked Karina to marry him, and had presented her with a ring – with a diamond as big as one of the smaller peas on Queenie's knife. Karina had been caught by Sister Ballantyne yet again, and was due to be up before Matron Throstle, but Matron was forestalled the moment she began to read the riot act by Karina handing in her notice. Ada Sawbridge was allowed to have a room of her own. Lastly there was the news that Liz was seriously ill in the nurses' sick bay.

'What has happened to Nurse Frankel?' said Ernst Jünger anxiously to Nurse Downs one night. He was walking about the ward now and making a rapid recovery. 'Is she on holiday?'

Nurse Downs shook her head. 'With God's help she will soon be back,' said Downs soothingly. But she wasn't really sure . . .

7

EXAMINATIONS

The nurses' sick bay was managed by the Home Sisters
and occasional auxiliary help. It was in the old Nurses'
Home, upstairs above the dining-room where there were
ten beds separated by floral curtains. At present only two
patients were there. One was Liz and the other was a staff
nurse who had hurt her back.

Liz lay there meekly. She had flaked out at the end of
working on the German POW ward. She had been standing in the duty room, in the morning, reading the night
report to Day Sister Starky. Liz had been the Night Nurse
in charge. Nurse Downs was off and there was another
nurse who was acting as relief runner between the
German Prisoners' ward and another one. At first she had
read through her written report in a steady and confident
voice. 'F.E. Baer: shrapnel wounds. Temperature normal.
He's had a good night, Sister, and has taken plenty of

fluids. I.M. penicillin given three hourly. Comfortable.

'H. Brugmann. He complained of stomach pains at two o'clock and Night Sister was notified. Seen by Dr Steiner. Written up for Kaolin Morph. Slept well afterwards.

'Planck. Slept well all night.

'Reis. Comfortable. Much better than last night.

'E. Jünger. Very depressed and unable to sleep. He received news from the Red Cross today that his whole family were feared lost in a bombing raid.' Liz had put her hand to her cheek nervously and slowly began to tremble. She gulped. Her pulse was racing. Her heart was thudding. The whole place was revolving and going dark and light in huge enveloping waves as she tried to control herself.

Sister Starky had glanced at her briefly, then said quietly: 'Carry on, Nurse.'

'He was prescribed Codeine, two tablets, and a hot drink . . .' She had finished reading the report and the Sister signed it. Then with a terrible moan she slipped to the floor in a dead faint.

When she recovered she was lying in the sick bay and Dr Frome, the Chief Medical Officer, was there with Home Sister Axton. Dr Frome examined her thoroughly. He took her temperature and felt her pulse, then he said with slow casualness, 'Are you on any medication of any sort?'

She shook her head. She did not mention the tablets, or her terrible nightmares. Her mind began to revolve as he examined her. It was flooded with thoughts of her family. Her heart thumped. Thousands of innocent people taken from their homes and carted away in railway trucks to somewhere unknown. Waves and waves of them – wheeling babies in prams, trying to help the elderly and infirm, holding the hands of children to comfort and console, remembering still the simple civilities of life. Lending each other ragged handkerchiefs to wipe their tears. Helpless, victims of her own birthright, some of them had dared to sing songs of hope only to be stifled by the barrel of a gun. She saw so clearly the relentlessly moving caravan of despair . . . Would the world remember it?

The doctor took her blood pressure, and as he was releasing the black air pressure band from the top of her arm to place it back in the sphygmomanometer, he turned to sister and said: 'Very quick pulse indeed. Tachycardia.'

He felt carefully at the glands all round Liz's neck. 'Complete bed rest, sister. Fluids only for the next twenty-four hours followed by light diet. No visitors for three days . . . Which ward did you say she was on?'

'GWP1, Sir. Night Duty.'

'When she's better get her back on to day duty. Try her on Female Medical with Sister Kinnon.'

Dr Frome had dealt with hundreds of nurses in his working life. Sometimes they caught skin complaints from patients; then there were the cases of nervous exhaustion; accidents with scalpels; various scaldings, from bowls of boiling water to the steam from sterilising units; fractured limbs cropped up, usually from falling or slipping over; the perennial bad back, and query pregnancies.

A middle-aged man, Dr Frome was pale and slim with a bald head and glasses. Nobody ever saw much of him unless they were ill. The only people who recognised him outside the hospital gates were Matron and the Home Sisters.

He scrawled something in large writing on a sheet of Liz's case papers and gave her a brief smile. Sister picked up the case papers from the end of the bed and they left the ward.

The first person to visit her after three days isolation was Nurse Downs. She came into the ward like a heavy-footed breath of fresh air. Her well-scrubbed face shone with concerned cheerfulness. 'Hello there. Glory be! My, but you've gone very thin, child. The men've all been asking after y'. Whatever happened?'

'I passed out, after reading the night report in the morning. I won't be going back there. I'm being put on days on Female Medical with Sister Kinnon.'

'Now, isn't that just where Nurse Nulty's on nights? It's a grand ward.'

Downs sat down on a chair by the side of Liz's bed and put her hand under her starched white apron. She drew something out of her uniform pocket. 'Jünger's been asking after you. He's getting on quite well since the awful shock about his people. Just between the two of us – and God – he has sent you this – the poor lad.' She handed Liz a wad of cheap, faded notepad. There were about four pages of closely written high German on it in pencil.

Liz thanked her and put it in the top drawer of her wooden bedside locker to read later.

'I'm fine now,' she said. 'I feel a bit of a fraud. I don't know what came over me.'

Downs nodded. Then just as she was going she said: 'Don't take any more of those metabolism tablets,

Frankel – unless you want to end up in an early grave. Everyone was very worried for you.'

Liz sat there in startled shock. Did all the girls know? None of them had ever said anything. She sighed slightly. No, she certainly wouldn't be bothering with them again. She had lost an amazing amount of weight but not quite in the way she'd imagined. They had speeded her whole system up to one of danger. All she wanted now was to get properly better. Slowly she took the letter out of the locker drawer and began to read it. How good of Downs to have brought it, she thought. Downs had taken a ter- rific risk. Liz couldn't imagine Nulty doing anything so kind and so dangerous as that.

She knew in her soul there was more than one reason why she had collapsed in the duty room. It was the terri- ble news about Jünger's family. She felt for him so deeply. They were almost in the same boat in different ways. Both victims from the same generation.

She stared at the words written so carefully in pencil.

And so it seems that there will no longer be anyone waiting to greet me if I ever get back to the home- lands from this awful war. What is to become of us all? Thanking you for all your kindness to me. Come back soon.

Yours respectfully,
Ernst Jünger

Tears came to her eyes. He had been her only real, true link with home since the moment she arrived in England. It had been a comfort to be able to murmur quickly to him at night in German, and to console him, and to understand immediately small nuances of expression between them. She liked the feeling of his hand in hers in times of anguish and to hear him speak of getting back to his family. The younger two of his three sisters and young brother were all still in school. She heard him mutter his longings in the early dawn before the daylight came. He hoped to carry on his work as a carpenter and joiner in his father's small business.

She lay back on her bed, then turned her face to the pillow and sobbed. Was her change of wards going to mean she would never see him again? It was almost like yet another death. He could vanish again in exactly the same way as all the other soldiers who had suddenly disappeared in the night. It was a wartime pattern; kaleidoscopic glimpses of nothing but destruction, death and hate, threaded here and there with fragile tendrils of tortuous and unforeseen love.

'Taken you off night duty? You lucky duck!' said Dizzy Oaklands as she sat in the sick bay with Liz. 'You'll be leading the life of Riley once you get on Female Medical with Sister Kinnon. I wish it were me. Nights on my ward are absolute murder. No wonder it's called B and B cottage. You'd think we'd be managing to get lots of studying done for our exams whilst we sit there guarding a lot of snoring patients, but not on your Nelly! Oh *no* my dear, far from it. It's one long cooking session of secret sausage and eggs, black market rashers of ham, and mystery bottles of booze. There's pontoon and gambling 'til it comes out of your ears, and all done with the knowledge that if any one found out about it, me and Fanny would be for the chop immediately.

'I was in trouble only this morning. You know how mean old Sister Flufton is with the sauce bottles? Well she suddenly accused me of stealing two bottles of HP, one bottle of Heinz Tomato Ketchup and a large jar of apple chutney donated by The Friends of St Alphonso's Hospital. It was all absolute rubbish of course. She found them all in Private Campbell's locker and reported him to the Army Office. Campbell just glossed it over by saying he'd been constipated and it helped his bowels. He pleaded with her to be able to keep the chutney, and all the men said let him have it as it was worse than a double dose of cascara.

'Quite honestly Liz, I've only managed to stagger on with this nursing lark by the skin of my teeth. But I'm thankful I have. I don't want to muck it all up just because of the antics of a lot of soldiers, even if it is a triumphant sign of their recovery, bless their cotton socks. So, roll on day duty.'

They both began to laugh. It was the first time a genuine giggle had welled up inside Liz for weeks.

'What's happened to that one you rather liked?'

'You mean Corporal Sanders?'

Liz nodded.

'He asked me to go out with him, but I refused. He's still a married man, even if he does claim his wife's already left him.

'After working there on B and B cottage for a bit, Liz, you realise they can feed you up with any old yarn. You can hear them actually discussing their conquests. You never heard such a load of bull. You'd think they were all God's gift to every female who ever walked on earth. Then the next minute they're slagging off half their conquests as nothing but common whores. They live this romantic life of hoping to find the impossible female dream. An eternal Betty Grable sweater girl to mollycoddle them to eternity. Even my brother Alan's a bit like that at times. . . . All the same Garry Sanders is rather . . .'

She suddenly shut up, then said: 'So when do you think you'll be out of here?'

'Probably by the weekend. Dr Frome says I'm almost back to normal.' Liz hesitated. '. . . In a way I shall miss the German ward.'

Dizzy nodded understandingly. 'Your ward, and my ward. There's always *one* isn't there?'

Liz looked away. 'How's May getting on?'

'She's got two days off at present. Did you know that Karina has left? She's supposed to be getting married to poor old Ada's ex-boy-friend, Ronny Ronson, and he's going to make her into an opera star.'

Liz was glad to change from the subject of soldiers. She gasped in wonder. 'Who would have dreamed that? Things go on for ages, the same, then the unexpected happens.' Her face clouded over as she thought of Jünger again.

Liz longed to reply to Jünger's letter, but she did not dare to. She tucked it carefully away with her most treasured possessions. They were a meagre bundle. She had put Jünger's pages in a small brown paper bag with his name written on it. It lay next to the letter she had received from

Alvina about Solly being lost on the bombing raid. She stared at her keepsakes, these records of her life. Were they always to end in tragedy?

Life on Sister Kinnon's ward gradually spread its more cheerful, comforting influence. It was a female medical ward and she began to feel quite at home there. The women patients were generous, kind and friendly. Some of them had heart conditions. Often they were only a few years older than herself, with young families at home. The women were severely bedridden. Even so they managed to keep cheerful, and one of them gave her a beautiful bathing costume. 'Take it love. It might as well be used.'

One day Nurse Downs stopped Liz on one of the paths in the hospital grounds. Downs was as usual hurrying somewhere in her dark blue, out-door uniform. She looked gravely at Liz. She never minced matters, and she never gossiped.

'I have bad news for you. Jünger has vanished. He went last night. Don't say anything. All the staff have been warned to say nothing. We're just carrying on our duties as if nothing has happened. It's an army matter.'

Downs carried on along the path as if she had never even spoken, and vanished towards the Hospital Lodge gates. In fact Liz began to wonder if she had imagined it all. She walked back blindly to Female Medical. She was in tears; surely it couldn't be true? Yet she knew that Downs was utterly reliable. What on earth would he do? Where would he go? How would he manage, in a bombed city like Manchester?

As she neared the ward she saw May in the corridor.

They did not see quite so much of each other now, since Liz had been given a single room because she was on day duty.

May was just going home. 'I shall be up to my eyes in last minute revision for our exams. They have arrived so quickly! It seems to be only seconds since we all first arrived – and now here we are – half-way through the course. Our moment of truth, next Monday and Tuesday. I'm absolutely dreading the spoken exams with the doctors, especially anatomy and physiology.'

All the girls had their off duty arranged so that their days off coincided with the days of their exams. Their rooms, before the dreaded time arrived, were awash with Evelyn Pearce's *Anatomy and Physiology for Nurses*. Some of them were feverishly studying Ballieres' small red-backed nursing books, which were full of surgical instrument displays and trolley setting for ward operations, such as setting up for glucose-saline drips, and lumbar punctures. Others were glued to studying the pages of *Materia Medica For Nurses*, a textbook of drugs and therapeutics. In the background was a large bible-like volume as vital as Mrs Beeton's *Household Management*, with recipes on practical nursing; listing things from bedbaths to tourniquets.

Dizzy Oaklands was dreading the exams more than anyone. She knew she would be bound to do something stupid. She was convinced that her mind would go a complete blank when they were confronted by the doctors in the spoken exams. Those questions about bones and the names of all their holes, cavities and tuberosities would be formidable. She frightened herself to death counting all the bits of bone in the human body and multiplying that amount by all the names for every groove and knobble on them. There were thousands!

Rumour had it that the year before, one of the orthopaedic surgeons, who had since left, and was as stern and ruthless as a Sergeant Major, had failed every nurse except one on the bones.

When each nurse had gone into his room, he sat with his own uncovered foot resting on a surgical towel on a chair. The first thing he did was to stare at each terror-stricken candidate and bawl: '*Os calcis*' twice in quick succession, as soon as they entered the room. The shock of this strange greeting made them completely befuddled. He would point to his foot lying on its towel, waggle his big toe and say: 'What's *that*, my girl?' to which each nurse immediately replied: 'Your big toe, sir.' Then he would wave his hand airily and say: 'Thank you. That's all. NEXT!'

After this he would put a cross against their name, which meant Fail.

Only one nurse passed in Bones. She was the one who replied: 'Calcium Phosphate, sir'. She said it because it was the first thing that came into her head, because she didn't know what he was booming on about. He gave her half a point because it bore some relation to the subject.

It was essential to pass these examinations by the doctors to qualify for a pass in the whole of the written and spoken preliminary exam. So Nurse Maude (Calcium Phosphate) Forsite was the only one to triumph.

However, this did not go unnoticed by the Senior Nursing Staff and the Sister Tutor. Nurse Forsite was not, in their opinion, one of their brightest hopes. Consequently there was a full enquiry into Dr Prodley's examination procedure. He was taken aside for a dry Martini by the Medical Superintendent, Dr Frome, who pointed to the failure list for the nurses. 'We can't have this, old boy. These girls are the future of this hospital. Sister Tutor Sorenson is kicking up quite a stink about it. What in heaven's name happened?'

'What *happened*? What d'ya mean; what happened? I actually gave the little blighters the answer to the wretched question the minute they entered the room. And I damned well went to the trouble of taking my own sock off and resting it there for them all to see. I'd even put some talcum powder on it.'

Dr Frome had already had three Martinis. He frowned. Why the devil was Prodley putting his sock out for them to examine, and why was it covered in talcum powder?

Prodley breathed heavily with exasperation. 'I shouted the bloody name I wanted, the moment they came in. They had only to repeat the words *Os calcis* to me and they'd all have passed! The point is, Frome, old man, if they can't cotton on to that simple procedure what hope is there for the human race?'

Soon afterwards Dr Prodley left St Alphonso's to take up a research post in a medical school and eventually became one of the chief examiners for medical students.

This year, all had changed, as Dizzy sat there on one of the chairs. This year, a small discreet bell tinkled as each nurse tripped demurely in turn from the room.

'He's ever so nice,' they murmured.

Dizzy waited with knees like jelly.

Tinkle. Tinkle. 'Come in.'

She walked into the room, and her heart fell a mile. The bed sock night! It was Dr Appleyard Sampson, one of the anaesthetists, commonly known as Fruity Sampson. He had been introduced to her by Julian at that party in the doctors' quarters. He was sat with a skeleton dangling from a stand next to him, and on the table in front of him was a human skull, accompanied by a few remnants of cervical vertebrae from a human neck.

Fruity Sampson had not meant to be there at all. It should have been Robin Bonsall-Cleaver but he was in the operating theatre. Fruity always found bones to be very boring. He had spent half his life administering long anaesthetics for bone operations. He had heard bones discussed ad infinitum. His real interest was motor racing.

He sat there gloomily waiting for the next candidate. They didn't seem such a bad lot, really. They all seemed to know what the eye sockets were, in a skull. But hell, what long faces. Why was life so miserable?

He wished to God the war was over and everything would get back to normal. Maybe he would pull out of anaesthetics altogether. Find himself a wife and settle down near a motor-racing track. Perhaps go to the Isle of Man. Maybe write a really good book on anaesthetics first though. Something profitable that would be used by all the medical schools world-wide. Though they did say the bestsellers were on cookery.

What he needed ideally was a good-looking wife who could write copious cookery books, and could stand in occasionally as a mechanic.

If only he'd gone into racing when he was younger, he

thought. He was getting so damned old. He was nearly forty-two. It was the end of the track now, not the beginning.

At first he looked at Dizzy with a quick lizard-like glance from lowered eyelids. He was slightly puzzled. Where had he seen her before? Why should he be so sure he knew her out of all these girls?

He pointed to the skull. 'What's that called?'

'Do you mean the whole thing?'

He nodded, and stared at her a bit harder.

'The human skull?'

'I think we've met before haven't we? Is your name Delyth?'

She smiled slightly and said cautiously: 'Delyth Oaklands.'

'You were at that dreadful party in our place weren't you? Your brother is a friend of Julian's and Julian introduced us.'

'Yes.'

'Are you interested in cookery books?'

Had he been drinking? Or had anaesthetics taken their final toll?

'I do occasionally. But it's all these wartime recipes now. But of course we study the special diets required for hospital patients, including diabetic diets as part of our training.' Her voice faded. What on earth was he getting at? 'Oh, and I am rather keen on lemon cheese. I always carry a recipe for that round in my handbag when I'm off duty.'

His face lit up. 'Do you? Do you *really*?'

'Yes. You never know when it might come in handy.'

'You don't, by any chance, happen to be interested in motor racing too, do you?'

Her own mind was racing. The main thing was to butter him up the right way, no matter how barmy he was.

'I'm sure I *would* like it. But nursing takes up so much of one's time.'

His smile weakened. 'It's the same with me and anaesthetics.

'Nice to meet you again anyway. Good to have a chat. Better get the next one in. Hoky-Doky. That's all. You've passed.'

Everyone stared as she walked from the room.

'You were *ages*,' muttered Dotsy Philips who was still waiting anxiously as Dizzy tottered past them like someone in a strange dream.

Later, when they were all back in the Nurses' Home talking about it all, they all agreed that the bones oral exam seemed to have been quite easy.

'But there again,' said Ada Sawbridge, 'we shall never know the whole truth until the results of the full thing are pasted on the notice board. But I must say he seemed quite reasonable to me. We discussed the bones of the vertebrae. And the sagittal suture between the two parietal bones of the skull.' She glanced across towards Dizzy and looked rather worried: 'Everyone said you were in there with him for about a month.'

'It certainly seemed like a month,' said Dizzy pulling a face.' He said he was interested in motor racing. It's a subject I know nothing about. But I did my best.'

A week later, the preliminary examination results came out, and they had all got through. Liz had come out top.

'What a pity Karina never stayed,' said Liz a bit later to May. 'I still miss her.'

Suddenly she wondered yet again what had happened to Ernst Jünger. There had never been a single mention of him since he'd gone. It was as if he had never existed.

8

ERNST

Ernst Jünger carried a small family photograph about with him. It showed his three younger sisters and his fair-haired baby brother, who was sitting on his mother's knee. His mother was wearing a patterned woollen jersey, a dark skirt, light stockings and sensible looking walking shoes. His father wore a bow tie. Ernst was sitting cross-legged in front of them all, a thin, enthusiastic looking child, smiling with proud pleasure. He was nine. He had a slightly pointed chin and he wore a white short-sleeved open-necked shirt. His brown hair was thick and tousled in an uneven fringe.

How different his life was now. Now he was pale and earnest and war stricken. He had fled swiftly from the hospital the moment he was fit to walk without too much pain. His previous birthday had passed almost unnoticed; nineteen had arrived to greet a boy turned soldier. Hair was cropped to featureless short bristles, he was of medium height and still thin and wiry. His face carried the marks of strain and his cheekbones were hollowed. The once perceptive and friendly eyes had now hardened to steely caution.

Ever since he had regained proper consciousness on the hospital ward, he had planned to escape. He had lain there listening to every scrap of information he could glean. He could already decipher speech and understand English conversation fairly well. His parents had often entertained English speaking visitors when he was a small boy. This had turned out to be a secret, heaven-sent advantage.

Pre-war Manchester was a cosmopolitan city and a place of world trade. Different languages, accents and nationalities were a familiarity. And although in wartime the message was that there might be a spy round every corner, the influx of armed forces and the effects of war damage and bombing had produced a pattern of survival rather than suspicion. People were there to help each other, whatever their accent or appearance. The main thing people had in common was to see an end to the war, to beat Hitler, and to be on the winning side. Nobody had time to ruminate on who anyone was. And even if some people were diligently on the look out, they at least expected the man to be helpfully hobbling about on hospital crutches wearing a German uniform with a large black swastika arm band to help identification.

Ernst Jünger walked out of his ward at Bell Lane Hospital during evening visiting time. On the German Prisoners' Ward some British male army staff were casually talking to some of the female nursing staff in the kitchen, next to the geyser as they made some coffee.

Jünger was wearing an ancient pair of brown suede shoes from a box in the ward linen cupboard, and thick hand-knitted socks which had been an unknown Christmas gift. He wore a coarse, grey and white, striped hospital dressing-gown over his pyjamas. Hidden around his waist was a belt he had woven from interlocking scraps of cellophane. Cellophane belts were very popular; everyone tried their hand at making them. Attached to his cellophane belt were all his meagre possessions: his means of identification, and family letters and photographs in a flat bag with press studs. His razor and toothbrush and a bit of soap were there too, in a small oiled cotton pouch. He had no money and no idea where he was going.

He walked straight past the kitchen, at a steady pace, never once hesitating as sounds of laughter from the open door of the kitchen followed him. He walked carefully down the stone steps past an army office at the bottom, and mingled with the crowds in the long ground floor corridors which branched off to ordinary wards. Nobody bothered about him at all except to give him a few sympathetic glances.

One woman, as she passed, muttered to another: 'Aren't those hospital dressing gowns awful?'

Jünger came to the end of the corridor where it met the dark and drizzly air outside. The visitors had all disappeared in small flocks to the various wards. He stood there sheltering close to 11A, thankful it was so quiet as he began to realise the full implications of what he had done.

The doors of 11A, with small glass port holes at the top, were closed. There were no lights on. To his alarm he suddenly glimpsed from the corner where he was standing, an army uniform. A man was walking in the same direction, but he was at the dimly-lit far end of the corridor.

Without a moment's hesitation Jünger pushed his way between the swing doors. At least if he was caught he could plead a lapse of memory or some other story, he thought.

Beyond the swing doors the area was divided into very small empty wards. In some there were signs of recent activity. Metal drums were lying there. Boxes of surgical dressings and packets of bandages were on a bed, which was covered with a white counterpane as if the place was sometimes used for packing the drums ready for sterilisation. A nurse's scarlet cloak was on a chair.

Jünger picked up a handful of folded squares of soft, cotton gauze and stuffed them up one of his sleeves. They did as handkerchiefs. He walked to the back and found a sluice and a bathroom. It looked as if it had been unused for years. Even so there were some thick rubber gloves lying on the edge of the old bath, next to a mop and zinc bucket behind the door. Hanging behind the door was a large, shapeless, brown boiler suit, with a pencil in one of its many pockets.

He stared at the boiler suit for a few seconds and felt at it. It was stained and smelt slightly of creosote. He took off his dressing-gown, took the boiler suit from the hook behind the door and began to struggle into it. His body was stiff and painful, but once the flat metal buttons were all fastened over the top of his pyjamas (the cellophane belt was still fixed round his waist), he felt fairly comfortable. He stared at the pair of rubber gloves on the side of the bath. Perhaps he would take those to. He put them in one of the pockets then looked towards the end of the sluice. There was another door there, an old heavy wooden door with an iron bar across it, and a sliding lock. It was well worn and well used. It opened the moment he put his hand to it and a blast of cold air met him. Outside was a thick iron mesh floor, high from the ground, and iron steps leading down to the untended earth below. Cautiously, he climbed down.

Soon he was nothing but a moving shadow lost in the undergrowth at the back of the hospital wings, where bins and rubbish containers waited to be emptied.

He decided to move as far away from the hospital buildings as possible. He stumbled along swiftly, gasping as small stabs of pain pierced his wounded body. Desperately he moved towards a high wall beyond some huts and out-buildings, breathing quickly. Heart racing, he began to realise the enormous step he was taking. In alien territory, completely alone in a hostile world.

To get to the wall he had to cross a place like a scrap-yard, full of pieces of rotting furniture and twisted metal beds. These were the remains of wreckage from when part of the hospital had received a direct hit from a bomb in the now distant past. Part of the wall had crumbled away, and a cursory attempt at a repair had been made with some barbed wire. Through the gap he could see small plots of land and little makeshift wooden and cor-rugated iron sheds dotted about in a patchwork of allotments, which local people used to 'Dig for Victory'.

He found a cold water tap and turned it on, cupping his

hands beneath it thankfully, gulping at the trickles.

Then turning to a broad, cinder-ash path, which led to some far gates, he followed it. Slowly with trembling hands and clumsy, unyielding legs, he gradually struggled over the top of the padlocked gates.

Soon he was walking along an ordinary, properly paved footpath by the side of a winding lane, towards a main road where people hurried past him with hooded torches in the darkness. He drew a deep steady breath of relief; he was free at last.

During the night he did not dare lie down and rest. He had already seen signs of patrolling policemen. Judging his direction by the number of buildings, the quality of the roads and the number of lampposts, he hoped that he would be getting towards the middle of Manchester.

On the way he picked up a crumpled sheet of newspaper, putting it in one of his pockets to read when the light came back in the morning.

It was starting to rain when he reached the back of Oxford Road, towards the centre of Manchester. He had become trapped in rows and rows of war-damaged back streets, and vast patches of land where buildings were reduced to heaps of rubble. He was pleased to see it, not because of the war damage, but because it was a natural haven to hide in.

He longed to rest. There was just a trace of dawn creeping to the sky and he could see a white dome-like building on the distant sky line. It was the reference library in St Peter's Square, next to Manchester Town Hall, but he did not know it. But he did know he was close to the city centre at last.

With a weary sigh he slithered down into a rubbled corner, deep in the bomb damage, and fell dead to the world in sleep.

'Wake up lad! What's up wi' thee?' An old tramp was standing there. He had a thick, yellow-grey beard, and wore a black felt hat. His ripped tweed coat was tied round the waist with string, and he carried a large tin box with a metal handle. 'Aren't thee supposed to be at work? They's calling for yer on't site near station.' He was gazing at Jünger's boiler suit with red bleary eyes. 'You'll be the plumber. There's another bust pipe, lad.'

Jünger stared at him uncomprehendingly.

The old man pointed his finger towards Mosley Street. 'Over there close to Central Station. Tha'd better look snappy.'

Jünger nodded and got up. The main thing was to move away from here. He smiled slightly by way of thanks and moved in the direction the old man was pointing. A group of ragged-looking creatures were already there and someone was giving out shovels. Jünger stood back a little behind two of them as they went forward to get shovels. The man dishing out the steel shovels, waved to him irritably to come forward and get one. He went forward and took hold of it. The men with shovels stood together in a group, next to another group who were resting against pickaxes. The shovel gang were all shuffling about and eyeing each other up. Some were smoking cigarette butts. Others were coughing and spitting, and rubbing their frozen hands together. Jünger stood with them silently. He felt weak with hunger.

The heavy-looking man in charge, in his striped, flannel

shirt, filthy waistcoat and dusty trousers fastened with
string round his calves, came across with a piece of official
paper clipped to a hard backing. The date was written at
the top and the time. He began to ask the names of the
men, and get them to sign the sheet.

For an instant Jünger panicked, then he noticed that
the first man had merely spoken his name, not written it,
and the overseer had scrawled it down in pencil. The man
then put a cross next to his name. There was only one
man who fully signed his own name.

The overseer came to Jünger.

'Name?'

'Ernest Jones.' The mumbled words sounded slightly
Welsh. Jünger put a wobbly cross on the work sheet.

The overseer stared at his ancient suede shoes from the
box in the hospital linen cupboard. 'Christ, lad. Them's no
more'n cardboard. Thy feet'll be mashed to bits in seconds in them! Come over t' work 'ut an I'll find ya some
buits.'

The work hut was on a flat stretch of ground, close to a
glowing brazier full of hot coals, which sent rays of hope
through the cold foggy air. Mucky old coats were hanging
on pegs inside the hut, and rough black leather boots with
large toe caps lay on the muddy floor, along with a few
more shovels and pickaxes.

Jünger took off his shoes and found some boots to fit.
He gave inner thanks for his thick woollen Christmas
socks, and clomped back to the rest of the group to shovel
the rubble.

'I'm bloody well starving,' said a middle-aged Irishman
next to Jünger. 'Two hours of this to do before we gets

anything. After that there's these two women comes round with a van and gives us cups of Oxo and lumps of bread. 'Bin ere before?'

Jünger gleaned what he meant. He shook his head.

The man nodded at him sympathetically in case the boy was deaf and dumb. This street work and general labouring round the bomb sites was the gathering place for all the unfortunates. 'Make sure you don't get your shovel pinched, lad, or it'll be the end of you. You never gets your money 'til you hands in your shovel.'

Jünger wondered if he would last out. He could hardly manage to lift his shovel any more. His insides felt like a burning cauldron of sharp knives, and he had broken into a cold sweat.

'What's up son?'

'Belly,' muttered Jünger suddenly crouching in agony, and hugging his body. 'Belly. Very weak.'

The Irishman could see it was genuine. 'God almighty you look done in. Get along to the hut whilst the gaffer's away and sit down in the warmth. He'll be out with the pickaxe lot. Then he goes for a drink at Tommy Duck's. By then the women'll be here with the Oxo. It's a hard life for four bob a day. But we're the lucky ones. You've got to be around just at the right time. Where are you from, lad?'

He didn't answer. Instead he turned and moved back towards the hut and the glowing brazier, using his shovel to lean on as he walked. Some of the other men called after him telling him to 'get on with it', and some who had missed being given any work shouted across from the streets and said, 'Pass us that shovel, lad'.

When he reached the hut an older man was standing

outside by the brazier drinking tea from a billy can lid. The man could see the state of him. 'Here, take a sup of this. It'll put a bit more fire in thee. Tha looks like a bloody ghost.'

Slowly with relief he sipped at the hot and strong sweet tea. Then after sitting down on the chair in the hut for about five minutes, he got to his feet again and walked back. The drink of tea had worked wonders, and two hours later he was able to queue with others at the travelling van, where the two women were busily handing out drinks of steaming Oxo and lumps of bread.

'Where do you live, then?' quizzed the Irishman as they both stood there drinking the Oxo.

Ernst shrugged his shoulders silently.

'Homeless eh?'

Ernst nodded.

'I know an old biddy that might put you up. She's a bit du-lally.' Then, half-ashamed, he added, 'It's one of my relatives. She lives on her own in some cellars in a lodging house in what's left of Brink Street. Bin there almost since she was born. The house was bombed. The top half has gone but she won't leave it. It's a big cellar. There's at least three beds down there. They shifted a lot of furniture into it from upstairs. It stinks a bit but it's better than nowt. What did you say your name was?'

'Jones, Ernest Jones.'

'It should do you all right Ernie. 'Til you gets summat better. I'm a married man – see. I've got seven kids. Me wife chars. If she didn't work we'd starve. My name's O'Brien. Paddy O'Brien.' They suddenly shook hands with solemn formality.

'Thank you, Paddy,' said Jünger in a low voice, full of bewildered gratitude.

'Have you a bag of belongings or owt that you'll need to collect?'

Jünger shook his head, and Paddy looked slightly puzzled but let it slide.

'In case we get parted during the day I'll meet you by the hut when we hand in our shovels and get our money.'

Jünger nodded.

Everything went smoothly. The women on the travelling van dished out more soup and bread during the day. The overseer gave Jünger an old overcoat from the hut to go home in, as well as his four shillings wages, because he thought 'Ernie Jones' looked very ill, and because he had spent a few hours drinking with some of his pals and felt a warm glow for all humanity.

Number 11 Brink Street, where Cissy O'Brien survived in the cellars, was about fifteen minutes walk away from Mosley Street. Paddy O'Brien and his family lived five minutes walk further on in a small terraced house in Frogbarrow Street, which had never been touched except by shrapnel. A few windows had been blown in with bombblast round about them. Jagged shapes in window frames still waited to be repaired; they displayed brown diamond criss-cross patterns of sticky paper. Others with thick curtain net pasted over the whole of the glass panes had escaped.

'Cissy is used to having lodgers in the cellar,' said Paddy. She needs someone there to help her out. It's not the place for women to stay. She'd drive 'em nuts, but it's a good standby for anyone out on a limb. The last lad of about your age joined up, before the bomb came. She owns the whole house but she's always lived in the cellar since the war began. She's got a bit of money tucked away so she never starves. She won't expect payment but she'll need a bit of help sometimes. Cissy's never bin one for having to put up with rent collecters or insurance men, or nosey parkers. She's been a real little boss in her time. All five foot two of 'er.'

Jünger nodded silently. He felt better after his first day's work. Mainly because of his four shillings, graced with the head of King George the Fifth, resting in his overall pocket.

He followed Paddy O'Brien with meticulous care, trying to memorise the cobbled streets among patches of bombed wasteland, as they made their way to Brink Street. When they reached number 11, he was overcome with horror and grief. The whole two-storey house was set like a shell above them. A ragged piece of curtain still trailed from a wrecked brick window, and a bedroom still held a mangled iron bedstead amongst its ruins, with a picture hanging tilted on the wall. Next to number 11 the house was no longer there, except for fire-ravaged timbers and a heap of rubble.

At the back of Jünger's mind lay the embedded dread of what his own family had suffered in a similar holocaust. He followed Paddy down four stone steps to the wooden basement door next to a small window covered with glued netting. On a stone window ledge were some crumbs put out for the birds, and by the door was a saucer with a black and white cat sitting there washing itself, as one last chaffinch landed bravely in the evening gloom for a final crumb. Cissy O'Brien peered at them from her frail rounded shoulders as she opened the door. 'Oh. It's you Paddy. Just the person. I want you to get me some more Pink Oil for the lamps and the heaters.' She stared at Ernst: 'Who's this lad then?'

'It's Ernest Jones. He's been working with me on't site. He's got nowhere to go. He needs a bed for a few days.'

'You'd better come in then. You've struck lucky. There's no one here at present and I could do with a bit of company. There's been a man round from the Town Hall wanting me to get out. Says the whole place'll come down on top of me. But I'm not budging. I was almost born here and here I'll stay. I'm not having those jumped up little knowalls telling me to get out of my own property! The next thing, I'd be homeless like all the rest and never see it again! Anyway, I'll put the kettle on the oil stove.'

She looked at Ernst. 'What's happened to you then Ernie? I'll just go and find some sugar.'

When she'd gone Paddy began to speak quickly in undertones. 'I won't stay. You'll find she never stops talking once she starts, and I've got to get home. Mind you get to work early again tomorrow. No later than six-thirty to be the front of the queue. There's lots of men sleep rough round there ready to get a job first thing. You were lucky this morning. It's nearly all luck except that I'm one of the proper regulars. I stand in for the boss when he's away.'

'Fancy him not stopping,' said Cissy when Paddy had gone. 'He usually has a cuppa with me on the way home from work, especially if I've got no one with me. So where are you from then?'

Ernst hesitated. 'I've been all over.'

'I can tell that. You've got one of them mixed up accents like seamen sometimes have. My brother used to work on Manchester Docks before the war, but he was killed in an accident. Just as well really. Losing this house would have broken his heart. I never was a real one for marrying. Always been single but always got on with men. They tell me all their troubles. Follow me whilst the tea's brewing and I'll show you your bed.'

Ernst began to relax. He could see she would never ever get far enough into his own personal history before branching off into a long lifetime of her own personal affairs. He followed behind her, politely.

'And you needn't worry about the bedding, there's no bugs in it. That's one thing I've always been very particular about. Paddy's wife Miranda washes for me as regular as clockwork, so the beds is always fresh. Yours is that big one in the far corner next to the wardrobe. I always sleep on my Put-U-Up in the living room, with Major next to me in his special basket. Black as night he is; a Heinz 57 Varieties, but mainly retriever. You won't have seen him yet because he's round at Moll Simpson's. Her boy Frankie thinks the world of Major. He takes him a walk after school every night, then he has dog biscuits there, and after tea Frankie brings him back. He should be back quite soon after we've had ours. What would you like? I always have plenty of food in. People make me pies and all sorts, and the butcher always sees to it that there's a bone for the dog and something for me in the same parcel.'

When they got back to the cellar living-room and were eating bright pink brawn and tinned tomatoes, Cissy pointed to the clock on a sideboard and said: 'Behind that clock are six ration books of the dead. Collected from the rubble. I'd be sent to prison if I was to use 'em as you well know. But I keep them for sentimental reasons. The same applies to the identity cards.' She got up and went across to get the pale blue, oblong identity cards, some of them crumpled, torn and scorched. She sat back at the table with him and formed the identity cards into a blue fan. 'Poor, poor Mrs Robina Jaxon . . . Ronald Blandings . . . Old Mr Burrows. Mervyn Stamp. And a boy only about your age: Edmund Young, aged twenty.' She handed the Edmund Young card over for Ernst to look at. It was the first British Civilian Wartime Identity card he had seen.

'Life can play cruel tricks,' said Cissy dabbing at her eyes. 'By the way, be a good lad before you go to bed and chop me plenty of wood into eight-inch length sticks and make it all into bundles. I'll show you where the wood's kept. It's in the proper coal cellar, and there's wire there and pliers to fasten the wire to put round the bundles. I gives them out to people who does me favours and I like to keep up the stock.'

When Ernst finally got to bed that night and lay both snug and warm beneath thick blankets and a feather eiderdown, he marvelled at his good fortune. Cissy had given him an alarm clock. She had left out some Sunny Jim Force for his breakfast, with some watered down condensed milk and in a paper bag on the table was a jam sandwich to take to work.

He arrived very early. It was still dark as he stood there, first in the queue, waiting by the hut.

Mat Truman, the overseer, smiled at him briefly as he

signed his name with a cross, muttering the name Ernest Jones.

'You look a bit better today lad. There'll be plenty of work to do.' He handed Ernst a shovel. 'I shall be away most of today at the back of Stretford Road. Trouble with a buried land mine. The army'll be sent in.'

The day was fine and clear and he shovelled away with no trouble.

During the afternoon there was a tremendous explosion which caused even more unsteady buildings around to partially collapse.

When work ended all the men stood with their pick-axes and shovels waiting for their pay. Paddy O'Brien held up his hand. There was immediate silence.

'It is my painful and unfortunate duty to tell you that this afternoon, in the course of their duties, two men were killed over in Salt Street. One was Soldier, Officer, Engineer Smithson who was mine detecting.' His voice became louder. He spoke firmly. 'The other was our over-seer Mathias Truman. There will now be two minutes silence. A hat will be laid here on the ground if anyone wishes to join in sending floral condolences for both men.'

The site, with its broken bricks and charred remains of buildings, was suddenly silenced as the ragged men stood there in total stillness with heads bowed. Nothing stirred but the sound of distant traffic. The late afternoon sky was dark and heavy.

Paddy O'Brien raised his head again and the men raised theirs.

After they were paid the men filed past the hat. Each man dropped money into it.

The following day, Paddy O'Brien became the new permanent overseer, and Ernst Jünger had a regular job and nightly bed at Cissy's.

Liz had called in the local paper shop, near Bell Lane, to take a *Nursing Mirror* magazine back to the hospital for May.

She stopped suddenly. Outside the shop was a poster. It said in big black letters:

WANTED
Ernst Jünger
German Prisoner of War
Aged nineteen
Wounded
Anyone with any information as to the whereabouts of
this man, please contact the nearest police station

Liz stared at the face peering at her from the poster. The shaved head. The blackened, badly printed eyes. It didn't look a bit like him.

At first when Ernst had run from the ward there had been a strange silence about it, and the girls had not bothered too much. None of them knew him or had seen him, except for Liz and Nurse Downs. The others were always far too busy with their own lives to notice anything about it in the newspapers. Main war stories were the proper news, there was also the ever-running German Propaganda from 'Lord Haw Haw' (as he was christened) on the wireless.

Apart from these minor distractions, the most important worries in people's minds were about the safety of their own loved ones. That was enough to cope with.

Liz trembled slightly as she asked for the *Nursing Mirror*. What would have happened now to Ernst Jünger? She blinked as she tried to stop tears forming. Then wiped her hand across her eyes, smiled at the woman in the shop, and said: 'I have a terrible cold.'

The woman smiled sympathetically. 'It's going round like wild-fire, love. You're the third in this morning with streaming eyes. Tarrarr then. Look after yourself dearie.'

About a week after the two men had been killed in Manchester by the hidden land mine, May and Liz went into town. Everybody was back on day duty again.

'The time's flying,' laughed May as they came out of the News Theatre on the corner of Oxford Road near the Ritz Ballroom. The News Theatre was a small, jazzy looking place. It had a revolving, hourly programme of news and short feature films. It was ideal for anyone who had no more than an hour to spare, but who wanted to relax in warm and comfortable surroundings. The News Theatre, the Ritz and Plaza dance halls were all close to each other near St Peter's Square, the huge Midland Hotel, and Central Railway Station. It was a place of night life for thousands of people. The multitude of small pubs were thronged by men from the armed forces. Music, dancing, love and romance were their medicine of hope.

Liz and May had gone into the News Theatre just before midday. It was a day off for both of them. There had been a short thriller about a drugged man being put in a cabin trunk. The newsreel which followed was dreadfully grim yet it was related in the usual brisk, cheery stiff-upper-lip voice. There had been a piece about the Red Army entering Auschwitz. Photographs were shown of emaciated human carcasses in grey-striped, prison-camp shirts lying in open trenches.

Liz closed her eyes and stood up to go out, with May following. Neither of them said anything until they got outside, then all Liz said was, 'she would collapse if they didn't have a cup of tea'. She was as white as a ghost and trembling. May was worried but tried not to show it.

'I was wondering whether we should try and find that place Dizzy's sister, Valda, runs – for a snack?' suggested May. 'It's a basement café. I think it might be round the back of the Tootal Broadhurst building. It might be worth a try?'

Liz readily agreed. She looked pale and still felt sick from watching the film, but she was determined not to show her anguish. They began to walk down the back streets, winding round from Gt Bridgewater Street.

'I think there's some bomb damage near by,' said May.

'Ada Sawbridge says there's a white-painted board with VALDA'S written on it in black writing, with a picture of a pie and chips, and a steaming mug of tea. She and Dotsy went there, but Ada said, "Never again". She said it was full of navvies. It's supposed to be a real bargain though: chips, bread and marg and a pot of tea for six-pence.'

There were some men toiling away on open ground as they drew near to the café. Some had pickaxes, others were wheeling barrows full of rubble, and others were shovelling.

One of those shovelling halted for a second, and

pushed an old tweed cap to the back of his head. He was only a few yards away. He turned away from his work and looked over at Liz. Their eyes met.

May was already going down into Valda's basement café.

Liz gazed at Jünger's pale and harrowed face. His hair was longer and more unruly, but she could not fail to recognise him. He bore no resemblance to the poorly reproduced WANTED poster. She was glad. She half raised her hand to him as if to wave, then stopped and followed May into the café.

Ernst Jünger turned back to his work as if nothing had happened.

9

PATHS OF PAIN

'You've hardly touched your food. Is it all right?' May looked at Liz's plate anxiously. The fried egg lay there heavily and the chips were beginning to sink into a soggy heap.

'Fine. It was much too big a helping anyway. And I've gone a bit off colour.'

'Have a toasted teacake instead. You'll need something . . .'

Liz shook her head. 'Just this cup of tea will do.'

May looked round. They were the only female customers. The tables were full of heavy looking men wolfing down massive helpings in seconds. Dizzy's married sister, Valda, who owned the café, was a charming woman. Big shouldered and blonde, in her late thirties, she was bubbling with friendly kindness. On one of the painted brick walls near the counter was a notice:

NO SWEARING

NO SPITTING

NO NECKING

NO FOREIGN COINS AND DEFINITELY NO
CHEQUES.

TAKE AWAY MEALS AVAILABLE AT ALL TIMES.
BRING YOUR OWN BASINS, PLATES, AND LIDS.

NO SLY DRINKING OF UNOFFICIAL LIQUOR.

SMOKERS PLEASE USE ASH TRAYS AND NOT
THE CROCKERY.

CHUCKED OUT CUSTOMERS BANNED
FOR ALL TIME.

Signed Valda.C.March.
Manageress, Owner, and Cook.

'The fact is,' admitted Liz with a look of anguish, 'I
think I saw Ernst Jünger from GPW1. He was working
amongst those men just outside here.' She began to back-
track: 'But it could have been my imagination, or even
wishful thinking.' Liz looked away and tried to pretend
she had not spoken.

'How on earth will he be managing – if it was him?'
May said. She thought over his predicament. To her
Germans were people in jackboots and iron helmets. A
ruthless enemy. Yet a wounded soldier in any language
was a human being needing help. He was a mother's son.

'Surely he'll be caught? The police check up regularly

on casual labourers. They usually require a list of names and addresses. They'll want to see identity cards.'

'That's what I was thinking,' muttered Liz in an under-tone. Sometimes I hear his voice in my dreams. I try to forget him and live my own life, and work to get my nursing qualifications. Then, in the night his face looms before me all mixed up with my own family and I wake up crying. It's awful.' Her voice cracked slightly with the pain of it.

She whispered the next words in a flood of fear. 'There was a "wanted" poster of him in the corner shop.'

May nodded gloomily. 'I saw it yesterday. He looked terrible. Just like a young forlorn schoolboy with wide staring eyes. But of course I never ever actually saw him at Bell Lane.'

'He's nineteen now,' said Liz. 'He doesn't look a bit like the poster, which is a good thing.'

'If it was him, do you think he recognised you when we came here?'

Liz shook her head sadly. 'He just turned away.'

'Perhaps he did it on purpose. He probably thought it would be safer,' said May trying to comfort her. 'In case we gave the game away. Or so as we wouldn't get involved.'

Liz blinked tearfully as they asked for the bill and paid at the counter. 'I shall never really know, and that makes it even more awful.'

On their way back to the hospital Liz tried hard to pull herself together, and changed the subject. 'How is your love life, May?' she said.

May smiled resignedly. 'It just doesn't exist at present.

She gave a quick laugh. 'I fell head over heels for Paratrooper Croxton, but he'll never know it. He was always ribbing me on the ward, but whenever we were alone together, like wheeling him to X-Ray or Physio he was as quiet as a mouse and so was I . . . We won't meet again either. He's being transferred closer to his home in Durham, next week. Just at the same time as we all go to do our three months' children's training at Booth Hall.'

Ernst had recognised Liz immediately. It was a moment of agony. He longed to rush towards her, but he turned away stiffly in a flood of self-preservation. When she and May had gone, a deep ache filled him. If only the world was a different place. If only they could meet again and go back home together, to a better life and both start again.

The three months at Booth Hall rushed by for the girls. It was completely different from Bell Lane; the hospital was smaller and on higher ground. Continuous, long red-brick walls wound round the outside. On the ground floor were the girls' bedrooms. Each one was separate. During their stay there was a slight feeling of insecurity, because a man had broken into one of the nurse's bedrooms at night, and attacked a nurse.

Most of the visiting nurses from Crumpsall and Bell Lane served part of their training on the Tonsils Ward, which was like a daily shuttle service. In the baby wards were some very sad cases of children who had been abandoned. One newly-born child had been found in a telephone booth by a policeman, and was called Edward after the policeman and Booth after both the hospital and the telephone box.

It was spring by the time the girls were back again. None of them were on the military wards now. They were advancing slowly to the status of Senior Nurse, and concentrating more and more on studies for their final examinations. They were all still in severe penury, with their pay just about covering the cost of weekly toothpaste. The only one to leave had been Karina, but she had kept in touch. She had settled down in bliss with Ada's rich boy-friend near Cheadle, and had become Mrs Ronald Layton Ronson. True to his word, he had encouraged her to have her voice trained, but that had been curtailed because she soon had a baby girl called Rona.

Quite often, some of the girls went round to see her when off duty. All except Ada Sawbridge, who had wiped both Ronny and Karina from her life for ever, and was now thankfully involved in wholehearted nursing. Living a life of 'sack cloth and ashes', she did not allow herself painted nails, cigarettes, or boy-friends.

'I'm very worried about Ada these days,' observed Dizzy. 'She's becoming just like a nun. I hope it doesn't last. She adorns herself with all those fawn jumpers and never wears an up-lift bra. I sincerely hope it's just a passing fad.'

'It won't last,' laughed Dotsy Philips.' Just you wait and see. By the time our finals are over she'll be fully qualified and back to her normal sophisticated self. She'll probably land up as wife of a chief medical officer or marry a lonely colonel.'

Both Dizzy and Dotsy were bereft of romantic attachments, although Dizzy had been out once with Garry Sanders before he was transferred from B and B cottage. Alas, he turned out to be extremely bossy and treated her as if she was a child in need of strict discipline. Yet he himself did not even accept the discipline of wartime queuing, which annoyed Dizzy. It wasn't simply because he had been a wounded soldier and was used to getting preference, but because he didn't believe in queuing and had not the patience to conform to it.

'One date with him was enough,' said Dizzy. 'He caused a real rumpus outside the Gaumont. I felt awful. And he chose very cheap seats too. Even though he'd just won a mint at pontoon. I'm glad I found out in time.'

Liz and May were also living saintly lives and completely immersed in their nursing. Often they spent their off duty time doing nothing more than capturing a precious sunny day by sunbathing on one of the flat roofs of the Nurse's Home, whilst others sat on the grass below them.

Liz still had hidden longings to find Ernst Jünger again. She thought about him constantly in quiet moments. Refrains of tunes echoed in her brain. 'Some day I'll find you . . . speak to me of love. You are my heart's delight.' Everyday she hoped to catch a glimpse of him. Twice she had been to Valda's café on her own, sitting there in the smoky haze, nibbling a Spam sandwich after surveying every outdoor worker on the bomb sites to see if he was there.

Meanwhile, the WANTED poster of him in the local newsagent's had become curled up and torn because of people pushing past it, and soon Mrs Hemmingway pulled it down and tossed it away. 'It's had a good innings,' she told her husband.

'Quite right, love,' said Alf who'd had enough of an army stint in 1914. 'Gloomy things like that don't do much for sales. Get one of them Marlene Dietrich posters up instead.'

Then one day, towards the end of a daffodil-strewn April, Liz saw him again. He was nowhere near the café. He was sitting quite openly in crowded Piccadilly Gardens; his wavy, slightly unruly hair wisping in the wind as he read a newspaper. He was wearing a sports jacket, collar and tie and cavalry twill trousers. She looked and looked again. He was just like a casually-dressed office worker or a university student. Doubts began to flood her mind. It couldn't possibly be him! Her longing for him was completely out of control, she thought. People often had doubles. This respectable young Manchester man, sitting here so innocently was her own projection, a wish fulfilment.

She stood at a distance, not wanting to take the chance of being mistaken. She wanted to cling to this image of him, the normal Ernst, a civilian, as if the war was over, here on this breezy April day with blue skies and pigeons strutting about on the garden paths, and sparrows chirping busily amongst the municipal flower beds.

Suddenly a woman, with a shopping basket resting further along on his bench, got up and moved away.

With a change of thought, Liz walked to the seat and took the woman's place. She sat there stiffly for a few seconds to control herself, then took a sidelong glance. She frowned. She took another look. Her heart gave a jolt.

Surely, surely it *was* him.? She was near enough to see slight shrapnel scars at the side of his nose. To anyone who hadn't known his face so well, the marks would have passed completely unnoticed.

She bent towards him. 'Excuse me,' she said. She planned to ask him if he had seen a parcel there, to pretend that she had left it a while ago. 'Did you happen to see —'

'Liz!' He moved towards her immediately, his face alight with true joy. 'Let's go somewhere quieter and talk.'

She felt quite faint now. It was almost like a dream come true. They walked through the crowds towards Market Street and then to a secluded spot near St Anne's Square, where they sat down on an empty seat beneath two trees. He held her hand, and told her what had happened.

'. . . I didn't dare acknowledge you when you went to the café that day. It was all I could do to keep working on the bomb sites and avoid being discovered.' He began to relate how lucky he was to have met Paddy O'Brien and to have been given shelter with old Cissie, as he described her basement beneath the rest of the bombed house.

Then he said quietly: 'I've been thrice blessed. I met you in my hour of need in hospital. And now my prayers have been answered again and here we are together. Oh, Liz, what will this world bring next?'

They kissed each other. It was the first time. Their mouths sought the warmth and comfort of each other's lips with longing and relief. It was like coming home.

'What was the third blessing?' asked Liz, a little later as they clung together.

'The third blessing was that Cissie gave me an identity card to help me get more work. She keeps some behind her clock. They were from dead people killed by bombs. She gave me the card of Edmund Carlton Young, aged twenty. He was an orphan, who had been one of her lodgers. She said it was better for it to be doing something for the living. She laughed and said I would have to change my name from Ernest Jones, but maybe the card would give me a better chance of getting more work.

'That was the day before she died. When I came back from work with Paddy she was lying there in a pool of blood. A piece of the wall had collapsed on her. Paddy told me to move out. He said he would report it. He wished me luck in finding somewhere else.

'For the last two months I have been working as an odd job man for a very rich old lady called Mrs Konrad Fortinscale. She has a very bad temper and lives alone in a huge house near Bury New Road. I answered an advertisement in the *Manchester Evening News*. I was interviewed by her daughter, Mrs Pracklin. None of the family will go near Mrs Fortinscale. There is only me there, living in the attic. She also has a daily woman called Franny who comes in to clean, and a live-out daily cook, called Mrs Walters. Mrs Fortinscale's husband was German but he died before the First World War. However, I have never said anything about my own background. As far as she is concerned I am Edmund Young, a Manchester war orphan. She agreed to take me on as odd-job man because she could hear me properly when I spoke, and that I reminded her of her husband.'

They both left the secluded seat and walked across to a

small café to drink coffee and eat rather strange tasting wartime bagels.

'I'm out near Boggart Hole Clough at present, on the other side of Manchester – at Booth Hall Children's Hospital, doing three months' training,' said Liz smiling. 'I'm quite close to you.'

'When can we meet again?' Ernst said anxiously. 'I still can't quite believe this is happening.'

'Neither can I. My next day off is next Tuesday.'

'Normally I only ever get Sundays off,' explained Ernst sadly. 'Except when I come into town on trips for Mrs Fortinscale. I never go out anywhere in the evenings. You understand why.'

She nodded sadly, then brightened. 'Perhaps we could write to each other, but we must write in English, and you must use your English name, just to be safe. I will write and let you know when my next weekend off is. We will keep in touch.'

They left the café and wandered like carefree dreamers along the streets, holding hands in the sunny spring air. Then they kissed once more and waved goodbye to each other.

Liz sat on the bus back to Booth Hall in a sort of daze as it made its trundling journey past the old red bricks of the huge Crumpsall Hospital. It had a resemblance from the outside to Bell Lane. She wondered about the future; her future and Ernst's future. She was filled with guilt and grief. How could she be in love with one of Hitler's soldiers – after the evil that had happened to her own family in her own land? Not so long ago she had been in love with Solly Meyer, who had been killed on a bombing mission. Yet Ernst's parents had been killed by bombs from similar missions. All of them were victims of the war for different reasons. She knew she loved Ernst now. Yet more and more she hated herself because of the fate of her parents. To some people she was now in love with a traitor, a runaway deserter disobeying the rules. Yet she could not abandon him.

What was to become of them?

10
TIME AWAY

The last week in April was very cold. It was as if winter was fighting with spring.

Mrs Fortinscale had stopped Ernst Jünger's Sunday off.

'I am staying with my daughter, Mrs Pracklin, in Wilmslow for the weekend. I'm going on Friday afternoon and shall be back on Monday morning. You can have the following Tuesday off instead.'

Ernst stood there silently in his overalls.

'Whilst I'm away you can get the old paint scraped off the back doors, and all of them re-painted.'

He nodded reluctantly. The amount of work he did for her, for a pittance of a wage, meant that she did not need to employ proper painters and decorators. She had done this before with another day off. It worked out that he had never made up on it, but worked a week with no time off at all, so that it had become one day off a fortnight.

'Don't look so petulant,' said Mrs Fortinscale peering up and down at him with shortsighted irritability. 'It's a wonder a young man as fit as you isn't in the fighting forces. Some of you don't know you're born. And remember not to turn any heating on or light fires while I'm away. We're half way into summer now, and it *eats* up the money. All my heating goes *off* when I'm out of this house. Let that be known here and now. I shall be able to tell if any of it has been tampered with. You've got a good circulation and plenty of work to keep you warm. If you light one stick or cob of coal, it'll be the sack for you my lad. My fuel bills have been too high this year, so I might as well go to my daughter's more often – to keep down the cost.'

The detached, Victorian house in an acre of garden was large and cold even with heating; but without it it was a total icebox.

He wrote a note to Liz.

. . . Alas dearest one I have to look after this great mausoleum for the whole of this weekend. My main job is to scrape and paint the back doors, including those of all the outhouses, and garages.

Please come and see me, but put on warm clothes as there is no heating.

Ring me up on Saturday if you can't come. But if you can I will meet you in Manchester by the cathedral steps on Sunday morning so that we can have the day together – here in frozen peace.

Yours, lovingly and faithfully,
Ernst.

Liz arrived at the cathedral steps fifteen minutes early. The buses were not very frequent on Sundays. She was wearing Dotsy Philips's light blue and dark blue, reversible, velour 'swagger coat' with a tie neck. A blue silk scarf covering her head had been borrowed from Ada Sawbridge. The price for borrowing anything was a full account to the rest of the girls about what happened on the borrower's time out.

Liz was staggered by the size of the house. 'And you mean to say she lives here all on her own with only two outside helpers, and you as the odd-job man?'

Ernst nodded. He was pleased at how freely they now spoke to each other as he took her to see all the work he had been doing over the weekend.

The back doors were scraped and sandpapered. The whole place was spotless. He had washed and ironed, sawn up a mountain of logs, tidied the gardens, washed all the greenhouse windows and swept the paths.

'I've prepared us some vegetable broth for midday.' His voice rang with happiness. 'We can eat it down stairs in the breakfast room. I have put a small fire in there.' He did not reveal the threats for even daring to touch a cob of coal. He was elated with loving kindness.

He led her upstairs to his attic room. The room was primitive and icily cold; it smelt musty with a tang of rotting apples. There was a gas ring, a tin kettle, an opened tin of condensed milk with a teaspoon stuck in it and some bottled coffee and chicory. Close by, on a rickety, green baize card table, which was covered by check oil cloth, were two breakfast cups without saucers and a chipped plate displaying two digestive biscuits.

'It won't take me a minute to make us a drink.' He beamed at her with pride and she smiled back. It was wonderful to see him looking so well after the terrible state he had been in when she first saw him. He was still very thin but he no longer looked so weak. He began to hum an old refrain which she knew immediately from her childhood. She joined in, murmuring the words gently and smiling.

He poured the coffee into the cups and added the boiling water. Steam rose from the cups into the shivering air.

'It's not much use taking your coat off up here,' he said, 'but it'll be warmer when we get down to the breakfast room.' His voice faded.

Suddenly in a moment they were close together and he was kissing her passionately. She had unfastened her coat and her scarf had fallen from her dark silky hair. Their hands were round each other's waists, drawing each other closer and closer until they could feel the pulsing of their hungry bodies and feel the passion of escape from sadness. He pulled her gently to a small single bed and they lay there fully clothed with their heads buried in each other's necks, snuggling and fondling with gentle and exploring hands. They kissed like a falling of melting snow until they lay back still in sublime and silent peace.

Then Ernst said in a small voice: 'Are you a virgin?'

Liz turned her face to him and there were still tears of happiness in her eyes. She looked at him and saw again the tiny shrapnel scars on his face.

'I am.' She recalled the true damage hiding on his covered body and did not ask him the same question.

His face clouded over. He said slowly: 'I have no feeling yet to be a real man. No urges. Ever since I was wounded it has been the same. This love we have at present is like puppy love. Yet I long for proper love with you. The moment the deep excitement comes it suddenly fades.'

She smiled at him. 'I understand.' She stroked his forehead and followed the shape of his eyebrows. 'Don't worry Ernst. I would never want more than this between us – unless we were going to marry. I know this is not our time yet. We must not spoil it too soon. It is enough that we have found each other.'

She got up from the bed.

He hesitated. 'If only it had been a better day . . . A day in summer. If we could have been swimming together or lying on a beach. Instead of here in this freezing attic with you in your coat and me in a thick jersey.'

Liz smiled. 'Perhaps one day it will all be different. We are lucky to have found each other. Lucky to have warm clothes. Lucky to be alive.' She shivered as she thought of her parents and her sister.

He knew what she was thinking. 'Come on. You look cold. Lets go downstairs.'

They went down to the breakfast room and soon they were sat down sipping and savouring the hot broth. A warm fire glowed in the small grate.

Towards the end of the meal Ernst switched on the radio so they did not hear Mrs Fortinscale arriving with her daughter until it was too late.

'I think I can hear my employer's voice,' said Ernst calmly. 'Take no notice if she comes in here. We are civilised people. Finish your broth. We are doing nothing wrong.'

Mrs Fortinscale, in her heavy fur coat (good enough for

sledging round the North Pole), took one look at them both sitting in *her* breakfast room with a fire roaring half-way up the chimney, and gave an almighty howl of anger like some animal in pain.

Her bony daughter, in tweeds and a green Robin Hood hat with a feather in it, stood behind her looking intensely worried. She had brought her mother back, merely to check up on the recruit. He was the last in a long list of her mother's 'handy-men', who always disappeared in a flaming row, usually without further trace. This present situation was a classic case.

They had arrived merely to tell Edmund to keep the heating off a bit longer, as Mrs Fortinscale was not going to be returning until late on Tuesday. This meant that his day off would have to be postponed 'for a few days' as he would need to get the heating back on in Mrs Fortinscale's vast bedroom and sumptuous sitting-room very early on Tuesday morning, as well as checking carefully on all the mouse traps (there were two hundred and three of them).

'You are sacked! Get out of my house this instant!'

Hildegard Pracklin flinched slightly at her mother's words. She had heard them many times before.

'Patience, Mother. Patience. If you sack him now. You won't have any heating when you get back and I certainly shan't have time to see to all the mouse traps. I shall be at a wartime food recipe conference with Lady Plunger at Saltly village hall.'

Her mother ignored her completely. 'Get out and take that little whore with you! I never want to see you again. I'll give you fifteen minutes to pack your belongings, and if you aren't out by then I'll call the police. No one trifles with *me*, my lad. No young upstart uses *ONE PIECE OF COAL* whilst I'm away from this house!'

Ernst was ready in five minutes flat. He fled with Liz by his side. He was owed two weeks' money. They walked quickly to Bury New Road and were lucky enough to catch a bus into town. Liz felt sick with fear. It was as well that he had escaped from the place, but what was to become of him now, and where would he sleep tonight?

She looked at his pale face and spoke to him quickly. 'The best thing would be for you to come back and stay the night in my room at Booth Hall. I know it's a terrible risk for both of us, but it's far better than you wandering about without money in your pockets. There's a seat, by the bus terminus about five minutes walk away. We'll go there now and you wait there for me while I let the girls know what I'm going to do.'

Liz left him and hurried to the main hospital gates. Her own room was at the end of a short corridor of ten bedrooms. She was between Dizzy Oaklands and May Greenrigg. The other two were there when she arrived, but were due back on duty after a split shift. She began to tell them what had happened. She was careful not to say that it was Ernst Jünger. She called him Edmund Young.

'. . . So he'll be here during the night. He can sleep under my bed on the floor out of sight – just to be on the safe side. I thought I'd better tell you all, especially with that terrible case of that man getting in and attacking a nurse, just before we came here.

'Edmund's lost his job today. The woman he worked for was a real monster; she dismissed him right in front of me. He has nowhere to stay the night. I'll tell you more about it when he's gone, tomorrow. It's just to say I'll be bringing him back about eightish tonight. Then if we manage to get in without being seen I'll stay in my room with the door locked, and the curtains closed just to be on the safe side. Then I'll see him out, over the wall, early in the morning before I go on duty again.'

When she'd gone back to find Ernst Dizzy said to May: 'It's that German prisoner isn't it?'

May looked away and said, 'I don't know. She called him Edmund. As far as I'm concerned it wouldn't be for me to say.'

Dizzy was unusually thoughtful as she stood at her bedroom door before closing it to go on duty. With a sudden change of mind she went back into her room, found a notepad and hurriedly scrawled Liz a note: 'If Edmund is ever short of a job tell him to go to Valda's. She always needs extra help in the kitchen. Dizzy.' Then she pushed the note under Liz's door, and rushed off to get on the wards.

Liz was surprised how easy it had been to smuggle Ernst into her room. It was as if the Gods were with them. Sunday was always a quiet day, and soon he was in her bedroom with the door locked and the curtains closed. They spoke together in whispers and drank fizzy lemonade and ate jam sandwiches which Dizzy and May had left for them.

She had picked up Dizzy's note from the bedroom floor and had put it in her pocket when she and Ernst had arrived. Then as the evening wore on, she suddenly remembered and pulled it out to read.

She handed it to him. 'It's from one of the girls. Her sister Valda owns and runs that small café near the bomb site. Keep the note in case you are stuck for a job or need to send me a message. You must not say anything about being at the hospital, Ernst. And you should always keep to the name of Edmund and always write in English.'

'Yes. I will.' He smiled with heartfelt gratitude even though her instructions were patently obvious to him.

He helped Liz to spread a blanket on the floor under her bed and a pillow, as they settled down to try to sleep.

At first, all that he could think about was what he would do from now on and how he would survive, but eventually sleep came and he passed into complete oblivion.

Liz lay there still awake, still worrying what she would do if they were caught, and telling herself that if it happened she would just have to face the consequences of harbouring an enemy deserter, and seeing the end to her nursing career.

At five o'clock the next morning they were both awake. She watched him washing himself. Much to her alarm he had stripped down. She stared at all the scars left by his war wounds; they were livid and disfiguring. She could see the stitch and clip marks scored into his body like lessons of history. One deep wound left across his stomach was still seeping slightly, staining his underwear.

Quickly she found a clean handkerchief and covered it, making it stay in position with zinc oxide sticking plaster, knowing that probably this might be the last decent wash he would get for ages.

It was an agonising parting – quietly tearful and quick

as she dressed and went with him to the hospital wall, knowing that soon the night staff would be coming round to wake up the day staff.

No sooner was he away, and she back in her own room with her bed made when there was a rattling of keys along the doors. There were voices and someone was unlocking all the rooms without warning. Swiftly she grabbed some of her study books and sat at the small dressing-table reading them.

She was not a moment too soon as the rattling keys reached her and the door burst open. A hawkish-looking Night Sister with quick darting eyes was standing there in a tall white hat and a scarlet and navy cloak. She stared at Liz suspiciously. 'You're up and dressed extremely early, nurse?'

Liz's heart thumped. 'Yes sister. I always get up very early. I like to get all my studying done before I go on the wards – and then the day is clear.'

The sister nodded. She could see now that Liz looked the studious type. Not like the other untidy room she'd just looked in: now *that* one really had looked suspicious except that Nurse Oaklands was snoring her head off. Rather too loudly, she thought. All the same she had taken a swift look under the earthquake of a bed. Disappointingly there was only something that looked like a concertina and six pairs of high-heeled shoes.

'Have you heard anything unusual, nurse? There has been a report of a man seen climbing over the hospital wall and a nurse was there.'

Liz looked straight at her and shook her head. 'The walls are very thick. I never hear anything.'

The sister nodded, departed and proceeded to rattle her way to the end of the row, flinging open doors as she went with a huge echoing crash, until finally there was silence again.

'How did you go on yesterday, on the date?' said Dotsy and Ada, the following afternoon when Liz was returning the reversible swagger coat and the blue silk scarf.

Liz smiled her thanks. 'I was dressed just right for a bitterly cold day.' She said no more.

'I expect the next borrowing will be that sumptuous gown of Dizzy's again,' said Dotsy tactlessly.

Ada stiffened suspiciously and moved away hurriedly, saying she had something else to do. Her memories of that awful frock, when Karina had worn it and it had snuffed out her own long term romance with Ronny Ronson still rankled deep down. However, her regimen of 'all work and no play' was gradually diminishing. She had been out a number of times with Dr Slater, who was a Junior Doctor. He had asked her for a date when they were on Outpatients together. He had noticed that she had a very firm grip when it came to clamping down on struggling and obstreperous patients.

Dizzy, who also happened to be on Outpatients at that time, had watched the romance blossom in happy silence. Thankfully, Berty Slater did not remember ever having seen Dizzy in the doctors' quarters when he was inebriated at Dr Blenkinsop-Barns's party. The effect on Ada of finding this faithful admirer had been heartening to see. Everyone agreed it was the perfect match: efficient, no nonsense, luxury-minded Ada and quiet, when sober, Bertram Slater.

'I think I might be the next one to borrow the gladrags,' said Dotsy, half to herself as Ada disappeared. One thing that puzzled her slightly though – was that May never seemed to wear the dress herself.

It was not until they were all back at Bell Lane again, and well into their final studies, that Dorothea Philips decided to try her luck in May's frock.

11
PARTINGS

On the first of May, in the centre of Manchester, huge cart-horses went about their work, their leather halters shining, their brasses glowing. They were decked out with brightly-coloured ribbons and rosettes, delighting workers and shoppers in the bombed city streets.

Only yesterday, on the 30th of April, in Berlin, Adolf Hitler had committed suicide.

The German soldiers had all been moved. They had disappeared as quickly and silently as when they had first arrived. Their ward had reverted to being a civilian male medical ward.

Nurse Downs, who was now working on Outpatients, recognised Ernst Jünger immediately when he was wheeled in on a hospital trolley. Ernst was in a cubicle lying on a trolley stretcher, semi-conscious. It was a hot sunny day. He had been knocked down by a van close to Valda's café where he was a washer-up and cleaner in the kitchen. He was groaning and mumbling in German and his eyes were closed.

A German Staff Nurse from one of the maternity wards was sent for to act as an interpreter. She stood there, thin and sunburned, with dark curling hair and a white cap. Her small silver and gold nursing badges glinted against her brilliant white, starched apron in a picture of precise efficiency.

'He says his name is Ernst Jünger and he's a prisoner of war – here at Bell Lane,' she said quietly.

Nursing staff and doctors looked at each other. The rest of the wounded German prisoners had been sent to a camp on the Welsh borders to fully recover.

Sister Villiers filled in his details on the case paper. She frowned slightly. Surely this was the name of the patient who had gone missing on GPW1? There had been an in-hospital, toned-down enquiry as to how it had happened.

Sister Villiers mentioned her suspicions to the Chief Casualty Officer, Dr Spencely. He nodded his head and noted it but said nothing. One could never assume that the words of a casualty case, who had been admitted in a state of semi-consciousness after being knocked down in an accident represented a true state of affairs. From now on observation would be needed, and careful investigation, whilst the patient was recovering. If this patient was the missing man, his notes would have to be found – which meant such things as comparing records of Jünger's teeth and the history of his war wounds – to see if they tallied with the groaning man who lay in the green curtained cubicles.

Nurse Downs, the nun, touched Ernst's hand. His eyelids flickered imperceptibly.

'We know each other from GPW1, when I was on nights,' she murmured.

His eyes were still closed but he muttered: 'Night Nurse . . .'

Nurse Downs's freshly-scrubbed face smiled slightly beneath her straight, chopped-off hair as she went about her duties. She made a silent prayer for him.

At first, to Ernst, it all seemed like a mixed up dream. He was in the cafe; he was on the bomb site with Paddy; he was in the house cellar with Aunt Cissie; he was at home with his family in Germany; he was at school; he was with the awful woman who cared more for saving a lump of coal than real warmth. He was with Liz . . . Liz! He opened his eyes wide for one staring, amazed moment, then lapsed into brief sleep.

The next thing he knew, he was being examined by doctors, with a nurse who spoke German whom he'd never seen before. He was extremely cautious and began putting two and two together: he had been knocked down outside the café; he was here in hospital; back in the one he had escaped from.

A doctor questioned him about his accident. 'Apparently you were struck by a van. Can you remember any of it?'

Jünger kept his eyes closed. He felt totally weary and did not answer. All he could remember was washing pans, cleaning the stove in the café, washing the floor, then getting ready to go back to the place he shared with other people in Moss Side. Valda had found it for him. It was a squat, an empty house full of homeless people. They all slept on mattresses on the floor. The largest room, which had been quite luxurious about fifty years ago, was now filled with women and children. As well as mattresses, there was a carpet on the floor and a dining-table, heaped with belongings. An ancient mahogany sideboard with an ornate, plate-glass mirror shone gloomily in the sparse day light which sifted through drawn curtains and half rolled-up black-out paper.

'Send him to X-Ray, first,' said Dr Spencely. 'Then to the side ward in Male Orthopaedic.'

By the time he was in the side ward, Ernst realised that his only hope of real salvation was to keep silent, and to claim only the knowledge of being on the German Prisoners Ward. As far as the world was concerned, his memory in between being in the ward and the accident was now a complete blank. He had gleaned from the X-Ray that he had a query fractured skull and a cracked shoulder blade. As he lay there, giving thanks to God that at least he was now settled in a place of care between clean white sheets, he thought of Liz again, but he knew that on no account must he try to get in touch with her, for the sake of both of them.

Liz was at one of the finals lectures when Nurse Downs came over to her.

'Ernst Jünger is back in the hospital,' said Downs.

Liz had not seen or heard of Ernst for over a month. She knew he was working at Valda's because Dizzy had told her, but Dizzy was on two weeks' holiday at present, so there was no regular report. Liz was due to take her own two weeks' holiday when Dizzy came back. She was going to go on a group walking holiday, to Ambleside in the Lake District, to a holiday centre known as Loughrigg. She had been told about the holidays by May who had already been.

Nurse Downs led her away from the rest of the girls. 'He's just been admitted and sent to Male Orthopaedic. He was knocked down by a van.'

Liz felt all the blood draining from her face.

She and Ernst had thought it safer for him to settle into his single life as Edmund Young in the homeless house until she had sat her examinations. It was a hard path to take but they both knew it was essential. Once, when she had called in at the café, and they had stood together in the sunshine at the back door, she had suggested that when she passed her final exams there might be a chance of them sharing a flat together. 'I will be a fully qualified nurse – and able to get a living-out job,' she had said.

After she had gone he felt terribly miserable. She at least was in a legitimate position, in spite of the horrors of her past life. He, on the other hand, was a hunted man, a deserter and prisoner of war. He had escaped but there was not a hope of him getting back to Germany.

'He is suffering from a gap in his memory,' said Nurse Downs to Liz. 'All he remembers is his time on the German ward. The period when he disappeared is a complete blank.' She gave Liz a straight look. 'Do you think you'll go and see him on Male Orthopaedic?'

'Do you think they'll allow it?' Liz looked back at her in an agony of despair.

'I'm going back there to see him when I come off duty tonight,' she said. 'Sister Gills seems to think it would be a good idea and might help his memory to improve. I'll ask for permission for you to see him, too?'

When Nurse Downs got to the ward that evening, her hopes were dashed.

'His X-Rays are clear,' said the Sister. 'But he has concussion. He has to lie flat in the darkened side ward with no visitors whatsoever.'

On the evening before she was due to go on holiday, Liz decided to go up to the ward herself and try to see him. She had heard from one of the day staff Senior Nurses at dinner-time that he was much better.

Nurse Partington gossiped: 'But he's driving all the Doctors mad because he claims a complete loss of memory for the time when he walked out of the German ward. It's so difficult because he talks only in German. His grasp of English is almost nil.' She gave Liz a sad look as they ate rissoles, cabbage and potatoes. 'It would probably do him good to see someone he recognises. You might be able to say a few words in German to him. I'm sure he'd appreciate it.'

Liz nodded tactfully. She prayed that he had not truly lost his memory.

'I'm on duty tonight with Staff Dawly,' said Partington. 'It's pretty quiet at present. Why don't you pop along about eight?'

Liz walked quietly into the side ward. The whole place

was peaceful and harmonious, in readiness for the night staff to take over at half past eight.

Ernst was lying there half asleep. He had been sitting out in his chair by the side of the bed during the day. He wondered what was going to happen, and where he would be sent. He had heard the specialist and one of the doctors mentioning that he was due to be transferred, but he did not know where. Supposing it was to a lunatic asylum? In those places it might be worse than being an official prisoner. He moved uneasily in the hospital bed and as he did so he heard someone whispering his name. Ernst. Ernst. Dearest one.

Just a voice in his head? He froze as he lay there with eyes closed, hoping. Hoping, but not daring to look.

'It's me – Liz.' She gazed down at him fearfully and touched his cheek, whispering tenderly: 'Nurse Downs told me you'd been admitted.' The words flowed from English to German in a soft torrent. 'The Staff Nurse says they think your mind is partly blank —'

'It isn't. It isn't.' He pulled her down towards him passionately. 'I remember everything, but I dare not admit it.'

She gave a trembling sigh of relief. 'They say that given time you will remember things again. They think it could be delayed shock from the accident. You are being sent to an interim hospital as a recuperating prisoner. But your escape from here is not going to be mentioned – it's too much of a blot on the security system, and would need a full and detailed enquiry. You'll be sent to work on a farm as an ordinary prisoner of war. It could be anywhere in the North of England. And when the war ends you'll be repatriated.'

He soaked up her words like a man still in a dream. He stared at her dumbly with tears in his eyes. 'Are you sure?'

'As sure as anyone can possibly be.'

He clasped her hands. 'My darling. Oh my darling one. My own sweet love. I still can't believe it. I will not be a deserter after all.'

She felt a sudden stab of pain. He seemed more pleased about not being classified as a deserter than anything else. Surely he wasn't still proud to be in Hitler's army? The hatred of it all flooded back to her. The indescribable crimes . . . the murder of the innocent. She blotted it out. She and Ernst had both been survivors; both been united by the death and suffering of their loved ones.

She saw his face – so pale and honest – yet so bound by the deceit of survival. She put her lips to his. For a few seconds they felt the magic flow of human warmth from one to the other. Tasted the salt of their tears. Felt the softness and the grief and joy, yet dreaded the desperation of the unknown paths ahead, in such a brief clandestine meeting. For both of them knew it was the parting of the ways.

There were sounds of footsteps outside the side ward. Liz hastily wiped her eyes and sat up stiffly in the chair by the bed. Ernst put out a thin hand and straightened the slightly crumpled sheet across his sheet.

Staff Nurse came in. 'I'm afraid it's time to go.'

Liz stood up smiling brightly but with a breaking heart. 'Goodbye then, Ernst. It's been nice to see you. I am going on holiday shortly. Let's hope by the time I return that you will be better and will have moved on like the other men, and that one day you will be home.'

She turned away quickly and hurried from the ward. Blindly she rushed to her room and flung herself on her bed to weep.

A week later she was on holiday in Ambleside.

12
SENIOR NURSES

Liz set off on her holidays feeling in the depths of gloom and misery. Reports in newspapers and newsreels at the cinema of what British troops had found when they entered Belsen concentration camp, and the Red Army at Auschwitz added to her despair. It left her with little but a grim thread of determination to survive – for the sake of her dead parents and sister. To survive at whatever the cost, whatever the future.

She blinked back the dry tenseness in her throat and eyes as she heard her mother's voice so vividly. She saw them, on that day never to be recovered, for the very last time standing there, calm, still, and proud. 'Our cherished child. At last you have the chance to escape . . . At least there may be *one* of us.'

She was still here. Still here to try and overcome their terrible past.

It was a consolation to find that once she was away on her holidays, her mood of desolation began to change slightly with the beauty of her surroundings. The early summer of dry weather, with a lasting touch of young leaves still fresh on oak and beech and silver birch; the lambs on the fellsides and in the fields; the splashes of light and warmth amongst the heavy purple shadows of deep valleys lifted her from her troubles. At the beginning she had felt alien to it all. It meant nothing. She was separate. Her whole inside was dead, but gradually, within two days, she began to change.

Each day she put on her stout walking shoes and, with about twenty others, walked up hill and down dale, across river bridges and rushing streams, along tracks and narrow footpaths to mountain peaks. One day it was Helvellyn and Striding Edge; another day to slaty Coniston Old Man; another to the Langdale Pikes. And, as she stood there with happy people gazing silently at the peaceful beauty of the earth in a patch of Lakeland, she began to feel better, feel part of life again.

When Victory in Europe was declared, the whole of Manchester around Albert Square, St Peter's Square and the Town Hall area was jammed with thousands of people, singing, kissing and hugging. It lasted until morning. Yet the six years of blood, sweat and tears had not quite finished. The final holocaust was in August when the atom bomb was used – to end the war with Japan.

*

By the time Dizzy Oaklands got back from her holidays, Liz was already on hers at Ambleside, and Ernst Jünger had been moved to an unknown convalescent home, to be eventually sent back home to Germany as a repatriated prisoner of war.

'Secondary loss of memory caused by delayed shell-shock,' was the term used to account for the gap in his stay at Bell Lane. No mention was made of his escape from the hospital, nor his return to it as a result of the accident.

Dizzy was talking to May in the Nurses' Home. They were in their blue hospital frocks with three horizontal white markers on the short sleeves. Their third year was nearly finished. They were truly Senior Nurses now, with final State Registration and Hospital Exams looming close.

'Did you meet anyone nice whilst you were away?' smiled May.

Dizzy laughed. 'It wasn't that sort of holiday. I went fruit picking down near Horsham. We worked like slaves filling punnets of blackcurrants. The fruit down there is absolutely enormous.' She produced a small yellow paper wallet of black and white photographs. 'We all had a marvellous time though. I met some more nurses there. There was every age and type of person there under the sun, and believe me it was *sun*. Just look at me! She sank back on the top of her bed in perfect bliss.

'Anything much happen here when I was away?'

May shook her head. 'I had a postcard from Liz. She seems to be enjoying herself at Ambleside.'

Dizzy suddenly remembered. 'Oh yes. There was one thing – did Liz mention that boy-friend of hers when I was away – Edmund?' Dizzy's face clouded over. 'He was supposed to have been knocked down in an accident close to Valda's café.'

May shook her head. 'Liz never said anything to me. I expect we've all been so tied up with our own affairs. And then with her being away, too.'

They both looked at each other silently. Neither of them mentioned it again. They knew very well that it was deep water.

Hurriedly May said: 'Did you know that Dotsy Philips is three months pregnant and swears she's expecting twins?'

'Never! Dotsy? I can hardly believe it. Are you sure? Does anyone else know?'

'Only us girls. She mentioned it when you were away. She said it would soon be too hard to disguise it anyway. She reckons it's Godfrey Pennylove's but he disclaims all knowledge.'

Dizzy's eyes bulged with amazement. 'Not *the* Mr Pennylove, the young Surgical Consultant who was in the RAF? He's supposed to be a ruthless womaniser. How ever will she cope?'

'You know what Dotsy is,' said May. 'She reckons she's going to *make* him admit it. She's not the type to cave in. It blossomed when she was on Female Surgical but she kept it secret.'

'Do you mean she actually went to his room in the doctor's quarters?'

'No. Never. It all started with them looking at surgical instruments together at Swainson and Simpson's in Oxford Road, and ended with her going to London to a surgical instruments exhibition. He was supposed to have booked her in for the night at a select Hostel for Gentlewomen, but when they got there he said it had vanished during the war. He didn't let on until the last minute because he thought she might be put off. Instead he had booked a double room at the Strand Palace and swore he'd sleep on a chair all night.'

Dizzy frowned doubtfully. 'It seems an awful way to start married life with him denying he's the father.'

'I think he's engaged to someone else, as well,' said May slowly. 'That's really the main trouble. The other one's an older woman, a niece of Matron Throstle's called Reeny Marsden, who is mad on riding point-to-point. Dotsy suspects she's pregnant too, caught on the hop in her forties . . . Dotsy only found that out by accident last week because she was talking to someone who knows Reeny and Godfrey.

'Godfrey Pennylove claims that Reeny's child will belong to one of the other steeplechasers when it arrives. He says he is completely sterile. It's a terrible situation.'

'Can't they test his sperm or anything?'

'He says he hasn't any.' May looked at Dizzy, and Dizzy looked at May with a comical expression on her face.

'Everywhere she goes these days,' said May, 'she carries that floral-patterned knitting bag full of white knitting wool. It's crammed with number tens and elevens knitting needles, and patterns of pram sets for bootees, mittens, bonnets and lacy matinee coats. All she ever talks about are the problems of slots, for threading ribbon through, and instructions saying Kl, Pl and K2 tg.'

Dizzy's mouth was wide with mock amazement. 'What

revelations! How is it I always miss something when I'm on holiday?'

May tried to look serious. 'All the time she's been working on the Female Surgical Ward, Mr Godfrey Pennylove has been a constant visitor in his course of hospital duties. So, if she has ever happened to be in the duty room when he's about, she has always endeavoured to have a knitting pattern of a baby in its pram set beaming at him from behind the covers of someone's case papers – accidentally on purpose —' She came to an abrupt end as Dorothea herself knocked at the door, then walked into the bedroom. She was blooming with good health. Her abdomen had a slightly curved look beneath her starched apron.

In June, not long after May and Dizzy had been talking about it together, there was a terrific showdown between Dotsy and Godfrey. He stopped her just as she was about to walk out through the lodge gates at the hospital. He was in his scarlet two-seater MG with the words DOCTOR displayed in it. He had hardly spoken to her except in his official capacity on the wards, since their jaunt to the fateful exhibition.

He drew up beside her and said coolly: 'Want a lift?'

She nodded and got in. What was this sudden kind action going to lead to?

He glanced surreptitiously towards her silky blue frock and loose velvet bolero. His experienced eyes were painfully aware of a slight bulge beneath the flared skirt. She looked beautiful; her complexion was like sun-kissed peaches. Her glossy brown hair glinted lighter from the sun along the edges of its neat waves. She was wearing small silk gloves and white sandals and carried an ivory leather sling-back hand bag.

'Going anywhere special?'

'Into town.'

'Day off?'

'Yes.'

'I'm going into town. My day off too. Fancy some nosh at the Kardomha and then a run out to Pickmere? Or are you going somewhere important?'

Dorothea looked hard at the noble profile and the slightly unruly hair. He had sharp grey eyes and well-kept hands, and wore a linen jacket, and very good quality summer flannel trousers. His open-necked sports shirt was one of Tootal, Broadhurst, Lee's best. Both he and she gave the impression that clothing coupons did not exist, even though neither of them were the type to buy extra ones from those who could not afford to spend their own.

'I had planned to go and see my auntie – but it was only casual,' said Dotsy. Then she added: 'But one *very* important thing I have to do is to get some more knitting wool for the baby's shawl. Knitting that will keep me busy until well after the Hospital Nursing Finals.' She stared straight ahead. Her voice had a slight ring of malicious humour. 'I was thinking about names in bed last night. I was wondering whether to call it Godfrey if it's a boy, and Dorothea if it's a girl.' She saw the lines of his jaw stiffen: 'That's just what I wanted to talk to you about.'

When they were in the café drinking coffee, he said: 'Do they know you're expecting, at the hospital?'

'How do you mean?'

'How the devil do you think I mean? The Matron! The powers that be! Do *they* know?'

She looked at him languidly and blinked her long lashes with indolent pleasure as he began to fidget. 'I haven't actually written it across the sky in huge letters. I don't want to kibosh my exams with any fuss.' She hesitated. 'All the girls know. Naturally . . . They're really looking forward to seeing if it looks like you.' Then she added: 'I expect it'll be the turn of a coin as to whether mine resembles you most, or whether Reeny Marsden's effort wins the day. Or will hers be named after one of the stable lads, in deference to you?'

He suddenly flushed to an angry red. 'Look – finish off that coffee and let's get away from here. Let's get out to some fresh air.'

They drove to Pickmere in solid silence, and drew up close to the lapping waters. It was a wonderful day with blue skies and sun. A few people were strolling about in the sparkling peace. Some others, with bicycles parked by the shore on the far side, were swimming. From the small hills and hummocks the houses of millionaires overlooked a lake, fed by three underground springs, that was one of the clearest and cleanest in Cheshire.

He pointed to some small wooden chalets, pointing out one which had pink curtains. 'Do you fancy a walk to that one? I have a key for it. It belongs to my brother and his wife. He and his family use it as a weekend place, away from the bombs.'

Dotsy walked beside him, entirely separate, with silent wariness. This was an unknown part of his background.

He never mentioned family details, any more than she mentioned her own. They usually lived entirely in the present. Yet here she was, already going to have his baby which would affect both their lives.

Inside the chalet was a brass oil-lamp with a green glass dome standing on a small square wooden table. Across the room at the back, in a recess, was a primus stove and a zinc mesh fronted food store on a kitchen table; also a sink and draining board and a small wooden kitchen dresser. The WC was in the garden. Beneath the sloping eaves of the chalet was a small attic bedroom with two bunk beds in it and some folded camp beds. A framed but faded magazine picture on the wall showed a woman and child standing in a rose-strewn cottage doorway.

They sat down in some wicker armchairs downstairs and neither of them spoke. She waited for him to make the first move.

He stirred restlessly. 'You're very quiet?'

'Haven't I a right to be?'

'I think you're making too much fuss about it all.'

She was absolutely staggered. 'Too much fuss. Have you gone off your head?'

'After all we both knew what we were doing, when we were away that time.'

'You said you would sleep on the chair all night.'

'Surely you didn't really believe that old ploy?'

'I didn't quite know what to believe. I'm not accustomed to sleeping with men in accidental circumstances. I didn't even know you'd got into bed with me at first.'

He smiled slightly. 'And then it was too late. Closed

eyes and complete innocence. A good bit of cover for any other "accidents" you'd had.'

At this point, most girls would have grabbed the nearest suitable object and battered him to death, screaming at his gross insults, but Dotsy didn't. She had no intention of making herself and the child in her womb suffer his nonsense. The icy streak inside her froze to a dagger of resolve. She would catch the devil if it meant waiting until the end of the world.

She stared at him as if he hadn't even spoken. 'Aren't you even going to find me a drink of tea? A pregnant woman has to be fed for two.'

He looked startled and began to hunt about for a tea caddy and a tin of condensed milk. He cursed because he could not find a tin-opener. She watched him idly. He was as helpless as a child in spite of all his surgical skills.

She walked over to the kitchen drawer. 'Use that meat skewer, *Doctor*. Make a couple of holes in the tin, then give the skewer a few taps with that old flat iron in the corner.'

She sat down again and waited. He was behaving like a little lamb now, as he fussed about, then poured out two cups of tea and offered her a biscuit out of a tin.

He gulped his tea quickly and said: 'Why keep harping on about Reeny Marsden? That whole tale is pure fabrication. To be quite candid, Reeny Marsden has been secretly engaged for the past ten days, to a galloping lawyer. The child that all the rumours were about, was never going to be mine. Oliver Streetfield and I knew it was his all along, but he was a bit slow in admitting it. So whoever told you otherwise was just a gossiping trouble maker – even though I grant that Reeny and I have always been very good friends.'

He looked at her with a pained expression. 'You seem to have some awful and false idea that I'm nothing but a womaniser. How on earth could I keep up with all my day to day work if that was the case?' he said pleadingly.

She didn't relent. 'I should think a man of your exceptional talents would be able to manage it fairly well. But one thing is certain: the father of this child inside me won't be a gadabout!'

His face brightened. 'You mean it isn't mine after all then?'

'I mean that when we're married it will be a different set of rules.'

They sat there for a solid five minutes with not a word, then Godfrey said: 'When shall we get it done?'

'Get what done?'

'Don't try to string me along. You know what I mean. Marriage of course.'

She gave a quick gasp of inward relief. 'As soon as possible. By special licence now you've asked me. I want it all settled before Sister Sorenson takes me to one side, demands a full explanation of my bulging outline and tells me that a pregnant and unmarried Senior Nurse has a poor chance of taking her finals.'

'There's a streak of blackmail about you, Dotsy.'

'And there's been a streak of playing fast and loose about you, Godfrey.'

He gave a grand, almost triumphant sigh. 'I suppose this is the proper "burning of the boats" at last. Should we go upstairs and seal it all?'

'Are you *serious*? And me your betrothed with not even a *secret* engagement ring or an official announcement in the *Manchester Evening News*?'

He looked down at the ground sheepishly.

She smiled at him with a sudden shaft of pure love. She had succeeded at last.

13
HOPES AND FEARS

'You mean you aren't even going to take your finals?' The girls all gaped at Queenie Marney as she shrugged her shoulders.

'You've worked for three years. Attended every single lecture, and passed every flipping exam and test we've ever been given!'

Queenie smiled faintly. 'That's how it is,' she said firmly. 'And that's how it's got to stay for the time being. Cyril Monkton has asked me to marry him, and at present the two paths of our working lives just don't join together. He's promised to make me an equal in the family business. We'll be proper partners in every sense of the word. Fish and chips have been in his family for the past forty years. It's up to him and me now – to make a go of it.'

'Sure, and it's only common sense what she's doing,' said Shirley O'Malley nodding with approval from her smiling, deep-blue eyes. 'What wouldn't I give to be in the same boat except that the Holy Mother seems to have different plans for me.' Her face clouded over. 'Patrick O'Dwyer married my sister and Herby Dawson, my second serious one, says he can't afford to marry or keep me in the manner to which he's accustomed. My only hope now is to build my own nest ready for someone else to share. Maybe it will be a nursing home or something.'

Everyone nodded. She would make a good matron in a nursing home. Homely, kind, and totally reliable. She was sure to come through her finals with flying colours.

Queenie gazed round at all the other girls again. 'I wouldn't have missed all this part of my life for a gold clock. Maybe I'll get back to nursing, one day. At least I'll know what I'm supposed to be doing if it ever happens. My old dad always used to say a bit of proper learning is never lost.'

'A person with more than one string to her bow,' remarked Ada ruefully when Queenie was out of earshot. 'She's the type who will take on anything and do well at it. Whereas me, I feel now that I'm doomed to spinster-hood for ever, as a quickly ageing Sister on a Gynae Ward. I can feel it in my bones already. Every time I see little white-haired Sister Tweddle and her flock.' She hesitated sadly. 'And to think how I hated it all when I first arrived. It seemed so restrictive. Maybe if Ronny and I had still been together —'

'It's no good saying maybe,' said May hastily. 'You've always got to try and look ahead.'

May was dreading the whole saga about Karina pinching Ronny from Ada being dragged up – just when it seemed to be finally fading away. She had always felt slightly guilty that the dress which Karina had worn at that dance had been hers . . . Yet on the other hand the result had been an extremely happy and fruitful marriage for kind Karen and Ronny.

'You've got more than one string to your bow as well, Ada,' said Dizzy, trying to be comforting. 'Think of all those years you worked in a bank, before you came here. I'm sure none of us would have had a clue about high finance. It takes me all my time to add up the change from a half-crown.'

A bit later that day, in her off duty, May decided to try on the dazzling gown that Mr Rooks had given her. It seemed ages ago now. She half wondered whether it would still fit her, considering all the stodge she had thrown down during her time as a student nurse. She was the only one who had never dared to wear her own property, except that first time when she had tried it on, for her mother and Mr Rooks.

She took it from the coat hanger in the wardrobe. It was as good as ever; the heavy oyster-pink satin, the ribbon rosettes, their tiny pearls and sparkling diamonds. The girls had been very careful with it. There was not a single mark or stain. She took off all her hospital clothes and slipped it on. It fitted her perfectly.

In the end, Ernst Jünger had not been moved out of Lancashire. He had landed, finally, in a very small prisoner-of-war unit where the men were sent out from a hostel in the middle of nowhere, to work under guard at forestry work. Thankfully it had not lasted long because final peace had been declared. But there was an interim period for the exchange of prisoners on all sides.

Every day he breathed thanks that he had managed to evade the life-long smear of being a deserter. He would be going back now, almost as a war hero.

He had never tried to get in touch with Liz again. His mind was on nothing else but returning home and finding out how things were in Germany.

Yet the peace declaration had also made Liz wonder about the state of things in her own part of Germany. All the time, in quiet moments, she brooded about going back to see if the house she had been born in was still standing complete.

There was no let-up in ward work when the Hospital Final Examinations began. The most important exams of all, the State Registration ones organised by the General Nursing Council, would come later. There was always a few weeks lull between them. There were questions on every conceivable aspect of nursing which required studying case histories of many classic illnesses and their treatments. A thorough display of nursing experience and specialist skills was essential.

Unfortunately for Dizzy Oaklands she had landed back as a Senior Nurse on Sister Mackonicky's ward, during the waiting period for the Hospital Exam results. Sister Mackonicky could never actually fault Dizzy for anything, but the barbs were still there. Mackonicky was a person who regularly picked one new student nurse out as a little jewel and if you were not that jewel, God help you for the rest of your career.

'Fancy you being back on Male Surgical,' said Staff Nurse Trencher humourlessly. 'Sister and I were just remarking how amazing it was that you were still here. Oh, and by the way – please remember that the new student nurses on this ward need to be set really good and strict examples of proper nursing. The ones here at present are almost as bad as your lot were. There's only one shining star amongst them and it's Nurse Posser.' Staff Nurse Trencher gulped dramatically and her neck began to flow rather pink. 'She is a perfect picture of what all the others should be aspiring to. Both Sister and I are in absolute agreement on it.'

Dizzy felt a simmering annoyance begin to rise.

Student Nurse Geranium Posser had realised quickly that she was the current 'chosen one' on Male Surgical. The legend was rife throughout her group's training school about being a 'shining jewel' of Staff Nurse and Sister. Some of the more spiteful girls, who were hardly likely to last out the course, intimated that she was nothing more than Sister's little lap-dog. They felt that most nurses shrank away from being singled out as a special case.

Geranium took no notice of any of it, as she sailed about with her nose turned to heaven half a millimetre more than anyone else's. She had known right from the moment she entered the hospital gates that she would be outstanding. Ever since she had arrived three months before she had had an acute sense of destiny. In fact she had been aware of her 'healing hands' from the minute she managed to screw the head back on her teddy bear when she was two and a half years old.

When Dizzy arrived on the ward as holiday relief for the ward's other Senior Nurse, Posser's face fell. She had been hanging round the duty room when the Staff Nurse and Sister were discussing the new off duty timetable. Clearly Nurse Oaklands did not appear to be their flavour of the month; she was being given the worst working schedule possible on the new off duty list, with not even a free evening before her following day-off.

'I'm willing to bet you a serious ten shilling note Oaklands'll not get through those finals,' said the Staff Nurse in a harsh rather pent-up voice to Sister Mackonicky. 'Look at all that scandal that went round about Matron's bed sock.'

'It was only a rumour, Trencher,' said the Sister with self-righteous innocence. 'Although I do agree with you. She has as much chance of getting those finals as anyone landing on the moon.'

Geranium Posser took special heed of it; she was not going to take orders from a Senior Nurse with such a terrible record! She felt a glow of zealous self-confidence and loyalty to the Sister. Her clear eyes and healthy-looking, flawless face shone with resolution. It was up to her to carry the banner of leadership and nursing propriety.

At first, Dizzy could make neither head nor tail of Geranium. Whatever was wrong with the girl? Was she hard of hearing? Everything Dizzy said to her seemed to go in at one ear and come out at the other.

'Nurse. Did you take the four hourly temps? There isn't a sign of them on the charts.'

There was the usual slightly impertinent look, thought Dizzy, then Geranium said, 'Staff didn't tell me to.'

'But Staff Nurse isn't here this afternoon. I'm in charge. Please get them done immediately. *Immediately*, Nurse Posser.' Dizzy fixed her with a look.

Dizzy began to get more and more suspicious. 'Did you test Mr Cleveley's urine specimen in the sluice?'

This time Geranium nodded and went on talking to one of the patients.

Dizzy went into the sluice. All urine testing was very important. She tested it herself. It went from green to orange.

'Nurse Posser could you come into the office for a moment please?'

Geranium followed her reluctantly.

Dizzy closed the door, and faced her accusingly. 'You never tested that urine did you?'

'Of course I did.'

'It wasn't recorded on the chart. What colour was it?'

'Green.'

Dizzy looked at her coldly. 'It was not green, and if you claim it was green you must be colour blind. Come back with me to the sluice.'

Hastily Geranium changed her mind. 'I was going to, but you keep giving me so many orders, I just don't know where I am. It's almost as if you're picking on me.'

Late the following day, after the Doctor's ward round, the final crunch came. Staff Nurse Trencher was on her day off, so the Sister was tending to soften slightly, in the absence of Trencher.

'Nurse Oaklands. Ask little Nurse Posser to make an enema tray and put it on Mr Broomhead's locker, with the screens round will you? I'll come over and supervise in a few minutes. She's the jewel in this group's crown. Her work reports are wonderful.'

Dizzy nodded and went to find Geranium. She was in the kitchen drinking tea.

'Please could you go and put the screens round Mr Broomhead and make up an enema tray. *At once* if you don't mind. I shall be away at the dispensary for a few minutes.'

Nurse Posser turned away with a haughty sweep of her nose. When Dizzy had gone she walked into the ward like royalty, and summoned Nurse Peebles to help her. They both carried the screens confidently to the wrong bedside, and placed them round Mr Brushley.

'Go and make up an enema tray and be quick about it, Peebles. I'm acting on Sister's instructions.'

Not for one moment did she really think that the order came from the Sister. As far as she was concerned it was merely Nurse Oaklands.

Mr Brushley looked at the tray apprehensively. 'Is that for me?'

Geranium pretended not to hear him. It wasn't the job of a mere patient to question.

He looked pleadingly at Nurse Peebles, who was more sympathetic and was nervously unrolling a piece of rubber sheeting to put on the bed. 'What's all this then, nurse?' he said.

'Don't worry Mr Brushley,' she whispered. 'Just an ordinary enema.'

Mr Brushley flinched. It was the last thing he wanted. 'Are you quite sure?' He looked round anxiously. 'Where's Sister?'

Nurse Posser had just got the nose of the rubber tubing poised ready for entry into his bottom when the Sister's face appeared round the screen. She was fuming with rage.

'*Not* Mr Brushley this morning Nurse,' she said with icy calm. 'It's not urgent. He can have one tomorrow, if it's necessary. Take this tray away and go and set a new one. And you, Nurse Peebles, take the screens over to Mr Broomhead's bed.'

Mr Brushley wiped his brow with heartfelt relief. He had never been constipated in his life, and he never intended to be.

'I said *Broomhead* in the first place,' said Dizzy with exasperation when she arrived back from the dispensary.

'As a matter of fact I heard you,' admitted Sister Mackonicky. 'Let's go in the duty room. I've an awful feeling that Nurse Posser isn't quite what I imagined.'

Dizzy said nothing. Nobody was ever quite what Mackonicky imagined. Even herself.

The Hospital Final Examination results were up on the notice board at last. Everyone was crowding round them, including Staff Nurse Trencher and Liz.

Staff Nurse looked with sour disbelief at the results.

Liz stared with sheer joy. She and Delyth Oaklands were joint first!

'I couldn't believe my eyes,' said Trencher when she got back to Male Surgical.

Sister Mackonicky said slowly: 'I noticed myself, on your day off, that there actually has been a bit of improvement in Oaklands since she started three years ago.'

Trencher sniffed, and her mouth became a hard line.

Then her face softened. 'Have you finished Nurse Posser's monthly report?'

The Sister nodded. 'Not *quite* as good as usual I'm afraid. But none of us is perfect, and she has a good way to go yet.'

Then the Sister said: 'I was just watching how well that young Nurse Peebles works. She's quite a little jewel.' They both smiled at each other with relief. They had found a replacement.

May had received a letter from a stranger. At least, she thought it was a stranger. Postmarked County Durham, it was addressed to 'Nurse Greenrigg', without even the initial of her first name, with the words St Alphonso's Hospital, Manchester. She sat alone in her room and stared at it. She had a vague sense of having seen the handwriting somewhere before but she could not place it. Carefully she tore open the top, and took out a single sheet of blue notepaper.

Dear Nurse Greenrigg,
I expect you will wonder who this is from after all this time, and you may not even remember me. I was one of the soldiers who came in after having my leg blown off in the parachute landings – over there. My name is Jamie Croxton.

May put down the letter for a second and gasped. Of course she remembered. How could she ever forget that night when the first wounded soldiers had appeared. Yet never in her wildest dreams had she ever expected to hear from Croxton again.

. . . My brother is now a student at Manchester College of Technology studying Civil Engineering. I am coming down to see him. I wonder if you are still a nurse at the hospital, and if so, whether we could meet again.

In affectionate remembrance,

Jamie Croxton.

May unfastened the top of her fountain pen. She found some notepaper and an envelope. Everything else was forgotten. Pleasure and excitement lit her face. She began to write back to him straightaway.

14
THE HOUSE-WARMING

After their first letter there was a flurry of correspondence between them. May arranged to meet Jamie Croxton, and his brother Craig, at Tiller's Private Hotel in Dodsbury. Tiller's Hotel was a quiet and select place with comfortable furniture and pleasant gardens. The food was all home cooked and at a very reasonable price. Some of the girls, like Ada and Dorothea, occasionally popped in for morning coffee on their days off.

She could hardly wait for the day to arrive. She longed to see how Croxton looked and how he had fared with his war injuries. He had now been fitted with an artificial leg and was working in local council offices in Durham as a clerk.

The weather was almost autumnal now, as May allowed herself the luxury of dreaming what she would wear when she went to meet them, and whether to buy a new pair of shoes, or have her hair set.

'I've never known you quite so excited about anything before,' smiled Liz. They were in Lewis's department store in Manchester, trying on kangol hats which were smart but inexpensive. May peered at herself in a large mirror. The hat this time was a small blue angora type one in a turban design. Liz was arrayed in a rust-coloured felt one with a turned back brim and dark brown petersham ribbon round the crown.

'At least it's keeping our minds off the Final State Registration results. I know we all did well in the hospital ones, but until we actually get our official certificates, I'll never rest.'

On the way back to the hospital they both sat there upstairs at the front, on a red double-decker bus, each of them clutching big, brown paper bags. They had bought a hat each, yet neither of them ever wore them much, except for very special occasions.

'We must stay away from shops for at least another two months,' said Liz. They both gazed out of the front windows with their own thoughts, as the bus rumbled along through Fallowfield and Withington.

Liz still worried about Ernst and wondered where he was.

On the morning when May was due to meet Jamie Croxton and his brother, May changed her frock in a rehearsal, full of nervous indecision. She was due to meet them at Tiller's at three o'clock. She planned to have her hair marcel waved at Dora's, just round the corner to the hospital, at half past eleven. It was getting quite late as she dithered about in her room, checking the stockings she would wear this afternoon to see they had no ladders, steeling herself to put pink pearl nail varnish on her nails without the small brush getting out of hand and wondering whether to put mascara on her eyelashes.

In the end she had to rush along Bell Lane at break neck speed to reach Dora's in time. She ran straight into a boy who was riding a bicycle on the pavement. She fell to the ground with a thud and her ankle bent inwards against the pavement. She was in agony.

The boy took to the road immediately and vanished as one of the girls from the hairdressers ran to her assistance. 'The little sod. I saw it all through the window! Are you all right?'

May tried to get to her feet. Her right ankle was so bad that she could not even put her foot on the ground.

Half an hour later she was sitting in Casualty. Her plans for meeting Jamie were at an end. Dreams of afternoon tea had vanished. An X-Ray was now on the menu. She looked mournfully at Liz.

'There's only one thing for it Liz. Seeing as you're off duty this afternoon, do you think you could do me the greatest favour in the world and break the news to them? It would be worse than awful for no one to turn up.'

May began to describe paratrooper Croxton to Liz. Liz had never seen him in those early days, her day-time ward had been a different one.

The moment Jamie Croxton saw Liz walking towards him into the hotel sitting-room he fell in love with her. There had been a phone call from May, full of profuse apologies and telling him Liz would be there instead. 'She's one of my best friends . . . A real last minute fiasco. I'm most terribly sorry . . .'

The phone call was completely forgotten as Jamie gazed at the small curvaceous girl with glossy black hair and shining eyes. She stood there hesitantly in a plain, light-coloured two piece costume, borrowed from Ada and her newly-bought hat from Lewis's. She was blushing, not quite knowing what to say next.

Shyly, she faced the two brothers: Jamie with his round and pale smiling face, dimple grooved cheeks and dark, well-shaped eyebrows with his walking stick resting by the chair; and Craig, thinner, fairer and more gangly. It was the first time she had ever been in such a situation in her life – in a hotel facing two strange men with no proper introduction.

Craig smoothed the way, unconcerned by the awkwardness of the other two. He asked Liz which ward she was on and spoke about his own course in engineering and how he found the flat he was now in. 'Some of them live in halls of residence but I've got a decent place in Victoria Park. A ground-floor flat. It means that Jamie can come and stay any time he chooses.'

Liz began to relax. By the time the cream cheese and cucumber sandwiches had arrived – she had poured out cups of tea and they had gone on to devour scones and blackcurrant jam, and cream cakes – she was almost a school girl again.

'How did it go?' said May when she got back.

'Oh it was *lovely*. I really enjoyed it. They were really sweet to me.' She hardly knew what to say next as May looked at her radiant enthusiastic face.

'Jamie says that as soon as your ankle's better, we must all meet again.'

May noticed it immediately. 'All meet again.' Somehow she had imagined it as a special thing for herself and Jamie Croxton. A picking up of past threads, a special bond. Now it was turning into something entirely different: a foursome. She felt a deep sense of disappointment, but she tried not to let it show. It was just a twist of fate and at least Liz looked happier than she'd ever seen her. Perhaps she was just being supersensitive. She would never really know until she actually met Jamie again face to face.

'Thanks for holding the fort until next time anyway,' said May loyally. 'I expect it will be after our final results now – before I meet Jamie – if this ankle is anything to go by. Anyway, it's something nice to look forward to.'

Two weeks later, when Liz was in town standing in a bookshop in her navy blue gaberdine raincoat, she suddenly felt a tap on her shoulder. She looked up into quizzical, friendly eyes.

'Hello there. We meet again! I've come over for a football match this afternoon. It's quite handy having a brother with such a convenient address. How's May's ankle?'

Liz became flustered by the sight of him. The last time they had met she had been dressed up for the occasion, but this time she was without make-up or fussy hats and her old gaberdine was fading with constant wear.

'It's getting better,' she said. She felt herself going hot

and cold. 'She has it strapped up with a firm crepe band-
age. She's on light duties in the ward. She's looking
forward to seeing —'

He broke in quickly: 'The match is this afternoon. Is it
your day off?'

She nodded.

'Do you fancy coming out for the evening? I could call
for you at the hospital. We could go somewhere and have
a meal?'

Her eyelids fluttered nervously. 'Do you mean all four
of us?'

He looked puzzled. 'All four of?'

'May, Craig and —'

He looked a little embarrassed. 'I hadn't thought of it
like that. I meant just us.' He stared at her suddenly. 'I
love you Liz. I want to marry you. I knew it the moment
I saw you.'

Time stood still. People in the crowded bookshop shuffled round and edged past them as they stood transfixed,
neither of them looking at the other.

He took her hand at last and led her outside into the
busy street. The cold, damp air brought them to their
senses.

He smiled. 'Did I shock you? I expect it was a bit sudden. I'm usually pretty slow on that sort of thing. Maybe
the battlefields have made me realise the folly of hiding
the truth. It's complete self-interest. I've not even waited
to see how you feel. I'm completely at your mercy.' He
spoke the last words quite jokingly. It was almost as if the
former intensity had never existed.

Liz's mind was at sixes and sevens. Not for one

moment had she imagined, since her one brief, sad romance with Solly Meyer, that any other man would suddenly fall in love with her so quickly. She had cocooned herself in her own on-going love for Ernst Jünger, which had vanished like her other affairs. Being swept off her feet was an entirely new and almost frightening experience. All that she knew of Jamie was what May had said about him when he had first come into May's ward as a wounded paratrooper. When she had gone to meet him at Tiller's Hotel he had hardly spoken to her, nor she to him. Yet now, she too was swept up in the passion of these sudden moments. Her brain raced in a tumult of relief and desire. This feeling, she knew only too well, was the longing to be wanted and protected, to have a love of her own, a man to turn to at last. Someone who would understand her and cherish her just as she would cherish them. A final loving security after the first brief spark between herself and Solly Meyer . . . That past spark . . . coming too late and taken from her before it had hardly begun. But now, this must be the proper love at last? It must, she thought.

'So do you think you will come out with me tonight? Just the two of us?' He looked at her with forceful pleading in his eyes.

'I will.' She spoke the words solemnly. It was almost like a marriage service.

They arranged to meet by the Hospital Lodge at a quarter past seven that evening as she waved him goodbye.

All the way back on the bus to the Nurses' Home she began to worry about what she had done. However could she tell May what had happened? Yet how could she deceive her by never mentioning it? She thought of Karina and Ada, and how Karina had inadvertently stolen Ronny Ronson away from Ada, and how it had caused a break in the friendship between the two girls. Surely this wasn't going to happen to her too? The last thing she wanted was to spoil her own friendship with May.

When she got back, the first person she saw was May.

'Did you find anything good at the shops?' said May.

May's words jarred at her conscience. They had a double meaning now. The whole meeting seemed tawdry when really it had been wonderful.

'I . . . Well, yes.' She took a deep breath. She would tell May everything, explain how it had been a purely chance meeting. How Jamie had asked her out tonight because it was her day off, just out of a need to keep in touch with both of them until May herself was quite better. Her voice faltered: 'I was in this bookshop . . . and I met . . .' Her hands were at her sides and her fists began to clench. 'I met a friend of Edmund's. What I mean is I met a man Edmund once knew when he worked on . . .' She faded out but May didn't seem to notice.

May smiled sympathetically. She knew that Edmund was really Ernst: 'It's amazing the people you meet from being a nurse,' she said tactfully. 'It has been just the same with me and Jamie. I was only thinking about him and Craig earlier on, when you were out. I think Craig was quite smitten with you. How amazing if it all grew into a double wedding. Me and Jamie, and you and Craig. I know Craig's a bit younger but always remember that age is only numbers. It has nothing to do with feelings. Are you doing anything tonight?'

Liz hesitated. 'I'm supposed to be going out with the person I met this morning.'

'*Supposed* to be? Don't sound so timid, Liz! It's a question of do you or don't you, and it's quite obvious that you *do* want to go. I can see by your face . . . Anyway duty calls. I must get back to the ward. Don't do anything I wouldn't do, and if you want to borrow anything special it's all there in the wardrobe.' May smiled cheerfully, and hurried away.

Liz did not borrow a single thing. How on earth could she, knowing what was happening. Feeling fatalistic about it all, she found a frock she had brought with her to the hospital, when she had first arrived over three years ago. It was a mottled pink and the skirt was far too long. It was a typical wartime effort; something raked up from a pre-war stocktaking clearance, substantially made and about a hundred years out of date. It had long sleeves and a white collar and cuffs.

She had slimmed down a lot and felt like Orphan Annie; but she did not much care now, or bother that the frock was far below the level of her old gaberdine. She felt that she would actually be glad if the whole evening was a complete fiasco and sank without a trace.

He was waiting for her with a beaming face, on time and just as arranged.

'My brother's gone out,' said Jamie, 'so we can go back there to Craig's place if you like. He's got plenty of food in. Or we could go out for a meal.'

She felt herself blushing with shame. He looked immaculate. His navy-blue striped suit was tailored to perfection and his hair shone in a closely cropped wave.

His eyes were bright with enthusiasm, yet here she was looking her very worst. How on earth could she say she wanted to have a meal out looking like this? She would put him to shame.

'I think I'd sooner go to your brother's. I wish I'd dressed up more.'

He didn't even seem to hear her words, as he described how good the football match had been. Then he said: 'I think you'll like Craig's place. He struck really lucky as far as flats go. It's ironic that he's got a vast, comfortably furnished place as a student, when not far away there are homeless families squatting. I think it's sometimes a case of absent landlords preferring to take a chance letting places out to the universities rather than having them occupied unofficially. He's even got a small refrigerator in the kitchen and there aren't many of those about! When he was interviewed for it, he got it because he was the only applicant who didn't smoke. Apparently there's a terrible lot of fire damage caused by cigarettes.'

They spoke to each other so easily. Soon she relaxed completely and by the time they got back to Craig's, they were as one, laughing and reminiscing about the best parts of their lives.

Together they sorted out the food, and finally they sat down to dine on cold meat and salad, and luxurious sliced bananas (never seen throughout the war) with cream.

'Shall I help you to wash up?' said Liz afterwards.

Jamie shook his head. 'There'll be time enough later.' He went over to the radio cabinet and lifted the smooth inlaid wooden lid. It was a streamlined affair in satinised light oak with four elegant angular legs. The knobs were all hidden under the lid. A selection of melodious dance music came from it: 'Won't You Change Partners and Dance with Me?' followed by 'Somebody Stole My Gal'. 'She didn't *even* . . . say she was *leavin'*,' Jamie murmured to it softly. Then he turned to Liz and said: 'That happened to me once, but now I'm happy again.'

Liz nodded. She was happy too, but the words of the music reversed themselves in her mind. Was she stealing May's boy?

The music changed to a recording of Al Bowlly singing 'Love is the Sweetest Thing' followed by 'I'll Get By'.

As soon as 'I'll Get By' came on, they both stood up from the chair, and began to sway together to the music. There was a passionate tension between them. Jamie slipped his hand round Liz's waist and they both held each other tightly in the fading light of the room. The refrain absorbed them as they stood rocking gently to the honey-sweet tones. '. . . But what care I? as long as I have . . . *you* . . .'

That night back at the Hospital Liz was happier than she had ever been in all her years in England. Her head fell against the pillow as if it was swansdown. Her eyelids closed to soothing thoughts of her next meeting with Jamie. Deep, untroubled sleep took over.

On the same night that Liz had been out with Jamie, Dizzy Oaklands bumped into Dr Fruity Sampson in Dodsbury village. He drew up with a screech in a clapped out MG missing her by an eighth of an inch as she tried to cross the road to catch a bus. As the car sprayed her legs with mud she exploded with anger. She did not see who the driver was, nor did she care as she bent down and yelled at the occupant: 'You blasted idiot! What the heck are you up to?'

Forty-two-year-old Fruity Appleyard Sampson, whose proper name was Fergus, gazed at the apparition bellowing in front of him, and frowned slightly. 'Aren't you Delyth Oaklands?' he said.

'Of course I am, you fool. And in another few seconds I'd have been a dead body!'

'Come off it.' He returned, 'This old banger won't go more than forty or the engine drops out. I was trying to be a gentleman and ask you if you wanted a lift? It also struck me that you might fancy coming to a bit of a do at Robin Bonsall-Claever's house warming. He's got a place of his own in Gatley, now. Or I could take you anywhere else you want to go first, and then go on to Rob's alone. But that would be rather sad?' He stared at her with his deceiving, droopy-lidded morose look. 'Get in anyway, and watch those muddy legs against my flannels.'

Dizzy got in. 'When you said you were going to a house warming – surely you didn't quite mean *now*?'

He nodded. 'Yes. Now. Where do you want to be dropped off then – or will you take advantage of a good offer and come and have a splurge?'

She glanced at him. She could never resist a party and he seemed perfectly sober. There was the advantage that if she went with him to Gatley, she could always walk back home afterwards because she lived there. It meant there was no risk in having to depend for a lift back with a drunken driver later on. She was not really dressed up for anything special but it was probably just as well. She certainly wouldn't have wanted to waste her best clothes on an outing like this. 'Right-O then – I'll chance it.'

'Chance it?' He looked quite indignant. 'You won't be going to a den of vice. Old Robin's as respectable as new mown hay, and his fiancée Myrna will be there anyway to keep him in order.'

Robin's little nest was a small Edwardian house with an added brick garage and a large garden. It overlooked an expanse of what had been fields, where some new houses were being built.

'It'll be goodbye to parties if the other houses reach his front door,' remarked Fruity as they parked in the unpaved drive and walked to the front door.

The whole place was ablaze with light. Through the windows Dizzy could see familiar faces; one of them was Rose Stansfield, who was waving a sherry glass about. These days Dr Stansfield held no terrors for Dizzy and she rarely saw her anyway, except in the corridor when Rose was on her way to the maternity wards. Time had flown since Matron's bed socks.

The first thing Dizzy did when she was inside the house was to ask the whereabouts of the cloakroom to wash all the mud from her nylons.

'Cloakroom, Delyth?' We haven't reached those Olympian heights yet. But the bathroom's next door to the bedroom where everyone can dump their coats. It's just at the top of the stairs on the right.'

The house had a lived-in look. In the bathroom, used razor blades were scattered across a window ledge in overlapping, rusty splendour. The bedroom, where all the coats were piled on an ancient oak three-quarter bed, had pale blue wallpaper with pagodas on it. Two obscure medical certificates in black frames hung uneasily on the walls, along with a picture of Bonsall-Claever in a cap and gown. The dressing-table mirror was completely blotted out by a large cardboard box of books casually topped by a lone white cotton mask, marked with lipstick.

At first Dizzy thought the room was just for women to use. Most of the coats were obviously female and someone had trustingly deposited a small mink cape over the top of the bed head.

She had just added her own to the heap when Robin popped in with a man. 'This is the cloakroom old sprout, so if you want to dump anything, stick it here.' Robin turned to Dizzy. 'This is Damian Clewlyn. He's a cousin, a librarian who needs mothering.'

Dizzy nodded towards him. Damian Clewlyn did not look a bit like the type who needed mothering, but he had a very interesting face with a humorous quirk to his mouth and a strange basin-like hair cut.

She smiled, and he smiled back. Then she went down stairs to the sitting-room. Everyone was talking animatedly, eating sausage rolls which looked heavy enough to flatten tarmac, and washing them down with liquids that ranged from Black and Tans to Gin and Its.

'Come over here,' bellowed Fruity when he saw her appearing again. He pushed a glass of sherry into her hand. He was well on his way to a sozzled state.

Halfway through the evening Dizzy began to get bored. Her consumption of alcohol remained limited to the same wine glass which she sipped occasionally. She had no intention of being the female victim in a house of hardened boozers.

She looked around. She wasn't the only one still sober. Damian was still walking in straight lines; and one poor little creature called Bertha Selwick was sitting like a lonesome pine, after doing sterling work administering first aid to a man who had banged his head on the corner of a massive gothic sideboard.

Suddenly, Dizzy saw Fruity Sampson flop down on the chair next to Bertha and heard him start to talk in a loud voice. 'Show you like motor racing toooo do you? It'sh sheldom I meet a deshent woman who likes proper carsh.'

At this point, the thought struck Dizzy that it was time to either wend her way home on foot, or find a more suitable companion.

She looked at Damian again. He was alone and wandering about politely.

She decided to go up to the bedroom where all the coats were and freshen herself up for another hour.

As soon as she got there Fruity Sampson followed her in.

'I shaw you dishappearing, shweetheart. Shorley you aren't going yet? The night ish shtill young.'

He flopped down on top of the heap of coats on the bed. Half of them fell to the floor but the mink cape landed on his head.

Dizzy stepped forward to rescue it, but too late. He grabbed her in a grip of iron and pulled her down on top of him. 'Shtay with me and be my true mate.'

She was furious as she struggled among tweed overcoats and delicate fabrics with very sharp fastenings. She tried to free herself in vain, going lower and lower into the heap as he tried to roll on top of her. She could hardly breathe and when she did so she was almost suffocated by fiery fumes. There was one saving grace – the coats had made a substantial barrier between their bodies. Fruity and his carnal intentions were completely smothered in a layer of mock fur, car coat belonging to a giant.

Dizzy blessed its presence as Fruity began to heave up and down on top of it. At first she thought he was actually giving a full male performance of sexual intercourse, and then she realised he was being sick.

At this point the bed collapsed and she managed to crawl out.

Hastily she escaped into the bathroom and locked the door, just as voices and footsteps began to ascend.

'I say. That was a hell of a thud. It nearly brought the bloody ceiling down.'

'Cyril – come in here and look, at all this.' A woman's voice shrieked with disbelief. 'My coat! It's ruined! I shall sue him!'

The place became a complete uproar, and when Dizzy finally dared to come out of the bathroom, she caught sight of Fruity Sampson's prone and groaning body being carried downstairs and dumped in the garden.

She decided to forget her own coat for ever. Thankfully it had been a very old one.

When she got back to the main room, there were only two people there. One was wallflower, Bertha Selwick, who was now looking quite perky, and the other was Damian Clewlyn.

'Is it true that Fruity Sampson has just been carried out

to the garden, after an accident?' asked Bertha showing genuine concern.

Dizzy nodded impassively. 'People say the bed collapsed when he was trying to put his coat on.'

'Surely the coats weren't as heavy as all that?' said Bertha. She looked very puzzled. 'How could the bed have collapsed? Unless he was standing on it, or something? Is anyone looking after him in the garden?'

Dizzy shrugged her shoulders as Bertha got up and went outside to give aid.

Dizzy looked at Damian and he looked at her.

'We seem to be the only sane people left,' he said. 'Can I see you home? My car's the first one outside.'

'I've decided to walk. I don't live far away.'

'I'll walk with you then, if you like.'

She nodded. It was as if she knew already what was going to happen.

It was a wonderful, clear starry night as they left the noisy house full of shouting voices and general upheaval.

By the time they parted on Dizzy Oakland's home doorstep, he had asked her to go out with him.

In bed that night, as she thought about it all, she knew without doubt that Damian Clewlyn was going to be the man for all her future life.

A few days later, when she was in the hospital corridor in her nurse's uniform again, she bumped into Fruity. He was striding along with his white coat wide open and a stethoscope round his neck. Looking as fit as a fiddle, his face lit up into a broad smile.

'Bit of a night at Robin's place – eh? Can't remember quite what happened, but I was rescued in the garden by the woman of my dreams: good-looking and mad about cars. Never happier than when talking about the Monte Carlo Rally and the thickness of car wheel treads. Her name's Bertha Selwick and she's training to be a lawyer. Just couldn't believe my luck. Did you get back home OK?'

Dizzy smiled back at him. He was completely incorrigible. She didn't dare to think what *might* have happened. Yet she could not ever bear him a grudge. She had known that the responsibility rested with herself the moment she had accepted his invitation.

'I had a wonderful time. That very nice librarian saw me home.' She wondered whether to ask him if anyone was still going to be sued for damages to clothes. And who was it that had the job of clearing up the bedroom and removing the ruined, sick-sodden coats.

Almost as if he was waiting for her to ask, he raised his eyebrows with innocent expectancy. 'Anything else?'

She tried to stop herself from laughing, then she said solemnly: 'Not a thing, it was absolutely perfect.'

The girls stared at the list.

It is hereby certified that the following candidates were admitted by Examination to the General Part of the Register maintained by the General Nursing Council, and that they are entitled in pursuance of the Nurses' Registration Act, 1919 to take and use the title of 'Registered Nurse'

D. Smith S.R.N: Chairman of Council

The Seal of the Council is hereunto affixed.
M. Henry. SRN. Registrar.

> Bridget M. Downs
> May Elizabeth Greenrigg
> Queenie Marney
> Liz Margarete Frankel
> Anne Nulty
> Delyth Oaklands
> Shirley B. O'Malley
> Dorothea Templeton Philips
> Ada Priscilla Sawbridge.

Queenie Marney made the sign of the cross on the bib of her starched white apron in pure joy. She had stayed on in the end to take her finals and she gave a thousand thanks. They had already received their own personal certificates by post. They had made it at last!

15
MAY

All the girls, including Downs and Nulty, had a mild celebration together as soon as the official declaration of their qualifying was on the notice board. They had gathered in the Training School with Sister Sorenson and had presented her with a thank you present. It was a leather-backed autograph album with all their names signed inside the front two pink and green pages. Dizzy's sister, Valda, had made a rich fruitcake iced in white and piped with pale blue lattice work, with the letters SRN in tiny silver balls.

Sister Sorenson cut the cake, and it was passed round in huge slices with cups of tea amid lots of laughing and talking.

The only person who was very quiet was Liz. May almost felt that Liz was trying to avoid her.

There was a shifting about in hospital life – now that

the girls had finished their training. Bridget Downs and Anne Nulty went back to Ireland to their convent straight-away, as quietly as they had arrived. Queenie Marney got married within a few months and retired into the chip shop empire. A few months after marriage, and the per-petual wrapping up of cod and chips and mushy peas in newspaper, she was pregnant. Then, when her small son Kenny was a year old, she escaped from the battered scal-lops and steamed steak and kidney puddings, and went to work at the Ear, Nose and Throat Hospital as a part-time Staff Nurse. A willing grandmother took care of Kenny.

Dorothea Philips was a large mountain containing twins when she had sat her final exams. She was already Mrs Pennylove. Her husband, Dr Godfrey Pennylove, had collapsed into an almost perfect husband, worried to death about the imminent arrival of their offspring and pleading with her not to take her finals. 'You just don't *need* to now, Dotsy. A doctor's wife has enough to keep her going for ever, without still wanting to be a nurse. It's all perfectly ludicrous. Your responsibility is to your hus-band and children. If you're looking for a paid job, you can be my typist, or even my secretary, or who knows in the future, my receptionist.'

'Don't talk such utter twaddle, Godfrey. For a start a woman is never properly paid if she works for her hus-band. I have a heaven sent opportunity to take this exam, just because I've redeemed myself by marrying you and I'm no longer single. Believe me, I'm going to take those exams even if the babies are born in the test room.'

The babies were not born in the test room, but Dotsy

left immediately after the results appeared on the board. All the girls were given an open invitation to the double christening: a boy and a girl.

Liz and May were in a different part of the Nurses' Home now. It was where all the other Staff Nurses were, and they all had single bedrooms. They were at opposite ends of the corridor to one another and were no longer 'The Girls'. May was a Staff Nurse on the female TB ward. Liz was a Staff Nurse on the Male Chronic Ward.

The role of official Staff Nurse meant a complete change of status signified by a stiff petersham belt, and colour of uniform. Their frocks were a very deep cornflower blue instead of the paler blue of student nurses and they wore stiff, white-buttoned 'dog collars' like the sisters, instead of ordinary soft collars. They also wore long sleeves and stiff white cuffs, the bottom half of which could be removed when doing dressings. It all gave a sharper impression of their new responsibilities and authority.

Liz had already been out with Jamie Croxton three more times. He now spent every available weekend at his brother's so as to see her. She was a mixture of joy and wretchedness.

'Over six whole weeks now and never a peep out of Jamie Croxton again,' said May to Liz one day in the dining-room. 'It seems an age since my ankle dashed all those romantic hopes and you stepped in for me at the last minute.' May sighed ruefully and smiled. 'I expect it was a pure fluke in the first place that he wrote to me and suggested meeting again. It would have been nice to see him though. I was quite smitten with him when he was on the ward. But even in those days he seemed to have lots of girl-friends near his home who kept in touch with him. I expect that – one day – for some peculiar reason, he thought back, then decided on the spur of the moment to try getting in touch, in a flood of nostalgia.'

May suddenly checked herself and stared at Liz's face. It was pale and miserable.

'Oh Liz! What on earth am I saying? Please don't think you were to blame by going instead of me. It was just one of those things and I'm eternally grateful to you.' May hesitated then said. 'The fact is I've been worrying a bit ever since it happened. We just seem to have drifted apart, since we've qualified.'

Liz plucked up all her courage. She just couldn't bear the situation any longer. It was even having an effect on herself and Jamie. They always steered themselves away from anything too passionate when they met at week-ends, but even the smallest kiss or show of affection between them was making Liz more and more guilty as she saw her own deep friendship with May slipping away.

That evening when work was over, she went to May's room and knocked at the door.

'Come in.' May was putting on her outdoor clothes. 'Liz! What a surprise. I'm just rushing out. It's my day off tomorrow. Barry Rooks and mother are picking me up at the lodge gates to take me back to Urmston. They've been out visiting friends.' She looked quickly at Liz. 'If it's your day off too and you're at a loose end, come with me. We'll wait for you at the lodge?'

Liz smiled. 'Mine's not for another couple of days. But

thanks. I'll see you when you get back, so have a good day off. There was just something I wanted to tell you about. I've been meaning to tell you for ages, but it can wait 'til you get back.'

May nodded, and went

On the way back home, her mother said casually, 'Barry and I are getting married, aren't we Barry?' Her mother was sitting at the back. She always let May or any guests sit at the front next to the driver, unless she and Barry were on their own.

At first May hardly heard her mother's words. She turned her head slightly. 'Did you say something about . . . *married*?'

'Yes. Barry and me. The registry office. We'll tell you when we get back.'

When they got back and Barry was out of the way, May looked round their flat. It was all exactly the same as it had always been, except that there were now some new red, cream and fawn folk-weave curtains at the windows and all the black-out paper had gone.

'What on earth has made you decide to marry him mother?' said May. 'You've always said that if you ever did, you would become nothing but his household drudge'

Lotty Greenrigg smiled wryly. 'To put it plainly, May, during these past three years whilst you've been away at the hospital and I've been working for him as his typist, we've become closer and closer.' She gave a quick laugh. 'And, fortunately, he's become richer and richer. He's not such a bad old thing and his heart's in the right place, but he just *has* to be kept in order. So now, with his finances improving every second, it's meant he's had no excuse to get me to do any of his chores. He can well afford to pay for domestic help, and with me knowing him inside out, I've been able to protect myself from his worst aspects of trying to use me as a slave. I've also managed to put a bit by, which gives me some independence. And what with you now being qualified and Coral almost grown up, I have succumbed to his charms and agreed to marry him.'

May looked round. 'What will you do about our flat then?'

'I shall leave it just as it is, but tidy it more. Then you and Coral can still use it whilst I live downstairs with Barry. We've also come to an agreement that if either of you two girls ever get married and need a temporary roof over your head, you'll be able to rent it. The house itself is even big enough to be converted into three flats – if it was ever needed.'

May sighed. 'Well you don't need to be worrying over *me* ever needing a flat, mother. I just never seem to meet any man, remotely suitable, to share my life with.'

'Everybody says that sometimes, dear.'

May didn't say any more as she thought how her chance of ever meeting Jamie Croxton again had slipped away. But by the time her day off at home was over she began to think slightly differently. Why should she have assumed so easily any way, that she and Jamie Croxton were going to be made for each other? Had she been blowing up their intended meeting out of all proportion, all based on knowing a wounded soldier in hospital? But on the other hand, why had he revived the memories by writing to her? The more she thought of it the more she realised there was more to life than worrying over one failed meeting. She might even send for particulars from UNRA about working abroad somewhere as a nurse, and widen her own horizons.

By the time she got back again to the hospital, Jamie Croxton had begun to fade away like a rather pleasant but unfulfilled dream.

Liz and May were out together for the first time in ages. They both had the same afternoon off and were sitting in Tiller's Hotel garden in Dodsbury at a very old wrought-iron table drinking coffee and eating walnut cake. The weather was idyllic. It was an Indian summer of blue skies and autumn tints, as late bees drifted over the tops of roses beside beds of deep velvety crimson and soft lemon antirrhinum.

It had been May's idea to go there.

Liz knew that she must keep her secret no longer.

'To think that Jamie Croxton actually once came here to meet me,' said May, with relaxed happiness. 'Anyway, perhaps it's as well it all ended as it did. Life plays strange tricks, and often when one thing goes out of the window it's replaced by something better.'

Liz smiled. 'As a matter of fact I'm a bit in your boat, May. Only this very morning I received a letter out of the blue. It was from —' she hesitated and decided to use Ernst Jünger's false name, the same as he'd used in his letter '— Edmund Young.' She didn't say any more, and decided not to mention that Ernst was now due to go back to Germany to be repatriated. When she had first read it earlier in the day and seen his familiar style of writing, in the solitude of her bedroom, her heart had seemed to lurch again with a mixture of love and sad regrets. There was no address on the letter, just the date. It was all written in English almost as if he was a casual tourist. Tears came to her eyes when she had read it.

How I wish you were coming with me to a fresh life all our own. Oh how I miss you my sweet one and pray every day that you will find great happiness in the future. I pray that one day we will meet again.
Yours for ever, Edmund.

'I expect you must have been badly hit – with Edmund suddenly leaving your life,' said May sympathetically. 'Somehow I always wondered what it was that was upsetting you. I knew there must be something. But never realised until now just what it was. Do you think you'll start to see him again?'

Liz felt herself blushing with embarrassment. She pretended it was due to the sun as she fanned her face with a small pink paper serviette. 'I doubt it. So much has happened since then.' Hurriedly she changed the subject and asked May how her mother and Mr Rooks were getting on.

Soon it was time for them both to go. Her heart sank. She had failed once again to break the news to May even though the time, the setting, and the mood had been perfect.

Then the following weekend the worst thing happened that she could possibly have wanted. She was with Jamie, in Manchester. They were just passing a second-hand jewellers and clock repairers. It was tucked in one of the narrow city streets, in the shadow of the Town Hall.

Jamie had spotted a beautiful brooch in the window. It was shaped as two finger-sized, double gold rings over-lapping each other, and in the overlapping space was a heart shaped ruby suspended at its centre. It was truly dazzling.

'A betrothal brooch,' he murmured. He squeezed her hand. 'Would you like it?'

She gasped slightly. 'It's perfect, but —'

'And you're perfect Liz. We're perfect for each other. Please let me buy it for you.'

'The cost . . . I just don't know what to say.'

He kissed her on the cheek. 'You don't need to say any-thing. It's the first token of our belonging together.'

He led her into the rather dark little shop. She sat down on the brown bent-wood chair next to the counter whilst the jeweller took the brooch out of the window and showed it to them both, allowing them to use his magni-fying glass:

'As you can see, it's absolutely perfect.' He handed the brooch to Liz to hold against her frock.

She nodded her head, and handed it back to Jamie as they all smiled at each other.

It was just at this minute that the doorbell tinkled and another customer arrived.

Liz could not believe her eyes! It was May.

May had seen the brooch in the window some days previously, but today she had noticed that it had gone. In her time off she thought she would just check up in case there was something similar but perhaps a little less expensive inside the shop on display.

'Liz!' Her voice faltered as she saw Jamie. 'Jamie! What a surprise. You look wonderfully well. How good to see you at last. How amazing to meet, here of all places, so unexpectedly.'

She saw the whole tableau of it, as if struck by lightning: Jamie holding the very brooch she had been going to ask about, Liz with her hand on Jamie's arm, the shopkeeper smiling at them both.

In one miserable second May turned and fled from the shop.

The nearer she got to the hospital, the worse the shock became. She thanked heavens it was her half day. She had been going to do so much, but now all she wanted was to lie on her bed and sob her heart out.

How could Liz, one of her best friends in all these years of hospital training, the girl she had shared a room with, and had shared her deepest secrets, have double-crossed her with such cold deceit?

May was still lying there with swollen, reddened eyes with the door unlocked when Dizzy popped her head round.

Dizzy stared at May's woeful state. 'What on earth's happened May? Has there been trouble on the ward?'

May stood up and went to the small washbasin in the corner to splash her face in cold water. 'Nothing as bad as that thank goodness – but —'

'But enough to make you want to die,' said Dizzy solemnly. 'I've felt like that at times and it's usually been something to do with a man.'

In a few minutes they were both drinking tea and May was telling her the whole tale.

'Honestly, Dizzy, it's absolutely the very last thing I would have expected. I just feel that I never, ever want to speak to her again or even see her face. It's not so much that she was with him. It's that she's never ever told me.'

'Perhaps she'd been too shy,' said Dizzy knowingly. 'Maybe she didn't want to hurt your feelings. Perhaps she met him quite by chance one day in town and it sprang from there. I always remember a similar thing happening to my sister Valda. She was once swept off her feet by a boy who was supposed to be courting one of my other sisters. The course of love hardly ever runs smooth, May. I can't imagine it being altogether her fault. She's never been the flirting type. And just remember what happened to Karina and Ada. Yet they're both nice, and we get on well with both of them. All the same it must be awful for you. Especially coming face to face with them in the shop and her with that brooch.' Then Dizzy said thoughtfully: 'I think if it was me – and of course it isn't so it'll probably be entirely different from what you should really do, well, I would try to forget you ever went in that shop and saw them both. I would wait and see if Liz comes to you to explain it all. Be patient for a while. You don't want to have some awful row based on a terrible misunderstanding.'

When Dizzy had gone, May sat there for ages thinking about what Dizzy had said. The next day she braced herself to take Dizzy's advice and behave quite normally if she saw Liz.

*

'What a strange thing, seeing May in the shop,' said Jamie, as he and Liz went back to his brother's flat. He seemed quite intrigued, but not in the least upset.

'I'm glad her ankle cleared up satisfactorily. She was such a comfort when I was on that ward. A real friend to me. I think I'd better write and explain to her about us. Then, one of these weekends we must try again and make up a foursome with you and me and May and another friend, or perhaps my brother.'

Liz tried not to show how upset she was about it all. She could have kicked herself now, for never having been brave enough to break the news to May when they were at Tiller's Hotel in the garden on that perfect day. Why was it that she never dared to take proper chances? She swore to herself that never again would she step back from what she felt she should do.

The chance came far sooner than she had expected, but not to do with May.

It was in the evening in the flat, and she and Jamie were alone. She felt quite drained with a deep sadness. All she wanted was to bury her face against Jamie. Have him there always to take her in his arms, so that all problems faded away in a welter of loving.

How they both wanted each other. Every time they met the longing became stronger and stronger, but each time she was the one to prevent their lovemaking going too far. Even though he had asked her to marry him so many times.

This evening it would be different at last. She was betrothed to him now. Her mind was finally made up as she put her hand across the brooch on her frock.

After a meal of scrambled egg on toast, and jelly and evaporated milk, Jamie took her in his arms and said: 'We need to go away together. We're never going to be able to really relax here. We can't have Craig accidentally bursting in on us, or you having to rush back to the hospital. We both need a complete change of scene. If only you could manage to have a bit more time off. Maybe on your next weekend we could go to Buxton in Derbyshire for our own special time, before the winter starts to set in. Craig and I used to go walking round there quite often with our parents, when we were small boys. We used to have an uncle and aunt who lived there in College Road.

Liz agreed straightaway. She had never been to Buxton. It was a spaciously set out spa town with a pavilion and a pump room where music filled the air and people walked round gardens close to a crescent of eighteenth-century houses similar in some ways to Bath.

They stood together and hugged one another, then without warning they were completely swept away. There was no question of set plans for lovemaking now. No wonderfully planned timetable, or worrying about whether Craig would arrive. They both dissolved on to the large well worn sofa, and from there they moved to the floor by the fireside, exploring each other's bodies in shameless nudity. Their clothes were spread about as if thrown by a tornado; neither was embarrassed by Jamie's missing leg, and they both murmured words to each other of relief and happiness.

When it was over Liz laughed with sheer joy and thankfulness. Spontaneity and longing had taken her over with such force that all care was swept away. She got up, gathered her clothes together and retired to the bathroom. A few minutes later she heard Jamie getting up and going to the bedroom.

About an hour later, when Craig came in, he found them sitting together on the sofa in drowsy harmony talking about Buxton again.

'What on earth do you want to go to Buxton for?' he said bluntly. 'Why don't you take her home to meet Mum and Dad in Durham, first. You'll have to in the end.'

Late that evening, when May was in bed, she was surprised to hear someone tapping at her door. It was Liz. She was still in her frock, and wore the brooch.

'May . . . I know how late it is but I simply have to explain. I've just never had the courage until now. When you came into the shop this afternoon it was the most awful moment. I'd meant to tell you that day at Tiller's in the garden.'

'Don't just stand there, Liz. Come in. Shall I make us a drink of Horlicks?'

'No. I'll make it, but not until I've explained everything. It's quite a long story. What a weight off my mind to get it told.

'First of all May, I'll tell you the main news first. He bought me this brooch as a sort of betrothal token, and on my next weekend off I'm going to Durham with him to visit his parents. He's going to announce our official engagement. We're planning to marry as soon as possible.' Liz poured out the words in a hasty stream, hardly daring to look at May.

'I never intended it to happen May. I never for one

moment imagined I'd be involved with Jamie. I was out of my depth at first. I didn't realise my own feelings, and it went on from there. He says he's going to write to you and explain.'

'What about Edmund then?' said May. 'What about the letter *he* wrote to you?'

Liz's face clouded over. 'I don't suppose I shall ever see him again. He didn't put an address on the letter.' Liz stared at May pleadingly. 'Can you ever forgive me?'

Suddenly May smiled. She gave a huge sigh. 'I'm glad you told me and it's all out in the open. If Jamie hadn't written that letter, none of this would have even happened. At least it's brought one of us some happiness, and I'm glad it's you Liz. I wish you lots and lots of happiness. Yes – let's have a drink! And if you want to borrow anything special when you go to Durham, just say the word.'

The next day, when May saw Dizzy Oaklands, she stopped Dizzy in the corridor.

'Liz told me all. I'm glad I wasn't too hasty. Everything's all right again and she's agreed to come to my mother's wedding next month.'

Dizzy beamed with joy. She grabbed May's hand and gave it an affectionate tug: 'It's the best thing that could have ever happened for Liz. I only hope I'll be as lucky with my librarian.'

As she walked to the ward again May thought about her own predicament. Maybe she would never get married at all. Perhaps she would never be swept off her feet by anyone? Perhaps she would never quite know what true falling-head-over-heels-in-love really meant. Perhaps it didn't even exist. Or, supposing it did and she fell for someone who was already married? Or worse still if she loved a man who didn't love her? Then she stopped brooding. Such thoughts were pure luxury really. She was suddenly feeling amazingly happy and very, very, single.

16

THE NURSING HOME

During the time after the war, and the girls had qualified,
there was a general turnover of nurses coming and going.
Other hospitals and specialist departments were expanding on the outskirts of Manchester. Some of their research
had been helped by experience gained from war injuries.
Plastic surgery was one of the main examples. This meant
that nurses who had trained at places like St Alphonso's
had more choice for specialisation.

The ravages of wartime destruction meant not only
more work for the medical profession, but more employment for everyone. Slogans such as 'Building a Land Fit
for Heroes to Live in' met the public ear.

Not that it was a magic-wand world. The constant
housing problem was always there, and was coupled with
long queues on council-house waiting-lists which lasted
for years. Many engaged and newly-married couples had

to live with parents or in-laws in terribly cramped conditions, or else hunt round to try and find rented accommodation, much of it shabby and ridiculously overpriced. And although houses were beginning to be built again, they were bought by those with steady jobs who could afford to take out a mortgage with a building society.

At this time there were also one or two individual enterprises of cooperative housing. They were rare, and usually stemmed from small groups of married couples, where the men had allied skills such as bricklaying, joinery, plumbing or electrical work. First the group had to find a piece of building land and then with their combined knowledge and craftsmanship between them, build a house each for themselves. This work took a few years, done in their spare time, whilst working at other jobs. It was one of these schemes that Liz and Jamie eventually joined.

They had married quickly. Jamie had moved to Manchester and found a clerical job at Manchester Town Hall. Meanwhile Jamie's younger brother Craig, who was still studying civil engineering, had found another flat where the three of them lived.

It was in the first year of their marriage, when Liz was pregnant, that Jamie found out about a small cooperative. He was full of enthusiasm as he told her: 'The other five couples will accept us because of my joinery apprenticeship when I first left school.' He pulled some copies of the plans from his briefcase. 'Just look at this perfect little bit of land close to the new Marlborough Housing Estate in Flexly. It's a handy, spacious area on the main bus route into Manchester. The building site for the houses is beside an already paved road. And just look at these designs. Three-bedroomed homes and each house detached. It'll be a dream come true.'

Liz smiled, but underneath there was a streak of fear. '. . . As long as you don't think it will be too much for you to take on, Jamie. You're always kept tremendously busy at the Town Hall and you would have to use all your spare time. Perhaps we should leave it till the baby is born? There's another four months to go, yet.'

His face fell slightly. 'We need to accept straightaway, otherwise someone else will jump in. It's a heaven-sent chance.'

Liz nodded nervously. She was thinking of his war wounds and whether it would all prove too much for them to take on at the start of their marriage. Then she wondered whether she was being too negative and too timid.

Suddenly her face cleared and she smiled. 'Yes I think you're right. It sounds a good idea.'

How little we know what is to become of us. Within two months, Jamie Croxton was dead. He had passed away quietly and suddenly, a shocking tragedy for Liz and the whole of his family. There had been a postmortem and the official description on the death certificate said: UNRE-SOLVED WAR INJURIES.

'. . . Out, out, brief candle . . .'

Numb with a broken heart, Liz felt she would collapse with the grief of it. Her in-laws pleaded with her to go

and live close to them in Durham. In a haze of stubborn-
ness she refused. But how it cost her. The loneliness. The
terrible quietness – even though Craig was still there. The
thought of never hearing Jamie's voice again – his quiet
humour. His softly lilting voice, his enthusiasms and conversation. No more the sharing of their plans, their joys
and aspirations. For now a huge chunk of the future was
hacked from her life where only weeks ago their hearts
had been filled with the plans for their own house.
Nothing was left now, she thought, only fading visions
scattered as casually as a dandelion clock. Where was the
plan to any of this? Was there even a God in this world,
where hell was so often here on earth?

If it hadn't been for the baby, Liz dreaded to think of
what would have happened to her state of mind. It was
akin to the madness of the past when she was a only
schoolgirl and realised she might never hear the voices of
her mother and father and sister again, except in her
dreams or nightmares.

One day, in one of her bleakest moments, she travelled
as if in a trance to the little bit of land at Flexly where the
houses were being built and stood there with tears streaming down her face, dwelling on what might have been.

Then as the days dragged by she finally consoled herself by strength of will – with more positive things almost
as if Jamie was still here beside her, guiding her.

Craig was an unforeseen blessing and an aid to her
gradual recovery. 'At least you have his baby inside you,'
he said, trying desperately to comfort her. 'A bit of both of
you – still there – together, to carry on living.'

*

'Liz Croxton, Nurse Frankel!' She was recognised immediately by Ada Sawbridge the moment she was wheeled into the labour room at Bell Lane. Ada was now a maternity Staff Nurse, along with Shirley O'Malley. The resident Doctor in charge in the obstetrics department was Dr Rose Stansfield.

Her baby son was seven pounds six ounces; a beautiful healthy baby who bellowed his way into the world from a red screwed-up face, with small clenched fists waving in a new, unknown world. He had a thatch of soft black hair.

She called him Nathan after her father.

Many married women now looked for part-time work to help the weekly pay-packet. Often SRNs did extra training to become qualified midwives or health visitors within the community. There were also other branches of nursing emerging, such as industrial nursing which meant working in large steel and chemical plants and in factories.

As soon as Nathan was a few months old Liz managed to find herself a job as an industrial nurse in a clothing factory. By now the flat she shared with Craig also contained Craig's girl-friend Amelia. Amelia had once been in the Land Army but now she worked as a hotel receptionist. Craig had finished at college and found a job working for some civil engineering consultants in Manchester who specialised in designing new shopping precincts.

Dr Rose Stansfield and Staff Nurse Sawbridge had just helped each other to deliver twins, assisted by Staff Nurse O'Malley.

With yet another proud mother and baby doing well, Rose and Ada were in the duty room having a cup of tea, whilst Shirley gave the mother a cup of tea.

'Fancy you knowing the Ronsons,' purred Rose. 'His wife's a terrific singer. She's in the Royal Northern Opera Society. I never realised she'd once been a student nurse here. I just couldn't imagine it. Ronald's such a *nice* man, and terribly *rich*.' Rose's eyes widened reverently.

Ada smiled slightly. She realised that she and Rose were going to be great friends. Apparently they both had a common bond – they liked rich men, even though at the moment Ada was playing a nun-like role.

'Do you think you'll carry on with midwifery then, Ada? Now that you've successfully completed parts one and two?' Rose stared at her earnestly.

Ada frowned slightly. It was the first time anyone had ever asked her about her future. Now that she had completed part two of the midwifery qualification – which had meant living in a small house in Moss Side with three other midwives, and spending six months delivering babies at all times of the day and night – she was having second thoughts. Was it really what she wanted to do for the rest of her life? It certainly wouldn't make her wealthy.

Ada shook her head. 'It's a good stand-by if you ever want to be a midwife or a health visitor. I think I'll stay here for the time being and give it more thought. Perhaps when I've been on my holiday to Spain, I'll decide. I'm going at the end of April.'

'Are you? Are you really? Have you ever been before?' Rose's eyes glowed.

'I did once go abroad with —' she was just going to say

"Ronny" but stopped just in time and said, "a friend".

'I've never been to Spain,' said Rose. 'I quite envy you.' Then she added: 'I have of course been to many other places like Iceland, Switzerland, Norway, South Africa and the Sahara, but that was when I was a child. I'd simply adore to go with you to Spain. I'm getting quite pale and feel the need for a proper change. Oh for a spark of true rejuvenation with a sun god! . . . Are you going with Cooks Travel?'

'No. It's a house that my old bank manager, where I worked years ago, lets out privately. Actually, I'm supposed to be finding a few others to go with me, but it isn't all that desperate, and I haven't the time to fuss around. There'll be at least one woman I know from the bank going at the same time. . . . There are four double bedrooms. They're all on a sort of carved wooden balcony which overlooks the main living-room inside the house. It's entirely different to houses here. The ground floors are heavy slabs of stone with hand-woven rugs, and there's a massive stone fireplace where all the cooking is done. And it's only a few minutes from the sea.'

Ada hunted in her handbag and began to show Rose some photographs.

By the time she had finished Rose was already on the plane ahead of her.

'Now are you sure you don't mind Ada? I mean . . . you did say you needed more people.'

Ada nodded with solemn primness. She felt she was getting back into her own type of society at last, even if it was going to be completely female. She quite enjoyed

Rose's morbid and exotic ramblings. At least they didn't sound too penniless.

'It's a pity Shirley can't come with us too,' said Rose a few days later, when they had just done another delivery of a massive ten pound boy. 'Have you asked her?'

Ada looked unenthusiastic this time. She didn't want a vast snowball of people developing, even though Mr Brand, the bank manager, did knock a bit off your own holiday costs if you found others to fill the house at the same time.

'Don't you think it'll be a bit much if we're all away from Obstetrics together?' said Ada uneasily, wishing she hadn't given up smoking, as the tension began to rise.

Rose offered her a boiled sweet. 'That's for Sister Casey to worry about, and anyway it's just when she'll be getting a fresh batch of newly qualified SRNs for the Maternity block. After all – it's only for a week.'

At first, when Shirley received the invitation to go with them, she turned it down straightaway. 'Yes, I am due for a holiday but I always go back to Ireland with Herby,' she said. A happy thought struck her. 'Could I bring Herby with me to Spain?'

Ada shook her head quickly. 'Mr Brand will only allow single sex bookings. It can be a full house of women or a full house of men, but never a mixture.'

Gradually Shirley began to succumb to Rose's pressure. She would never have thought of a holiday abroad, either with Herby Dawson or without him, if this had not cropped up. It would mean telling Herby she wanted to go for a holiday without him. She began to quail slightly. Until quite recently she had always imagined that her relationship with Herby was rock solid for ever. It had lasted like that until they agreed to become engaged, but before he actually bought her a ring. Now she knew deep down that it might not be so stable after all.

Shirley smiled valiantly. 'Yes. Sure an' I think I'll try it. But I'll have to tell Herby first. After all, if it was him that went away to some far-flung land without so much as a "how's y' father" to *me*, wouldn't I be a bit nettled miself?'

Yet for some deep-seated reason she could not bring herself to tell Herby, even though Ada kept mentioning the holiday.

'I need to tell Mr Brand within the next two days, Shirley. The inevitable has happened – a whole host of other women are now – according to him – howling at his door to book the place.'

Shirley O'Malley gazed at the statue of the Virgin Mary on her dressing table. Her own frank, blue eyes looked at the Virgin's eyes. Her dark eyelashes fluttered slightly. 'Mary, Mother of God, what am I to do about telling Herby? Sure, he'll slaughter me and no mistake?'

The Virgin Mary looked as passive as ever. The message Shirley received was to take her fate in her own hands and just trust to God.

Herby was two years younger than she was. One of six brothers, just as Shirley herself was from a large family, his family were market traders in the fruit and vegetable trade. Herby was at work at five each morning, buying fresh fruit and vegetables to sell on their market stall. Tough, handsome and muscular, Herby's working life was the sort that bred authority, decision making, independence and firmness.

That was why Shirley had fallen for him. It wasn't until now, when she was more independent herself, with plans and dreams of her own, that she began to waver. The truth of the matter had arrived one day, when Herby had kicked up a fuss about a frilly, sleeveless blouse she was wearing to go out for a meal with some friends. Shirley had fallen in love with the blouse, but out of love with Herby.

'You'd better keep your cardigan on whilst we're out with Mirabelle and Cyril. And get something tucked in round that neckline, Shirl. Clip it together with a safety-pin or summat or they'll see your belly button.'

Shirley seethed with anger. 'And you want to mind your own business and get your fingernails seen to. I never make remarks about *your* clothes.'

But the rot had set in. Shirley felt distinctly awkward now about her blouse and wore her cardigan, which made her sweat and fume at the same time. Why was she being such a fool as to take any notice of him? The situation was not made any better when Mirabelle slipped off her coat in the cloakroom and displayed a similar style of blouse to Shirley's. It was sleeveless and snowy white with a frill down the front. The low V neck showed a cleft as deep as a crevasse, accentuated even more when Mirabelle spilt some ice-cream down it at the dining-table, and Herby quickly came to her rescue with his serviette, his nose almost buried in her chest.

'There's one thing about Mirabelle Stubbs,' said Herby on the way home, 'she always dresses like a complete lady.'

Shirley controlled an impulse to batter him. Yet most of

the rest of the time, they were as happy as larks.

'Herby . . .'

'Yes, my love?'

'I've got other plans for my holiday this year. I shan't be going home to Ireland.' Her words quickened before her resolve weakened. 'I'm going away with two others from the maternity department. We're going to have a week in Spain.'

Herby seemed not to hear for a few seconds, then he said: '*Spain*?'

'Yes. We're all sharing a house together. You won't need to worry, it's women only.'

'You can't go to Spain, Shirl!' He stared at her with complete and confident amazement. 'What about your parents? What will they say? They'll be expecting to see us both. They trust me to look after you.'

Shirley faced him resolutely. 'Look Herby. I'm not a baby. I'm over twenty-one. I'm my own boss. I'm a person who is responsible for the care and lives of others. Whatever you say I'm going. And that's the end of it.'

There was an awful silence.

Herby Dawson slowly went red. He looked like a throbbing, simmering bull.

'If you go to that bloody place, Shirley, it'll be the end. Mark my words. You can please yourself – if you want to go and be a tart for a week – but that's not the type of woman I want to look after me all my life. So just think on. Think on . . . deep and serious.'

Shirley stayed silent a bit longer to let her news sink into his skull, then she said: 'I've thought on, Herby – and the situation is still the same. I'm going.'

That day when she got back to her room at the hospital she looked at the Virgin Mary. 'God forgive me for upsetting him. He means well. Did I do the right thing?'

The statue stared straight across the room.

The holiday was a great success. The sun, the sea, and the sparkling air had such an effect on the three women that they were loath to return to the hospital at all.

'We should stay out here and set up a small nursing home,' joked Rose Stansfield.

'Or better still,' said Shirley with a glint of steel, 'a place of our own in Manchester.'

Ada nodded triumphantly. Never for one moment did they doubt, in this present holiday heaven, that when they got back they would bring it about. It was as if their guardian angels had heard every word.

When they got back, there was an invitation waiting for Rose from one of the Consultant Obstetricians, Mr Lawson Longsight.

. . . After thirty-three years of dedicated hospital service I am retiring.

My wife Mitzi and I will be pleased to see you at a farewell get-together on Friday the fourteenth of June at Appledore House, Wilmslow.

Yours Sincerely,

Lawson Longsight,

casual dress. R.S.V.P.

Rose was euphoric when she read it. She had always felt that she irritated Dr Longsight, ever since she had told him there were some strands of cotton wool stuck to his nose when he was speaking to Sister Tadworthy, who was like a blonde angel and had an hour-glass figure.

When she arrived at Appledore House, her enthusiasm cooled slightly. Monty Middleton the GP from near Edgely was there, along with Elaine Driffield, who was now a hospital almoner at Stockport. She did not seem to have suffered at all from carrying buckets of coal for them both, as Elaine lived with him in the vague disguise of part-time, pseudo cousin, housekeeper.

'How are you getting on?' said Elaine to Rose when Monty was helping himself to some more chicken livers cooked with marjoram and cream, a far cry from tinned spaghetti on toast which Elaine often provided.

'I'm getting on exceedingly well,' said Rose with rather a cold but challenging flourish. 'I've just come back from an absolutely stunning holiday in Spain with friends, and we're getting a consortium together to start a private, *very* high quality nursing home.'

Elaine's tight lips began to quiver with sudden interest. 'How perfectly wonderful, Rose. Will you be needing someone for the administration side – like me?'

Rose smiled slightly. 'It would all depend on whether you could manage to break away from Monty, wouldn't it? Anyway there's a lot of preparation to do yet. We haven't actually got any money at present.'

Elaine's face fell as she moved with undisguised speed to find some whole shell-on prawns lightly cooked in garlic butter, served on a bed of salad leaves.

Secretly, Lawson Longsight was in a bit of a panic about

retiring. It was his wife Mitzi who had forced him into it. Some consultants had been known to stagger on in their nineties, muttering bring back more leeches, and where's the chloroform?

Mitzi continually went on about her life being chopped into pieces because of her husband's professional activities. 'I'm not a whole woman any more, Lawson. I'm a splinter group of conditioned reflexes. When are we going to settle down into a dignified pattern of life, not dependent on me always being the one who tags on behind the Specialist, who has to entertain your friends for ever more, and keep a cupboard full of interesting X-Rays to bring out with the wine and cigars? When are we going to be able to follow the Silk Road to Samarkand instead of a quick trip to North Wales?'

Dr Rose Stansfield's idea that Lawson Longsight didn't really like her (dating back to the cotton wool) was completely erroneous. He was far too busy to bother about such trifles even if he could remember every detail of trim Sister Tadworthy. At this moment he gazed across at Rose from the buffet table, with its heavy, white embossed cloth. On his starter plate was Parisienne of melon chilled in gingered coulis. He was looking straight – he hoped – into the eyes of Darling Obstetrics. His face was filled with sad admiration. Oh to be back to her age again. To be back in the thick of it with all the eternal turmoil of new, bawling life and bouncing babies.

His chance of speaking to her happened the moment he was about to start his second course of poached supreme of salmon Véronique. They had both chosen the same thing, and by the time they sat together for pudding

(Victoria cup filled with chocolate and Cointreau bavarois), and his wife Mitzi was in the kitchen hurriedly nibbling a solitary ungarnished cream cracker, he was completely reborn and resuscitated with talk of ideas for a private nursing home.

'I know many pregnant friends who would welcome such a place and be ready to pay for it,' pressed Rose. 'And I even know of ideal empty premises in Dodsbury, which are almost going for a song but need a bit of doing up. There'll be no problem about fully qualified staff either because there are already four of us ready and willing this very second. First, there's Staff Nurse O'Malley who would make a *perfect* Matron. Then there's a suitable Senior Sister available called Sawbridge who is at present staffing on obstetrics, and finally there's my dear friend Almoner Elaine Driffield. She is more than keen to take over the accounting and general administration . . . All it needs now is the money.'

The money . . . Lawson's eyes glazed over for a moment. There was always a snag, but . . . His mind began to tabulate likely financial support: Lord and Lady Cottingly-Spence, who'd been wanting a decent private place for years . . . Firebright Smith, the scrap-iron millionaire, whose wife had been one of Lawson's satisfied patients . . . Professor Inskinskope, who had once proposed something similar about a year ago . . .

By the time Rose left, she had a genuine assurance that the scheme would definitely go ahead.

And go ahead it did, as Mellowdays Private Maternity Home became a reality in the following eighteen months, with the new company directors and shareholders. The four women moved happily to their new surroundings, which caused a complete break-up of both Shirley O'Malley's association with Herby Dawson, and Elaine Driffield's with Monty Middleton.

There was only one sentence of criticism against the whole project.

'They use ordinary tap water for douches and charge five shillings a time,' said Herby Dawson to his new girl-friend, when they were engaged. 'So don't ever think for one second that you'll ever be going there.'

'No dear,' she said meekly, gazing at her huge diamond ring.

17
LONELINESS

Have you ever been lonely?
  Have you ever been blue?
  Have you ever loved someone one
  Who has never loved YOU?

That lilting music. Those words. May Greenrigg knew them from childhood radio days. They circled round her brain. She was feeling more and more lonely now that Lotty was married to Barry Rooks.

Everything was entirely different when she went home. The flat was still there to use, but now bereft of all the loving familiarity of the past. It seemed to be merely a meeting place for sixteen-year-old Coral and her girl-friends from school to play very loud records on the old radiogram, and do the 'jitterbug'.

Soon Coral would be in the sixth form. She was staying on and planned to be a junior school teacher. In another two years she would be the same age that May had been when she started nursing at Bell Lane. May felt as old as the hills. On her next birthday she would be twenty-four and not even a hint of marriage on the horizon. Her own mother, Lotty, had been married before she was even twenty-one.

Slowly, May put on her new hospital Sister's uniform. She was now in her own bedroom in the Sisters' quarters, along with Dizzy Oaklands. Both had the privilege of a small padded chair in their room, each with a cretonne cover. She was now a Junior Sister on Gynaecology Ward, but it was a far more sober world than during her training years. She hardly saw Dizzy, because Dizzy was now a Junior Night Sister, and spent all her spare time with her fiancé, Damian Clewlyn, who had just become a Senior Librarian. They were saving up to get a deposit for a house. Was she doomed to live for ever in a clutch of dedicated Florence Nightingales with not even a proper place of her own? Just when she was in the depth of this gloom something strange happened.

It was a hot Saturday in July, and her day off. She had just bumped into Liz in town and Liz had invited her back to the flat for a snack. She and Liz still kept in friendly casual contact, but this time Liz seemed quite excited about something.

'I've just got to tell you, May. I met someone in Platt Fields Park absolutely by chance. I was near the boating lake with Nathan, and Nathan was playing with a ball I'd bought him. It rolled under a bench where this man was sitting reading a book, and he threw it back to Nathan.' Liz's face was alight with happiness.

'Nathan was being a real little fusspot. He would not leave Paul alone. He expected Paul to play ball with him the whole time.'

'Paul?'

Liz nodded. 'Paul Rothsen. He's a physicist at Manchester University. He's over here for a year on a university exchange visit from Berkeley in California . . . I wanted to ask you, May, would you like to make up a foursome for a meal with Paul and me and Paul's friend? The thing is – you and Craig are the nearest people I have. But I can't just ask Craig and you because Craig's already tied up with Amelia.'

'Who is his friend?'

'Joe Selbyson. He's from the digs where they live in Northenden Road, Sale. Actually it's Joe's mother who owns the digs. Paul says she was a very young widow as a result of the First World War. Joe's a musician who works in the record library at the BBC. Both Paul and Joe are in their thirties.' Liz's cheeks bloomed a gentle pink. 'Paul said something about driving out for a meal to a place Joe knows – near Prestbury, one evening next week.'

May nodded enthusiastically. 'I'm off next Wednesday and Thursday evening if that's any good?'

'I'll ring you next Monday evening then and tell you which day.' They waved to each other, and parted.

All the way back to Bell Lane, May thanked her lucky stars that she had met Liz. Already she wondered what Joe Selbyson and Paul would be like, and what she should wear for the outing. She felt cheerful for the first time in weeks.

*

Joe Selbyson had short-cropped, dark curly hair. The skin was taut across his cheek bones and there was a cheeky, humorous looking glimmering from his deep-set eyes, which belied his general polite solemnity. He was thin and lean, and an exceedingly snappy dresser; the sort who might well have become Best Dressed Man of the Year. He wore a honey-coloured waistcoat and finely-woven beige suit with a subtle creamy herringbone pattern, a crimson silk handkerchief dripped casually from his chest pocket. May looked at him goggle eyed. She could not believe her luck.

Paul was quieter looking and plainer. He had dark red hair and a sandy, freckled complexion and was very neat. A solid gold watch gleamed from his wrist; whenever he glanced at his watch his arm shot out then bent in a precise angular movement, to display a gleaming white shirt cuff of highest quality with an engraved gold cuff-link.

The small whitewashed pub they went to, said to date from Tudor times, had purple clematis climbing its outer walls, and an arch of entwined pear wood round the iron-studded wooden door.

Joe owned a ten-year-old Chrysler that shone with luxury. It had hardly been used during the War. It used a lot of petrol, but he didn't seem to worry.

May noticed how pleasant and easy going he seemed. She was glad. She could see plainly that Liz and Paul had eyes only for each other. They held hands all the time as they walked to the small wooden tables and benches set out in front of the pub. What a glorious evening it was – so calm and dry and warm.

Honeysuckle drenched their senses, overlapped by the

mellow smell of local beer on tap from the barrels inside the small crowded pub. On the walls were hunting prints and pewter tankards hung gleaming from oak beams.

Most of the time the four of them sat outside chattering quietly in the evening light. They leaned with their elbows on an old oak trestle table in a peaceful paradise. Across the cobbles was an ancient row of well-built cottages with tiny-paned windows and heavy slate roofs. Most of the small cottages were decorated with flowery window boxes.

For a few seconds May had the feeling it was almost too good to be true. She decided to have a port and lemon. Until now she had been sipping Pimms. 'I think I'll just slip across and get myself a glass of blood red wine,' she murmured jokingly to Liz.

'Are you quite sure?' whispered Liz. 'It isn't too wise to mix your drinks. I think it's time we went back. I don't like being too long away because of Craig and Amelia having to act as baby sitters.'

But May wasn't to be put off. Her lonely feeling was coming back again as she stood up and walked towards the open door of the pub.

'Here – let me . . .' called Joe as he sprang to his feet with courtier-like politeness and followed her, but she didn't even hear him. She had already decided in her mind that she was a loser where men were concerned.

The pub bulged with people. She had to shove and thread her way amongst shouting and laughter to get to the bar. The sweating barman who needed to have six pairs of hands and three heads eventually spotted her. 'Yes Miss?'

She gave her order and took the glass with slightly wobbly care.

'I'll pay,' called Joe's voice just behind her.

She turned quickly to remonstrate, and within seconds the glass tipped sideways and port wine drenched the front of Joe's jacket. She stepped back in horror, right into the arms of a man waving a pint of Guinness. The Guinness went flying and drenched a woman in a pure white, pleated tennis dress. The place was swimming, with clothes flapping and arms waving, as May put her empty glass on a table and pressed through the crowds in a panic-stricken escape to try and get back outside and find the Ladies.

There was a small arrow pointing around to the back of the pub. She had to walk along some very worn paving slabs into the garden where there were two WCs. One said HIS and one said HERS. Both had a Horse Shoe nailed to the door. In HERS there were young dandelions growing in the crevices of the stone floor and the door had a wide gap below it big enough for your ankles to be seen from outside.

She leant against the inside of the door. Her heart was racing – she felt that they must leave the pub this very minute. She must get back to the hospital, and forget it all. Sleep it off. She thought of Joe's suit and shuddered. She knew only too well from Barry Rooks and *his* clothes, and how finicky *he* was not to get the slightest spot on them when he was dressed up, that it would be exactly the same with Joe. She knew well that men did not like disasters thrust upon them, particularly by women with wobbly hands and chicken brains. She felt her eyes smarting with despair. She would never be able to look Joe Selbyson in the face ever again.

When she got back to the table Joe was already there.

He looked up and smiled. 'We thought you'd either got lost or decided to go back on foot.'

She gazed at his jacket. Surprisingly it looked nothing more than a little damp.

He saw her looking and said: 'I washed it off in the pub. It was my fault for being so pushy.'

All three of them smiled at her apologetically. She began to feel a bit better.

Before they went, Paul Rothsen changed the conversation completely and said casually: 'Would anyone fancy a weekend at Mottram Hall some time? It's quite close to here. Some of the married guys at Owens College have been with their families. They say it's great. The Scientific Workers' Association sometimes organises Saturday night stay-over weekends – country walks and all that sort of thing.'

He looked straight at Liz as he spoke, and Liz nodded. 'I could bring Nathan with me too.'

She turned to May. 'What do you think, May?'

Joe was looking at May with quizzical blue-grey eyes.

'Me?' said May.

'Yes, you.'

She was taken aback. 'I d'dont know really. But if Liz is coming and is bringing Nathan – well, yes. It would all depend on getting a weekend off at the right time.' Suddenly her face was wreathed in smiles. 'Yes, I'd love it.'

*

Two weekends later, it was all properly arranged and the four of them plus Nathan went to Mottram Hall for the weekend.

The food was very good and the surroundings perfect. The place had a winding carriage drive to the front entrance, with unpretentious gardens and green country-side and no sign of other buildings except for a few ancient cottages on its outskirts.

Liz and Nathan and May slept in a large room over-looking the gardens. Paul and Joe were in a separate wing near the stables.

At the end of August Joe asked May tentatively if she would like to go away with him. By now they had been twice to see plays together at the Opera House in Manchester, once to the Halle Orchestra, and twice to the Ritz Dance Hall with Liz and Paul. Yet they had only kissed twice, and that was at Mottram Hall in the moon-light. It was almost a platonic relationship.

May wondered what to do. She had a week's holiday due. She adored going out with him even though it wasn't passionately romantic, but to actually go away on a holiday with him seemed an entirely different matter. Supposing it was a complete disaster, and she was left with no companionship whatsoever afterwards? Back to work, work, work at the hospital and not a male in sight?

Then one day she mentioned it to Dizzy. '. . . So he wants me to go away with him . . .'

'To sleep with him?' said Dizzy with cheerful blunt-ness. 'Well it would certainly be better than being in a huddle in the back of a car. Damian and I have been lucky in that respect,' she said. 'One of my sisters lets us guard their house in Chorlton about once a week. Which reminds me, I'm getting married in October so I'll be inviting you to the wedding.'

Dizzy stopped and looked thoughtful. 'Only kissed you *twice* up to now? As long ago as Mottram Hall. He must be made of stone. Well at least there's a slight spark of passion somewhere, and he chose an apt moment. . . . On the other hand he might be . . . He might —'

May stared at her with anxious impatience. 'Might be what?'

'Might be burning with hidden, well-controlled desire. There's no real knowing unless you do accept his holiday offer. He may be so full of passion for you that he simply dare not let himself go at present and a holiday would just iron things out a bit for both of you.'

May looked at her anxiously. 'I think I'll chance it,' she said at last.

Ernst Jünger was still single and was working as a commercial traveller for a German Drug company. As soon as he got home he had gone to college on a scholarship for past members of the forces.

He could not believe his luck when he was sent to London for five days. He thought immediately of Liz, and his time in Manchester, and wrote a letter from Germany. This time the letter was in German and signed with his proper name. It was cautious and formal.

Dear Liz,
I am coming to London on business, and am hoping to visit you for old times' sake. It is no use suggesting

we meet in London, because I realise that you may be otherwise engaged, and I too have many places to visit connected with my work.

As you can see by my visiting card I have changed my way of life completely. I live in West Berlin, as you will notice by the address.

How are you going on? I expect you will be fully qualified by now. Do you ever see Valda from the café? If you do, please send her my kind regards. Also Nurse Downs. I often think of you all, and hope I may see you soon.

Yours Respectfully,

Ernst Jünger.

There was no mention of the nostalgia and thankfulness for her being in his life at just the right time to save him. Or the memories that often swept over him from time to time.

The letter landed in the letter rack, in the dining-room of the nurses' quarters at Bell Lane. It stayed there for months, quiet and unopened. Other letters covered it like a small snow-drift – coming and going – leaving it to a lost and lonely fate.

Every day, Ernst waited for an answer, trying not to show – even to himself – his disappointment. He knew deep down that she might have moved, but somehow he never pursued that idea. Instead he preferred, sadly, to think she had forgotten him at last. After all, their short time together was all gone now. Everything was changing so rapidly. He already had a very faithful girl-friend called Germaine, who like himself, had lost many relatives during the war. Was it some strange greed, holding these romantic memories so close to himself? He had hardly mentioned that part of his life to Germaine, except to say that he had been a wounded prisoner of war, like countless others of his countrymen.

Nevertheless, as soon as he arrived in London in his new role, the need to revive old memories of the north of England haunted him again. Had it all really happened as he imagined? Four other men accompanied him on his business trip to London. One day out of the five had been put aside for sight-seeing and relaxation, visiting the Tower of London and sailing along the Thames in a barge.

Ernst decided not to go with the others on the outings. Instead, he slipped away on his own and caught a train to Manchester.

By the time he had walked from the railway station to Valda's café in pouring rain, and had stared at some of the bare dereliction, now covered with layers of weeds, wild flowers and twitch grass, he knew it was just as he had imagined. He realised it was true. And if that was true, Liz was true.

He decided to go inside the café. He pushed open the familiar, old wooden door. It had hardly changed. There was no sign of Valda. Two young, fourteen-year-old girls in nylon smocks were dishing out pie and chips with lots of gravy. The place was the same old mixture: there were a few down-and-outs smoking cigarette butts, keeping warm and drinking hot tea out of saucers, and a few office workers eating toasted tea-cakes and drinking mugs of tea.

One of the young girls asked Ernst what he wanted. She called him 'sir', because he was so handsome and neatly dressed. The other one wondered if he was a food or health inspector and began to examine the newly washed-up plates extra carefully, in case there was any egg still stuck to them. She polished a few cups vigorously to remove all traces of lipstick, made sure that gravy had not dripped onto the counter and that no stray cats were lurking near the back larder.

'I'll have Welsh rabbit,' said Ernst, speaking in perfect Mancunian.

The pale yellow Lancashire cheese on toast, with its bubbly brown freckles on top, arrived on a thick white pot plate. He sat there alone in the corner, dousing it with Heinz ketchup.

'That was very nice,' he said later, as the girl gave him his bill. She took the plate away, brought him his change and began to wipe the table with a rather grey looking dishcloth.

'Does Valda still own the place?'

The girl nodded. 'She's having it all done out in pink and cream soon. She's busy with her other branch in the basement in Mosley Street, that used to be part of a furnishing place, near Gibbs' Bookshop. It's going to be blue and orange, and very select.' She wiped some long blonde hair from her eyes and ogled at him.

'Tell her I called,' he said and smiled. 'Tell her Edmund Young called, for old times' sake.'

He was just turning towards the door when a huge woman with carefully set, pale blue hair and wearing a long black velour coat with a velvet collar arrived. He did not recognise her until she opened her mouth and bellowed at one of the girls.

'Kate! Get rid of that dishcloth immediately. Get a new one from the cupboard.'

'It's locked, Valda.'

'It is not locked. I unlocked it this morning when I called in. Do it now, Kate. Not next Preston Guild.'

Ernst turned to her, his face alight with smiles. 'Valda! How are you? It is good to see you after all these years.'

She glanced briefly at his immaculate clothes.

'No doubt you hardly remember me? I was a friend of Liz Frankel's. My name is . . .' he hesitated imperceptibly . . . 'Edmund Young.'

Valda stared at him almost stagestruck. Then she said with breathless bluntness: 'Not that escaped German POW, Jünger?' She began to look flustered and glanced towards Kate and the other girl. They both pretended to be busy getting new dishcloths.

Valda tried to cover up her admission, yet in a way Ernst was glad she had said it. Every spark of true recognition was like honey. He looked at her with a smiling bland expression, and repeated his former words with a slight bow: 'Edmund Young. A friend of Liz Frankel's.'

'We all knew about it, see? But never said,' gabbled Valda apologetically.

'It was Liz I came to enquire about. Those wartime days are thankfully gone at last. What happened to Liz?'

'My sister Dizzy said she married, and her husband died.'

Ernst felt a saddening of his expectations. Somehow

this bit of news was too realistic. He had never included in his ideas that she might have married.

Valda was still covered with confusion. 'She has a little boy called Nathan. I think she works as a nurse in a factory somewhere. Excuse me, but I must hurry, I've got to get back to my other premises.' She gave him a wide smile. 'Good to have met you again. Tarraar then. I'll tell Dizzy to pass on the message that you called.'

When he'd gone she wiped her brow with relief. She glared at the two young girls and said: 'And remember this much you two. Never believe all you hear because it could be a load of baloney.'

One of the girls nodded, and hurried out of sight. When Valda had gone, Peggy said to the other one: 'Thank God he wasn't a health inspector, anyway. They can take dishcloths and put them under a huge microscope. It shows up microbes by the million.'

Kate said disgustedly: 'He must have been much older than I thought. Them old ones should stick to their own old fashions. He could have lead us astray – all dolled up like that.'

Ernst caught the bus from Piccadilly to West Dodsbury. The journey took about half an hour, and the walk to Bell Lane about five minutes. It was afternoon visiting time and people were walking through the main gates. The place did not appear to have changed at all. It was almost as if it was waiting there to welcome him. He slipped in with the crowds and kept on walking along the broad inner road towards the Main Hospital block and its long corridor. Sometimes he saw nurses in their blue and white uniforms and scarlet cloaks. He caught his breath with a strange nervousness as if he was still on the run.

When he came to the entrance to the Main Hospital corridor he did not go in with rest of the small army of visitors, who were all talking and carrying bunches of flowers. Instead he branched away to his left and walked along a narrower path to the back of the buildings.

His heart filled with joy. It was actually still here, with all its gloomy workhouse image! All the old iron fire escapes. All the old hospital dustbins. All the wild and yellowy looking grass leading across to the fenced-off allotments in the distance. Tears came to his eyes. It had not changed. He was standing here a free man in a different world – and he had not imagined any of it.

He looked up at the sky and gave thanks to God. Then turning away, he hurried towards the main gates again, and within an hour and a half he was back on the train returning to London.

18
THREESOMES

In the year of the Festival of Britain, three things happened within months of each other: Dizzy got married and left Bell Lane; Liz became engaged to Paul Rothsen and she and Nathan went back to California with him; but, before either of these, May took the plunge at the end of April and agreed to go on holiday with Joe, to Nice.

At first she did not actually say who she was going with. She merely mentioned 'a friend, whose mother owned a private house there.' She tried to make it sound as casual as possible.

'How on earth will you afford it,' gasped Lotty anxiously. 'You were only saying the other day that the prices were far too much for you, even to travel to Bournemouth!'

May hurriedly ignored her, and carried on talking about Monaco and Monte Carlo. '. . . And anyway we'll have to travel cheaply because you aren't allowed to take much money out of this country – even if you have it.'

It was Coral who got down to the nitty-gritty. 'Are you going with someone we've heard of before? Is it one of the other nurses? What's her name?'

May brazened it out and said: 'Joe. Joe Selbyson.'

'Is it short for Josephine or Joanna?' asked Coral rather bumptiously.

May shrugged her shoulders vaguely. ' Don't ask me.'

By now Lotty and Barry were perking up.

'Perhaps it stands for Joceline,' laughed Lotty.

'Or even plain Joe from the name Joseph,' remarked Barry shrewdly. 'I once knew a couple called Freda and Clive Selbyson from Sale, with a small boy called Joseph.'

May was a poor liar. She felt herself going red. 'I might as well admit it. Yes – J is for Joseph. He's invited me away with him for a week, and I've accepted.'

There was a terrible silence. May had never seen her mother look so shocked.

'Are you quite sure you know what you're doing? He might be any old Tom, Dick, or Harry, just out to take advantage of you. You'll be in a foreign place with some-one you haven't even had the grace to introduce us to.'

May felt her heart sink. She knew it was true. It was even true that she hardly knew Joe herself, if ten years of courtship was the general criteria. She had never been introduced to his mother either, or actually been to his home.

She tried to bluff over it. 'Nonsense mother. I'm not as

green as that. I'm a responsible person. It's a perfectly simple *friendly* holiday. It has nothing to do with being men or women.' She looked round at them all. Barry was grinning and nodding his head like a Cheshire cat.

May began to get annoyed. 'You needn't look like that Barry. There *is* such a thing as platonic friendship. I don't care what anyone says.'

Barry's smile became wider and wider. Lotty dug him in the ribs with her elbow, and said to May: 'Let's hope there is, for your sake, May. I expect you've burned your boats already if it's all arranged, but if you want my honest opinion I think it's the road to ruin. In fact I never thought that a daughter of mine would ever – *ever* go off on holiday with a man she hardly knew, with not even an engagement ring on her finger.'

'I wouldn't put it quite as dramatically as that, Lotty,' said Barry toning down to more solemnity. 'May isn't a fool.'

'Thank you *very* much, Barry. I'm really grateful.'

Nothing more was said. But the following week the whole fuss about her holiday was put in the shade by Coral breaking the news that she thought she was pregnant. The place was in an uproar. Coral said it was one of the boys from school, Aldred and had happened during a game of 'sardines' in a cupboard at someone's birthday party, and everyone was mad on him, including her.

'I just couldn't help clicking with him straightaway,' she said. 'He's the image of Humphrey Bogart.'

'Which must make him the same age as your grandfather,' said Barry, as Lotty stood there dabbing her eyes in hopeless agony with a handkerchief.

Coral's announcement was thankfully a false alarm. What she had thought was resting against her in the cupboard was in fact a small piece of pink wet carbolic soap, which had slipped from a nearby washing-up bucket. And in any case, as Aldred himself said later, he could not possibly have undone all the buttons of his fly with as much speed as all that, because they were found by the other sardines in about ten seconds. And as for Coral's three-day's-late menstrual period, which started all the panic, the doctor put it down to either examination stress, or wishful thinking to escape from the exams. Nevertheless the incident, thankfully, had taken all the attention away from what May was doing.

May had spent a small fortune on clothes for her week's holiday: a green and white striped button-through skirt with matching small sun shorts and sun top; a shoulderless, intricately patterned, sea-blue dress with a slightly boned bra and a long matching stole; lastly, two beautiful, flowing creamy nightdresses of transparent, flowered cotton voile, with thin, narrow-rolled shoulder straps. Deep in her heart she regarded it as a sort of honeymoon.

The house was tucked away up a sharp winding hill which looked across in the direction of Corsica. May and Joe slept in separate bedrooms. A housekeeper came in daily. The days were pure paradise, with outings to Grasse, in the perfume country, and Antibes down the coast.

Joe had insisted on paying for their stay right from the beginning. 'Stop fussing about it, May. I invited you to come with me and you accepted. I can well afford it, otherwise I should never have invited you in the first place.'

Already, after only a couple of days away from Manchester, their faces were taking on a sun drenched bloom, as they talked and explored like two children, free of adult cares.

Yes, it was proving to be all perfectly platonic, thought May to herself. There was not even a kiss between them, but sometimes they did hold hands. One thing Joe did not mention though worried her slightly. He ignored anything in his own past not linked to living with his mother at her guest house, or working in the record library at the BBC in Manchester. It was almost as if he was carrying some secret deep inside himself.

Then on the final night, just as May had gone to bed, after a romantic boat trip, Joe tapped at her bedroom door. She got up and went to open it in a long, flowing diaphanous nightdress. He was standing there in a maroon silk, Paisley dressing-gown and blue pyjamas. The sun had made them into god and goddess.

'I've something to tell you May. Do you mind if I come in?'

She stood back from the door and nodded, her arms golden from the sea air. A small spark of uneasiness gripped her. The holiday had been perfect. What on earth was he going to say? Please don't let it all be spoiled by some awful revelation on this their last night together, she thought.

As things stood she would be going back home with her conscience as clear as any medieval virgin. She would even be able to convince Lotty and Barry of the truth about their platonic friendship.

She turned and looked nervously towards the bed with

white cotton sheets and a fringed, beige counterpane. It took up nearly all the room. Was it best for her to sit on the side of the bed and hope he would deposit himself in the bamboo chair? Or should she claim the chair?

He came in and stood there. And she stood there. An almost unbearable tension existed between them, and he began to speak quickly.

'The reason I brought you here May, was because I once came here with her before we were married. It was before the War.' He put his hands to his face. 'It was a complete disaster.'

The tension drained away. May felt quite faint and sat down on the side of the bed. He sat next to her putting his hand in hers. What a thing to be faced with – who was this other 'her'? It was almost as if she was his next victim. Yet the holiday had been paradise.

'Don't look so shocked May, for Christ's sake. I know it sounds strange but I love you so much. I just had to bring you to the same place to make sure it all worked out all right. I needed to check if that other visit long ago was – maybe not altogether my own fault – but was simply a case of Aylise and myself being completely incompatible.' He gave a wry smile. 'It was all so petty really. We were very young. I was eighteen – but at the time the little things and the bickering caused disaster from the start. We even squabbled eternally over things like bed covers and who had the most of the sheet or the pillow.' He stopped then hurried on. 'It was a most foolish thing to ask her to come away with me and for us to sleep together. It meant that I was pledged to marry her after that, whatever happened. It was a question of honour or, as she pointed out, she would have faced life as a ruined woman.'

They sat in silence for what seemed ages. He looked a picture of misery and remorse. Anger began to rise in her against the other woman. But was she a 'woman'? Maybe she was just a girl? She realised sadly that she had passed that stage now.

'Was she eighteen like you were, Joe?'

'She was nineteen.'

May thought back for a fleeting second to herself at nineteen. She'd been completely enveloped in nursing. She thought of him now – in this room. He was older than she was and already had a history of divorce. No wonder he still lived at home with his mother.

'Divorce is a terrible thing to have to go through,' she said. She stopped suddenly. He hadn't really told her *anything*. For all she knew he might even have some small children somewhere about. 'Especially,' she said to him slowly, with an awful feeling of doom, 'especially if you happen to have any children. That must be the worst thing of all. It must make it extremely sad and complicated . . .'

He stared at her in amazement. 'That's just it, May. I'm *not* divorced. I haven't any children, but Aylise refuses point-blank to divorce me, even though we parted after only three months. She told me to get out. Yet she says we are bound together until we die. She vows she will never give me a divorce.'

May sat there. Her body felt cold as stone. What an awful ending to this wonderful week.

He left her room without saying another word. She lay

in the darkness thinking and brooding, thinking of his slow confession and his awful dilemma. She felt tired and disillusioned.

Just as she was drifting off into a sad sleep some of his words came to her again: '. . . I love you so much . . .'

He loved her, and she loved him. She knew in her bones that it was true. She closed her eyes at last and slept.

The following day in brilliant sunshine, as they packed their bags and got ready to go home, it was just as if last night had never happened. Yet in some ways it was better that it had, thought May, for at least she knew the true situation, and she knew that he loved her and meant it.

But there was one thing neither of them knew – a telegram for Joe Selbyson arrived at the house half an hour after they had left to get back to Manchester.

Joe saw her back to the hospital by taxi from Manchester, and as they parted he kissed her with sudden passion. It was their first really natural show of hungry affection.

'I'll phone you tomorrow. As soon as you know your off duty, I'll take you to meet my mother,' said Joe. 'I'll be able to tell her that you know the state of things with regard to Aylise.'

The next day she was waiting by the phone in the Sisters' Home. May paced up and down, until finally in desperation she tried to calm herself by sitting on a nearby chair in the corridor, moving her hands about restlessly on the lap of her starched white apron. The call, if ever it was to arrive, was terribly late now, but still she kept hoping and hoping. This was quickly followed by more despair. Becoming surer that he would never ring after all, she thought that perhaps he was letting her down lightly and had just decided to call the whole thing off. Perhaps he had told her too much about his past and regretted it. Surely it hadn't all been a pack of lies?

Suddenly the phone rang and she grabbed it thankfully.

His voice seemed rather flat, as if he was trying to be enthusiastic and normal, but there was a strangely false streak.

'Have you got safely settled in again then?'

'Yes. Have you?'

He didn't answer. Instead he said: 'I'm afraid there's bad news at this end.' He hesitated as if to brace himself. 'I'm not ringing you from work. I'm still at home. My mother died in the small hours of yesterday. My sister Binny sent me a telegram but it must have arrived after we'd gone . . . It was a terrible shock for all the family . . . I think it will be at least a fortnight before things are sorted out, and I manage to ring you again. It saddens me so much to think that you two never met.'

By the time May replaced the receiver she was in tears.

Paul Rothsen had planned to ask Joe and May, and Joe's Mother, as well as others, to a celebration party before he, Liz and Nathan went back to America in two weeks' time. The sudden death of Mrs Selbyson had put a tactful end to the idea. Instead, Joe and May, Liz and Paul, Delyth and Damian met for a last goodbye at a small country pub on the outskirts of Baguley.

'I hope you all live happily ever after in California,'

murmured May fervently to Liz, as they kissed and put their arms round each other.

Liz was blooming with good health and happiness. 'I'm sure we shall. I'll write to you the moment I get there.'

About a week after Liz and Paul had departed, Dizzy said to May at the hospital: 'It's the end of a whole era and we're the only two left from all our group. We're the sole survivors of a strange happening.'

'I wonder what happened to Edmund Young?' said May broodingly.

They both shook their heads. Even though they knew the whole story, neither of them had ever divulged the full details of it to any of the others, and Dizzy always pretended that Edmund Young was someone completely separate from Ernst Jünger.

'Maybe we will never know,' said May quietly. 'And perhaps it's just as well. Time changes all things and it's different now. I feel as old as the hills . . . I'll soon be twenty-seven.'

'I feel the same,' laughed Dizzy. 'My daft days are well and truly over. Damian is one for trying to keep me in order. I once showed him Matron Throstle's blue bed sock. I've always kept it in my dressing table drawer as a souvenir. He was most unimpressed and didn't see the funny side at all. He just thought we were all barmy.' Dizzy chuckled, quite unabashed. 'But I think he's soon due for a shock. I'm pretty sure I'm already expecting, even though we aren't actually married yet.' She put her finger to her lips. 'Not a word to a soul. I shall walk down the aisle as pure as driven snow in a white taffeta gown without a scruple of guilt. After all it is *his* child, and all children should be regarded as a blessing.'

May felt a slight jab of envy. Dizzy – all set for a posh white wedding and – bar mishaps – their first child already guaranteed. Whilst she? Why – she hadn't even met Joe's older sister Binny yet. Nor had she heard any more about his clinging wife, Aylise.

Some days later May was invited to Joe's detached home, the Bel Accueil Guest House. Its name and the words 'Guest House' were set in a tastefully understated piece of carved oak, next to black wrought-iron double gates. It was in an avenue of bright pink, double-flowering cherry trees in Sale. Lying in half an acre of garden, it had three garages, six bedrooms and a box room, and a magnificent kitchen.

May was quite overcome by its opulence. It was far from what she thought of as a 'lodging house'.

'There's just me here at the moment,' said Joe as he showed her round. 'We only have two guests at present; they're a couple of engineers staying for three weeks, who are out all day and only take breakfast and supper.

'It has been such a terrible jumble since mother died. That's her portrait over there.' He pointed to a very skilful watercolour sketch of a lively-looking young woman of about twenty-two with a chestnut bob of hair wearing a light brown jumper. May warmed to the picture immediately.

'My sister Binny is staying for another fortnight, and we have some daily staff who come in. I can't introduce you to Binny yet as she had to rush back to North Wales to tell her own family she'd be staying here a bit longer, and to collect some more of her belongings.' Suddenly Joe looked at her pleadingly. 'Is there a chance you could stay the night? We have plenty of spare bedrooms.'

She was surprised. 'I expect I could – with it being my day off tomorrow.' She smiled with sudden joy. 'Do you think I could just pop back for some night things and my toothbrush?'

'Of course. I'll give you a lift right now. It shouldn't take more than half an hour or so.'

Soon they were speeding back in the Chrysler. May could see happiness returning to his face. He waited for her in the car whilst she went to get her things.

When she got in the car again he said: 'Will you marry me May?'

She could hardly believe her ears. She did not answer. All she saw was his serious looking profile as he drove the car.

'But – I thought . . .' She remembered everything so clearly from what he had told her on their holiday. Aylise was already engraved on her own heart. So what about Aylise? 'What I really mean to say is . . .' She gulped nervously. 'Where does Aylise live?'

'I'll explain more when we get back,' he said then went on to mention something more trivial, as they drove along.

When they were back in the house again he went to a bureau and took out a small photograph album. It was full of little black and white snaps. There was one of himself at about eighteen in shorts and an open-necked white shirt with his sleeves rolled up. He was standing next to a slim, pretty woman with frizzy hair wearing a long narrow skirt. She was holding a holiday bag and wore a tiny straw hat.

'That's me with Aylise in Nice.' He stared at the photograph in silence, then he said: 'She lives in Sweden now.' He said nothing further.

In Sweden? May didn't know whether to be pleased or sorry. At least Aylise wasn't likely to be popping up every five minutes. All the same, it was awful to think that he was tied to her against his will, for eternity.

That evening when the meals were over and the two engineers had gone out, and the cook and the washer-up had gone home, they sat together in the private sitting-room drinking coffee. But by now as May simmered away inside, it was as if the damage was done. She could see it was a hopeless situation. What on earth had induced him to propose marriage suddenly, when both of them knew it was impossible, unless he wanted to become a bigamist and be sent to prison?

She could contain herself no longer. She sipped the remains of her coffee, and as she replaced the Royal Doulton cup in its saucer she said: 'Did I hear right when you asked me to marry you?'

He almost hung his head in sudden shame. 'I should never have said it. I love you too much to ask you to live with me as my secret common-law wife, and yet I love you so much that I want to take you in my arms this very minute . . . I want to take you to bed and make love to you. But I dare not. I just dare not do it unless you agree. I have been stung once and it proved to be a complete disaster.'

May stared at him in anguish. She could see he meant

every word of it, yet how could she possibly agree to such a situation? She would be lowering herself to be almost a strumpet. She knew people too well. They would regard her as his tart, or his 'other woman'. She would be as nothing. Soon their love would fly out of the window like the last wraith of smoke from dying embers.

She stood up, and turning to him with her eyes smarting with sudden tears, and her voice cracking with a terrible tightness she said: 'I love you too, Joe. I love you almost to madness but I cannot take the plunge. I shall never be able to until you are completely free of her and tear up that photograph in the album.' She turned hastily, grabbed her small bag of night attire and rushed from the house.

'May – May! Come back for God's sake. Don't leave me!'

She ran and ran. She heard him starting the engine of the car. Soon he would catch her up, but she was determined it was not to be. She turned away from the avenue down a small driveway and he drove past.

Slowly now – all passion spent – she found the nearest bus route and soon she was on a red double-decker speeding back to the hospital. She sat there in dull oblivion. What on earth was she doing with her life?

When she got back Dizzy met her to say there had been a phone message for her. 'It was Joe. He sounded terribly worried. He wanted to know if you were back? Whatever's been happening?'

May flopped down on her bed and Dizzy made her a drink of tea. 'You look all in.'

May sighed, partly with sheer thankfulness. She was

already beginning to feel better. It was such a relief to be back in the same familiar old surroundings.

'It's a long story, Dizzy, and I'm already beginning to wonder if I did the right thing or whether I was far too hasty . . . Joe asked me to marry him.'

'Congratulations, May!' Dizzy's face flooded with pleasure.

'It's not all it seems, Dizzy. He already has this wife who won't divorce him.' Depression reigned again as May began to explain what had happened.

Dizzy was silent for a while then she said: 'No one else can ever really give advice. The only people who know us best are ourselves. We're all on our own in the end – but it is nice to have friends.' Then she changed the subject and said: 'Take me, for instance. You'd never believe it, but I've just been promoted to Senior Night Sister! It'll mean more money, and just when I'm going to need it – which is always.'

'B – but – I thought you said you were —?'

'Expecting? Yes. Given with one hand and taken away with the other. I shall accept the new role with delighted thanks and not say a word for the time being. Such is life.'

As Dizzy made her way to her own room that day, she thought sadly of May's dilemma. May was such a well-meaning, honest girl. She deserved a happier state than a man tied up to some woman, who was out to get revenge for ever. She liked Joe. She liked May. Please let it all get solved in the end, she thought.

It had been her day off today and she had been in town with Damian looking at furniture. Feeling quite tired, she got into bed. She put her hands to her belly and stroked it.

It didn't look the least different yet. She would be able to get at least six months work in as a Night Sister, she thought, before it began to show and by then she would already be a married woman, ready to look after a family threesome.

But after that – who could tell? How could anyone ever tell what was going to happen in life?

19
LOOSE ENDS

'Get on that bed and be quick about it.' Dizzy could hardly believe the cheek of it. The tone was bossy and hard. Even if this firm looking Maternity Staff Nurse was efficient, it was her *attitude*, thought Dizzy.

Obviously the nurse realised that the now secretly married Mrs Delyth Clewlyn was about to have a premature baby, but need she have been so brisk and sharp? No – Dizzy thought.

The whole place was like alien territory now. Ada Sawbridge and Dr Rose Stansfield had long since flown. They were doing very well with their private nursing home, and the expensive tap water.

Dizzy had retired as a very busy Night Sister in her seventh month, but, three weeks later, she was now paying the full price. As well as the catastrophe of the baby arriving before it was due, she had been criticised by her family about the folly of taking on too much work.

'Being able to afford a nice new bedroom suite is all very well,' said her sister Valda bluntly, 'but have you sacrificed a nice little baby for it?'

Dizzy lay there in the bed in a depressed panic wondering and praying it would not be so.

The baby was born – a little girl. She called her Joy. Joy spent her early days in an oxygen tent and survived, but alas from that time she suffered with eyesight problems. This was thought to have been caused by giving too much pure oxygen to premature babies.

After that, Dizzy never went back to nursing again, but stayed mainly at home to look after an ever expanding and happy family. She also had the advantage of Valda being in the background, who was going from strength to strength with her two cafés, and could always provide some part-time work.

May had received a handwritten letter in a blue envelope with neat, unknown writing on the envelope. It had a North Wales postmark, and as soon as she opened it she knew by the address it had come from Joe's sister.

Dear Miss Greenrigg,
You will probably wonder who this letter is from, but I am Joe Selbyson's sister Binny. I hope you won't mind my writing to you. I have heard such a lot about you from Joe, all of it nice! so it's a pity we've never met.

This is to say I am coming over to Sale during the next week as Joe has had to go to Sweden. I was wondering if we could meet some time whilst I'm there? Yours Sincerely, Binny Williamson.

May read the letter again and frowned slightly. She was in a dilemma. She had been chugging along in her usual familiar pattern, and had finally decided to try and forget about Joe, and all there was between them. Over the past few months the whole affair had begun to fade; there was a need growing within her not to be disturbed by all that again, as she began to rue even the fact that she had gone on holiday with him.

It had not been helped either by her last visit home.

'What happened to that fellow May went away with?' said Barry one day to Lotty as they washed some pots together. 'That "platonic" one?'

May could hear everything he was saying, even though she was in the bedroom above the kitchen. This was because new central heating was being put in and wide gaps had been left in all the floorboards where the pipes passed through.

'She hasn't said another word about him,' replied Lotty, smoothing out the tea towel and hanging it up. 'And a good thing too if you ask me – though I did hear a whisper from Coral that he's supposed to have a wife who won't divorce him.'

'Won't divorce him?' laughed Barry incredulously. Any man can get rid of a woman if he rally wants to. 'Any man can get a divorce. The law's on our side. Don't forget my sister. Look at how she suffered with those children when that bastard husband of hers cleared off and got a divorce on the grounds of adultery by her that didn't even happen! Oh no, Lotty, we have it the jammiest, even though I says it myself. We're king of the jungle.'

May bit her lip in suppressed anger as she thought of Coral blurting out her personal confidences to Lotty, who had immediately told Barry. She must have mentioned it to Coral in a lax moment – probably when Coral was having one of her dramatic heart-to-heart talks about her latest boy-friends. And now May's most secret remarks were common news. It just showed you could never trust anyone, particularly the nearest and dearest.

Barry launched into the subject with even more gusto. 'Men like that are a bit dicey,' said Barry knowingly. 'It's a difficult situation what May's in now. To put it plainly, Lotty – if they're a normal man – they aren't exactly going to remain with their pride and glory dangling down doing nowt for years. Quite often it's a case of calling in at the local knocking shop for a quick one.'

'Barry! How *can* you? I never heard such awful talk as that in all my life!'

'Come off it, Lotty. You've only to read the *News of the World* on Sundays to see that.' Barry was an ardent *News of the World* reader. There was nothing he liked better than to read aloud a juicy scandal with a vicar in it. Whereas Lotty was more prim, and kept to *Reynolds News* which had a more wholesome, idealistic tone, full of soothing family and socialist values.

'Believe me, Lotty, that there platonic lover could have been trampling his way through a female vineyard. And another point, did you realise that we're going through one of the biggest rises in VD ever? It's always been there in these hot countries, but we're a real cold lot here.'

'You wouldn't think it to hear you talking, Barry,' said Lotty with dagger-like, icy precision.

May moved out of earshot in exasperation. Barry had always had a very coarse streak tucked away. Usually she turned a deaf ear to it, but this time . . .

Yet his words had disturbed her and she began to think about them deeply. What did these men normally do when they were left high and dry without a permanent woman about? Did even the most respectable ones resort to local prostitutes, or did they try to find an amenable if slightly imperfect girl-friend? More to the point – did they remain completely chaste?

She thought back to the way she had run out on Joe. He had sworn he loved her and she had sworn she loved him. Yet neither of them had even been in touch again. It was beginning to seem like something that had never even happened, as she pursued her nursing career, and visited Dizzy once or twice at her new home, in Gatley. Was she burying her head in the sand? She found it absolutely incredible that she was the sole survivor of all the girls, and was still an unmarried virgin.

So what about Joe, then? Was he at this moment trying to recapture his own virgin days, or was he satisfying his desires in some secret rendezvous?

She decided to accept Joe's sister Binny's invitation and go to visit her.

Binny Selbyson was a tall, rather ungainly, dark-haired woman of about forty with a warm welcoming manner. She wore a plain jumper and skirt, and flat shoes. Brisk and down to earth she had been a Red Cross driver during the War. May felt at home with her straightaway.

Binny got up from the occasional table, where they were just finishing coffee and cake, and took a photograph off a bureau. 'I don't know whether you know who this is, but it's Joe's wife, Aylise. I've always kept in touch with her over the years. She's a charming person, but of course they're completely incompatible.' She looked shrewdly at May as May stared with shock at the photograph. It was bigger than the small snapshot Joe had shown her of himself and Aylise when he was only eighteen. The picture was of a woman sitting in a wheelchair. She was smiling.

'I don't suppose Joe ever mentioned the accident? He hardly ever does.' Binny went over to the bureau and put the photograph back, and just at that moment the bell rang.

'Excuse me. I shan't be a minute. I'm expecting something back from the dry cleaners.'

Binny left the room and May stood up and went to have another look at the photograph. She could not get over it. What else had he not told her? Her glance wandered to an open diary on the bureau; with a shock, she realised it was his. She recognised his writing immediately. The diary was open at a full page of carefully written names and addresses from all over the country. They were all women. Some of them had ticks against them. One even had 'not very good' written in minute writing by the side of it.

May turned away with a feeling of nausea. Her legs had turned to jelly, so she sat down again. How ever had she managed to get herself involved in such a shabby affair? Barry's past warnings and sage lectures on there being no such thing as platonic friendship, along with his somewhat lascivious delight in describing the life of womanless males, was taking its inevitable toll. She could see quite plainly now that Barry was right. Barry had always been a man who mixed with all and sundry. There was no doubt he knew the ways of the world even more than she did, and this diary had proved it. It was plainly a list of likely women. Everyone knew that most men had a few names and addresses, but this list was just as Barry had forecast in his summing up of Joe's situation.

'I'm sorry I was so long,' Binny said smiling when she returned. She went over to the bureau and closed it. 'I thought I'd better show you that photograph. Joe's gone over to Sweden to see her. Have another piece of cake? Or shall I make some more coffee?'

May shook her head. 'I'd better be getting back. It's been so helpful being able to meet you and hear about Joe.'

'But I haven't told you anything yet. He made me promise I'd tell you. He wrote it in his diary along with all his other important necessities. Before you came I was busy sorting out all the names and addresses of countless women he knows –'

May switched off immediately – she never heard the beginning of what Binny was saying.

'He has to sort them all out for his music programmes.

All of them are musicians but they live everywhere. It's quite a job gathering them together for programmes. Many of them are in orchestral quartets or trios and some of them are singers. He has to decide which ones to choose.'

May blinked at her.

'Am I tiring you? I am rather a talker when I get going. Are you quite sure you wouldn't like some more coffee?'

Suddenly May came to. She smiled. 'Seeing you've asked me again – yes, I think I will have another cup. I hadn't realised how involved Joe was with his work. He hardly mentions it.'

'He hardly ever does with us either. He's been with the BBC since he left school. He likes to leave work behind as much as possible and just relax – if you could call helping mother to run this place as a guesthouse relaxing.' She smiled ruefully. 'Sadly I think that era will be drawing to a close once our present guests have gone.

'Excuse me, whilst I bring the coffee. I don't like to have Lorna from the kitchen hopping backwards and forwards. She's got enough to do.'

May sat there and looked round the room. It was as if a veil of deep mourning had lifted from her. The sun was streaming through the French windows and she could see blue and buttery yellow tom-tits hopping about amidst the glorious gold of forsythia blossom and smell the scent of cut grass as someone mowed the lawn. She looked with pleasure at the pale green Wilton carpet and the deeply embossed, oyster-shaded silky tapestry of the three-piece suite. It was built to last for ever. She gazed lovingly at all the family knick-knacks, the silver-framed photographs, the walnut bookcase, the pieces of ornamental china and the glass-fronted cabinet full of crystal wine glasses.

The whole place glowed with sober, reassuring, decent permanency. This was Joe Selbyson's background. Perhaps she had not been wrong about him – after all. Maybe he was as good as she'd always hoped, before she had overheard all Barry's macabre predictions, and had become so unsettled.

When Binny was back, and they had both sipped more coffee, Binny said: 'I was thinking when I was in the kitchen, I hope I didn't mislead you with that photograph of Aylise in the wheelchair? She's perfectly fit now, but Joe has always kept the snap there on that shelf inside the desk. It was such a shock when the accident first happened years ago – they were on a skiing holiday, and she damaged her leg. The prognosis for recovery was very bad indeed at first, and Joe felt terribly responsible.

'Aylise insisted on going to stay in Sweden to recover because she has a sister there. She was only supposed to be going for a few weeks but it's now three years. Joe has been torn apart by it. She keeps him like a puppet on a string the whole time.

'When mother died so suddenly it changed his views, and he decided he must go and see her and get things properly sorted out.' Binny hesitated and smiled slightly at May. 'He told me he wanted to marry you. I know I shouldn't be putting it so badly – but that's the truth of it.'

May felt her face flushing with deep embarrassment but Binny didn't seem to notice.

'I don't know for certain,' said Binny, 'but I seem to

remember Aylise's sister once mentioning that Aylise had some other man in tow. Here's hoping she'll find true happiness with someone else, and Joe will be free at last. He's been a real martyr really. He has sublimated himself to his work and has spent much of his spare time running this guest house – to help mother out. No one could have had a better son.'

May travelled back to the hospital that day lost in thought. She knew it was time she made her mind up. It was now or never. Just imagine if he did propose and it was all a dismal failure once they were together? She knew things could be a bit of an anticlimax at first. People were always describing the pitfalls of early marriage years. It was hard to get used to being tied to another person after a life of single autonomy. There was a trend to try out the marriage bed beforehand – just as Dizzy had done, but there was always the trap of the dreaded 'bun in the oven'. And anyway what earthly good was all that experimenting going to be if all the passion suddenly went cold? What would be left but drudgery and subjugation?

Each day she waited to see if he would write to her from Sweden, but nothing happened. For some reason she did not seem so worried now; she had a feeling that eventually everything would work out. There was now something else happening: she had been promoted to Senior Sister on the new Outpatients Clinic which dealt with female ailments. This meant she would be able to live out if she chose.

When she told Lotty and Barry they were absolutely

delighted, and Barry said he would soon find her a decent flat close to the hospital.

'Thank goodness you never got entangled again with that platonic friend,' said her mother.

The day after that a long letter arrived from Sweden . . . Aylise wanted a divorce at last and Joe yet again was pleading with May to marry him . . .

20

MEETINGS

'You can talk all you want, Joe. I mean what I said. I'm not giving you a divorce. I know I said I would the last time you came over but I've changed my mind. Instead I am coming home for a while at the end of this month.'

As he travelled back rather wearily all the way from Sweden to Manchester, yet again, Joe Selbyson wondered what to do. It was an ironic situation. Aylise refused all offers of a divorce even though they'd been separated for years.

His own sister, Binny, had always claimed that Aylise was absolutely charming. This could have been because Binny did not have to haggle with her all the time, like he did. All the same, a feeling that it might have been his own fault in the first place – including her skiing accident – made him resist the impulse to stride across the realms of decency to get a divorce by swearing that she was the guilty party. Thank God there were no children to worry about in this interminable tangle, he thought.

When he had seen Aylise he had taken great care not to mention wanting to marry May. The thought of her chewing over another piece of his shredded life would have been total hell.

'I shall be back by the end of this month to live with my cousin Pauline in Macclesfield,' Aylise had said imperiously. 'Perhaps you'll be able to get your act together this time and be a *proper* husband. If by some exceptional chance this happened, I *might* come back to you for good.'

Who knows what she meant by 'proper husband', thought Joe. But there was one thing certain – he would not be getting his 'act together' with her again. Particularly since a large photograph of the 'other man' had faced him when they were eating a meal of baked mincemeat cabbage rolls in her flat. Even her good cooking was not enough to tempt him. The man in the photograph had been fair-haired and plump; his head and shoulders had taken up all the space. He had worn a complaisant smile. Diagonally across one corner of the picture, on his pin-striped suit, had been scrawled the words 'Love you for ever. Rollo' in thick black ink. The photograph had rested provocatively next to a large wooden bowl with fruit in it.

He had stared at it with rising anger and thought how she was having her cake and halfpenny at the same time.

'What on earth do you keep glaring at that bowl of fruit for?' Aylise had said irritably. 'Isn't my face good enough for you?'

'I was just avoiding gazing at that Swedish lover boy – next to it.'

'That's the trouble with you Joe. You always did jump to the wrong conclusions didn't you? That picture happens to be of a very great friend of mine. He's a *Manchester* textile manufacturer who comes over here on business and we have a lot in common.'

'I can see that.'

'You always did *see* too much. So shut up for now will you? And I'll *see* you when I get back to Macclesfield.'

It was the Easter holidays. Dizzy Clewlyn was clearing out an old handbag. She was giving it to nine-year-old Joy to play at dressing up. Joy was in a small wooden summerhouse in the garden.

The bag had been kicking around the house in cupboards and wardrobes for years. It was full of ancient and disintegrating bus tickets. Some creased yellow paper stubs were still there, recalling films from well over ten years ago – like *Oliver Twist* and an Italian film called *Bicycle Thieves*, which was about a little boy and group of men who worked on a city rubbish collection wagon. Memories were revived for Dizzy – large capital letters in block printing saying: ROW H – SEAT 6. There were old bills from Lewis's department store for gramophone records such as 'How Are Things in Gloccamorra?' and 'It's Almost Like Being in Love'.

Dizzy smiled wryly to herself. Thank goodness the war was past, even if she did not dare to recall the awful thought that she was now twelve years older.

She turned the open handbag upside down with a

flourish and shook it. A bigger piece of folded, rather better quality paper slipped reluctantly from the lining. She unfolded it slowly and looked at the enthusiastic free flowing writing. It was a memento from her long dead mother – The lemon cheese recipe, simple and straight-forward with every cooking move clearly stated and always guaranteed to be perfect.

Dizzy gazed at it lovingly as she thought back to earlier days. She never had time to make lemon cheese now, though sometimes she bought a violently yellow concoction of it at the shops for the children. The sort she bought was usually like sticky glue with a strong flavour and smell; it had as much resemblance to homemade lemon cheese as tinned salmon to fresh salmon.

She folded the paper up again, gave it a small nostalgic kiss and put it in her best handbag. She had won it from a women's fashion magazine. It was dark navy and was the sort used by the Queen. Dizzy lifted the ledge-like, shiny gold clasp along the calf leather top and placed the recipe gently in its own soft suede compartment. As far as she was concerned this was its eternal home.

What a day it was today – so mild and summery and full of hope. Most of the older local children were revelling in fresh air and freedom. Frog spawn like large jelly rafts of tapioca lay amongst mossy fronds of wavy grass and waterweed held in beery looking brown streams and brooks. Hedges and small muddy paths lay invitingly along the sides of seeded corn fields – gathering places for boys and girls who guarded two pound jam jars, which were looped round with string handles.

The houses in Dizzy's avenue were all quiet, except for

the sound of *Moon River* floating through the air from a distant window.

The telephone rang. It was May. To think she was still working away as a Senior Sister at the hospital and *still* not married, thought Dizzy.

May often came round to see them all. She adored the children. These days she never mentioned men friends or love affairs. That aspect of her life seemed to have faded away completely. She had a very comfortable flat only a few minutes walk from Bell Lane, and her own garage for her car.

May sounded quite excited on the phone. 'Shall I pop round for coffee? I've got some news.'

'Come over this very second,' laughed Dizzy. 'Whilst the house is quiet.'

Not long afterwards Dizzy saw a small, buff-coloured Ford saloon pulling up outside and hurried to the gate to welcome May.

May looked wonderful. She was slim and slightly sun-burnt, and wearing an expensive duck egg blue two-piece linen suit and a pale coffee-coloured blouse. For a moment Dizzy envied her. She herself was getting plumper every second. Her stomach, after having chil-dren, resembled a pumpkin that swelled out as soon as food was consumed.

As they sat down May said: 'I've had the most astound-ing bit of news and don't quite know what to do. This very morning a letter arrived from Joe. He's moved from the radio to television. He's arriving back in Manchester next week, permanently. But more than that, Dizzy, much more than that – he's got his divorce at last!'

May's face changed suddenly to one of uncertainty, as her smile faded. 'It's all so late in the day Dizzy. What an anticlimax to get all this news heaped on me out of the blue. It's years ago now since our affair first began, and I was so young and romantic. I can even remember the two nightdresses I had when we went to Nice.'

Sadness enveloped her face. 'I've never seen or heard of him all the time he's been away. I don't even know whether he still keeps the house in Sale.' She looked a bit shy, then said slowly: 'And you know me, Dizzy. I hate to say it, but I'm still very much a speedily ageing, but reasonably happy virgin.'

Dizzy giggled good naturedly. 'You don't need to *apologise* for it May! But I know what you mean. What you've always got to remember if you ever do take the plunge, is that it often takes time to adjust. It's no good having the romantic idea that it will be heaven on earth the first time you do it – even if it might be. Sometimes it doesn't work out properly until you've actually had your first child . . . No wonder sex is the most favourite subject on earth. But its ramifications these days are too numerous to even think about as far as I'm concerned. And it's always easier for men – they are only interested at the time when *they* feel like it.'

May nodded vaguely, only half listening. 'It's just that *if* – and it's a very big if – Joe got in touch again and expected things to be the same as before, I just don't know whether they would be. So much water has gone under the bridge for both of us.'

'You'll never know that until you come face to face with him,' remarked Dizzy, 'But good luck anyway.'

When May got back to the hospital she answered Joe's letter in a rather plain impersonal way:

Dear Joe,
It was a very pleasant shock to hear from you again after so long, and to know that all the problems are ironed out at last, and you are a free man. Everything is plodding away much as usual in Dodsbury, Gatley, Urmston – and even Sale – from all accounts.

I have just been round to see Dizzy this morning.

Do you still keep in touch with Paul Rothsen? Liz writes to me regularly from California. Did you know that she has just qualified at university for a chemistry degree? She has also had another baby – almost at the same time. The new child is called Ruth. She is very happy over there.

I will call and see you next Friday evening as it's my weekend off and look forward to your telephone call on Thursday.

With all very best wishes, May.

'I still own the house in Sale,' said Joe to May when they met at last at Tiller's Private Hotel in Dodsbury. 'But it's rented on a long lease to a family who've been there since I moved to Newcastle, so we shall have to look for something else.'

May knew she would not find anyone better. She had agreed to marry him, but things were not the same. They were both polite and friendly to each other but that certain something between them had entirely disappeared. It was because of this that she had avoided any passionate advances before their honeymoon arrangements.

She had taken him home to meet Lotty and Barry in Urmston and they had been over the moon with gladness.

'You can stay here with us whilst you both look round for your own place if you like'? Barry said.

Joe thanked him profusely but said he would be lodging with a cousin in Timperley.

Eventually, much to Lotty's secret disappointment, May and Joe arranged to get married at the Registry Office in Manchester.

'I just wouldn't be able to stand all the palaver of a church wedding, Mother. Not after all the fuss. And anyway the ceremony isn't what counts. Joe had the most elaborate wedding imaginable when he married Aylise and it didn't do either of them much good. If God knows everything and sees everything he'll give us his blessing whatever we do.'

Lotty fell into subdued silence.

As far as May was concerned, the only thing that livened the whole thing up was the thought that Liz and Paul were flying across from California, and Damian and Dizzy were coming. At first both May and Joe had been reluctant even to mention the honeymoon to each other. It was as if they were skating on thin ice.

'Where do you fancy going, May?'

'No Joe. Where do *you* fancy?'

Then, just when everything else was arranged but they still hadn't fixed up a place to go, and Liz and Paul were on their way over, May suddenly decided that she could not go through with it.

Joe was absolutely horrified. 'You don't know what

you're saying, woman! Whatever's got into you? You've been leading me along the garden path for years! I've gone to almost every length on earth to get this divorce, without hurting anyone. I've been as patient as the biggest fool on earth. I've led a life completely without other love affairs and now – on the very last bloody second – you come out with all this claptrap.' He looked at her in simmering anger. 'Jesus Christ – I don't think I can stand any more of it May.'

'And neither can I!' yelled May with tearful passion. 'You cleared off to Newcastle and left me high and dry with never a word. Is it any wonder I built myself my own little single world in this flat? Women don't *need* men. I'm beginning to find that out pretty quickly. I'm too old for all this romantic love. The pleasure went years ago in Nice when you tore my heart to pieces by telling me you were still married. You wrecked the whole of my life! All my young days gone for ever in worthless hopes and waiting.'

'I DID THAT? I never heard the likes of it! What about *my own* worthless hopes and waiting? What more can you accuse me of?'

She raised her fist to him in anger and he grabbed it. They glared like tigers into each other's eyes, each staring the other out. Neither of them was prepared to give way, even a fraction.

'Leave go of my wrist, you brute.'

He lessened his grip, but they still stood there.

Suddenly she was aware of him. Aware of every hair on his head, every eyelash, every part of his taut body as it began to slacken. She felt the warmth of his hand. It was quite gentle now.

His eyes fluttered for an instant like a woman, and he smiled at her. His mouth relaxed into smile. Both of them were breathing quickly.

May felt her heart thumping and her own body quickening.

'How about making a start,' he murmured.

'M – making a start. Whatever d'you mean?'

He bent forward and kissed her forehead. 'You know exactly what I mean. Let's have our own secret honeymoon right here. Now.' He released her hand.

For a few seconds she was taken aback, but before she could even reply he had taken her in his arms, and was kissing her with a gentle passion which she couldn't resist.

'We've both been single far too long, May. It's time to break the pattern.'

She became flustered. Did he mean them to go to her bedroom? Had she made the bed? Should she pull the curtains to and lock the doors? Why was she such an innocent quivering fool?

He kissed her again, pressing his mouth hard against hers. Their teeth clashed, then all cares dissolved as if they had never been. He followed her to the bedroom. She did not bother any more about the sundry details she was usually so fussy about.

He watched her undress and did the same. She realised now that there was no need for specially chosen nightdresses. Their naked bodies were quite sufficient as they intertwined with the warmth and freedom of their rekindled love.

Two hours later they heard loud knocking at the front

door of the flat, but they ignored it and lay there in a quiet bliss that nothing could spoil.

When they got up May said: 'Let's go to Scotland for our honeymoon. Let's go to the Isle of Skye,' and he agreed.

The wedding invitations and the reception were organised by Lotty and Barry, with help from Joe's sister, Binny. The meal was at the Orange Grove, Valda's posh new basement café along Mosley Street, opposite the Art Gallery.

When the new bride and bridegroom had waved goodbye, and set off by car to the railway station, Dizzy laughed and said to Liz jokingly: 'It's quite a relief to see the back of them both. Who would have thought it would have taken them all these years to get spliced?'

Liz smiled, then said: 'Has anyone ever seen anything of Edmund Young again? Do you still remember how he sometimes visited Valda's café on the bomb site? I was quite attached to him in those days.' She looked at Dizzy with frank dark eyes.

'We've never seen him – or Ernst Jünger – from that day to this,' said Dizzy meeting her gaze.

'I love California,' said Liz. 'I hope I never have to leave it. It's my proper home now.'

Dizzy opened her handbag and said: 'Take this souvenir back with you in remembrance of us hospital girls, Liz. It's a copy of the lemon cheese recipe my mother once wrote out for me. I've given a copy of it to May as well. One day I hope to make my fortune marketing it in Valda's café. Maybe I'll start a café myself and call it the

Lemon Tree ready for when we all meet again . . . who knows.'

There were tears in everyone's eyes when they all parted: it was as if half their lives had already sped away. Yet there was comfort in the fact that there were children springing up beside them.

Joe and May were sitting in bed with cake crumbs round their mouths. They were at last settled in their own house in Fallowfield, and May was seven months pregnant.

Liz and Paul and their children were due to fly over from America for a ten day tour of Europe. They had asked Joe and May if they would like to meet up.

'We can't possibly go and meet Liz and Paul in our present state,' May said. But maybe one of these days we'll be able to go to America and visit them. We might even be able to arrange a sort of family group with Dizzy and Damian and Co. I really feel that even though Liz did invite us to meet them in Germany it would be better if she and Paul explored the past alone.'

Joe nodded, and wiped his hands on the sheet with careless boyishness. He lay back and stared at the ceiling he'd just decorated. Tomorrow it would be May's birthday. She was an elderly expectant mother of thirty-seven. They were both thrilled to bits and he had bought her a Mini Minor car. It had cost £500.

Liz was glad, in a way, that May and Joe had not accepted the invitation to meet. The sightseeing tour was proving more traumatic than she had ever imagined. She could not have undertaken it without Paul and the children by her side.

At present they were standing with others from the touring party in some rose gardens, a place where a whole village had been massacred in the last war. People stood silently in the sunshine in their best summer clothes.

As Liz stood there peacefully, her thoughts went back over the old days at the hospital with Ernst Jünger on the German ward. She thought also about the girls and marvelled at the way everything had turned out. Inside, she wept a little for Jamie, her first real husband, and looked up thankfully to her eldest son Nathan. He had known no other proper father but Paul, who was Jewish like herself. She gazed with motherly pride at her small daughter, Ruth. Liz could already see her mother's eyes there. Standing there she knew that she would never forget the past, for their sakes. And she felt that she would have more children. Suddenly she stretched her arms to the broad sparkling skies in a gesture of solemn thanks.

'I'm glad we took the tour of Europe,' said Liz to Paul when they were back home again. 'It brought back such a host of memories. It set things right at last. The past is gone but not forgotten. But now it's our new future.'

She smiled quietly to herself, then, taking some photographs brought home from their travels, she sat down in an armchair and began to stick them into the family album.

A Very Loud Voice

To Jimmy Eadington and all my friends

CONTENTS

I

THE INVITATION

1920

'That child is stuck in this rambling old house – like a dried pea in a penny whistle,' said Mrs Dawn as she ate bread and jam in the kitchen with the gardener. 'It's pure tragedy, that's what it is. Pure – very pure – tragedy.'

Inga could hear every word. She was peering into a broken shopping basket in a corner of the scullery where the washing-up sinks were. Her attention was glued to it. Over an hour ago a stray black and white cat had slipped in through the back door and had produced kittens there. At first the howls were awful, but now the cat was busy licking itself, and some strange unseen squealing, squeaking creatures were suddenly moving about but hidden in the cat's fur.

Inga stood there, thin and slight, her straight fair hair flopping forward untidily as she peered down. Her short blue serge frock was plentifully covered by a heavy, linen crash pinafore her mother, Daphne, had once embroidered with borders of lazy daisies. Her bare legs were as thin as blanched rhubarb.

'Anyway, those kittens'll be *something* . . .' said Mrs Dawn, standing up at last and looking towards the mop bucket, as she lowered her voice to a deliberately inaudible level: 'at least it's a bit of company for the child. Especially with her mother taking the dog when she went.'

'Ay. Mebbe just as well she did tak' dog,' muttered Albert. 'It were a right one for mucking up the borders. It were never trained proper from start. And to think I christened it Rainbow.' He put a weathered hand into his trousers pocket and drew out a huge red cotton hanky to wipe his mouth. 'I'd best see to planting them onions, before the mistress gets back from town.'

When he'd gone Mrs Dawn sat down for another few minutes. She drained the big brown teapot into her cup and added a drop of milk as she stirred in a heaped teaspoonful of sugar in thoughtful, unharassed solitude.

Aye . . . it was a very, very unsettling situation in this house. The Great War had done it, she thought. If that poor little soul hadn't been left fatherless before she was two years old it could all have been completely different. But instead she was now entirely alone with her grandmother, Margot Abbott, in a seven-bedroomed home in Harborough Road West, in Sale. The place was big enough for a boarding house and the child's own ma, Mrs Daphne Abbott, gone off in mad desperation only two weeks ago with a man who was already married.

Mrs Dawn had always distrusted Osmond Beardsley:

forever hobnobbing with a young orphaned woman of twenty-eight – a widow with no near relatives, who was living with her mother-in-law. He looked about the same age as her Tom, when Tom had got his teeth in – so that made him at least sixty-nine and a half. She knew quite a lot about him. Her best friend Mrs Phelps was the Beardsley's cleaner and was there when Maud Beardsley found the goodbye letter from her faithless, escaping husband Osmond, and collapsed in hysterics.

'Of course, if you ask me, Cissie,' said Mrs Phelps to Mrs Dawn, when it had just happened, 'them two Beardsleys was never ever what you might call a proper couple. They allus slept in single beds, with thin sheets and all the windows open, and she's wrapped up in Good Works and giving lectures on how to boil cabbage to the poor.'

Mmmm . . . thought Mrs Dawn, life was full of the most awful, *awful* tragedies. She sat there for a few moments longer, gazing at the old grandfather clock and wondering whether to take the kettle from the range and drain the tea leaves again. Then, bracing herself, she dismissed temptation and stood up, ready to fill the bucket with hot soapy water and Jeyes fluid to mop the floor.

Grandma Abbott was a very tall woman, thin and bony with large dark eyes and a regal appearance. She had practised walking with a heavy book on her head for hours when she was her granddaughter's age and it had stood her in good stead. Wherever she went in her fur coat, male underlings would hasten to bow slightly and

3

open doors for her. She was fifty-five, and had been a widow for eight years. Her husband, Lawson, had made a great deal of money from the cotton trade. She'd had six children – five girls and a boy. One of the girls had died as a baby and her son Tarvin had been killed in 1914 in the war.

Her four daughters were, thankfully, all married and prosperous. They were well-educated and could all play tennis. One of them also played golf and three of them played the piano. They all had children of their own. The only feature which linked them now was that they had all escaped their mother's iron will as soon as was humanly possible. They lived well away from Manchester, in places like Ross-on-Wye, Denham in Buckinghamshire, Oxford, and Haywards Heath.

Until now, the only person who had been trapped into sticking with Margot over the past years was her widowed daughter-in-law Daphne Abbott. And now Daphne had finally fled – leaving her small daughter, Inga, behind. It was an act everyone considered to be callous and traitorous, both to the child and to the whole of womanhood.

Daphne Abbott had been in a mad, almost deranged, panic when she had realised she was three months pregnant by her longtime friend and confidant, Osmond Beardsley, a shipping agent old enough to be her father. Yet it was almost a father she craved for. Her own father had died when she was very young, and her mother was dead. She had been left as an only child, just like Inga, her own daughter. So when her mother-in-law Margot had introduced her to Osmond, just after Tarvin had

4

been killed in the war, and he had been so warm and consoling and fatherly, she had clung to him like a seashell to a rock.

He had accepted the clinging gratefully. And then one day, when the house was quite empty – Inga was at dancing class, Margot had gone to Buxton and Mrs Dawn and the gardener were out – he had strolled along Harborough Road West in his best linen jacket, light flannels and creamy light felt hat with its slightly rakish wide brim and its petersham ribbon round the crown. At the Turrets he had taken the stairs to mad ruination where, in one of the unused bedrooms, the pair of them had clung together, naked in each others' arms, with the sun blinds down in a vain endeavour to blot out the restrictions of their lives.

'When will Mummy be back home again, Grandma?' Inga was following Margot round the glass conservatory.

Margot lowered her noble nose and peered at huge green leaves through her lorgnette, inspecting the undergrowth for small, marauding insects. 'I'm not quite sure dear. Mummy may be away for some time. It could be for the whole of the summer. These health cures take quite a while. You run along now, and answer that invitation in the library. Rule some lines *very* faintly on a piece of Grandma's best mauve notepaper, and make sure they don't slope. Then copy out that reply I gave you, in your very best handwriting. When you've finished, bring it to me to check and I will find you a special soft rubber to rub out the pencil lines so that it will all be perfect.' Margot gave her granddaughter a steady affectionate smile, and Inga – knowing that the smile would go on, very meaningfully, until she did what she was told – turned and hurried away to answer the invitation card which had R.S.V.P. at the bottom and coloured balloons on it.

The card was from Ruby Selwyn. It was an invitation to Ruby's birthday party; she was eight. Her mother Ermyntrude (known as Trudi) was a friend of Inga's mother and the two children went to Miss Cossett's kindergarten.

Inga knelt on the big leather-covered seat of a desk chair in the library, and slowly set about her meticulous task with the ruler and pencil. Her thoughts about her mother were soon forgotten. It was at bedtimes that she thought of her the most and then, when she had prayed to God to bless Mummy and bring her home safe and well, she felt happier. The times she felt most miserable about Mummy being away were when people shouted at her or blamed her for things that weren't her fault. There was no one here now to really understand and comfort her. Her grandma was kind but she never had time to 'understand' anything, because she knew everything already. To Grandma, comfort was graded by the thickness of cushions. Whenever Grandma went anywhere she always prodded a cushion discreetly to see whether it contained cheap flock, bran, straw, hen feathers, goose feathers or silky down.

Sometimes cushions did help, thought Inga. You could cry into cushions; you could hug them; you could nurse them; you could tell them secrets. But cushions could never talk; they could never answer back.

Grandma never seemed to hear people who answered back.

'You look absolutely wonderful, doesn't she, Mrs Dawn?' Margot set the taffeta bow more precisely on the pale blue silk poplin frock, then stood at a distance to make sure the white silk knee socks were even.

Mrs Dawn nodded. She put Inga's copper-coloured kid party pumps into a small shoe bag with 'I.A.' embroidered in the corner. 'She looks a real little picture.' Then she looked warningly at Inga and said, 'And if that little pest Leroy Spinks nips you on the arms with his nasty little fingernails, tread on his fancy slippers real hard.'

Inga's straight fair hair gleamed. It was fastened in position with two kirby grips and a diamanté slide. She felt like a fairy-tale princess. Mary Mullins and Mary Mullins's mummy were going to call for her in the car and take her with them. Mary Mullins was her best friend. She wished she had a proper mummy and daddy like Mary.

She had been to lots of parties. Some were nice and some were horrible. This one at Ruby's was turning out to be a bit of a mixture.

The best parties had a conjurer and treasure hunts or hide-and-seek. Often there was someone's big brother looking after it and blindfolding people for blindman's buff or helping with musical chairs. But this one of Ruby's was being run by lots of ladies who talked a terrible lot and were urging all the children to do a 'turn'.

'We're going to have our own little concert,' said Mrs Selwyn after the children had eaten all the jelly and egg sandwiches, blown out the pink cake candles and trampled food into the pale fawn carpet. 'We know you are all good at dancing and singing. You sang "Happy Birthday" to Ruby loud enough for the roof to fall in. We're going to divide you into two teams of entertainers, and Mrs Mullins and Mrs Forsyte and Miss Fitzackerly and I will be the judges.'

Some of the children began to look unsettled, and one boy in a neat little shirt and tie and shorts said he felt sick and wanted to go home. Hastily, Ermyntrude made him into the captain of one side with Ruby captain of the other. There were five children in each team.

Ruby never chose Inga to be in her team. Today she picked her best friend Clarissa who had a very drab frock on with a trace of her vest showing at the neckline, and Peter Dawson who had a pony. Ruby also chose Janey Jackson who sometimes gave people Chinese burns by squeezing and twisting their wrist flesh in two directions at the same time and she chose Brenda Frogmorton who had come with her very protective nanny and had long golden ringlets. The ones left over, after Captain Robin Stubbs had chosen his best friend Leroy Spinks and then lost all interest as they began to swop cigarette cards, were Inga Abbott, Mary Mullins, and a girl with a runny nose and a pure gold bangle called Cherry Minton.

Ruby hadn't wanted to invite any boys except Peter

Dawson but her mother thought there should be two more because she knew their mothers.

'I think,' said Trudi Selwyn to all the captive children with firm, rather coy bossiness, 'I think we'll have one person to recite a poem from each team . . .'

'*Me*, Mummy, me,' shouted Ruby, bouncing about excitedly.

'. . . and someone – someone to do a *dance*?' Trudi looked hard at poor little rich girl Clarissa Dunkley whose mother tried so hard to make her as inconspicuous as possible. 'A little bird tells me that Clarissa can do a very pretty little ballet dance.'

'I haven't got my ballet shoes, Mrs Selwyn.'

'You can do it on tiptoe in your socks,' said Trudi firmly. 'We shall all love it.' Then, turning to Brenda's nanny whom she had once seen being kissed in the park by a scraggy youth and over whom she had ever since held a position of power, she said, 'Did you bring Brenda's tap shoes then – Nanny?'

The nanny, who was really paid only the meagre salary of a nurse-maid, nodded reluctantly.

'Can anyone here do magic tricks?'

'I can make a penny disappear,' said Peter Dawson.

'I can do a cigarette card trick,' said Robin Stubbs.

The children were all beginning to fidget. Peter Dawson had a new watch and looked at it very hard and muttered a sentence with 'home' in it.

Mrs Selwyn sensed that she hadn't the strength to go further. She had collapsed like a pricked balloon, and suddenly decided she preferred washing up, any day. She looked round with appealing eyes to where Miss

Fitzackerly, who was the best organiser of the lot, was wiping away traces of chocolate blancmange from a curtain. Trudi Selwyn beckoned to her in anguish. 'I think I've got my monthly gripes, Cicely. I'll just have to dash to the lav.'

Cicely nodded gravely then, in a loud no-nonsense voice, she said, 'We'll start off with singing. Who's got a good loud voice? Anyone who can sing on their own will get a small prize. Come along now – I know you've all got *very* good voices . . . and when this—' (she nearly said 'awful' but stopped just in time) 'concert's over we'll have a treasure hunt in the garden.'

There was silence.

'Come on, liven up. Let's see which team does the best. A poem, a bit of magic, a dance, a please-yourself-what-you-do, and a song. How's that? And if you want any help just ask me.'

At last, the fire began to glow slightly again and soon the teams were being sorted out. They were all going to sing 'Three Blind Mice' together. And then each team would start with a poem and finish with a song and all the mothers and helpers would judge which team was best.

The whole enterprise (thought up originally, but not thought out properly, by Trudi who was now sitting well away on a sofa, with two aspirins inside her) began to chug along successfully, as everyone did their 'turns'. The do-as-you-please ones had both decided to be statues: Peter Dawson just stood there and said he was a policeman. Everyone was given a small dolly mixture as a prize the moment they'd finished. Cherry Minton, the 'statue' in the other team, kept moving to wipe her nose but swore she was a statue of Queen Victoria.

Soon the tension began to rise all round. Everyone, children and grown-ups, was dying to get to the end of the wretched concert and explode away from it for ever – into the final garden treasure hunt.

They had come to the last turn – the singers. Janey Jackson was the singer for Ruby's team, and Inga Abbott was the singer for Robin's team.

Janey Jackson stood there like a small innocent angel in a white silk frock with tiny pearl buttons all down the front and sang in a small whispering voice a song to the tune of 'Onward Christian Soldiers' which went:

> I am small and pow-er-less,
> Help me to be good.
> Let me help my par-ents,
> Doing what I should.
> I am small and ge-entle,
> Loving all around,
> Bringing joy to everyone
> From stars to earthly ground.

She curtsied to rapturous applause from all the adults, then sat down and jabbed Brenda with a strong little elbow for sitting too close.

Inga was feeling a bit nervous. She hadn't really wanted to sing but everyone else had chosen what they wanted to do and she was the only one left – along with the singing bit.

They had all done 'Three Blind Mice' at the beginning,

so she couldn't do that . . . All she could think of was one that Albert Rain the gardener sang when he was in a good temper. It was called 'Boiled Beef and Carrots'. He always sang it really loud. He said he had made up his own words to it as they were better than the originals.

She stood up in her lovely party frock, and looked round hesitantly. All the ladies clapped encouragingly. She closed her eyes tight and yelled it as quickly as she could:

> Boiled beef and carrots.
> Boiled beef and carrots.
> It keeps you fit and it keep you well,
> It gives you strength for your Darby Kell.
> It makes your muscles grow and swell . . .
> If you use your legs you can run like hell.
> Boiled beef and CARROTS!

She curtsied again and sat down proudly. All the children in her team, except Leroy Spinks who was seething with jealousy, jumped up and down and clapped, but the grown-ups didn't do anything. They simply got together in a group and started to talk very quickly. Then Mrs Selwyn turned to them all with a rather frozen smile on her face and said hastily, 'You were all wonderful. We've decided to give the prizes to Ruby's team. I think Janey's small semi-sacred prayer just tipped the scales by a fraction of a whisker.'

Quickly, Ruby's team were each presented with a small white paper bag tied with coloured ribbon which contained five jelly babies each. The other team got exactly the same but without the coloured ribbon and then they were all hustled outside for the treasure hunt in the vast garden, with its bubbling ornamental stream, huge umbrella pine trees and stone statue of a shepherdess.

Just as Inga was going outside she heard her name mentioned by one of the ladies. First, the voice said, 'Oh, you mean Inga Abbott? She's the one whose mother ran off with that man. Mmmm . . . all that child has is a *very* loud voice, but she has absolutely no idea how to sing . . .'

When they were in the garden doing the treasure hunt, Leroy Spinks came up to her and pinched her really hard on the bare arm with his scratchy fingernails. 'You made a real muck-up of your song and it had swearing in it. It was you that made our team lose.' He tried to nip her again but she stamped heavily on his toes just like Mrs Dawn had told her to, and they had a fight.

Mrs Mullins took her and Mary home extra early. All the way back from the party Inga thought about how the woman had said her mother had gone off with another man . . . Whyever had she said that when Grandma had said Mummy was away on a long health cure? Suddenly she felt sad and quite tired. The jelly babies hadn't been very nice ones. They tasted more of glue than fruit. And fancy them saying she didn't know how to sing when she'd sung the song so well and had remembered all Albert's words. All the children except nasty Leroy had clapped really loudly.

'Did you enjoy it, dear?' said Margot when she got home at a quarter to eight, after a lot of waving good-bye and thank-yous to Mary Mullins and her mother.

Then Margot said, 'What on earth's happened to your lovely frock? Surely the treasure hunt wasn't as rough as that?'

She nodded silently and went upstairs quickly. Just after Grandma had tucked her in and kissed her good-night, Inga said, 'Has Mummy run off with another man, Granny?'

'Good gracious child! Whatever made you think such a terrible thing?'

'Some ladies said it at the party; I heard them. And they said I had a very loud voice but I didn't know how to sing.'

Margot Abbott began to seethe with anger. How could they be so cruel, so unthinking, as to gossip like that at a children's party? 'Mummy will be back for you my darling, never fret. And *never*, never take any notice of gossiping ladies. Always walk past them very quickly. Listeners never hear any good of themselves. As for your voice, Inga, it's absolutely beautiful!' She tucked her granddaughter up, and soon Inga was smiling contentedly again.

Margot trod with heavy anger down the well-padded stairs. A very loud voice, eh? *She doesn't know how to sing?* She snorted with noble determination . . . We'll soon see about *that* . . .

2

THE ROOM

The moment Daphne had spent one night in seedy, furnished lodgings in Chorlton-on-Medlock with Osmond Beardsley she regretted it. Her heart sank as she realised, too late, that she had been driven there by explosive desperation born of that previous comfortable prison of deception.

Lying here now on a thin hair mattress which had been used by countless other past lodgers, she watched a small beetle crawling slowly up the badly pasted, dark, mottled green wallpaper. She felt she was in living hell. What had made her behave so stupidly? And worst of all why had she forsaken her own darling little daughter?

How could she ever be redeemed? What would happen when this next child arrived? She was now five months pregnant, and although Osmond was fully aware of the fact he seemed to be impervious to it, as he dressed up to go to business in the city as if he were still at his old address.

She thought back with hidden tears to the day she had succumbed to Osmond's warm pressure. Yes, it had been a mutual need; a heady release for both of them. Rich, confident, worldly, well-dressed, caring Osmond had seemed, on a warm, sunny day in salubrious Sale, like the only answer to her prayers. It had been a comfortable answer, in a way. For they were never together long enough to annoy each other, and always had the luxury of their own cosy bolt holes – whatever their tales to each other of the agony of other ties.

Theirs was a happy life of cleanliness and comfort. From what they could see, their secret in Sale was not harming anyone else and was based in a mutual and honest affection. Or at least, that was how Daphne had imagined it then. And no one could ever, she thought, forecast the future . . . nor imagine anything too different.

Osmond on the other hand was revitalised. He wasn't interested in children; his son from his first marriage – before Maud – never even sent him a birthday card and lived abroad with a worn-out wife and seven children. Osmond's periodic secret escapes from sixty-eight-year-old Maud had knocked forty gnawing years from his life, as he bedded Daphne with youthful zest at every opportunity. He was indeed in heaven. His Spartan life of thin sheets and open windows had in no way affected his virility: in fact, it had probably enhanced it. He had no problems in that direction.

He had, with hardly any compunction, burned his

boats and left Maud the final billet-doux: 'Lots of love, old thing, but it just had to be. Some things are bigger than us both, in this world.'

His present lugubrious life of flat hair mattresses and a few beetles made hardly any deep impression, as he planned a future where he and Daphne would eventually move to Southport, and a decent bed.

It was a year now since Mummy had gone. She had sent Inga a furry monkey which jumped about when you squeezed the blue rubber air ball which was attached to it. Inga left it in the box along with the birthday card which had *The Sanatorium* written inside and the words: 'Love and kisses to my own darling little daughter, Inga. Mummy will soon be home. xxxxxx.'

Inga knew it was false. It was what was called Telling Lies. She knew her mother wouldn't come home.

Grandma called lies fairy tales. It was very wicked to tell them. Grandma took a farthing from Inga's two pennies pocket money, whenever Inga told them – even though often it was a real accident. One day Inga told Grandma she had seen Mummy when they were in town. And Grandma said it was the biggest fairy tale she had ever heard. That week Inga only got three ha'pence pocket money to put in her money box.

Inga opened the lid of the padded Ottoman and pushed the monkey right to the bottom beneath all her worst toys. She began to wonder what it was really like in heaven. She was always getting told by Mrs Dawn that she would never go there.

She looked round her bedroom dolefully. There was

a new thin paper song book of popular songs, with an orange cover, lying high on top of the tallboy. She was having to learn some of the songs off by heart and sing them to Grandma whilst Grandma played the piano. Grandma was getting rattier and rattier about her singing. 'Sing louder, child. Sing *louder*. Expand your chest. Don't sound so timid.'

Every single day now she had to practise, and on Sundays her voice was one of the loudest for the hymns in church. Yes, she did her very, very best to be able to get to heaven.

Then one Saturday there was a terrible accident. She was eight and a quarter. It was early in the morning and the tulips were out in the garden. Everything was sprinkled with early-morning rain. Grandma came in and woke her up. It was seven o'clock. Grandma sat on the side of Inga's bed in her beautiful quilted dressing gown. Her grey hair was tightly wound round lots of hairpins and she was holding the orange music book. 'I want you to learn a completely new one today, child. Off by heart. It's very important. Mr Protheroe, the famous music teacher, is coming round for supper this evening and I want you to be perfect. He will only accept the very best children as his pupils.'

Inga shrunk beneath the bed covers and tried to pretend she was still half-asleep. Mr Protheroe? Surely not Mr Protheroe with the white side whiskers and striped trousers? The one who smelt of sickly scent and scratched himself a lot? She'd once been with Mummy when she was very, very little and he'd been there. He was Ruby Selwyn's great-uncle. Ruby had once by accident left a half sucked peppermint on the chair he sat on. It stuck to his trousers and he got in a rage with her mother about it.

Grandma opened the music book. 'Get up and have your breakfast straight away, then go into the study and copy out the words from this song.'

The song was named 'Macushla'. She already knew its rather mournful tune. It was one of Grandma's favourites. Once, one afternoon in winter, Grandma had invited someone called Miss Pansy Jefferson to sing it in the drawing room to about six other ladies whilst they all did embroidery. The sound was so loud Inga could hear it booming through the air outside while she was making a snowman in the garden.

> Ma-cush-la! Ma-cush-la!
> Your sweet voice is calling.
> Calling me softly, again and again.
> Macushla! Macushla!
> I hear its dear pleading.
> My blue-eyed Macushla, I hear it in vain.

'You only need to copy that first bit,' said Grandma. 'The rest, about white arms, red lips and death, isn't really suitable for children. But it's a nice piece of soulful music which will show Mr Protheroe what you're made of.'

Reluctantly, Inga got out of her warm, cosy bed, washed herself, squashed the soap though her fingers, blew two bubbles, brushed the top surface of her hair, then put on her clothes. What an awful day it was going to be.

After nibbling at a boiled egg and leaving the crusts off her bread for the birds she went to the study to get the terrible task done. Copying things out was slow and laborious but she knew that practice made perfect. It took her all morning to get it done properly with no mistakes and to sing the words and the melody together off by heart. Macushla, Macushla – there were no sweet voices calling *her*. It was all what Mrs Dawn would call nag,nag,nag.

At dinner time it was liver and onions, and she felt more miserable than ever. She hated liver staring at her from the plate, so smooth and brown and bitter with all its little tubes hidden in it, but she knew she would have to eat every single scrap. Grandma was sitting opposite, her heavy, silver-plated knife and fork poised above her boiled potatoes and Brussels sprouts, as she demolished her own helping with swift methodical efficiency.

'As soon as your pudding has settled,' said Grandma, being very careful never to talk with her mouth full, 'we will go into the drawing room and have a small rehearsal. It is absolutely essential that you produce a real musical gem for Mr Protheroe . . .'

Her stern enthusiasm was suddenly interrupted by Mrs Dawn with an urgent message, 'There's someone to see you at the door – very urgent, Mrs Abbott.' Mrs Dawn's eyes were rolling hither and thither in their sockets as she tried to send a special silent message across to Margot Abbott's eyes. 'It's a lady you know quite well – that's all I can say . . .' Mrs Dawn looked meaningfully towards the top of Inga's head.

Immediately, Margot left the dining room and followed Mrs Dawn. Surely it wasn't – surely it couldn't be . . . Daphne? Surely she wouldn't have just popped up out of the blue without any warning? Surely she would realise the upset something like that would cause to Inga?

Mrs Dawn had tactfully disappeared into the kitchen. She began to hang up some pans, as she waited with dry patience to find out what the outcome would be. It would all come out in the wash.

'Oh . . . It's you . . .'

'Yes, it is *me*, Margot. I'd like to come in if you don't mind and have a few words with you. It's about Osmond, and Daphne.' Maud Beardsley's voice trembled slightly. 'I haven't given up yet.'

Margot hesitated imperceptibly. This was the last thing she would have expected. Maud had never been in touch about the fiasco before. A growing irritability took over. Maud had always aggravated her, with her plain ways and her flat shoes. But on the other hand Margot felt a righteous indignation at the way Osmond had so selfishly and heartlessly upset the applecart.

'Come in, Maud,' she said coldly. 'I'm very surprised to see you. It's one of my rather busy days today . . . I have a music teacher coming to listen to Inga sing this evening.' She led Maud to the sitting room. 'I'll just go and tell Mrs Dawn to see to the child, while we talk.'

As they sat there with the afternoon sun streaming warm yellow across the room, and a pink and white Royal Doulton tea set between them, Maud Beardsley's voice gathered momentum with droning determination.

Margot had never heard her talk so much, in over thirty years. Yet, there again, they had never been really close, even though – years ago – Margot had been a matron of honour at Maud and Osmond's wedding.

Maud had always been well hidden in Osmond's house, like a piece of domestic camouflage.

'I haven't given up yet – don't alarm yourself,' said Maud fiercely. 'I haven't kept a house full of polished furniture and honest-to-goodness silver just to be treated like this! I haven't spent cold nights with the windows wide open and thin sheets on our bed, and worn flat shoes for Osmond's sake, in order to get such a brush-off as this at the end of my life.' She glared at Margot. 'Why do you think I've worn my hair in this Eton crop all these years? You know full well, I had the most glorious hair when I was young. It flowed like silky waves to below my waist. But after our honeymoon at Torquay, Osmond pleaded with me to get it cut off and be more modern. It happened after another man had stared at me rather a long time and complimented me on my "shimmering cascade".

'Oh what an innocent fool I was, Margot. I would have done anything to please Osmond at that time, and once the deed was done I let it be – like so many other things. But it wasn't really *me*.' She looked plaintively at Margot who was now sitting there with her mouth slightly open in genuine surprise. All these years of summing up this mousy woman in front of her and she had been getting the wrong end of the stick.

Of course it had always been apparent that Osmond Beardsley was the dominant partner but she hadn't realised the extent of it. She could hardly have imagined herself submitting like that in the past to her own husband. She patted the carefully hairpinned pile lying on her own scalp and felt a sudden flood of superiority.

'And as you know,' said Maud pointedly, 'Daphne has every attribute Osmond stifled in me from the very beginning. But now the worm has turned—'

'I wouldn't call yourself a *worm*, Maud,' said Margot hastily. 'Slightly young and misguided at the beginning, perhaps – but certainly not a worm. It's Osmond who's the worm. And at least wearing those beautiful flat-soled brogues all your life will have kept your feet in perfect condition. They do say that health starts from the ground up. My own feet are a mass of corns and bunions.' She smiled consolingly and glanced quickly towards the clock. 'Anyway, I hope for all our sakes it gets sorted out in the end. I just couldn't imagine what had got into Daphne at the time . . .'

'Osmond had got into her,' said Maud triumphantly. 'The same as he got into me, except that in my case I was denied the ultimate – because he already had a son from his first marriage who's now abroad. Osmond swore to me by God and the Holy Ghost he would never produce again. I was devastated. But I haven't given up getting him back, Margot.

'When the news seeped through that he and Daphne had conceived a child and had called him Ralphie *Osmond* Beardsley I felt like throwing in the towel, and lying on the railway track. All the same, I swear that – bastard or no little bastard – my husband will return to me in the end.'

'Don't you think it's got a bit too complicated for that – now?' murmured Margot, fixing her with a cool, bland gaze. 'A child makes just that bit of difference to everything . . . I know it from my own experience of being left high and dry with Inga.'

'He *will* come back,' said Maud with mounting, feverish passion, 'and when that day arrives it'll be a relief to all of us – including you, Margot. You – left in your old age with a small girl to look after in this rambling dungeon, because of him and Daphne.'

When she'd gone, Margot was simmering with anger. Her slight sympathy for Maud and her willingness to admit she might have misjudged her had completely vanished. She disliked her even more than before. Her shoes had flat rubber soles and the pattern from them had left zigzag marks on the shining parquet floor. And that reference to this beautiful house being a *dungeon* had been the last straw. No, the less they saw of one another the better. And as for all the other ramifications, like Osmond's baby and Inga being without a mother – well, Margot thought she had dealt with her side of it with amazing aplomb. Inga was going from strength to strength with her singing, which would never have happened if Daphne had been here.

Inga could hear her grandmother's voice calling urgently. It had a sharp edge to it. She clutched her music book and hurried to the drawing room. Grandma was sitting on the large oblong tapestry stool at the grand piano, tapping her foot on the carpet irritably. 'I hope you've been practising hard. I was held up by an untimely visitor.'

Margot began to thump out the introductory refrain of 'Macushla'. Maud's visit had upset her more than she had imagined. Especially the mention of the other child, even though – thank God – it wasn't a blood relation. But oh, the ramifications . . .

Inga's small voice began to sing, but Margot could hardly hear it. This was obviously a disaster day for both of them. What a total embarrassment it would be if this was the standard of performance she gave for Mr Protheroe this evening – and after all the trouble she'd taken to impress on everyone the wonder of her grandchild's melodic charms. A desperate simmering rage began to rise inside her as she got up from the piano and closed the lid. 'Go up to the attic bedroom straight away – and don't you dare come down until you can sing really loud!'

Inga flinched with horror. The bare attic bedroom with its iron bedstead and small wooden chair was the punishment cell. It had been a servant's room in past days, before she was born, but now Grandma sent her there when she had misbehaved really badly – like the time she ran away to play with Charlie Musgrave and fell in a pond. Yet she wasn't misbehaving this time. Yes, she knew she had a bit of a sore throat and the snuffles, and didn't really feel like singing. But everyone got those from time to time and it wasn't called misbehaving. Inga stood there, unable to quite believe what she'd just heard.

'Go along then,' said Grandma impatiently. 'Do as you're told, immediately! And take your music book. I shall come upstairs in ten minutes to listen to you again.'

With tears in her eyes Inga climbed the narrow back stairs to the attic. She knew she couldn't do any better. She felt even worse, now. She felt she wanted to forget singing for ever. She began to long for her mother to come home. These days, now she was eight, she thought about her mother more than she'd done when she was little. Especially when Grandma was being horrible. Oh – if only darling Mummy would come back. Mummy had never bothered one tiny scrap about her being able to sing.

In the attic she drifted about, aimlessly, and coughed and sniffed and wiped the back of her hand across her nose. She looked down at the back garden and her old doll's pram, and watched the birds and a cat on a wall.

But, in no time at all, Grandma was suddenly there again. She came in and sat on the bentwood chair. 'I want you to sing the words really loudly – off by heart from the beginning, Inga – *now* . . .'

Inga opened her mouth fearfully. Nothing came out except a hoarse whisper. Grandma took one hard, awful look at her, then she got up from the chair, stuck her chin in the air haughtily and left the room. With mounting panic, Inga heard the click of the bedroom key in the door.

'You will stay there until you come to your senses and sing *properly*. I will return in a few minutes and listen to you from outside this room,' called Margot. 'I expect your voice to be loud and tuneful. And you will stay there until it is.'

There was total silence again. Inga was in a tearful

26

daze. What on earth was happening that Grandma had gone so strange?

She went over to the door and tried to open it but it was firmly locked. She went to the window and looked out again with mounting dismay. Supposing Grandma kept her here for *ever*? Supposing Grandma was a real witch in disguise or was like the old woman in *Hansel and Gretel* who kept the children caged up? Supposing her grandmother left her to *starve*?

The church clock in the distance chimed four. Miserably she dragged the chair to the small window. Perhaps, if she opened it and called out, someone would hear her. Perhaps Mrs Dawn, or Albert the gardener. The catch on the window was an iron latch with a curled handle and opened fairly easily. She had just unfastened it when there was a knock at the door, and Grandma called her. She got down from the chair quickly.

'Have you decided to sing properly yet?' Grandma's voice was as cruel as ever. 'Come along then . . . I'm waiting. You aren't coming out of there until you try really, *really* hard. When that happens we'll go down to the drawing room again and practise with the piano. Start now!'

There was a moment's silence. Inga went to the door and stood close to it in dumb dismay. She took a deep breath: 'Ma-cush-la! . . .' She screeched the words for all she was worth then broke down in sobs. 'I want Mummy. Bring back my Mummy. I hate you – I hate you!' But all she heard were the muffled, steady footsteps of her grandmother going downstairs again.

She rushed across to the window and pushed it open,

calling for help at the top of her voice as she caught a glimpse of Albert in the kitchen garden but he did not even turn his head. Then as she leaned forward and tried again her voice gave up altogether. She squeaked in a powerless whisper as, in one memorable instant, she felt herself propelled through the window by unknown forces – to topple on to the flat roof of the jutting out half-moon bay window of the dining room. She fell with a terrible thud, lying there senseless on the heavy lead covering of the bay, and knew no more.

When she awoke she was in her bed. Grandma was standing looking down at her with a worried expression which changed to a smile. 'Awake at last! No, don't try to move. You must lie there quite flat until Doctor Renshaw gets back. You fell out of the bedroom window, but fortunately no bones were broken.'

Everything came flooding back as the word 'Macushla' began to form on her lips in a murmur.

'Forget all that,' said Grandma touching her hand gently. 'All you must do now is to rest and get better.'

'Is it the next day?' Inga stared at Grandma anxiously.

'No, it's nearly seven at night, but you have to be kept in a semi-darkened room with the blinds drawn, and you will be covered in bruises for at least a fortnight. Thank the Good Lord in all His Heavens you aren't suffering from concussion.' Margot clicked her teeth together in exasperation. 'And after all that trouble we had – getting you ready to meet Mr Protheroe this evening – the wretched man sent a message of apology saying he had important visitors and couldn't come. The name Dame

Clara Butt was mentioned. What a blessing if you could be like her, one day . . .'

Inga closed her eyes with weary thankfulness. She would not have to sing for Mr Protheroe after all. She would probably never have to sing any more. Her face relaxed into angelic bliss as she drifted into a deep satisfying sleep.

'What a mess you look, and no mistake,' said Mrs Dawn the following week as she stared at Inga's pale face with its mauve patchiness and the fading yellows and greens of bruising. 'You poor little soul . . . but there again, it was bad of you to get at that window. You should have been a good girl and waited for Grandma to let you out. You knew very well she would in the end.'

Inga bowed her head in silence. She knew nothing of the sort. She felt she could never trust any grown-up again, what with Mother telling her lies in letters and Grandma locking her in the bedroom. She looked up at Mrs Dawn's plump, reliable face. 'Anyway, Mrs Dawn – I know one thing: at least I'll never need to sing again after this.'

'Don't you be too sure, child . . .' muttered Mrs Dawn as she filled a pan with cold water.

That afternoon the doctor arrived for the final time and pronounced Inga fit to return to school the following week.

'All's well that ends well,' said Margot briskly when he'd gone. 'The main thing is that it hasn't affected your voice.'

She began to walk round the room, pulling off one

or two petals from flowers which weren't quite perfect, and running her little finger across two picture frames to check for dust.

'Whilst you're still at home this next day or two, you'll be able to get a bit of practice in again. I've been busy arranging some special events for you. The first one will be a real toe in the water: a small *conversazione* at Mrs Willoughby's, two weeks on Saturday. Madame La Bouche is coming to talk about her life as an opera singer and you will be able to do your little piece just before she arrives, then sit there quietly for the rest of the afternoon and listen to what everyone has to say. It will be a real education. You can sing "Macushla." You know it so well now and it's a pity to waste all that practice.'

Grandma sat down next to Inga and stroked her head gently. 'You might have to put a bit of powder on your face if any of the bruising still shows, but everyone will understand.'

'Going to try to perform that song *again*?' said Mrs Dawn, a bit later, to Margot. 'I think the poor child thought it was all over and done with for ever.'

'It certainly is *not*, Mrs Dawn.' Margot glared at her imperiously. 'Nor will it ever be whilst I've a single breath left in this body. Sometimes one has to be cruel to be kind, and when I've passed on to heavenly pastures that child will bless me with all her heart. No, Mrs Dawn, the train is on its track and the whistle has only just blown. It's full steam ahead.'

'I certainly think she's overdoing it a bit,' said Mrs Dawn to Albert as they drank tea in the kitchen. 'She was babbling on about herself going to heavenly pastures and the train being all set for full steam ahead. It's a most unhealthy situation. I wish the child's stupid mother would come back . . .'

Albert looked up from his copy of *Tit-Bits*. 'Stop going on so. She's a right little strong 'un, is Inga. She's a chip off the old block. There's nowt to worry about there. That child'll flower and flower as long as my best roses. She'll climb and climb as tall as these chimneypots – you just mark my words.'

3

THE HUBBY

1924

THIS IS A WARNING THAT YOUR HUBBY IS SEEING ANOTHER WOMAN. FROM A WELLWISHER. The blunt message of doom was written in fountain pen and neat block capitals on a piece of respectable notepaper with the small purple imprint of a violet in its corner.

Daphne stared very hard, then tore it up briskly and burnt it. Thank goodness it had been written by someone who thought Osmond *was* her 'hubby' – if only for little Ralphie's sake. She knew it was complete nonsense.

She went into the back kitchen to get the lead for Rainbow, her old wire-haired terrier. The dog had been a blessing of companionship over the past four years. She thanked heavens she had brought him with her when she left The Turrets, even though he was getting a bit past his best. Each day when she took him for a walk she always thought of Inga and wondered how she was getting on and prayed that she would be kept safe and well in Margot's care.

This summer of 1924 was vanishing swiftly. A cold panic gripped her. Was this to be her life for ever? July was almost over. Life crowded her with a hundred things to worry about now compared to her passive days of being ruled by Margot.

Until three months ago, Ralphie had consumed almost every scrap of her time. She had taken him with her when she was at her market stall. Twice a week, she sold her home-made toffee there. Soon he would be going to school. What a lot of water had passed under the bridge since she had run away with Osmond, she thought wryly.

Unfortunately they had not yet bought their own house in Southport which he'd so faithfully promised her. They were now in a small rented place in Apple Street, Ancoats, not far from Ancoats hospital, in a haze of chimney smoke.

'It won't go on for ever,' Osmond kept saying. He was still holding on to his dream of eternal paradise in a tree-lined avenue of new, modern houses, in fresh seaside air.

Each day when he came home his stiff shirt collar was finely dotted with black smuts. 'At least, my dear,' he murmured consolingly as they lay in bed with the windows tightly shut, 'you can afford to have my clothes laundered. You don't need to slave over a washtub all day, like so many others. Better still, you have the luxury of expanding your personal income from that little hobby of the home-made toffee. How many other women round here are as free as that, untrammelled by loads of howling babbies clinging to their skirts?'

How wonderfully easy her life sounded when Osmond described it.

Often, when Daphne took Ralphie for a ride out on the tram, she wondered just what Osmond's own business life entailed in those vast, glossy, granite shipping offices where he worked; for he never mentioned his actual occupation as a shipping agent.

Sometimes, Daphne was haunted by terrible thoughts that he didn't go to 'business' at all each day, but was one of those unemployed people, driven to desperation as they left the house at the accustomed time each day and just wandered the streets or visited public houses and billiard rooms, unable to reveal to their wives and families the state they were in, until final collapse overtook them. Maybe it was this basic fear that stopped her from ever asking him what sort of a day he'd had.

Deep down, the remorse about Inga still lingered. Leaving her with Margot had seemed to be Daphne's only escape from madness at that time. But now her guilt about Inga's fate was fading as she reassured herself with thoughts of the comfort and love available in Grandma's care at The Turrets.

As for Osmond, he revelled in casual happiness – living a life of steady comfort. He was in a perfect niche at the shipping agents where no pincers would ever reach him. He wasn't exactly one of *the* shipping agents; he wasn't Mr Harris or Mr Prosser or Mr Gilfinnigan of Harris, Prosser and Gilfinnigan, but he had worked in their accounts department since he had left grammar school and had saved a tidy bit of cash over his past long years with Maud.

Looking back, which he rarely did, he accepted that his other, proper, wife, Maud, had been a Godsend: she was a competent, thrifty, domestic manager, who had money of her own, inherited from her rich widowed mother, whose husband had been a corn merchant.

Osmond knew he was in a strange situation, living where he was in a grimy backwater – but, balancing one thing against another, it wasn't working out too badly for him. As far as his firm knew, thanks to his own bit of carefully managed subterfuge, he was still officially living at home, in Sale, with Maud. Osmond was never a man to discuss his personal life with anyone.

One item he had never mentioned to Daphne was the fact that every month he did the right thing and sent Maud, via his solicitor, a regular sum of money which more than covered Maud's cost of living. It was the manly thing to do. It was this outgoing expenditure which had rather hindered his earlier plans for a decent existence in Southport with Daphne and Ralphie, but he realised it was the only way of showing how much he had valued Maud in past years. Hopefully it would, at the same time, snuff out too much female squawking.

Daphne had found a baby minder for Ralphie, from a notice in a sweet shop window, and for the past three months it had been working well. She took him to Annie Murdoch's home on weekdays. Annie was a war widow too and lived in Blossom Street, just off Great Ancoats Street.

'I only put the advert in this morning,' said Mrs Murdoch, at their first meeting.

'Have you been looking after children for long?'

'No, madam,' she said, respectfully.

Daphne sat there in her well-cut coat and neat hat in Annie's tiny parlour with a pleasant smile on her face. The place was clean and plain. The pale blue wallpaper looked new and was patterned with Japanese lanterns and small hummingbirds.

'To be honest, I've never done child minding before, madam, but I don't want to go out to a mill or be in t'rubber factory; I'm too chesty for it. I've got my boy working now but the girl is still at school. I do a home job for a local man, making posh little radio crystal sets for them as doesn't want to make their own. I'd enjoy having your little boy here.'

To Daphne she looked far younger than a mother with a son of fourteen who worked in a clothing factory, and a daughter aged fifteen, said to be very clever, who had won a scholarship.

'I was married when I was my young Florrie's age,' said Annie Murdoch, becoming less formal and putting a pale thin hand to her fair, faintly freckled face to push away strands of wispy hair. 'By the time I was seventeen I had the two of them. Then I had one that miscarried and one that grew in a tube instead of the womb, so they took everything away, because they thought it was best, as I had asthma quite bad. My husband Danny was in the British Machine Gun Corps on the western front. He was killed after only four months.' She gazed sadly at Daphne with her large grey eyes.

The arrangement for looking after Ralphie worked well and he thrived. Daphne gave thanks to God for her good fortune. Sometimes horrific tales came to light of baby minders who kept children in conditions like those of a small prison. A child would be in a pram or locked in the same room all day and given 'baby powders' to keep them quiet. There had been cases of minders hitting the children in their care, and putting any bruising down to a childish accident. 'Boxing children's ears' with a heavy, flat-handed blow was a common form of discipline, causing terrible pain and sometimes deafness for life. Daphne had always dreaded any of that happening to Ralphie.

The day after Daphne had received the anonymous letter, she received a note from Annie Murdoch. It came by the Saturday morning post. *'Dear Madam, I shall not be able to look after your little boy next week. I have been called away. Yours respectfully, A. Murdoch.'*

Daphne stared at the letter in its large, neatly looped writing and it suddenly struck her that the notepaper, with the violet in the corner, was exactly the same as yesterday's warning message. She looked at the letter again then put it in the kitchen drawer. It was the style of paper you could get at Smith's the stationers. Sometimes it had a violet in the corner and sometimes it was a carnation.

There was no intimation of when Annie would be back again. Tomorrow was Sunday so it meant that Daphne would have to have Ralphie with her the whole time, even at the market. A streak of frustrated annoyance welled up inside her.

The following week another letter arrived. This one was much longer. All letters to Daphne were addressed to Mrs Trent, which was Daphne's maiden surname. She had planned this with Osmond right from the start and he had even bought the house in the name of D. Trent. It worked quite well, as Osmond never received any letters there himself and all the gas bills and other sundry, impersonal communications were automatically addressed to D. Trent Esquire. Osmond had already gone to business when the second letter arrived, and when Daphne began to read it she felt a streak of shame at her own selfishness. It went on at length about Annie's father who had been in a terrible accident at work when a crane had run against some buildings and crushed three men. '. . . and so I cannot say exactly when I shall be back, but if ever you want your little boy looked after on Saturdays, my daughter Florrie would be glad to oblige.'

Saturdays . . . Daphne put the letter back in its envelope thoughtfully. Until this moment she had never thought of having Ralphie looked after on Saturdays. She never went to Saturday markets with her toffees. Osmond always had Saturday afternoons and Sundays off. But now with this offer of child minding on Saturdays she could be free to work Saturday mornings on a market at a time when business and buying was at its best, and it would not disturb Osmond's own working pattern.

The following Saturday morning, Daphne went round with Ralphie to see young Florrie, to get more details of when her mother would be back again and perhaps to make some arrangements about the child minding on Saturdays.

Daphne had never seen Florrie at close hand but there was a seaside photograph of her and her brother on a tiny sideboard, where she looked about ten. Florrie greeted her with a smile fit for a toothpaste advertisement. She was stunningly beautiful with black wavy hair and her deep blue eyes were shaded by bushy eyelashes. She was taller than Daphne, and was blessed with a natural aura of authority.

'Mother is having to stay on longer, to look after Grandad, Mrs Trent. But I'll willingly look after Ralphie on Saturdays.' She beamed at Ralphie and he smiled back. She turned towards a school bag which was hanging on the back of a chair and took a notebook and pen from it. 'Are there any special instructions you'd like me to write down, Mrs Trent?' She unscrewed the top of her elegant, pale green mottled fountain pen with its gold nib, and wrote 'Ralphie' at the top of a new page in the lined notebook and the date.

Daphne stiffened slightly. There was something about it that reminded her of the anonymous note. 'What a lovely fountain pen . . .' she murmured ingratiatingly.

'Yes, I got it as a prize at school.' Florrie smiled confidently. 'As a matter of fact, I think I've seen your husband, Mr Trent, once or twice. My friend's hubby works in the shop where Mr Trent buys his cigars and I sometimes go there to do some tidying up before school.' She gave Daphne a cool, bland look.

Daphne went quite sick. 'Fancy that . . .' There was an awkward silence.

'What shall I put down about Ralphie then?' said Florrie. 'Has he any food fads? Is he allowed sweets? I know you make them but they can sometimes rot your teeth. Has he got any favourite toys he should bring with him or a favourite bit of rag or dummy as a comforter? I'm not like Mother. I like to have everything written down and cut and dried, so there's no mistakes. Mother works from what she calls instinct.'

Daphne's mind was still swirling around. '. . . *Your hubby is seeing another woman. From a wellwisher.*' She tried to stare Florrie meaningfully in the eyes. 'Are you a *wellwisher*, Florrie?'

'A wellwisher?' Florrie looked at her hesitantly then her face cleared. 'I expect I am really, Mrs Trent. I love wells. It's a bit like coins in a fountain, isn't it? You chucks your pennies in and makes your wish. I once went to one in some rocks near Matlock.'

Daphne smiled. 'I'm not *quite* sure about the Saturday mornings yet but I'll let you know as soon as possible.' She turned to Ralphie who was playing in the corner with a tin of small lead soldiers belonging to Florrie's brother. 'Come along, darling.'

All the way back to Apple Street, Daphne's imagination bubbled. What a philanderer! Even now she could hardly believe it. Naturally there was nothing for it but to try and find out the whole truth about Osmond, but which was the best way to approach it? Especially as she had thrown away the letter of warning which was her main evidence. And there again, was Florrie the actual seductress or was it that friend she'd mentioned whose husband worked at the wretched tobacco shop? Daphne's

41

imagination expanded even further: perhaps the tobacco shop was one of those undercover brothels where they had shabby, red velvet settees and the girls upstairs pretended to be in the cancan! She began to tremble slightly with panic. There had been a case quite recently in the local news where they were so busy doing the cancan above a grotty greengrocer's shop for an ex-Lord Mayor and his two cronies that the wooden floor which was riddled with deathwatch beetle collapsed and they all landed amongst the dried up cabbages and lethargic carrots, in a very bruised state. But the main scandal of it all was that the council was accused of repairing the floor out of local public funds.

All that day Daphne waited impatiently and uneasily for Osmond to arrive home from business, but he never appeared. Visions of the Moulin Rouge almost set Daphne's brain on fire.

Then at nine-thirty that evening, when Ralphie was fast asleep upstairs, Osmond arrived back at last. He was having trouble getting his key in the front door. Daphne peered through the curtains and could hardly believe her eyes . . .

By his side, and completely unrecognisable to Daphne, was this strange apparition in a black and yellow striped silk frock. Surely this wasn't young Florrie's friend from the tobacco shop? Daphne had automatically presumed that Florrie's friend would be as young as Florrie; this woman was old enough to be the girl's grandmother . . . Daphne went weak at the knees and turned away from the window as she heard Osmond still fumbling. It was obvious they were both drunk. People usually filled themselves with gin in those seedy palaces of ill repute. Should she go swiftly to bed and ignore it all? Or was it possible to get to the front door and lock it at the bottom before he managed to open it with his key? The back door was already fully locked. It would not be the first time in Apple Street that a man had been forced to sleep off his madness elsewhere – but God forbid that it was happening in this house.

In seconds she was kneeling down swiftly to pull the heavy bolt across at the bottom of the front door, but she was a moment too late. She jumped back just in time to avoid a crack on the head as the door swung open. Osmond stood there uncertainly. In the gloom just behind him was his lawful wife, Maud Beardsley.

Daphne had no idea at first that it was Maud, but slowly it began to dawn on her.

Years of single blessedness had transformed Maud from an Eton-cropped mouse to a colour-rinsed, bushy-haired slightly snarling tiger. And within the next few minutes she was plonking herself down on the small sofa in Daphne's front room with Osmond beside her, as meek as a little lamb in his neat office suit, stiff white collar, and beautiful hand-made calf-leather shoes. There wasn't a trace of drink anywhere about either of them.

Daphne listened in horrified silence as the whole of Osmond's deceitful pattern was revealed by Maud, now swollen to the flushed, gleaming triumph of the conquerer.

'And so he's coming home with me at last, Mrs Abbott.'

The words were sieved through Maud's clenched porcelain teeth like wayward tea-leaves. 'I've waited long years for this moment . . .'

Daphne stood there. The room began to go round and round but she gripped the table hard then sat down on an upright chair. She looked across at Osmond. 'Should I get the brandy out?'

Osmond flapped a flaccid hand across his face in weary abandonment: 'Not tonight, de—' He was nearly going to say dear but remembered just in time to say 'Daphne', in rather strict tones. For it seemed to him now that in one flash his circumstances had altered completely and he was in a different war zone.

It had all happened like a rather horrible dream one morning when he had just popped into the tobacco shop. When he came out, an elderly woman with slightly purple-white hair accosted him and persisted in walking along the street by his side. And all the time she kept saying, 'Found you at last, Osmond. I wonder what they'll say at the office when I start coming with you in the mornings on the way to my hairdressing appointments and my shopping. You can thank God I found you. I would never have known if I hadn't met Mr McAlpine from the accounts department. He asked me if we'd moved, and I said certainly not. He said he always saw you every day going into the tobacco shop because the tram stopped right across the street . . . I shall keep on meeting you every day at the tobacco shop until you come back home, Osmond.'

Finally, Osmond had wilted like a worn out lettuce. With one acquiescent nod of defeat he had promised

Maud he would go back to the straight and narrow. With one stroke he crossed Daphne and Ralphie and the house in Ancoats out of his life for ever, as if they had never existed.

This evening was the first time in four years he had ever been back to see what he still regarded as his proper home. He had blotted that out in much the same way as he was now blotting out his present one. He was amazed to see how wonderful everything looked. The garden was blooming with orange and lemon dahlias and the grass was velvety green. The house itself, with its lead-lighted diamond-shaped window panes and emerald green glossy paintwork, still had its windows open as muslin curtains fluttered gently in the breeze.

That night at eleven p.m. Daphne found herself in Apple Street wide-eyed and entirely alone in the small double bed. Three times she crept into Ralphie's bedroom and looked down at his chubby, peaceful, sleeping innocence, her own face wet with tears. What was to become of them now? How could she explain to one so young that his father had deserted them? And worst of all, how on earth was she going to manage financially? No longer was the sweet stall on the market going to save the day for it was no more than a comfortable whim. By five o'clock in the morning Daphne was distraught with the whole situation. She was driven to going down to the cupboard where the brandy bottle was kept. Then, like a saving grace, Ralphie woke up with a bout of bad coughing and she checked herself. Her life now must be to protect him . . . He had no one in the world but her. She went upstairs to comfort him.

Osmond was an amazingly cunning man. He went home that evening with Maud in almost complete, but tactful, silence as they sat together on the bus to Sale. He let her pay his fare. He knew it would please her as much as the last nail in his coffin would have done. He had become secondary to Ralphie in Daphne's affections. Everything had been a mistake.

He hadn't brought any belongings with him except his shaving tackle and a clean collar yet he didn't seem to be at all perturbed.

'I've put you in the boxroom, for the time being,' said Maud, when they arrived back. 'The big alarm clock is set for six-forty-five in the morning and Maria, my new live-in maid, will get your breakfast ready.

'You will find the car in complete working order in the garage. It's hardly been used except when Mr Wentworth came to take me out occasionally, so you'll be able to use it again to go to business. Goodnight, Osmond.'

'Goodnight, Maud.' A glimmer of thankful satisfaction flitted across his face. He slept in the narrow single bed in the boxroom, like a log, and was up the next morning like a young greyhound.

Maud stood at her bedroom window and watched him drive off to business. The dark green Daimler shone in the first rays of sun. It was a perfect summery morning. Then she got dressed and went downstairs for her own breakfast.

'The master has been unavoidably detained away from home for some time with urgent family matters,' she explained to Maria, 'but he will be here permanently from now on.'

Seventeeen-year-old Maria nodded solemnly.

Later that morning Maud rang up Margot at The Turrets. 'I just thought I'd let you know that Osmond is back, Margot.'

'Back? Where on earth has he been?' Margot sounded genuinely exasperated. 'I'm sorry if I'm not quite following you, Maud, but I'm having a very fraught time at present. Inga has just sprained her ankle at a tap-dancing class. The doctor has said she's out-growing her strength and she's on Parish's Food three times a day. It's all terribly trying. You've no idea what it's like bringing her up by myself. We had a frightful time last week. I took her to a *conversazione* at Mrs Pemberton-Marsh's – to sing "The Trout", by Schubert, in the interlude. It was completely marred by that snobby Hetty Reece choking on a glazed cherry, added to which Miss Pritchard played completely the wrong piano accompaniment. The whole thing was an awful disaster.'

'Why don't you ask the child's mother to come back then, Margot?' said Maude with icy sarcasm. 'She's entirely free to do so. Osmond's back with me now – for good.'

Maud heard Margot gasp. 'Of *course* . . . forgive me Maud. It's so long since I heard from you. These past years have absolutely galloped along. I'm completely out of touch . . . So Osmond's *back*, then? How truly amazing . . . Does that mean that *you* now have a child

47

to look after too, just like I have?' Margot spoke with silky stealth.

Maud carefully replaced the receiver and went into the garden. She had fired her bolt.

4

THE TRUTH

Inga could hear Mrs Phelps going on for ever to Mrs Dawn. They were always very cheeky when Grandma was out. Especially in the afternoons.

This particular afternoon, they were in the small sewing room having a cup of tea. They were using the very best forget-me-not tea set and the best silver teaspoons on Grandma's best rosewood tea tray, covered with one of Grandma's best embroidered-linen tray cloths.

Inga hovered about near the slightly open door as the teapot lid clinked for yet another cup. She had almost given up hope of ever seeing her mother again, but gradually over the past five years she had formed her own picture of what had happened: her mother had left the sanatorium where she had been ill for so long and now lived in a very healthy place called Apple Street where she had to do what was called 'recuperate'. Even Grandma didn't know it was called Apple Street, but

Inga did because Mrs Dawn's best friend Mrs Phelps who worked for the Beardsleys had once mentioned it in undertones in the kitchen.

Inga knew her mother must still be quite ill because of her not being able to come back to visit The Turrets. Probably she had something wrong with her legs. There were an awful lot of people who walked round with their legs in irons. She yearned and yearned for her mother to be cured and for her to be able to walk again. Her mother never wrote much but she always sent birthday cards and presents and never forgot Christmas. Inga kept all her letters and cards in a small white cardboard shoe box, with 'Mummy' written on it and flowers crayoned all round in a curling border.

'What will happen in Apple Street *now*? That's what *I* want to know,' said Mrs Phelps in the sewing room, with a triumphant edge to her voice. She was a large sprawling type of woman and reminded Inga of the sort of lady the giant in *Jack and the Beanstalk* might have chosen to be his wife before he started eating people.

'How does he like being back then?' said Mrs Dawn. 'It'll be like having an entirely different wife, with her all dolled up and changed out of recognition. Not that I've ever seen her, since the day of that scene, years ago, when she called round here, all set for a bit of rousting. But from what you say she's changed completely. For the worst, it seems to me. I like plainness better.' There were sounds of the teapot being drained. 'How does he like that young maid of all work?'

'I wouldn't trust him with my own great-grandmother.'

There was a sudden, sipping silence. Inga lost interest and moved away. It sounded as if some man had turned into a pickpocket. Fancy them even having him in the house.

She went upstairs to her bedroom. It was hardly the end of September, but it was forever raining. Even the wasps had disappeared. Already she was practising for a children's Christmas *Messiah*, at the Sunday school. It wasn't a Sunday school she ever went to until Grandma had found out what they were doing and sent her there so that she could take part in it. She hated it there. No one seemed to like her. Some of them said she was stuck up, and her voice was too loud and she did it on purpose to swank. Most of them were a lot older than she was. Some of the girls were as old as fifteen, and she was nearly twelve. Their pet girl was Mimi Garter. Everyone said she had a voice like a nightingale, but Inga could hardly hear it once the organ began to play. And once, Mimi fainted.

There was also a boy there with a voice like a nightingale, too, called Oscar Stewart, whose mother made him suck throat lozenges all the time. He was going to have his voice put on a gramophone record.

Inga looked down at one of the rugs in the bedroom and began to walk round in very small steps, tracing its pattern. She seemed to have fewer and fewer of her own real friends now, because she was always practising her singing or performing in the evenings.

Even Miss Mitford at the Kellerways Private School thought she did far too much, and remarked on the dark rings round her eyes. 'I must have a word with your grandma,' she said. Then in the next breath she said, 'although I think you'd be perfect as Little Red Riding Hood, at Christmas. Doctor Harmons has set it all to music, and Leroy Spinks has developed a *beautiful* voice. He could play the big bad wolf. Dr Harmons has written a wonderful duet where the big bad wolf is pretending to be the grandmother, and Little Red Riding Hood is just saved in time by her father . . .'

All the way home from school one day, Inga wondered what it would be like to have a real father who could come and save *her*, instead of only her grandma all the time . . .

She had noticed too that Mrs Phelps sat and gossiped to Mrs Dawn far more these days because Grandma was out so much, dealing with what she called 'making you into a musical star, dear'.

Quite often Grandma was with famous Dr Harmons who gave Inga, and many other children from school, private singing lessons. He was a short, stout man with white hair and a red face who wore an old buff-coloured nankeen waistcoat and made them all do lots of breathing exercises as he pushed at their stomachs, gripped their ribcages or set their posture like a mechanical vice. 'Breath stoomach,' he would bawl from the piano. ''Old the breath, 'old the breath. Let go, let go. No parrots.' (Crash of piano chords.) 'No *parrots* – Canary! Canary!' Then he would give a final thump at the keys and lean back with his head bowed, looking very sad.

It was just at the beginning of September when, suddenly, like a bolt from the blue, Inga found out the full and devastating truth about her mother from Mrs Phelps. As usual, Mrs Phelps was there at The Turrets, spread out in comfort, having a drink of tea in the afternoon with Mrs Dawn.

'This'll have to be my very last cup, Cissie. Maud's beginning to jib, even though I do come here in my own bit of time off. She hates Margot Abbott like poison underneath. She's never forgiven her for saying Maud's wedding cake was too gritty – all those years ago when Margot was matron of honour at her wedding. She let it out only a week ago when I was stoning raisins for some Christmas puddings.'

Inga was off school with a sore throat. She was hanging about, listening, and wishing Mrs Phelps would go back to her own domain. It was awful having her parked here like the Queen of England. When the two of them were together they seemed to change into quite nasty people. Even Albert kept his distance and stayed in the garden shed looking at seed catalogues.

The telephone rang. Mrs Dawn went to answer it. 'Now who on earth can that be?'

Inga slid away from the hall hastily, but not far enough to be out of earshot.

'Yes Mrs Abbott. Yes, I'll do that, Mrs Abbott. As a matter of fact, I'm busy with them at the moment. I'll get on my bicycle and bring them along to you this very minute.' She replaced the receiver and went back to Mrs Phelps. 'She wants me to take ten jars of chutney round to the Walshes in Cranmore Road. You'll have to help me to get the labels and the date written on them, Dora. I should have got it done a bit earlier. She wants me to take them round to The Pine Trees on the bike. I'll just have to put some of 'em in the basket on t'front and the rest in a boxed up parcel on t'back carrier.'

There was a great scrabbling round for the chutney labels, and heavy breathing as they wrote them out, with no mistakes – they knew that careless labelling could ruin Margot's reputation for ever.

'I'll have to get back myself, Cissie,' said Mrs Phelps.

'Oh, not yet, Dora. I'll only be gone a few minutes . . . Albert's nowhere to be found so I'd sooner you stayed with Inga whilst I'm away, if you could? She can get up to all sorts when she's on her own . . .'

'Right you are then. But only fifteen minutes at the most, and that's definite . . .'

At last Inga heard Mrs Dawn go. She was still treated like a small child.

'You can stay with me in the kitchen, Inga, whilst I do some more of these labels for Mrs Dawn, then I can keep an eye on you,' said Mrs Phelps bluntly. 'I don't want you going off and being a Meddlesome Matty whilst I'm in charge. All I can say is that it's a pity your mother hasn't been here all these years to keep proper charge of you.' Her voice softened. 'Here. You stick these labels on some more of these other jars but for heavens sake, don't have them sloping.'

Inga nodded solemnly as she painstakingly licked the back of one of the blue-bordered small white labels and stuck it on slowly and perfectly. Then she stopped and stared at Mrs Phelps who was speeding away at hers like a busy bee.

'Mummy would come home if she could, Mrs Phelps,

but she can't walk. I know she lives in Apple Street, but she's been very ill in a sanatorium.'

Dora Phelps's plump face went an angry pink as all caution went to the winds. 'Can't walk?'

'No. I think her legs are in irons, like Mr Pendel's at the paper shop.'

'In *irons*?' Dora looked completely dazed. Her hands drooped away from the chutney jars.

'How long will it take for her legs to get completely better, Mrs Phelps? I pray every night for her to come home one day. I try to be patient, but sometimes I think that even God doesn't care . . .'

Dora's brain ticked round angrily. Perhaps she should help God, by telling the poor child the truth. After all – God loved truth above all things. Perhaps she had been sent here this very afternoon to do His secret bidding. God moves in most mysterious ways . . . Everyone knew that.

'Your mother doesn't have to wear leg irons, Inga,' she said a trifle coldly, but with a streak of zealous determination. 'She's as fit as a fiddle. She does live in Apple Street, though, and you have a little half brother you never knew about. He lives there too. His name is Ralph and he's nearly five. I'm telling you because you're getting into a grown-up girl now and I believe in telling the truth.' Then Dora said firmly, 'And don't do any more chutney labels, dear, in case they suddenly start to go all crooked. I'll do the rest.'

Dora Phelps fished in her skirt pocket and drew out a crumpled white bag of rather posh transparent oblong mints all wrapped in transparent cellophane. 'Have one of these to suck, dear.'

Inga's spirits soared to the sky. Her normally slightly gloomy face lit up with joy. Her mother could walk! And as if that wasn't enough, she, Inga Abbott, had a real live baby brother! The past mysteries were completely wiped out.

'When will they be home then, Mrs Phelps? Will I be able to go and see them?' Her face glowed with excitement.

Dora stared at the transformation in amazement. It was as if the Good Fairy had suddenly appeared from *Cinderella* and turned Inga into a princess, ready for the ball. Surely God would be pleased to see such a wonder, even if the rest of them wouldn't.

'I don't think I'll *quite* wait until Mrs Dawn gets back, Inga. She'll only be a few more minutes. I think I've just seen Albert in the garden, through the window, so at least he's not far away.' Hastily, Mrs Phelps went to fetch her coat. To Inga's eyes she seemed unusually flustered and in a terrible hurry as if she'd just had an urgent telegram. 'Goodbye, dear. Be a good girl. And I hope you see your mother and half-brother soon.' She was out of the door like lightning.

Inga went into the garden to find Albert and tell him the wonderful news. Albert was standing next to a small bonfire poking at it with a piece of old iron railing. 'Albert, I've got a young brother, and his name's Ralph. Isn't it *lovely*? And Mummy's well again. I might go to see her in Apple Street!'

Albert gave an extra poke at the fire and stared into the bluish, curling, dampened smoke. 'Very nice indeed, very nice . . .'

'Albert . . .'

'Yes?'

'What's a hearth-brother?'

He turned and looked at her with wise eyes. 'A hearth-brother, lassie, is one born in a place where it's quite warm and cosy; where there's plenty of coal on the fire.'

'His name's Ralph.'

'And very nice too, Inga. Very nice too . . .'

'Do you think Mummy might bring him home to live with us?'

'Who knows, lass. There's one thing in life I've learned and it's never to forecast anything where women's concerned. Bring me a few more twigs, there's a good girl.'

She gathered him some good big bits of branch blown down in gales. They stood and watched them as they began to spit and crackle. Bright iron sparks rusted the dusk as orange flames burst through. The smell of wood smoke blended with the surrounding backgound quietness. It was perfect, a garden of peace . . .

Then, almost immediately, it began to fade as Mrs Dawn started to call to her from the back door of the house. Reluctantly, Inga turned to go inside again. Somehow the joy of relating her good news had evaporated. Somehow she felt that Mrs Dawn wouldn't tell her the same amazing things as Mrs Phelps had told her, and it would all be spoilt again.

She drifted inside very slowly. She would just have to tell it to Grandma – when Grandma wasn't too busy . . .

5

HELL BREAKS LOOSE!

Margot was going out again. It was Saturday morning and Inga was standing next to her, shivering slightly in her best clothes. Mrs Dawn was polishing the bannisters and smiling at them.

'Well, all I can say is, Mrs Abbott, the very best of luck to both of you . . . I hope Inga shines like the true star she is and carries off the Junior Rose Vase. It'll be a long way to travel just for nothing. Oh – and that reminds me – talking of shine. This new polish you bought isn't doing a bit of good. There's no shine at all. I'd be better going back to vinegar and water . . .'

Margot stared at her irritably and hurried out. Her creamy white fox-fur with its purple lining flapped away from her shoulders, checked by a thick silk crocheted chain and firm, fancy button, as Inga trailed after her.

What an ignorant woman Mrs Dawn was, Margot simmered. Mrs Dawn had no finesse whatsoever and she was getting worse. Especially now that the Bearsleys were back together again. In some ways *that* had been a disaster because Mrs Phelps from the Beardsleys' now spent all her spare time coming round to see Cissie Dawn on the least pretext. And Margot knew they took advantage because one day she'd returned to find two kirby grips and a couple of long grey hairs, plus cake crumbs, in the drawing room.

Inga sat in the back of the car, with all its brown leather seating and chromium plating: a small lone figure clutching her music case. She was dreading the Rose Vase competition. There was a very complicated test piece with lots of trills and tra-la-las. You had to control your breath and plunge up and down, higher and higher, like sharp mountain peaks, without actually squeaking. Then you came down to almost a sombre whisper. It was about a stag caught by the huntsman's arrow in a forest, and was translated from a foreign language. It made people cry if it was sung properly. But Dr Harmons said it was usually sung excruciatingly badly, and made him weep buckets.

'And remember,' hissed Margot when they eventually reached The Belvedere Music Academy, which was within sight of Blackpool Tower, close to the promenade but hidden by trees, 'don't *ever* be seen chewing your handkerchief, or it'll be the end of you. I know for a fact from Dr Harmons that the adjudicators have a closed cabin with a viewing window on the balcony in the music hall, and they can see every single thing that goes on from the moment the entrants begin to arrive.'

Inga clutched at her lump of hanky nervously and moved it further up her sleeve, on the inside of her wrist so that Grandma wouldn't even know it was there. Surely it was better there than in the leg of her knickers? She began to think of Mummy and the new brother Mrs Phelps had told her about. It cheered her up to think that Mummy could soon be home and that she might even go herself and visit her in Apple Street. She hadn't mentioned anything to Grandma because Grandma seemed to think of nothing except the singing . . .

The Academy was a frightening-looking building; it was like a massive church. And today it was buffeted by squally, sea-swept weather. Inside was a huge hall with a parquet floor and a big wooden stage with a glossy black grand piano on it. There were doors leading from the hall to passages and cloakrooms.

The minute they got inside, who should they see standing there by the heavy iron clothes hooks, in a long lavender taffeta frock with frills round the edges, but thirteen-year-old Mimi Garter. Her mother was next to her, holding a music case. Mrs Garter was exeedingly thin, and wore a faded, navy blue serge coat. Her hair was thin and wispy, her nose was slender and pinched looking, and her fingers were bony enough for the two plain gold rings there to rattle.

Inga stared at Mimi enviously. Grandma never allowed her to wear long frocks. At present she was dressed in her best fawn barathea coat with a Fair Isle tammy, and underneath her coat was a knee-length, inky blue velvet dress with a lace collar. Oh, how she wished she was as grown-up as Mimi Garter in that long frock, and with those short black curls, big dark eyes and pale face, even if Mimi did faint sometimes.

Margot nodded towards Mrs Garter, but at first there was no response. Mrs Garter wasn't really Grandma's type. It was quite obvious that Mimi's music case wasn't very good quality. It had a suggestion of grey cardboard about it where it was scuffed.

Mrs Garter glanced back at Grandma hastily then turned away, and told Mimi to be quick and change into her satin party slippers. Inga knew they weren't real diamonds on the front because Grandma had once told her about slippers with false diamonds on. But all the same – oh, how she would have liked some . . .

'What piece is she singing to start off with?' said Grandma forcefully to Mrs Garter.

'"Nymphs and Shepherds" . . .' murmured Mrs Garter evasively.

'Inga's is different,' said Grandma. 'There's no comparison between a mature thirteen-year-old and an eleven-year-old.'

'Oh . . . they won't be in the same *sections*,' said Mrs Garter suddenly coming to life. 'Although that one about the forest stag does seem a bit hard for the inexperienced ones. It was used at the Alderport Music Festival for adults! Surely you saw it in the Alderport instruction book?'

This time Margot turned away. Her instruction book for that event was buried under piles of other instruction books, all set for more and more Rose Vases, Bowls, Silver Trophies and Golden Sound Awards stretching on into an unending future. Quite frankly, she knew that Inga wouldn't quite walk off with a top prize this time. The Belvedere Junior Rose Vase was one of the most prestigious competitions of all. But all the same, the practice gained from this constant competing was essential.

'What has she got for her own choice in round three?' said Mrs Garter as she dabbed some powder on Mimi's nose.

Inga stared in amazement. Powder! For beautifying, not for bruises . . . Make-up was banned for her.

'"Rose Among The Heather",' said Margot.

'I think most of the young boys have chosen "Oh for The Wings of a Dove",' said Lena Garter, melting to normality at last, 'though I did hear that Oscar Stewart was singing "Pure Are the Sounds From Heaven" if his throat is better, and perhaps a sea shanty if his voice is uncertain. He's approaching "That Age" now. But at least he's made the gramophone record, which is more than most.

'Leroy Spinks is quite a different kettle of fish, though. According to what I've heard, his mother's chosen "The Road To Mandalay". He's here with his Aunt Mabel; she always sees to him. I think "The Road To Mandalay" is quite out of keeping for a child of his age.' Mrs Garter smiled briefly at Margot. She had two teeth missing.

Leroy Spinks! Not him, here! Inga's heart sank.

The audience in the hall was made up mostly of women, and there was rather a lot of coughing and crackling of toffee papers. Quite often there was a scraping of chairs too as the unfortunate coughers, clutching hankies or scarves to their wicked mouths and heaving slightly through gritted teeth, tried to shuffle quietly from the hall to have a really good cough outside; whereupon they found the cough had completely vanished, and proceeded to discuss the fate of their protégés with fellow sufferers.

Even Margot had succumbed to a coughing bout and was outside in the vestibule amongst the small huddled groups which included Leroy Spinks's Aunt Mabel.

Margot beamed at Mabel with triumphant relief. 'I *thought* I recognised you, but I wasn't quite sure at first. Altrincham High, wasn't it? I was a prefect and you were nine. I had to take you from the dining room when that gravy boat got tipped all down your blouse. Then we met again years later when my husband was alive and we were both on holiday in Torquay.'

'And *you* were trapped in that little sandy cove in that awful striped bathing costume, and had to be rescued by a fishing boat,' said Mabel, beaming back, swathed in outlandish, tangerine silk, bordered at the neck with flouncy frills. 'Yes, I'm here with my great-nephew Leroy and he's done very well this morning. I'm keeping my fingers crossed for "The Road To Mandalay" this afternoon. It'll be crucial. How did your granddaughter go on then?'

'Not too well, I'm afraid. It was a bit of a trial for her this morning. She's so highly strung. The minute her turn comes she always wants to rush off to the W.C. Then afterwards she complains of pains in the stomach. I'm hoping she'll have settled down more for "Rose Among The Heather".'

'We're both starving; we only brought a bit of fruit cake.'

Inga's heart thudded with anxiety as the afternoon wore on and people moved backwards and forwards with their pieces of music for the pianist to play at the grand piano. Supposing her voice disappeared? Grandma was already telling her to stop whispering all the time.

She had noticed three different pianists: two men in evening dress with bow ties and glasses kept popping up then marching out again, interspersed by a lady in a long, autumn-tinted, figure-clinging frock with an artificial lily of the valley corsage.

Inga waited dolefully with others in an awful waiting room at the back of the stage. She stared at Leroy Spinks in his long-trousered silk twill sailor suit with its big white square shoulder collar and its braided border. His Aunt Mabel was talking to everyone, and he was looking at pictures of racing cars in a small, twopenny paper story book. He ignored Inga completely and she was glad. She rarely saw him these days. He went to a small private prep school for boys, but she knew from others that he still bullied people.

Phoebe Strangeways, the accompanist, always wore lilies of the valley at music festivals. She was a lonely woman, whose heart's desire (an explorer) had disappeared many years ago. Her artificial lilies of the valley, which she doused with scent, were a torch for her eternal love and, lying against her breast, kept hope alight. She was a pianist *par excellence*. Her playing was faultless: no one ever complained that she galloped ahead like an unrestrained cart-horse or lagged behind like a funeral dirge. She was experienced, professional and utterly reliable. Perfection was her constant watchword.

But today, after the midday dinner break, she was in a goggle-eyed, dizzy whirl of happiness. Her crotchets and quavers, usually second nature to her, were all in a muddle. The cause of this uncharacteristic behaviour was a totally unexpected proposal of marriage from Mr Forwardly, the Director of Education for Stanton-on-Medlock, and an avid member of the Junior Silver Vase Committee.

His passionate declaration had taken place behind a holly bush close to the front door of the Academy. He had followed her outside, touched her elbow and then pulled her to him, kissing her full on the cheek, with his rather floppy hair brushing gently against her forehead. 'Phoebe,' he had said, 'I've been plucking up the courage to ask you for two years. Will you marry me? Don't say no, for goodness' sake; I'll never be able to get this far again . . .'

It was the first definite proposal of marriage Miss Strangeways had ever had and the enormity of it made her feel quite faint. She was suddenly caught in a rash, entirely new, venturesome world.

Phoebe said yes, immediately. And forthwith, the whole afternoon was to become, for her, nought but a strange, jumbled dream of joy.

But to some, like Inga Abbott, it was to remain a nightmare for ever.

It started with Leroy Spinks's 'Road to Mandalay', which Phoebe played at an alarming rate with a seraphic smile on her face. This didn't trouble Leroy Spinks at all, for, although everyone said what a wonderful voice he was developing, he was quite immune to the potential blossoming as his mind was full of racing cars, joke comics full of cannibals, and how much money he'd get from his Aunt Mabel for performing well. Leroy just stood there at the front of the vast wooden stage in his blue sailor suit, closed his eyes tight and galloped along with the ungainly music, remembering to bow very carefully at the end to the judges. They were on the first row of wooden chairs in front of the stage, where they jotted down things in small notebooks to chew over later, in their box on the balcony.

The rest of the audience in the hall applauded loudly. They just couldn't get over the way this boy had kept up so well with the speed of the pianist with such courage and discipline. And the way he had bowed to them all at the end was completely charming, even though they had no idea what he had sung.

There was someone else performing before it was Inga's turn, but by now Phoebe Strangeways was in a dream of her own, with her brain full of other melodies: For tonight . . . For tonight . . . Let me dream all my dreams of delight, tra-la-la, tra-la-la, la-laa . . . Phoebe was completely swept away as the next miserable child did her best to battle with unforeseen circumstances. At this point the judges began to huddle together on the front row of chairs and it was decided to replace Miss Strangeways with someone else before any more harm was done.

Inga climbed on to the vast stage, quivering like a small

jelly, as one of the men with a bow tie and glasses came hurrying out to take over the grand piano. Mr McCloud didn't mince matters. He sat down and began to thump out the introductory notes to 'Nymphs and Shepherds' for the umpteenth time as if he were blindfolded. Then, realising that no small voice was joining in, he looked at the sheet of music and saw that he should have been playing 'Rose Among The Heather'. He was a kind man. He could see Inga was petrified, so, to make things better, he gave a quick melodic sweep of the piano keys and began very gently to play the refrain for 'Rose Among The Heather' in perfect timing. It was one of his favourite pieces.

Inga stood there numb with shock. She hadn't even caught up with the false beginning of 'Nymphs and Shepherds'. And as for this morning – struggling up mountain peaks and down to the depths of thick forests to cope with a stag caught by the huntsman's arrow – it had left her white-faced and fearful.

Mr McCloud mouthed the words slightly to get her started: 'Saw a youth, the mo-or-n-i-ing rose . . . Blooming in the hea-the . . .'

Inga stood there blankly. She felt her hanky sliding from her sleeve. She put it to her mouth and began to chew it.

Mr McCloud had seen many such collapses. He kept on playing and his voice became louder and louder, to counteract her dilemma. He sang the words with dramatic, challenging conviction. The audience could do nothing but sit there and succumb, as he wound himself through the verses with massive concentration.

They stared like startled stoats at his glinting glasses until he reached the final sadness of the youth and the rose. 'Rose stung sharply as he pulled. But alas their da-ays we-ere tolled . . . Woun-ded bo-th tog-e-e-ther . . . Rose thou pretty rose so-oo red . . . Rose among the Hea-ther . . .'

Mr McCloud stood up and nodded quietly to the audience. They all applauded, timorously now, wondering vaguely what had happened to the child and whether she had been there as some sort of symbol of a higher meaning for the music.

Mr McCloud looked across comfortingly to Inga, but it was a complete waste of time. She had vanished. She had rushed out of the first open door she saw where a lady was coming in from outside with a yellow umbrella which had just blown inside out.

Inga fled past her away from the Belvedere Music Academy. She ran along the pavement, shocked by the blustering, swirling winds which tried to push her back again. She saw giant, grey, splashing waves at the end of the street. They roared and frothed across the promenade. The smell of cold sea enveloped her, and her ears were numbed of sound by spray-lashed gulls shrieking in the air. She felt herself perpetually beaten back by the force of the high tide and the wind. Then, when it lulled for a second, she ran across the tramlines to some stout green iron railings and clung to them. She was completely lost. All she knew now was to catch a tram to anywhere, to tell the ticket man to get her back to Manchester, to her mother. She would leave Grandma for ever. She would go to Apple Street . . . And then she knew no more.

She knew nothing of the massive, rising, foaming breakers that swept over her flattening her small thin body as if it were a mere swathe of heavy seaweed; sliding her from pavement to sea like a rag doll . . .

She knew nothing of the man who jumped into the cold, raging sea to save her, followed by two other people forming a human chain until she was finally dragged back to safety.

When she woke up properly again it was dinner time the next day and she was back, warm and snug, in her own bed at The Turrets. She lay there contentedly, with the music of 'Rose Among The Heather' strumming in her head. Soon, she thought, she would have to get up and go to Blackpool with Grandma to try for the Junior Rose Vase . . .

Then, as she sat up, it all began to come back – right up to the part when she had seen the lady with the yellow umbrella coming into the Belvedere Music Academy.

'It seems to me, love,' said Mrs Dawn a couple of weeks later, when all the hullabaloo had died down and she was, as usual, peeling the daily potatoes, with Inga watching her idly, 'it seems that you are fated to have trouble with all this singing business for ever more. It's just not doing you any good, child. Why on earth can't your grandma ever see it?'

'I expect it's because Mummy's not here, Mrs Dawn.' Inga looked at her pleadingly. 'If Mummy was here she'd stick up for me even more than you and Albert . . . Perhaps, if Grandma had Mummy and my young hearth-brother were here as well, she'd forget all about making me into a famous singer.'

A long, curling piece of potato peel dropped slowly from Cissie Dawn's ancient, foreshortened steel knife. Her hand clutched the potato. Her other hand gripped the worn bone handle in sudden shock. 'What did you say? Just then . . . half-brother! Who *ever's* told you that tale?'

Inga eyed her fearfully. She had kept her wonderful news a secret except for asking Albert on that special day what a hearth-brother was. She hadn't told a soul that she knew her mother wasn't ill any more and that Mummy was living in Apple Street, and that she, Inga, wanted to visit her as soon as possible. In fact, only yesterday, when Mrs Phelps had been sitting in the sewing room again with Mrs Dawn using the best silver teaspoons, she had waited in vain for Mrs Phelps to be on her own so she could ask her the best way to get to Apple Street.

She took the plunge. 'It was Mrs Phelps who told me, Mrs Dawn. It was one day when you were getting all that chutney ready and you had to go out on your bicycle. Mrs Phelps always tells the truth. She says you go to hell if you don't.'

Cissie Dawn gulped and put down the potato. 'Did she say where your mother was living? In all that squalor in the worst part of town?'

'She said Mummy lived in Apple Street, and that's a lovely name. I wish I could go and see her . . .' Inga's voice petered out helpessly.

'Believe me, child – that street could never grow a nice fresh apple tree in a month of Sundays. Even the applecarts round there are full of rotting and bruised leftovers. Dora Phelps had no right to tell you all that about your mother. It's nothing to do with her and it's nothing to do with you, so the less said the better.'

Cissie's mouth set into a grim, hard line. She was hanged if she was going to be blamed for Inga getting to know the truth and she was extremely disappointed in Dora. What a disloyal friend she was, to have let it all out the moment someone's back was turned. Obviously Dora had no idea of the real repercussions. Cissie began to simmer with downright hatred for Dora Phelps. What sort of viper was she herself harbouring at these afternoon tête-à-têtes? What was the point of ever speaking to Dora again if she was going to disclose their secret confidences? After all, she herself never, ever breathed a word about other things. She kept as silent as the tomb over spicy bits that Dora let fall. She had never breathed a word to Albert or anyone else about Osmond Beardsley's little 'how d'ya do' with Maria that Dora had kept on about: Maria, who had suddenly changed from Maud Beardsley's living-in maid to a living-well-away one with an ever-expanding waistband . . .

So, the very next time Dora arrived here expecting to see the silver-lidded Wedgwood jasperware biscuit barrel open, she would have another think coming.

The following afternoon Dora arrived, as usual. It was pouring down. Dora shook her umbrella from the back porch and rang the bell. Every second Tuesday was Margot's afternoon for bridge at Trudi Selwyn's.

Mrs Dawn opened the back door stonily, and placed

her foot deliberately in the way of Dora's as Dora tried to step inside.

Dora pushed forward resolutely. 'What a *dreadful* day, Cissie!'

'It certainly is, Dora. A very dreadful day. A day that I thought would never come. A day when I never dreamed I would have to admit that one of my best friends had betrayed my innermost confidences.'

'Who was that then, Cissie?' said Dora, taking off her rubber overshoes and leaving them on the coconut matting. 'I can't stay too long. Maud's interviewing a new girl to do all the heavy work because of my bad back. She might be another living-in one. I've only enough time for a quick cup of tea, today – and a small chocolate wafer . . . Did she ever notice the butter mark on the sewing-room wallpaper from the scones last week?'

'I soaked it off with bread and pumice powder.'

'You should have used borax.' Dora gave her a brief confident smile. 'How's Inga getting on?'

Mrs Dawn's anger began to wane. She went to put the kettle on. 'I've got something important to ask you, Dora. It's about Inga . . .'

Ten minutes later, when they were both sitting in state with the open biscuit barrel between them, Cissie said, 'Is it true that you actually told Inga about that Other Child in Apple Street, when I wasn't here?'

Dora hastily wiped some crumbs from her mouth and looked away. 'Yes, I'm afraid it is true, Cissie. Inga said something to me and I thought it best to come out with it. The divulgence of it isn't just your private property. My lot's just as involved in it all. It's a blessed shame, the way she's been kept in the dark. Someone had to tell her, and the Good Lord gave me the job.'

Cissie stared at her in silent shock. 'Little do you know what damage you've done, Dora. It'll cause ructions in the end, from here to Timbuctoo.'

Later that day, when Dora had departed, Cissie Dawn said to Inga, 'Mrs Phelps had no right to tell you all those things about your mother. It was supposed to be a sort of secret until you were older. Your grandmother would be fuming if she knew . . .'

Inga looked puzzled. 'But I am older, Mrs Dawn, and I'm glad I've got a baby brother.' Slowly, tears began to fill her eyes. 'I want to see Mummy again. *Please*, Mrs Dawn, please take me to Apple Street to see them. I swear I won't tell anyone. I swear it on the Holy Bible – or God cut my throat!'

Mrs Dawn looked embarrassed. 'There's no need to carry on like that about it, seeing as you think you're so grown-up. The main thing is not to worry your grandma with it, because she's a very busy woman.'

'But if Mummy was back home, Mrs Dawn, Mummy would be able to help Grandma and I'd be able to look after my baby hearth-brother for them both.' Her face shone with earnest, enthusiastic hope. 'Please take me – just once, to Apple Street, to see them, and I'll promise not to breathe a word to anyone else in the whole world.'

Mrs Dawn began waver. Perhaps after all she could take Inga to Apple Street and just point out where Daphne was actually living. It would at least teach the child one of the hard lessons of life . . . that nothing is quite as rosy as one expects and that there's more to things than meets the eye. She had led such a sheltered life . . . Then, after giving her a quick glimpse, they could go into Manchester, look in the toy shop windows, and come back home again. At least that much might shut her up for a while and stop all the fuss about her knowing more than she should. The longer Dora Phelps's busy-body blundering was kept away from Margot's sharp ears, the better.

'All right then, p'raps we will go. But not a word to anyone, mind. Not a single hint to a soul. Not even to Albert. I'll just take you to have one peep at where she lives. We'll go there tomorrow, Saturday morning, when your grandma's away on her Good Works doling out the soup to the down-and-outs, round the back of Sampson Street with the other ladies.' Mrs Dawn's mouth quirked with a streak of cynicism. She gave a deep sniff of disapproval.

'Oh, Mrs Dawn, what a darling you are!' Inga stared at her rapturously and Cissie Dawn's face creased into a slight, softening smile. How that child did suffer, and no mistake. If she had her way, she'd shove Margot in a tub, along with that idiot Osmond and a few others, and push them all off to sea.

That night, Inga couldn't get to bed quickly enough for the next morning to come, and Margot was slightly puzzled. 'It's nowhere near your bedtime yet. I want you to practise your singing. There's a chance you might be able to sing at another Masonic Dinner, in the near future.'

'I don't think I'd better, Grandma. My throat feels

slightly sore.' Inga gulped and put her hand to her neck nervously. She hardly ever dared to fob Margot off; it never seemed to work. And it wasn't working now.

'Fetch me that Ever Ready torch from the sideboard drawer.'

Inga stood there tremulously with her mouth wide open as Margot shone the torch into it. 'Your throat looks perfectly all right to me.'

Inga began to retch and gulp.

'Here. Take the torch back. Perhaps we'll pass over the singing tonight. You can have some extra practice singing your scales tomorrow afternoon before you perform at Mrs Hobson's musical evening. I don't know how that woman has the temerity to even have them. She hasn't a note of music in her whole body. But at least it's all practice for you. You can go to bed now if you want but take the words of "Your Tiny Hand Is Frozen" with you. Adult operatic pieces like that go down very well in drawing rooms when sung by a child.'

The next day, Inga was up with the lark. She was already washed and dressed by seven, but she stayed in her bedroom reading *Peter Pan*. She was a bit late down for breakfast; she didn't want Grandma to see she was excited about anything special.

Margot herself hardly noticed. Saturday mornings were always a rush of activity, involving last-minute messages, phone calls, and the tooting of car horns accompanied by ladies in rather old Singer coupés.

'We'd best get out quick, now your grandma's gone,'

said Mrs Dawn, standing there wearing a dark basin-shaped hat with a large central feather display springing from its petersham band. 'Don't put you best coat on. Put your navy blue one on. We don't want to show up too much . . . We'll go by train, and get back by tram.'

Inga was silent with overwhelming joy. She hurried along beside Mrs Dawn, never leaving her for one second. She obeyed every command like a noiseless, moving doll, so much so that Mrs Dawn some times looked down hastily to make sure she was still there.

'That's Apple Street,' said Mrs Dawn, stopping at last amongst smoke-blackened streets where the only brightness was from creamy, donkey-stoned steps, and where horse manure steamed on the cobbled roads. She pointed to a sign high up on a grime-ridden red brick wall. A cast-iron sign said Apple Street in black letters but there wasn't a tree or an apple to be seen.

Inga stared in disbelief.

'Come on then,' Mrs Dawn glanced at her a trifle sadly, 'but make sure you hold tight to my hand.'

6

RALPHIE

Her mother's house was the only one without heavy lace curtains. Inga stared at it from across the street.

Mrs Dawn stared, too. She had been down Apple Street only once before. She'd been out with Dora and they'd both chewed over the whole scandalous situation as they went back into town for tea and buns. There had been lace curtains that time, like all the rest.

Cissie Dawn was a bit sorry Daphne's house looked more modern. Those out-of-place loose-weave 'folksy' curtains with no covering on the dusty glass were a mixed blessing. She didn't want Inga to get too much of a view of the inside in case she blurted something out to Margot when they got back.

'Why can't we just go across the street and knock at the door, Mrs Dawn?' Inga stood there uneasily.

A rag-and-bone man's horse and cart had pulled up right in front of Daphne's house and was completely blocking their view. Mrs Dawn's mind registered happy release from any further revelations. 'I think we'll go now, dear. At least you know for certain where your mother lives. Perhaps, one of these days, we'll share our little secret again and pop back to have another look.'

Inga's face fell a mile. An awful sense of panic rose within her. 'We haven't seen a thing, Mrs Dawn! Supposing it isn't even Mummy's house after all? Supposing you've made a mistake? Mummy might not live in a place like this.'

'I'm afraid she does, dear. I know for a fact it's the right house.'

The horse and cart began to move on. The thin little man in baggy trousers, torn jacket and flat cap was bawling out his message for 'any-ole-cloes' in strident high-pitched tones over the cobbles.

Inga threw caution to the winds and rushed across the road. Mrs Dawn followed her. Her temper rose dramatically. She knew they were already being viewed by a hundred pairs of concealed eyes.

Inga stood in front of the window and peered through. Her heart thumped fearfully. She half expected to see some witch of an old woman sitting there: the sort who worked on a street stall and smoked a white clay pipe; a dark figure in a thick, plaid shawl in a rocking chair with a gleaming black cat beside her, and a yard broom lying against a wall, rocking to and fro as she puffed at the brown stained-stem, with her toothless mouth below a hooked nose and fiery eyes.

The colour drained from Inga's face as sheer fright took over. Meanwhile, Mrs Dawn's face was colouring up to angry scarlet. 'Come away from that window, you silly girl!' Mrs Dawn stood on the pavement, a yard or two ahead, hissing back at her. 'Everyone'll be *watching*. I wish to heavens I'd never brought you.'

The moment Inga looked through the window properly, she knew it was her mother's room: there was Mummy's clock, from her bedroom at home. Hope and surprised joy flooded her whole being. There it was, exactly the same, with its shiny black marbled pillars on either side of the clock face! And on the wall was a framed sampler in cross-stitch which Mummy had done when she was about ten. It said 'A Lady Should Be Full Of Grace, In God's Sweet Realm To Take Her Place'. It was decorated with garden flowers, a bee, a butterfly and a bird.

Then, to her amazement, like something from a story book, the door of the room opened and in came a chubby little boy with thick wavy hair, wearing a very pale, rather posh, blue cotton suit with large pearl buttons fastening trousers to blouse, and topped by a long woolly fawn cardigan, and he was carrying a tattered stuffed toy horse.

Inga's heart overflowed with joy. It was true; It was *all* true . . . She turned away from the window and bellowed at the top of her voice, 'Mrs Dawn – Mrs Dawn, I've found him! I've found my hearth-brother at last . . .'

Cissie came hurrying to her and grabbed her hand forcefully. 'That's enough for one day, *madam*. We can't stay another second or the whole street'll be out to see what's going on.'

As they hurried away Inga pleaded and pleaded to return. 'If my hearth-brother's there, Mrs Dawn,

Mummy'll be there too. I wanted to see Mummy the most. Please, oh *please*, Mrs Dawn. Please let me see Mummy.' Her cheeks were crimson as she hurried along beside Mrs Dawn who was almost running.

'The sooner we're out of the way the better,' chuntered Cissie breathlessly, and the child is not your "hearth-brother".'

'He is, he is . . . Albert said so.' Inga pulled at Mrs Dawn's hand, to turn back, to try again, to actually knock at the door in Apple Street, but it was no use. The few amazing minutes had flown for ever and even the toy shop was no solace.

They were both silent on their way back to The Turrets. Mrs Dawn was regretting every moment of it. She must have been mad to have taken Inga there in the first place, she thought. By now, she had a doom-laden presentiment that the whole episode would turn into a sea of boiling repercussions, and the only one who could be blamed was herself.

She glanced sideways at Inga's solemn face as they travelled back. The child looked tired; there was a smudge of soot on her forehead and traces of sticky toffee round her mouth. 'As soon as we get in, go straight upstairs, wash your hands and face, and put some clean white socks on. All I hope is we're back before your grandmother. And whatever you do, don't breathe a word about going to Apple Street.'

Inga sat there like a small statue.

'Do you hear me? *Not a word* . . .'

Inga nodded faintly.

They hardly had been back at The Turrets for ten

minutes when Margot arrived back. She sensed there was something slightly wrong; there was an emptiness about the place as if it hadn't been used all morning. Usually Mrs Dawn was busy in the kitchen and the house was warmer and more noisy. Usually Inga was wandering around in her blue felt ankle strap slippers, or playing in the garden with a friend, in her wellingtons.

'Dinner won't be long,' said Mrs Dawn defensively.

'What sort of a morning have you had?' said Margot with idle suspicion. Then she added rather sharply, 'I noticed Inga had changed her socks.'

Mrs Dawn pretended not to hear at first. She took the slowly roasted meat from the oven and began to thicken all the fatty juices around it into brown gravy with a wooden spoon. Its warm, mollifying aroma soothed her. Then she said, 'So how did *your* morning go? Did old Mr Bakeup arrive for his soup? Folks do say he's a millionaire.'

Margot bridled slightly. 'That is *not* the point, Cissie. Ask and you shall receive is our motto, and who knows – he may well leave us something when he dies, for our Warm Welcome Saturday Club. But, from the way he gobbles down two helpings so religiously every Saturday, he might be with us for another twenty years.'

Cissie breathed a sign of relief. At least Margot had been sidetracked . . .

Weeks went by and October had coloured the trees to russet and scarlet. The leaves of lime trees were as pale as straw and some pure gold. Men with small deep-box hand barrows moved slowly along the roads around The

Turrets, sweeping up the leaves in the quiet autumn sunshine. Inga had turned twelve. Her birthday was as quiet as the grave. There was a half-term holiday at school.

Margot hadn't been quite so pushing with the music recently, mainly due to a warning from Dr Harmons. 'The child is getting stale; let her rest a bit. I get the impression these days that she has some deep worry . . .' He had looked at Margot shrewdly over the top of his glasses.

'I'm sure I can't think what it is,' countered Margot briskly. 'She has a life of perfect comfort and, bearing in mind that Christmas will soon be here, I hardly think she can afford to let things slip.' Margot fixed Dr Harmons with challenging eyes but he was unabashed.

'She is a young girl, Mrs Abbott. She needs to grow and expand in her own childhood. She is the type of child who, if you push her too much, will dissolve before she reaches maturity and never sing again. But if she rests a little she will blossom.'

Margot had never heard such nonsense in all her life. 'Of course, I do realise that you are a very experienced teacher, Dr Harmons, but I am the one who has to deal with her at the end of the day. And we both know of many famous singers who have been trained and trained from a very early age to become the worldwide stars of the present.'

Dr Harmons had shrugged his shoulders. He was never upset by bombastic overseers. 'I am not here to make stars, Mrs Abbott. I am here to help, encourage, and sometimes chivvy the talent that is already there.'

At half term, Inga was surprised to find that, for once, Grandma had not got the whole of her life mapped out with singing practice and afternoon performances for local ladies' circles.

'Perhaps the time has come for you to have a little rest, dear, especially after that traumatic epsiode at the Junior Rose Vase. I don't want you to get stale. After all, the singing itself is our main concern. It isn't just trying to be a top star, like some of these other ones seem to think. You need a bit of space to grow and develop as an ordinary schoolgirl.' Margot smiled at her brightly.

Inga smiled back in genuine amazement. What on earth had happened? 'Does that mean I've got the whole week of half term *free*, Grandma?'

Margot nodded hurriedly and left the room. But two seconds later she was back. 'By the way, dear. There doesn't happen to be anything *worrying* you, does there?'

'No, Grandma.' Inga frowned slightly. What on earth did she mean?

Margot gave a slight gulp of triumph. 'That's all right then.' She left the room, feeling completely at ease.

By now Inga was thinking deeply about why Grandma had asked her such a strange question. She had always been told in the past that little girls didn't suffer from 'nerves' or 'worries'. Those two ailments were adult territory. Because of this she didn't really know what they actually were, but she realised she would know when she was properly grown-up. Maybe Grandma thought that she was starting to get a bit grown-up now that she was twelve. It had brought good luck anyway . . .

She became wrapped in the pleasure of having a whole

free week to play with her friends, and dwell on the idea that had been haunting her ever since she went to Apple Street with Mrs Dawn. She would call back, on her own, to see her mother in secret. She would be able to plan it now, quite easily. She would pretend to be going round to play with Mary Mullins one morning, but really she would catch the tram into town. She would get a kitchen knife and rifle her money box which was in her bedroom; it was quite easy to do. A thrill of excitement ran through her.

By Tuesday morning she was all set to go, and luck was with her. Grandma was going to have her hair set, and she was taking Mrs Dawn with her to do some shopping. Albert had been left in charge of dealing with messages.

'You can go round to Mary's house this morning if you want,' said Margot. 'I had a word with her mother yesterday. But you aren't *forced* to go . . .' Margot was still suffering slight pangs of guilt from her bit of straight talk from Dr Harmons. 'The main thing is, during this week, to have a nice, restful, pleasant time playing with your friends.' Then she added ruthlessly, 'So as to be really up to scratch for all your future singing.'

Inga nodded dutifully. Inside she was flooded with excitement. Everything was prepared. Her best coat lay on the back of her bedroom chair, her new dark green beret and her woolly gloves were beside it. Her small leather purse had two half-crowns in it from her money box, and on the floor near her bed was a small carrier bag with her favourite teddy bear in it to lend to her 'hearth-brother'.

It was a slightly damp, misty morning when she set off, with signs of sunshine merging from higher skies. She ran and skipped her way along the leafy roads towards the trams which led to Manchester. Never once did she doubt that Mummy would be there to greet her.

'I want to go to Apple Street,' she said to the tram guard, handing him half a crown, imperiously. 'Please tell me when we get there.'

He nodded and took the money to put in his large flat leather money bag which hung across his chest from a shoulder strap. It had thick, well-worn leather divisions inside for coppers and silver. He smiled as he fished out the change. 'Goin' on 'oliday, love?'

'I'm going back to see my mother.' She beamed up at him and he winked.

'Been on 'oliday then, and going back? Right?'

She nodded happily. In a way that was what had happened: she and Mummy had been separated by a very, very long holiday . . .

'Apple Street.' His voice rang out loudly for her, as the red and cream-coloured tram clanked to a stop on its inset metal lines.

Old and young began to alight from the winding, cast-iron stair which led from the top deck. Others, down below, trailed slowly along the dark grey wooden ribbed floor with its scattering of old tram tickets.

'Apple Street is first one on the right, love,' called the ticket man cheerfully.

Inga jumped from the tram and stood there as it rattled away with its swift whirring sounds. Two women were about to shepherd an old blind man in a shabby suit and flat cap across the noisy, horse-ridden street. He had a white stick, and she joined them all: a small, hopeful, fresh-faced schoolgirl, sucked into the smelly, noisy city.

When she got to Apple Street, she stood there again in exactly the same place as she'd stood before with Mrs Dawn. This time there was no rag-and-bone cart blocking the view. It was perfectly quiet except for a man wearing a raincoat who had a bicycle with a carrier on it and was going from house to house. He was the sort of man Mrs Dawn always called the insurance man, or the rent collector.

Inga looked round. Were there really a hundred pairs of eyes watching her, like Mrs Dawn had said? Quickly she ran across to her mother's house, her heart beating with sudden fright. Please God and Jesus and all the angels in heaven, please let Mummy be in . . .

She knocked timidly at the door with her fist and, the moment she did so, the next door in the row of houses creaked open and a huge woman in a pinny, holding a doormat, greeted her. 'You'll not get any answer, love. They're out.' The woman began to bash the mat against the wall and clouds of dust rose.

Inga edged away from the dust. She stood there, suspended in time. She looked at the windows for a sign of movement inside her mother's house but there was nothing.

'Have you come far?' The woman eyed her briefly then sneezed once or twice. 'Shall I tell 'em you've called?' The woman gave the mat an extra thump against the wall as if to teach it a lesson for making her sneeze.

'I've come from Sale to see Mummy and my hearth-brother.'

The woman threw the mat inside hastily. She was now all ears. 'Are you little Ralphie's half-sister then?'

Inga was puzzled. She didn't understand . . . She wasn't used to big bossy charlady-people who scrubbed steps suddenly asking her strange questions.

'Are you that little girl who came once before with a lady, then went away again?'

Inga nodded.

'So Mrs Trent's your mother?'

Inga's face was a complete blank.

The woman, whose name was Mrs Collywood, tried again. 'Were you expecting them to be in?' Her sharp little eyes above the mound of pendulous double chin were soaking up every detail of the girl. Her ears, once the pink shells of love, before she went to waste, still worked exceedingly well.

'Mummy's not called Mrs Trent,' said Inga slowly. 'Her name is Mrs Abbott, and I'm Inga Abbott.'

'You'd better come in and wait for her,' said Mrs Collywood, bursting with secret curiosity. 'They should be back before dinner.'

Mrs Collywood went to wash her hands in her scullery. Inga followed her and watched. Mrs Collywood dried her hands on a shabby old towel then she looked on a small shelf in the back kitchen and lifted down a tall, scratched, slightly rusty-looking tin with a picture of King Edward the Seventh on it. Breathing heavily, she struggled to open the lid and produced some ancient gingerbreads.

Inga nibbled at one half-heartedly.

'It won't kill you, child!' said Mrs Collywood, sharply. She looked at the clock. 'They shouldn't be long; she usually goes to the fish stall on Tuesdays.' She looked down at Inga's brown carrier bag. 'What have you got in there, then?'

'It's one of my teddy bears – for my hearth-brother . . . for Ralphie.' She mouthed his name with careful pride.

Mrs Collywood shook her head. It was a rum do, she thought. She couldn't quite make head nor tail of it. There'd never been a whisper of any other child in the background of her next door. Though the tales about Mrs Trent's disappearing husband varied from his being sentenced to ten years' hard labour for secret robberies in a very posh area, to being sent abroad on a secret mission linked with cough mixture.

She went to her front door again and peered out anxiously. She hoped Daphne Trent and Ralphie would soon show up. She would be in a bit of a jam if she was landed with this unknown girl in her lap for too long. Her own family wouldn't be at all pleased. No proper jobs, any of 'em. Just standing at street ends talking to others and hoping to get enough for a pint of ale or a packet of cigarettes from scraps of casual labour. But lucky to be alive. Thank God, it hadn't quite got down to begging yet. Though her brother, who'd once played in a proper band, was already trailing the streets in a small weary group with other Great War veterans, playing from the gutters to the theatre queues, in the centre of Manchester. A couple of trumpets, a clarinet, a mouth organ, and a concertina – their only means of subsistence. She could just see the looks of her sons if they came back and found this rich waif sitting here eating all the food.

Mrs Collywood went into the street and shaded her eyes with a plump hand. Her mournful expression dissolved into profound relief as she saw Daphne and Ralphie coming round the corner into Apple Street. 'Yoo-hoo . . .' Her hoarse tones crackled as she stood half in the road and waved towards them madly.

Daphne saw her and waved back slightly. What on earth was Christabel Collywood up to, standing there in that awful pinny and her hair for ever in rag curlers? Why all the fuss? Usually it was hard to get even a mutter out of her, though she had given Ralphie a halfpenny chocolate bar in a small, crumpled white paper bag on his last birthday.

Mrs Collywood hurried towards them now. 'I thought I'd better just warn you, Mrs Trent – you've got a young visitor and she's in my front room. She's come from Sale to see you and she says her name's Inga Abbott. I thought it was best to say . . .'

Daphne stood stock still. Inga – here? On her own! She felt quite weak. 'Thank you for letting me know, Mrs Collywood.' She began to hurry towards home in a nervous daze. Her mind was in a whirl of what to do next as Ralphie trotted beside her.

She opened her front door. She stood for a minute, in a flood of panic. She walked into the front room and glanced round at all the small items left from her days when she had lived at The Turrets. Then, with trembling hands, she took off her outdoor things and removed Ralphie's little blue coat. She stood uncertainly.

How was she going to deal with a young daughter she hadn't seen for over five years – except by accident on some rare occasions in the distance? A child who was fast becoming a proper schoolgirl, living in an entirely different setting to herself and Ralphie? And what on earth was Inga doing here on her own? Daphne knew for certain that Margot would never have allowed it. There must be something terribly, terribly wrong . . . She braced herself, then, taking a small box of wooden farm animals from her shopping bag, she handed it to Ralphie. 'You can have the toys to play with for a while, Ralphie. I just want to go next door to Mrs Collywood's. You stay here – there's a good boy . . .'

Ralphie looked at her in amazement. 'But I thought these farm ones were for Billy Swanson's birthday present, Mam. To take to him this afternoon.'

Billy Swanson was now his best friend. Billy Swanson's mother sold dress material on all the markets, and Mam said they had a lot of money. She was Mam's best friend, now.

'We'll get him something else, on the way there. One of those chocolate pipe-smokers' selection sets – with the toffee cigars and sugar cigarettes.' Daphne hurried from the house and went next door.

Mrs Collywood's front door was wide open. 'Come in, Mrs Trent. I'll just make a pot of tea.'

'Please don't,' said Daphne, quickly. 'I mustn't leave Ralphie on his own. He gets up to all sorts, and we're going out again soon.' Daphne stared at her daughter like someone seeing a ghost: the neat tailored coat and green beret; the expensive shoes; the well-cut hair; the perfectly shaped eyebrows and large, bright eyes. She was standing there, clutching a bag with a teddy bear poking out of it.

'Mummy! Mummy!' Inga's eyes flooded with tears. She dropped the bag and rushed to her mother, flinging herself against Daphne's body. 'Mummy, I've come to live with you and Ralphie. I want to live with you for ever and ever. I never want to go back to Grandma's again.'

Mrs Collywood stood in the background, looking on.

'There, there . . .' said Daphne in total confusion, as they huggged each other. She turned to Mrs Collywood. 'Thank you ever so much for looking after her. We'd better get back to Ralphie. I do appreciate your kindness . . .'

'That's all right, love,' said Mrs Collywood blandly. 'Just let me know if there's anything else you want. I'm always here to turn to.'

When they'd gone Mrs Collywood sat down with a cup of tea and went over the whole incident in her mind from start to finish. What a nice day, she thought, better than fights and brawls. It was pleasant to have ladylike people living next door. What complicated lives the better off ones had . . .

She would go out in a bit and look in Annie's secondhand clothes yard for a good-quality felt hat, like these smart ones wore, p'raps with a pheasant's feather stuck in it. She heard the door next door bang to in a sudden breeze and sat back comfortably to wait for the next instalment.

Next door, Daphne, Inga and Ralphie were all standing there looking at each other. Inga bent down and took the teddy bear out of the bag. She handed it to

Ralphie. 'Here you are, Ralphie. I brought him specially to lend to you. His name's Augustus, but I call him Guggles.' Her face was wreathed in smiles of happiness.

7

THIS WAY AND THAT

'I want Inga to come with me to Billy's, Mam . . .'

'I'm afraid she won't be able to, Ralphie. She has to go back to her own home . . .' Daphne was in a turmoil of shock and panic. It was as if Inga wasn't her own daughter at all. All Daphne knew was that she would not be able to think straight until Inga was back at The Turrets where she was supposed to be. And after that? Well, she, Daphne Abbott – Inga's mother – and she, Daphne Trent – Ralphie's mother – would have to try and work something out. Perhaps Inga would be able to visit herself and Ralphie occasionally . . .

But all along, she knew deep down there was still the proper hurdle: the ultimate, awful confrontation with her mother-in-law, Margot.

'Inga never wants to go home again, Mam. She wants to stay with me for ever and play with the teddy bears.' Ralphie's mouth was set firmly into petulance. 'And

I don't want to go to Billy's birthday now, Mam. I want to stay and play with Inga.' His eyes were full of challenge.

Daphne's temper flared. 'Inga's too big to play with teddy bears, and you're going to Billy's whether you like it or not. Inga can come with us to the door. Then I shall take her home whilst you are at Billy's, and call back for you. You'll be able to see Inga another day . . .' Daphne turned to her daughter. 'We'll make some arrangements . . .'

Inga nodded miserably. She was already slightly disappointed with her mother. Why on earth couldn't she stay with them for ever instead of going back to Grandma's?

Ralphie's bedroom had a folding camp bed in it, and Ralphie seemed to like her, even though she could see now he was rather bossy and spoilt. But all the same he was her hearth-brother and it was better to have a hearth-brother than being on her own all the time. And it was far, far better to have Mummy back than anything else in the world.

The best thing would be for Grandma to live in Apple Street and for her and Mummy and Ralphie all to go and live at The Turrets with Mrs Dawn and Albert. But she knew it would never be like that because Grandma only liked very big houses, and Apple Street was far too small.

All three of them walked along in silence now to Billy's. Billy's was a big house on the corner of a busy road. There was a small green motor coach in the driveway with 'Swanson's Silks and Satins' written on the side of it.

They climbed the stone steps to the front door of the double-fronted, smoke-blackened Victorian Gothic brick mansion, with its pointed arch windows: Holly House, 3 Barlow New Road.

As soon as the front door opened Inga could see lots of other little children in the background with party clothes on, playing about with balloons and making a terrible din.

'This is Ralphie Trent,' said Daphne, with hurried apologies to the maid standing there in her black afternoon dress and pleated white headband. 'I'm afraid I have to rush away to take this little friend of ours back home, but could you please tell Mrs Swanson I will try to be back on time to collect Ralphie – but to hold on to him till I arrive . . .'

Hardly had she finished the long-winded instructions when Vinny Swanson herself pushed forward to the front door, dressed in a maroon, crushed-silk velvet knee-length frock with a lampshade fringe around its hemline. She was swamped in loops of pearl beads. 'Don't worry, Daphne, dear. He'll be fine. His little friend can come to the party as well if you want. We've got twenty-four of them altogether, and another one will just add to all the fun whilst we're waiting for the Magic Man.' She smiled at Inga as she spoke to Daphne. 'Has Ralphie's friend got far to go?'

Inga stared at Mrs Swanson. 'He's my hearth-brother,' she said proudly. 'Mummy wants to take me back to Grandma's again, but I'd sooner stay with Ralphie and her, and come to your party.'

Daphne blushed to the roots of her hair and grabbed

Inga's hand. 'It's all rather complicated, Vinny. I'm afraid I'll have to dash . . .'

Vinny Swanson smiled and turned away slightly. She'd hardly heard a word; other people's worlds were far too much to bother about. All she was praying for was that the conjurer was a good one.

'Do you think I could just use your telephone, Vinny, to get in touch with Inga's grandmother, before we go?'

'Of course you can, dear. You know where it is, don't you? In the hall vestibule.' Vinny hurried away, surrounded by popping balloons.

'Disappeared?' Margot Abbott was simmering with fury. 'How can she possibly have disapppeared, Albert?'

'Don't ask me,' muttered Albert truculently. 'She has. And that's all there is to it. I'm not a nursemaid and you all knows it.'

Margot had returned from having her hair set. She was in a bad temper. In the hairdressing salon, the hair dryer had been set far too hot, and every time she called out no one had seemed to hear her.

Mrs Dawn wasn't making things any better either. She seemed to have gone all to pieces. 'That lost child must be wearing her best coat and that green beret, Mrs Abbott. There isn't a sign of them. She never goes out to play in her best clothes . . .'

Mrs Dawn became more and more nervous as Margot became more and more irate. Dinner time came and went with never a sign of Inga. There was one tiny seed of fear lurking in Mrs Dawn's sharp mind. Supposing Inga had decided to go back to Apple Street on her own?

Later that afternoon, just as dusk was setting in and Margot had phoned up everywhere she could think of and was planning to get in touch with the police, she received the phone call from Daphne, with a lot of noise going on in the background.

At first she had no idea at all who it was except that the voice was familiar.

'Is that Margot?'

'Yes.' Margot answered with puzzled caution.

'This is Daphne. I've got Inga here and I'm just setting off to bring her back to you. She visited us today, in Apple Street.' The phone clicked, and there was silence.

Margot replaced her own telephone receiver in stunned silence. How on earth had Inga got round there? She had purposely kept the whole ghastly story about her mother a complete secret from her. What the head didn't know, the heart didn't grieve over . . .

She went to find Mrs Dawn, and as she walked into the kitchen her temper began to rocket, fuelled by a mixture of fear and anger, as some of the implications surfaced in her unwilling brain.

Mrs Dawn was pouring Albert a mug of tea.

Margot stared at them both, defensively. 'I've just had a phone call to say that Inga is safe and well.'

'That's good news,' said Albert evenly. 'Where is she?'

Margot hesitated. 'She went to see her mother.'

'That's good news.'

'Daphne is bringing her back . . .'

Albert sipped his tea, and Mrs Dawn asked Margot if she would like a cup.

Margot ignored her. 'When Inga returns, the least said about all this the better.' Margot swept out of the kitchen.

'God knows what'll happen now,' said Mrs Dawn gloomily when she'd gone. 'Between the pair of them, that poor girl's being knocked from pillar to post, to suit their whims . . . Her own mother won't ever want her back now; Daphne'll have enough on her plate with the other child, what with Osmond sailing back into port to dock with Maud again.

'Daphne'll not be able to support two children, the way she's been left. She's not the type. Not like you and me who's come from large families where we was all used to scraping.'

Albert supped his tea and stared silently into space.

'And as for Margot, I can't see her letting go of Inga, what with all that there music bug. Margot always was a one for playing the fiddler's tune and everyone dancing round her. She'd be completely lost now without the child to hang on to. All I can say is, the sooner Inga's grown up and able to escape from all of 'em, the better . . . providing it's not out of the frying pan into the fire . . .'

Albert finished off his mug of tea and wiped his mouth on his hanky without a single word. Then he packed up and went home. He lived in a small cottage nearby with his wife. He'd lost two sons in the last war, he had a daughter who was married and lived in Canada, and his wife, Lottie, was deaf and suffered from arthritis.

Margot paced the drawing room like a caged animal. Where on earth were they? It was getting quite dark. Then suddenly the doorbell rang. Both she and Mrs Dawn rushed out of different doors at the same time to answer it, with Mrs Dawn slipping back into the kitchen, biting her thumbnail apprehensively.

Margot took a deep breath and swung open the front door with purposeful aplomb. 'At last! Where on earth have you *been*?'

Inga looked at her meekly. She was standing close to Daphne, with the empty carrier bag hanging from her wrist.

'She came to see us, all on her own,' said Daphne, in tones full of meaning. 'I was very surprised. If it hadn't been for one of my neighbours looking after her I don't know what might have happened. I was out with my son, Ralph.'

Daphne faced Margot with a deliberately frosty, distant look. She was surprised how much Margot seemed to have aged. She no longer felt afraid of her. She almost wondered why she had left The Turrets in the first place and was living in such an awful place as Apple Street. It seemed quite shameful that Margot now had all this vast house to herself, plus Daphne's own small daughter to keep her company, whilst she herself was living in penury with Ralphie. What a fool she'd been to rush off in the first place, considering how life had all worked out, thought Daphne wistfully.

They followed Margot inside.

'I'll get Mrs Dawn to bring us some tea and scones.' Then, turning to Inga, Margot said abruptly, 'Mrs Dawn will bring yours up to your bedroom, Inga. You can get up there straight away. You've caused enough trouble for one day.' Her grandmother's eyes pierced her like steel.

Inga fled from the room. She lay on her own bed and sobbed as if her heart would break, and when Mrs Dawn brought the drink she turned her face away and hid under the eiderdown. How could her own mother have been so cruel as to bring her back here and then go and leave her again?

A strange cold feeling she had never felt in her life before rose within her. Did it mean that nobody really loved her? That she was all on her own except for Mrs Dawn and Albert? Did it mean that from now on and for ever she would have to look after herself and could never expect anyone else to really care for her? She knew quite well already that Grandma only cared for her singing voice and not truly for her alone. It was also plain that Mummy only cared for her hearth-brother, Ralphie. If Mummy had really loved her she would have let her go to that party Ralphie was going to. She would have allowed her to stay the night at Apple Street in the camp bed.

Inga gave a last violent sob, and fell fast asleep.

Downstairs in the drawing room, Margot and Daphne were trying to come to terms with each other. It was extremely difficult because Margot had no intention of giving way one inch. She knew full well that to do so could wreck her own well-planned life in seconds.

Ever since Daphne had abandoned Inga and had run off with Osmond Beardsley, Margot had sworn never to forgive her. It was an insult to the name of Abbott and to her dead son, Tarvin, killed in that terrible war. Sometimes as she looked back she even surmised what an awful life he might have had living with a woman who was fickle enough to abandon his child and run off with another man.

Well, at least she had been able to save *that* day . . . At least the child was being properly brought up and was being trained to take her place in a civilised world. It would be a disaster now if Daphne suddenly wanted her back. All that voice training would be completely wasted.

Ever since her own children were born Margot had longed to produce a singer in the family. Her four daughters had shown no talent for that sort of thing whatsoever. But Tarvin, her one and only adored son, had almost fulfilled her dreams. He had been accepted for the cathedral choir when he was very young but his promise had all faded away due to a near-fatal attack of diphtheria. Then, when Inga was born and Tarvin was lost, it was like a second chance to renew Margot's personal family dream.

Daphne sat there politely chewing at a scone, and averting her eyes. The scone rolled round her mouth like gravel as she waited for Margot to make the first move. She was filled with a sense of hopeless fate. She had no idea what to do except to suggest that Inga should come and see her and Ralphie sometimes. She knew Margot far too well to imagine that she would ever let Inga go. She herself had been in that trap when she had lived here – lulled by all its comfort and the heavy presence of a mother-in-law who held all the purse strings. It had come home to her only recently that, if Osmond hadn't been an older man with an assured aura of confidence and financial prosperity, she might not have gone with him at all.

Often she sat alone in Apple Street when Ralphie was asleep upstairs in bed and imagined what would have happened if Ralphie had been born at The Turrets. Somehow she knew that Margot would never actually have turfed her out, because of Inga being Tarvin's child.

Daphne was the first one to speak. 'I shall have to go soon. Ralphie has gone to a party and I have to collect him.'

'Is it in your street?' Margot looked at her with a faint flicker of cattiness.

Daphne ignored the jab. 'Perhaps Inga could come and see us sometimes. Ralphie would love it.'

It was Margot's turn to be silent. Then, like the stab of an icicle, she said, 'You'll never get her back. She's used to better than you can provide. I owe it to the memory of her dead father. What you do with your illegitimate offspring is entirely your own affair.'

The meeting came to a sudden end as Daphne stood up and Margot showed her out to the front door.

The next morning when Inga was having her breakfast, her grandmother said, 'How on earth did you manage to find out where you mother lived?'

'I just *knew*, Grandma . . .' Inga stuffed her mouth with porridge and the milk dribbled down her chin. She began to eat very quickly so that her mouth was always full – Grandma insisted she should never speak with her mouth full.

'How could you possibly just "know"?' Margot glared at her. 'Someone must have told you how to get there.'

'The man on the tram told me.' Inga pushed a big piece

of toast into her mouth, but when it was finished she couldn't resist talking again, to rest her jaws from the toast. 'It was lovely seeing my hearth-brother . . . but I love Mummy best. Could Mummy and Ralphie come and live here?'

There was silence.

'Grandma?'

'What?' Margot scowled.

'*Could* they? I'm sure they'd like it.'

Margot looked at her through narrowed eyes. 'What did you call Ralphie? A *hearth*-brother? What on earth's that? Surely you know how to speak correctly, after all the time I've spent with you, pronouncing words. What you really mean is *half*-brother. There is no such thing as a *hearth-brother*.'

'Albert says there is, and Mrs Phelps and Mrs Dawn. Mrs Dawn once took me to see where he lived and I caught a glimpse of him . . .'

Margot could hardly credit her ears. She began to tremble with rage. 'Do you mean to say that *Mrs Dawn actually took you to Apple Street*? It's almost unbelievable!'

Inga's head drooped with shame.

'Ask Mrs Dawn to come here immediately. And *you*, you can go up to your bedroom and stay there until I tell you to come down!'

Inga hurried from the room like a startled rabbit as she went to find Mrs Dawn. For once she was glad to be banished to her room. She dreaded what might happen now between Mrs Dawn and Grandma.

Mrs Dawn was sitting at the kitchen table writing in the groceries order book. She looked up calmly. 'What is it?'

'Grandma wants to see you in the breakfast room.'

'Is it about you going to see your mother?'

'It might be . . .' Suddenly Inga's face crumpled into tears and she began to weep. 'She knows we went to see Mummy and Ralphie. I've to go to my bedroom and stay there.'

'Don't worry, child. It's not your fault. I'll deal with it.' Mrs Dawn looked unperturbed as Inga left her and scuttled upstairs, but inside Cissie Dawn was quaking with a mixture of annoyance, pride and a sense of injustice. She was heartily fed up with Margot and all this present trouble. If people had been straight with Inga in the first place it wouldn't have come to this.

She closed the order book, got up and went to the outside W.C. She came back and washed her hands and face, carefully, in the scullery. Then, after looking at herself grimly in the small cracked mirror, she went to see Margot, taking a tray with her to clear the pots at the same time.

Margot was still sitting at the breakfast table with the tea-cosied teapot in front of her. She was pretending to read the Manchester *Guardian*. She looked up at Mrs Dawn through her reading glasses, then deliberately pretended to read a few more lines, to make Mrs Dawn stand there. She looked up again. 'What's all this I hear, about your taking Inga to Apple Street, Mrs Dawn – to show her where Daphne lives with her illegitimate child?' Margot's bodice was moving up and down with every frenzied breath.

Mrs Dawn sucked her lips against her teeth, and stood there in stubborn silence.

'I'm waiting for a reply.' Margot cooled down and looked at her like a lean cat with a trapped bird, but Mrs Dawn was more of a domestic fowl, and didn't intend to be trapped. She gave a huge disparaging sniff and fluffed her shoulders about.

'I'm absolutely flabbergasted by it all!' said Margot. She pushed the morning paper away, dramatically. Even that hadn't been to her liking this morning, it was getting far too liberal. She was thinking of going back to the *Daily Mail*, it was a firm, reassuring paper. 'That you, Mrs Dawn, a domestic employee in my establishment, should take it upon yourself to interfere in my personal affairs, wholly against my wishes. Apart from that, surely you can see all the terrible trauma and heartbreak you have caused?'

She'd caused? Cissie had never heard the likes of it. Over five years of deception, and she was being blamed. Just wait till she told Albert that one . . .

'I would never have dreamed, in all my born days, you to be so disloyal.'

Mrs Dawn walked forward to the table without a word and began to clear the dishes on to the tray.

'You can just stop doing that.' Margot stood up haughtily with blotches of red glowing feverishly on her cheeks. 'You are *sacked*! Go and get your coat and *leave*!'

Slowly, Mrs Dawn stopped piling up the pots. She left the wooden tray where it was on the table, turned

silently, and walked with dignified funereal steps from
the breakfast room back to the kitchen. Then she took
the order book from the table, threw it across the floor,
put on her hat and coat and went home.

8

GENTLEMAN FRIEND

1928

'To think, you were only just twelve when Margot gave me the sack,' said Mrs Dawn to Inga in quiet triumph. 'I nearly took her at her word. It was you as made me come back when she changed her mind a week later. I've never seen such pleading from her, before or since. But all the same, she never put my wages up, or apologised.

'Three years ago to the month, and I'm still here. The only thing that's changed is your mother being allowed to visit you and bring Ralphie. He's a bonny lad for a seven-year-old, isn't he? You were a mere wisp at his age.'

Inga sat on the scarlet-cushioned kitchen chair near the table, hugging a hot water bottle to her groins. She was always the same when the monthly curse started. Sometimes the gripes were so bad she had to take an aspirin and go to bed with a glass of hot milk.

It was funny how Mrs Dawn didn't seem to think much

had altered. Nearly everything had changed for herself except living here. She had left school in the summer and was working at Mrs Marsden's knitting wool shop in School Road but, most of all, she was in love with a man of twenty-five.

Grandma hadn't changed though. She was in the drawing room this very minute, talking to her friend Shelma Dayton.

'Fifteen, did you say?' Shelma gave Margot an old-fashioned look. 'And hasn't she got even one solitary boyfriend?'

Margot shook her head vehemently. 'She has more to do in her life than that, Shelma. Her singing is her *all*. She works in Hetty Marsden's wool shop and Hetty allows her all the time off in the world to get on with her proper profession. Hetty's mother was once a singer.'

Shelma raised her eyebrows. 'What marvellous luck . . .'

Shelma Dayton had been abroad in Singapore for ten years, but had returned home a rich woman when her husband died. She had since remarried. She was a couple of years younger than Margot and had been at school with her, together with Mabel Spinks who was now fifty-six. Margot was sixty-three and the eldest of the trio. She had kept in touch with Mabel ever since they'd caught up with each other that awful time in Blackpool at the Junior Rose Vase. In fact she was with Mabel when they met Shelma quite by chance at the Warm Welcome Saturday Club – dishing out the soup, over two years ago. It was like a reuniting of lost souls.

'I had many a beau at Inga's age,' said Shelma, 'but it was all strictly chaperoned.'

'The Great War changed all that,' said Margot, suddenly looking bleak.

'And is her mother still living in that awful place in town with Osmond's offspring?' Shelma's bottom lip tilted to a slow grimace. 'I heard only the other day he's had another heart attack but his wife, Maud, is going from strength to strength . . . Thank goodness I never had any children. Maud and I have that same advantage.' She stared idly at Margot. 'Not like you — tied by four grown-up daughters with hordes of their own, and Inga round your neck.'

Margot felt a sharp jab of indignant anger. 'It's not like that at all, Shelma,' she said reprovingly. 'All my daughters are down south. We never worry one another, and I hardly ever see their children. I don't think Inga realises she has all those cousins. She means more to me than any of them. It's been like bringing up another late child of my own, and doing it exactly how I wanted to. I expect, in a strange sort of way, I have Daphne to thank for that.'

'What on earth does Daphne do with herself, living in Apple Street?' said Shelma languidly.

'She's in business now with a friend of hers called Vinny Swanson of Swanson's Silks and Satins. She's making enough out of it to be able to send Ralphie to a private prep school shortly, before he starts at Manchester Grammar.' Margot frowned. 'I expect she's bettered herself, really. I would never have imagined her being up to that when she lived here with me.'

'Does she still call herself Mrs Trent?'

'Probably. And it's a blessing as far as I'm concerned.'

'Do you think Osmond will leave them anything when he dies?' Shelma narrowed her eyes hopefully; money was her favourite subject. 'After all, it is his son, and they did live as man and wife.'

'Not him! Not now he's back with Maud. He wouldn't dare. He ignores Ralphie completely. According to Mrs Dawn's friend, Mrs Phelps, he's already had trouble over another child by a servant girl who once worked for them, but she kicked up such a stink she gets a sworn monthly sum from him until that child reaches fourteen.' Margot sighed deeply. 'All one can say is that Osmond's adventures have ceased dramatically these days. Mrs Dawn says he spends his time listening to his wireless set and tottering to the Liberal Club.'

Inga retired to her bedroom at last, still hugging the hot water bottle, and Mrs Dawn brought her a hot drink.

'You'll be as right as rain in another hour, lovey. It takes womenfolk all sorts of ways. Sometimes they has to go through actual childbirth before it disappears proper.'

Inga looked at her, aghast. 'Don't say that . . . surely it won't go on for years and years? And supposing I don't want any babies? I don't even want to get married till I'm thirty . . .'

Mrs Dawn gave her a strange, consoling look. What it was to be that age and so innocent.

Mrs Dawn was right. An hour later the pains faded as Inga lay there, warm and reassured, dreaming idly of Dermot Farthingale, the wool salesman from Bradford who had told her to call him Dobbin.

'Dobbin?' She had gazed up at the alert, teasing grey eyes suspiciously. 'D-dobbin? Surely that's a name for a horse?'

He had looked back solemnly. 'It's a horse I am, carting all this stuff round every day to shops like this. And you the only beautiful young lady in all my travels to lighten the load and cheer me on my way. Every time I get to Sale, I say to myself: soon, soon I shall be reaching Hetty Marsden's where the light of my life will greet me.'

Their eyes had met in a sudden glow of total brilliance and she knew it was this thing called love. It was the forceful vivid firing of an untried Roman candle from the flame of a handsome, smoothly waxed taper: the preview to a panoply of a million silver stars . . . and they would live together for evermore in a mansion with a shining copper dome . . .

'Alas, Dobbin is my true name and Dobbin it will always be.' His soft, honeyed tones lapped over her.

Dermot 'Dobbin' Farthingale fixed her with a gaze of rapture, omitting to say that the reason he was called Dobbin by all his friends was because his main interest was betting on horses.

In her spare moments, when the shop was empty and at home at The Turrets when she needed a bit of comfort, she dreamed of Dobbin, but when she met him he was always Mr Farthingale, the traveller. It was exactly five commercial traveller visits ago that he had invaded Inga's heart, and now she dreamed in all her spare moments of this tall, dark stranger with his well-shaven face, his beautifully cut, amazingly light, grey striped suit, and his spats. He looked almost as if he wasn't visiting wool shops at all, but constantly going to weddings – with that small rosebud in his buttonhole. His next visit was due in a week's time . . .

That following week, fortunately or unfortunately, Hetty Marsden had to go into Manchester.

'I shall only be away for a couple of hours, love, so you'll be completely on your own. If, by some chance, an emergency happened that you couldn't cope with, just pull the door blind down, lock the shop door and put the CLOSED sign in the window. I don't suppose you'll ever need to do it in a month of Sundays but it's always best to know what you're about. Robbers and rogues must forever be taken into consideration.'

Plump little Hetty stood there mentally checking through everything before she set off. 'Oh, and if Mr Farthingale happens to arrive in the morning instead of this afternoon, get twelve more sets of number thirteen steel knitting needles and fifty hanks of the pink and the blue baby wool that I had the last time.'

Inga nodded dutifully. Her whole being quivered even at the mention of Dermot Farthingale's name these days. She just felt like lying on Hetty's chaise longue, in her back parlour, and swooning away in pale dreamy splendour. But it was her deep, deep secret and she hid it completely whenever Hetty mentioned him. And that was quite often, as Hetty was intrigued by what she called his devil-may-care attitude – even when she complained about some wool he'd once left them with thin strands in it that had to be sent back. Oh if only, if only he would call this very morning – whilst Hetty was away in town . . .

To her amazement, like some divine bolt from heaven, her wish came true about half an hour after Hetty had set off. The little shop was as friendly as a silk and wool padded cocoon. The small bell on the door tinkled and in he walked, bending his head slightly to miss the low wooden beam.

Inga felt the blood rushing to her face. For a second, because of her shyness, she was flooded with panic; all she wanted was to escape, to turn away and rush through the back door, never to return. But instead she was rooted to the spot behind the counter, with some knitting patterns in her hand, wearing her blue silk crêpe-de-Chine smock, with its white polka dots, her whole being as pink as boiled shrimps.

'What a wonderful day,' smiled Dermot Farthingale, shrugging his broad shoulders beneath his Burberry raincoat, and removing his trilby.

He stamped his feet on the doormat and stood there with his black umbrella dripping. 'That's a bit of a lie really, isn't it? It's a hell of a day: gales blowing slates off roof; newspapers landing in trees and, to cap it all, I've just trodden in a huge gutter overflow and drenched my feet.' He came over to the counter. 'Could you lend me a duster or something to wipe my dispatch case?'

'Yes, yes of course . . .' Inga came to life and hunted quickly beneath the counter for a clean duster.

It was strange how different things seemed when she wasn't actually dreaming about them. Now that Mr Farthingale was here, in all his rain-washed flesh, he seemed sort of untouchable and matter-of-fact. It was usually when he was leaving the shop after a visit and made some small joke and smiled at her that the dream would grow enough to carry her on to his next visit and add fuel to her dreams of love.

She stood up straight again, holding the pale, cleanly laundered duster in her hand, and was almost shocked to find how close Mr Farthingale was now, as he stood beside her. She could actually feel his heavy breathing fanning her ear and, as she turned with the duster, he plonked a warm, fruity kiss straight on to her mouth, then caught her in an iron-like embrace which almost deflated her to a squashed sardine.

'I have been waiting for this,' he murmured huskily.

Suddenly, a bit too late, it dawned on her that this was not how a proper gentleman, let alone the man of her dreams, should behave. She began to push at him, to try to escape, but she was no match for him once she was in this belly to breast contact. His mouth had left her lips and he was actually biting her neck. Horrific thoughts of Dracula rose within her.

She began to panic. She prayed for the shop bell to halt it all. She asked God to send in Mrs Watkins, who weighed fifteen stone and carried a heavy gnarled walking stick. Come this instant, Mrs Watkins, and order your weekly ounce of angora wool, she prayed.

'I want you to be my regular woman,' groaned Dermot Farthingale in a hoarse voice cracking with heavy emotion. 'I've always wanted it since the moment I first saw you.' He tried to bite her neck again but at last she had come to her senses: she struggled and flayed and kicked. She shrieked in his ears.

'Leave me alone, you horrible, *horrible* man, and never come to this shop again!'

His hands fell to his sides and in seconds he had removed himself, complete with all his belongings, and had vanished.

Hurriedly, Inga pulled down the door blind, locked the door and put the CLOSED sign in the window. Then, breathing heavily from shock and anger, she went to give her face and neck a thorough wash and attempt to calm herself down.

The cheek of him, to call her a 'woman' in the first place; surely he knew she was either a young lady or a schoolgirl? The way he'd mentioned her being his 'woman' sounded as if she was going to be his weekly charlady. And as for trying to bite her neck, it made her feel as if she was being mauled by an animal.

After washing her hands and face, she carefully began to comb her ruffled hair. Suddenly she felt unspeakably sad as two huge tears rolled down her cheeks. It was the complete end to her beautiful dreams. How could she ever trust another man ever again? How could she ever mention with pride that she had clicked with someone who desired to spoon with her? Spoon, beneath the light of the silvery moon . . . like they did in songs. Not *this* . . . This being attacked by a savage who wanted to eat her and had almost made a meal of her neck, which at present looked quite unsettled and blotchy.

She walked slowly to the front door of the shop, put the blind up again and removed the CLOSED sign from the window. And not a moment too soon, as the woman she had prayed for earlier suddenly appeared with her gnarled walking stick.

'I'll 'ave my ounce of angora please, Inga.' Mrs Watkins sat down on the brown bentwood chair by the shop counter. ''Ow come you was closed earlier on?'

'C-closed . . . Oh – *that* . . .' Inga tried to keep calm. She found the wool quickly and concentrated on wrapping it up very carefully. 'I've always liked angora, Mrs Watkins. I can remember having a very pretty little cardigan my grandma once bought me when I was little . . .'

'Yes,' said Mrs Watkins with stout perseverence. 'It was just after that traveller had been. I was across at the cake shop, talking, and we saw the CLOSED notice put up – otherwise I'd have come a bit earlier.' Mrs Watkins began to open her voluminous black crocheted handbag and hunt for her thick black leather wrapover purse with its silvery metal clasp worn down to brass.

Inga shivered slightly with relief as she took the money and gave Mrs Watkins her change. At least she hadn't had to explain . . .

Then, just as Mrs Watkins was grunting and chuffing her way out of the shop, Hetty appeared. She stood back on the pavement, smiling politely, to let Mrs Watkins get out.

'I was just asking Inga why the shop was closed up whilst the traveller was 'ere,' said Mrs Watkins with a voice like a foghorn, her head bowed away from any confrontation, as she began to shuffle away with her stick.

Hetty walked into the shop, frowning slightly. 'What

on earth was Mrs Watkins babbling on about, Inga? Something about the shop being shut? Surely not. I almost *thought* I heard her say it was shut whilst the traveller was here.'

'She was wrong. I swear to you on my honour the shop was not closed when the traveller was here.' Inga went scarlet.

Hetty stared at her. She was slightly shocked to see such a violently defensive reaction to her queries. And why was the child (for that was all she was in Hetty's eyes) looking so terribly guilty?

'There's no need to be so upset, Inga. I was just surprised to hear Mrs Watkins saying the shop had been closed at all.'

'Well, I can assure you, Hetty, that it was *not* closed when Mr Farthingale was here. She was completely mistaken.'

There was an awkward silence between them for a while but gradually it eased off during the day as the customers came and went. Even so, Hetty felt there must be something Inga was not telling her, but she decided to let sleeping dogs lie. Inga was a capable, hard-working assistant and Hetty's own arrangement with Margot about employing her worked out very well. In return for Inga having time off for her musical activities, Hetty didn't have to pay her as much as she would have done for a more regular employee. It was the difference between nearly three shillings a week for an older, more experienced full-time person, to one shilling and ninepence halfpenny.

All the way home that day, Inga went over what Mr

Farthingale had done . . . How could she ever have been so stupid as to worship him? Why was nothing ever quite what it seemed? How could she ever face him again? How could she go and work in that shop, knowing that one day the bell would ring and in he'd come?

But there again, if she complained to Grandma and said she didn't want to go there any more, there would be an awful fuss and Grandma would be sure to prise the reason from her. Then Hetty would get to know and she might accuse Mr Farthingale, who would deny it. And Hetty might never get wool from him again – especially Mrs Watkins's angora. It would all be such a terrible muddle. And every single person would blame her . . .

But worse than all of that, she would be left at home with Grandma, and Grandma would step up her singing practice, and send her out to more afternoon performances in front of ladies with chins covered in cream cake who stared at her very hard then muttered between themselves and ignored her, except to say that one fine day she might become a proper singer. Yes, that would be her sorted out and completely forgotten as they all talked about who was going to entertain them the next time. And another thing – she would get not one smattering of pocket money from now on. Oh yes . . . she knew exactly how it would be.

She had just reached the broad drive of The Turrets when she stopped. The best thing to do would be to go somewhere right now and try and find another job before any fuss started. Perhaps her mother would be able to take her on. She began to run full pelt to the kitchen to tell Mrs Dawn what she was going to do.

Mrs Dawn groaned inwardly. She stopped peeling some carrots for the evening meal. 'I wouldn't be too hasty, dear. Whatever's made you want to leave there so sudden? I thought you loved every minute of it. At one time you just couldn't wait to rush out of this house to get there.'

'It's quite boring sometimes, Mrs Dawn, and I do miss Mummy.' Inga began to take off her coat and hat carelessly, to hide her embarrassment. 'It was just that I thought that with Mummy having her friend who works with all the silks and satins they might be able to fit me into it.'

Mrs Dawn put down her knife and shook her head slowly. She looked at Inga sadly. 'I very much doubt it, love. Everyone seems agreed that you're cut out for something better than that. Your grandmother has visions of you singing at Manchester Town Hall for the Corporation, or that Albert Hall in London. And your mother seems to agree with her, or she wouldn't leave you to live here would she?' Then she frowned and said, 'Whatever's happened to your neck? It looks terribly blotchy. Do you think it's that shellfish poisoning?'

'Of course,' said Mrs Dawn to Albert the next morning as he sat there stirring his mug of tea, 'they're love bites, and they were all black and purple and in full bloom today. As soon as I saw her I told her to put her high-necked jersey on. Thank God Margot was out before her.'

Albert sat there silently, staring into space.

'God knows what'll happen now, she's shot off to Daphne's like a rocket. Margot doesn't know a thing about it. I hope the poor girl isn't on the slippery road to rack and ruin. One thing's certain, and that I *do* know: no good'll come of turning up at Apple Street. Just you mark my words.' She took the woolly, tea-stained cosy from the teapot, lifted the lid and peered in. 'Shall I fill it up again?'

Albert nodded. In some ways, being a bit deaf was a blessing at times like this.

Daphne had just arrived at Vinny Swanson's. She almost lived there these days. Half of the huge house was converted into the business side of 'Swanson's Silks and Satins'. The silks and satins had emerged from a second generation of Swanson's the coal merchants. Vinny Swanson was Cyril Swanson's second wife. Cyril was now a melancholy invalid who left her to do exactly as she wished. Money meant nothing to him now; it just mounted up all around him like a fortress. He had married Vinny some years after his first wife died of cancer at an early age.

Vinny had met Daphne on the market years ago when Daphne was making the toffee. The fact that they were both with much older men had united them. By now they were so close they knew each other's deepest secrets.

But there was one secret that was yet to be divulged. It had all started the day before Inga's unexpected visit.

'I know you,' said Constable Kelly, grabbing Ralphie Trent by the scruff of the neck and taking two large soil-ridden potatoes from his pockets. 'You're that boy from Apple Street. That rather posh little boy . . . So what's you doin' mixed up with the Ragbottle gang from Back Gunners Street? 'Ow old did you say you was?' Kelly grabbed his ear and twisted it hard.

'O-o-w!' Tears of agonising pain flooded Ralphie's eyes. He blinked them back resolutely. 'Please, sir, nearly eight, sir.'

'An' why aren't you at school?'

'I'm ill, sir.'

'In that case, you should be 'ome in bed, lad. I'll take you there now. What's your name and what number Apple Street is it?'

'Me name's Ralph Trent, sir, but me Mam's not there, sir. She has to go out to work.'

Constable Kelly was a large six footer. He got out his notebook and pencil and placed a heavy black boot on Ralphie's foot whilst he slowly wrote down the particulars. Then they set off to Apple Street.

Vinny paid Daphne a small sum to do a bit of typing and help her out generally with office work and accounts. They sat together in a tastefully furnished office with Persian rugs on the floor, while Daphne confessed her latest deep, dark secret. This time it concerned Ralphie. '. . . Yes, Vinny, he was *supposed* to have been part of a gang caught stealing vegetables from outside a corner shop. He was brought home by the local bobby. Unfortunately, I was here, working, at the time. I'd waved him off to school as usual, so you can imagine my shock when I got home from work and received this message to call at the local police station for him. He had a very sore ear from it and the back of his coat collar was ruined. He was obviously innocent; it's all been a dreadful mistake. He

123

told me he had to take another child home from school who was ill and just happened to be near Mrs Sprinkler's shop when this gang of little ruffians appeared. It was a truly awful tale to hear. These things happen a lot round there. All I can say is the sooner I get him into that prep school the better. Then I'll look round for a better home. But I must choose *carefully*.'

'Have you ever thought of going back to live with your mother-in-law again?' said Vinny bluntly. 'She's got enough room for the army. I know those houses in Sale very well. A friend of ours used to live in one.'

Daphne shuddered. 'Oh no! I could never entertain anything quite like that again, not unless I was entirely self-contained in my own apartment.' She gazed up at the creamy, fancy, fleur-de-lis plasterwork garlanded around the high ceiling of Vinny's office. Then she said to herself silently, *something like this would do . . .'*

9

MUMMY, MAM, MOTHER, GRAN

'She's gone to see her mother, and that's all there is to it,' said Mrs Dawn very firmly to Margot. 'I'm no match for her these days. You went out first, so she probably missed telling you. No one in this house can be her keeper for ever. You know that just as well as I do, Mrs Abbott. She's been brought up in a very muddlesome set of circumstances.'

'And I'm telling *you*, Mrs Dawn, not to get too impertinent. Surely you knew she should have been going to work as usual – at Hetty's? I called at the wool shop on the way back here and there hadn't been any sign of her. Hetty thought something might have upset her yesterday but she couldn't say what . . .'

'She told me she was bored there.' Mrs Dawn was rolling out some pastry dough on an old marble slab in a corner of the scullery and shaking flour over it from a cannister. 'She seemed to think she might get something better to do, linked with where her mother works.'

Margot sniffed angrily. 'Hetty's been so good to her. Inga just doesn't realise how lucky she is. Hetty was most concerned; she thought Inga might be sickening for something. She said she looked a bit flushed and inflamed. Strangely enough, I thought the same when I saw her last night . . . It could be some sort of throat condition, and that's the last thing we want.'

Mrs Dawn turned over the dough with a hard slap against the cold marble. Thank God Margot hadn't seen the true rainbow colours of the girl's neck this morning.

'If she isn't back by tea time I shall go and bring her home.' Margot frowned grimly. A perpetual set of worry lines grooved her forehead these days. 'Inga has a diary full of singing appointments. She's not going to play fast and loose with me after all these years!'

Their conversation was interrupted by the crackling ring of the telephone. Margot hurried away to answer it with a simmering sigh: 'Hello. Mrs Abbott; The Turrets . . . Who's that speaking please? . . . Oh it's *you*, Mrs Phelps . . . No you certainly can't – she's just making an apple pie. . . . Yes all right I will take a message, but only this once. *What*?' There was a shocked silence.

'But why are you asking me to pass on a message like that to Mrs Dawn? . . . No it was *not* more polite to go that way round when it was *me* you wanted. *I* was the one who should have been informed directly.

'Oh.' Margot's bossiness subsided. Her voice went flat. 'Yes. Yes, of course. A terrible shock – even though we can't escape it.' She took a deep, troubled breath.

'Oh . . . yes . . . I know . . . Mmm . . . she will be feeling it awfully . . . very sad indeed, Mrs Phelps. When will the funeral be?'

Eventually Margot replaced the receiver and walked slowly back to the scullery where Mrs Dawn was now washing her hands. 'It was Mrs Phelps wanting to speak to you, Mrs Dawn. It was to let us know that Osmond Beardsley has just passed away. As you well know, he and Maud were two of my oldest friends – in spite of all the trouble there's been.' Margot drew a delicate muslin handkerchief from the concealed pocket in the side of her long, neat, tweed skirt. She blew her regal nose with bony fingers and went upstairs to her bedroom. She had forgotten all about Inga.

Towards tea time, just when Margot had finished looking mournfully through a bulging photograph album at some very old sepia photographs taken over thirty years ago, there was another phone call. It was from Daphne.

'I'm speaking from my friend Vinny Swanson's, Margot. It's just to say that Inga will be staying the night at Vinny's with me and Ralphie. I'll bring her back safely, first thing tomorrow.' There was a moment of silence then Daphne said slowly, 'I don't know whether you will have heard, but Osmond died early this morning. I received a telegram.

'Vinny has been very good about it. She says we can stay with her for a few weeks until everything is sorted out . . .'

'Until everything is sorted out?' Margot's voice

sharpened aggressively. 'What do you mean, Daphne? What on earth is there for *you* to sort out?'

Margot felt a streak of satisfaction as she heard Daphne's firm tone suddenly wilt.

'It's just that I don't feel I can stay in the house in Apple Street whilst it's all on my mind, Margot, and as I work at Vinny's she suggested that Raphie and I should stay there for a little while – I accepted.'

Daphne didn't mention quite everything. There was also another reason she wanted to escape from Apple Street. It was because she was desperate to shield Ralphie from any more contact with the Ragbottle gang and the police. The thought of him as a fatherless child, gradually drifting into that other life of petty crime leading to harsh physical punishment and a reformatory, filled her with dread. She could almost see him now, with his fair, round, winsome face and big blue eyes, in one of those terrible residential industrial schools where they all wore uniforms akin to those of convicts and spent their time making boots and chopping wood.

No – she must use her savings to get him into a private prep school as soon as possible. Hopefully, it would be the one Vinny sent her son Billy to. Billy was nearly ten and due to leave there shortly for private secondary education elsewhere. The school was called Erudine Hall. It also catered for the girls of very rich parents. The girls often stayed on there until they were seventeen, then sped on to final finishing schools in France or Switzerland where they had all their rough northern edges smoothed away and learned about elegance, cooking, and finding a suitable husband.

The only snag was that the fees at Erudine were exorbitant. Daphne was hoping that Ralphie would at least manage to get a scholarship from there very quickly to the equivalent of a grammar school. Her dreams of Manchester Grammar were fading fast though. She had noticed how slipshod Ralphie's own grammar was becoming and how Penny Dreadfuls and lurid comics seemed to appear from nowhere in his bedroom. Only yesterday she had seen a coarse-looking paper called *The Magic Dagger* in his room, containing pictures of ghosts, skeletons, apes and snakes. She realised it was a far cry from *A Child's Garden of Verses*.

Often she comforted herself with the thought that surely, one of these days, he would be educated enough to breathe the word mother in her ears instead of just mam . . .

Inga went to bed at Vinny's that night before her mother Daphne. It was a huge bedroom as big as her grandmother's drawing room at The Turrets. There was a double bed in it and a divan. The walls had a broad frieze of hand-painted flowers and foliage which had yellowed with the gloss of an over-varnished surface. The rest of the wallpaper was pale, fawn-coloured, and modern. The mahogany wardrobes shone with ancient gloom, but their mirrors reflected the light from a truncated back garden – part of which had been sold off just before the Great War in order to build some small, garish, box-like semi-detached houses where people kept bicycles in their halls instead of in their back yards.

Ralphie was sleeping upstairs in the attics with Billy. Billy had two attic rooms to himself. One was his study and old playroom. On the wall was a picture of a big game hunter tackling a tiger.

Billy was a placid, generous boy, although his general quietness was deceptive. He spent much of his time when he was alone playing with his Meccano set. He had been a late, only child for his ageing father and hyperactive mother.

Vinny slept on the second floor in her own bedroom which had a large adjoining dressing room with a locked door between herself and her husband, Cyril.

'Billy?'

'Yes?' Billy looked up from some small brass wheels he was counting. They belonged to his red and green Meccano set with its innumerable strips of smooth flat metal of all widths and lengths, and all stamped out with small, round, amenable holes and oblong slots.

Raphie was looking at some story books. 'You remember I told you my father had one of those apoplectic fits when I was little?'

'Yes?'

'And how he went away to live with a relation called Maud and never came back?' Ralphie took a deep breath. 'Well, he's dead now. I haven't got a father any more.'

'Oh,' said Billy.

'What do you think it'll be like – now I've not got one?'

Billy shrugged his shoulders and put two metal wheels

together next to a large piece of red Meccano. Then he said with prosaic bluntness, 'Fathers make the wheels go round. They make the money that makes the wheels go round. It probably means you'll be poor now, unless you know someone else who's very rich . . .'

'Are you very rich, Billy?'

Billy shook his head. He was a tall, well-made, ordinary-looking boy blessed with complete good health, intelligence, and widely spaced front teeth. 'No, but my father is.'

'Is your mother rich, too?'

'I don't know. The only way I'd be able to tell that is if I hadn't got a father – like what's happened to you . . .' The conversation came to an abrupt end, and they played a game of Snakes and Ladders together. Then, later, Billy showed Ralphie a copy of *Popular Wireless* and told Ralphie that one day he, William Swanson, aimed to be a sports commentator. 'The *Daily Mail* paid for a man to describe a boxing match between Ted "Kid" Lewis, and Georges Carpentier at Olympia in London, two years ago. My father went to it.'

Ralphie nodded. He wasn't quite sure what Billy was talking about, but it sounded good. He hoped he himself wouldn't be poor, now that he had no father. He hoped he wouldn't need to go and steal things again like the Ragbottle gang.

Maud Beardsley was furious about Osmond's will. Never for one moment had she imagined he would leave a single penny to Daphne Abbott or his illegitimate son, Ralphie. She had been quite convinced that they had been blotted from his memory the moment she scooped him away from Apple Street. In fact his will was quite a disaster for her. And what made her even madder was that his wealth had accumulated. The fact that she had her own private income and they had never had to spend anything on any offspring, or bringing up a family, meant that Osmond, with typical devious panache, had somehow over the years managed to accumulate a small fortune. And much to the surprise of the local gossips he had bequeathed something to all the recipients of his extra marital mistakes, leaving them not only fond memories but also much-needed cash for the support of their offspring.

He'd managed to leave his distant elder son from his first marriage the price of a motor car. He'd left instructions for his last splurge, Maria – Maud's young domestic drudge – to receive a continuing sum for her child, from the interest from some of his shares in a cigar company. And finally, he had left Daphne a comfortably large amount of ready cash which, if used carefully, could keep her and Ralphie ticking away at a standard of living far higher than any ordinary working man with a wife and children to support.

It was the luck of the angels and Maud was furious. Finally, Osmond's will had stated, 'I leave to my dear wife Maud all the rest of my financial wealth, knowing that she is already well padded . . .' Maud seethed with anger at the way he had worded it. As well as all his old clothes, he had left her about enough to pay the window cleaners for life.

Although the contents of the will had, at that time,

cheered Daphne no end, the news, brought to her via Mrs Phelps and Mrs Dawn, had filled Margot with a terrible dread. She had realised that from then on Daphne – what with her windfall and her involvement with rich Vinny Swanson and the silks and satins business – was becoming a real force to be reckoned with where Inga was concerned, especially now that Inga was nearly sixteen and virtually grown up.

Sadly, at present, Inga was now living in Apple Street with her mother and Ralphie. There was hardly a peep out of her, but deep down Margot never gave up the hope that she would return to The Turrets, and resume the life she had been fashioned for.

Suddenly Margot had begun to feel unsure of herself, and her own life. These days, she spent more time brooding about her past times when all her own children were small. She bemoaned the way all her daughters had left the north and never came to see her. She wept yet again for what might have been if Tarvin hadn't been killed in the war. She realised she had been harsh with Inga at times, but to her mind it had been for the child's good – so that Inga might have a sparkling future.

Often these days, now that Inga had gone to work for Vinny Swanson, helping her mother with clerical work, Margot was filled with a terrible sadness. Had all that past work and care she had spent on bringing up Inga been a complete waste of time? For the past nine months now – almost since the day of Osmond's death – Inga had been living in Apple Street with her mother, and had never been back to The Turrets once. There had been no more contact except by letter and telephone. Daphne had written a firm letter saying it was time Inga had a complete rest from the singing so that she could be more free to decide her own future life.

Henceforth, Margot had been in the humiliating position of having to cancel all Inga's further musical performances and singing lessons. The whole change of circumstances had even affected Margot's own social life. Wherever she went, she was asked about Inga and what had happened, as she tried to be confident and somehow justify the unwelcome pattern of events.

A few months later, on a murky day in February, just when Margot was feeling at her very worst, she received a brief letter from her eldest daughter, Petunia Shoreditch, who lived in a beautiful little spot close to Oxford. Margot stared at the smooth pale blue envelope. It had a soft imperceptible swelling to it, due to the expensive dark blue paper lining. Delicately, with cool suspicion, Margot opened the envelope with her silver paper knife.

In the dim past Margot had occasionally received a letter from Petunia and once, when Petunia first got married, she had stayed for two days at The Turrets with her six-week-old baby. Petunia had always been a very solid, humdrum child of regular habits. She had married a man who became an Oxford don and they had one daughter, Ronalda, who was now fourteen. They had always wanted a boy and had planned to name him Ronald, after his father, so the baby girl was a bit of an anticlimax.

Petunia spent a great deal of time playing golf and

was the epitome of domestic efficiency and household accounts. She had rosy cheeks and red hair and bore no resemblance whatsoever to Margot, except for her very strong personality. In turn, Petunia's daughter Ronalda was a different kettle of fish altogether. She was a wide-eyed, shrewd, fluttery girl with mousy hair crimped up in rows on her scalp, and pencilled-in eyebrows. She was normally surrounded by a lot of boyfriends who all had motorcycles and side cars.

Margot looked at the handwriting. It was as firm and undeviating as ever. It reminded her of her dead husband's handwriting.

Dear Mother,

I expect you will be surprised to hear from me after all this time, but I was thinking of coming to see you and bringing Ronalda with me for a short stay. Ronald has gone to America to lecture at Radcliffe College For Women which is closely linked to Harvard University in Cambridge, Massachusetts. He will be giving lectures on Shakespeare at their faculty of arts and sciences. He will be away for some time.

I thought it would be rather nice for Ronalda and Inga to get to know each other. How is Inga's singing going on?

Hoping to see you very soon,

Your affectionate daughter,

Petsy.

Margot placed the note back in its envelope with some

trepidation. She had a doomed feeling that if Petunia's visit materialised the whole situation of Daphne, Inga and Ralphie would be uncovered in the blaze of a family searchlight beam, busily spotting its worst aspects. Over the years Margot had never mentioned the true state of things. Her cover-up story involved vague references to Daphne being away in a convalescent home because of chest problems, and that she, Margot, was busy looking after Inga who was something of a child prodigy with a wonderful voice.

As her daughter and granddaughter's visit loomed, Margot grew more and more nervous, even though she still immersed herself in the hope of bringing Inga to her senses and getting her back to her singing again. Then one day a small chink of hope beamed through, which she regarded as a tiny step in the right direction. Her friend, Mabel Spinks, Leroy Spinks's great aunt, had some spare invitations to go and see a private performance of the opera *Madam Butterfly* at Whittleshaw Hall in Lancashire.

10

ENTICEMENT

At first, Inga had no intention of going to *Madam Butterfly* especially with the name Leroy Spinks hovering in the background. She knew he was doing very well for himself; she had actually seen his name mentioned in the *Manchester Evening News* as a rising young singer of great promise. It had caused her to sniff with slight derision and to bless her own lucky stars that she had escaped it all. That side of her own life had gone for ever, thank goodness.

Margot's daughter and granddaughter were arriving far sooner than Margot had bargained for. There was a telegram to say they would be there the following day – just when she was immersed in planning to get Inga, come hell or high-water, to *Madam Butterfly*.

Gatherings at Whittleshaw Hall were always important social functions. The Storell family had listed the hall as one of their many possessions in times when it was only a small wattle-and-daub building set stoutly on a raft of stones. Now, centuries later, it was this magnificent conglomeration of period architecture. Structural appendages of every shape and size graced its noble presence like a tempting array of knick-knacks and folderols adorning the tray of a wandering pedlar. Stone monkeys peered from the tops of drainpipes; twin angels swooped in solemn prayer above the family chapel, with hands together like diving swimmers; unknown humpy-looking stone creatures, weathered by centuries of rain and gales, stood valiantly at the main doorway, willing to be bears or lions – according to one's individual choice.

The old black and white timber-framed part of the house had been reduced to a small offshoot of the present magnificent dressed-stone mansion. Scores of leaded-glass windows twinkled in occasional sunshine beneath at least twenty tall, fancy brick chimney stacks, some of them curved like sticks of corkscrew barley sugar . . .

These days, the present middle-aged Honourable Mrs Storell, noteworthy for her business acumen and commonsense frugality, spent much of her time holding 'occasions' there. These ranged from annual church outings for the poor to large musical functions for people who paid a society subscription, and helped to distribute the tickets.

Yes, it was just the place for Inga to be with young people of her own age – like handsome, up-and-coming Leroy Spinks . . . Margot dissolved into sentimental, wishful dreaminess. Leroy was growing into quite an Adonis; perhaps this outing would lead Inga back, like a lamb to the fold, to her proper life – her singing.

Even so, it was a pity Petunia was arriving so soon. Margot began to glower with annoyance; that telegram from Petsy had been sent purposely to by-pass any letters arranging for some later date. All her daughters down there were like that. They planned for no one but themselves. Margot had no idea where such traits came from.

She began to think about Inga's fleeting sixteenth birthday. If Inga had still been living at The Turrets there would have been a proper celebration party. She would make up for it in a different sort of way when Petsy and Ronalda arrived.

She went to her bureau and opened the top drawer to take out a box of notepaper and envelopes. She never stinted herself on good-quality notepaper and took a delight in changing the shade occasionally. This set was a deep straw colour, the edges of the paper thinned out to delicate tissuey edges. She never had her address printed on it, but she did have some cheaper postcards with The Turrets printed on them in a curving copperplate style embossed in deep, shining blue.

Taking out a small gold-nibbed fountain pen from her favourite crocodile handbag she wrote a short note to Mabel about *Madam Butterfly*, explaining that unfortunately she had two extra people to cater for whilst *Madam Butterfly* was on at Whittleshaw Hall, '. . . so do you by any chance have a couple more tickets still left over?' Mabel duly approached the Honourable Mrs Storell, who agreed to 'fit them in on some of our nice leather chairs from one of the barns and we'll knock a shilling off the tickets'.

'So you've decided to go after all?' said Daphne to Inga as the time for the opera approached. They were sitting in the parlour at Apple Street.

'Yes, I think I will, Mummy. Grandma's kept on about it so often, and seeing as she's got the tickets . . . I'd really, *really* like to meet my Aunty Petsy, and my cousin Ronalda. It'll be quite amazing to see them for the first time. It's only just sunk in properly about so many cousins living down south.'

Her face glowed with sudden joy. She spread out her fingers and began to count them all up: 'Aunty Petsy and Uncle Ronald with Ronalda; Aunt Alma and Uncle Tom with Matthew and Pauline; Aunt Josie and Uncle Bert with Len, Stewart and John; and Aunt Yvonne and Uncle Dennis with their adopted daughter, my age – called Sybil.' Her eyes shone with affectionate triumph.

Daphne felt a shiver of unease. It sounded like the gathering of the clans – but for what purpose? She had always been vaguely aware of them all when she had been living at The Turrets but it had never concerned her much. Margot's daughters had sent presents from a distance when she had first married Tarvin, and she had written to thank them, but that was about all.

'Grandma has invited me to stay at The Turrets the whole time Ronalda is there – for about a week.'

'A week?' Daphne's voice rose in horror. 'How will you get backwards and forwards to work at Vinny's from there? I know just what Margot is . . . once you're in her clutches you'll find it very hard to get out to work by bus every morning – especially with the others there on holiday. It's exactly the sort of situation your grandmother's been waiting for. She's absolutely dying to get you to leave me and go back there. And if you ever do that for any length of time she'll ruin your life with all that singing again.' Daphne stared at her beseechingly with rising hysteria. Surely there wasn't going to be another family battle about where Inga was to live?

'Please let me go, Mummy. Please?' Inga looked thoroughly miserable. It wasn't as if she was leaving Daphne for ever. It was just that she enjoyed meeting new people. It was like an expanding life – to find out about cousins you'd hardly known even existed who all lived in places you'd never even visited. Besides, it could get very boring working at Vinny's – almost as boring as the wool shop. Mummy and Vinny of course didn't find it in the least boring; they prattled to each other for hours. They were twin souls and never ever seemed to quarrel.

But it was different for her, especially now that Ralphie was immersed in his day prep school at Erudine Hall. Mother fussed on about him for ever and a day, even when he wasn't with them.

Distant memories of herself as a small child grew bitter when she was fed up. She felt ashamed that her mother had left her. Yet, according to Daphne, it had all been because of Grandma and her bossy ways. These days, in her more charitable moments, it was beginning to filter through to Inga that there were more sides than one to everything. More and more, she was unsure which side she was on.

'I asked Vinny yesterday if I could have a week's holiday, and she agreed, Mother.' Inga spoke with growing defiance. 'I explained about going to The Turrets and *Madam Butterfly*. She said it would be all right.'

'And you never even let me – your own mother – know?' Daphne stared at her with hurt reproach.

Inga blushed. She was going to explain. She gulped, then instead her mouth closed and her lips set together very firmly.

Daphne blinked nervously once or twice. She knew her daughter was fast outstripping her these days. 'Well there you are then. I don't suppose there's a thing I can do about it. It's entirely up to you, but don't say you haven't been warned.'

Inga was away from Apple Street and from Vinny's like an arrow through the air as she headed back to The Turrets. If the truth were told she was glad to swap both Apple Street and Vinny's 'Holly House' for the The Turrets. She was even pleased to get away from Daphne for a bit. She realised that her worst memories of living with Grandma were fading now that she was no longer involved with the music. Looking back she saw what an advantage it had been to have Mrs Dawn and Albert close by, to talk to and spend part of her life with. She marvelled that they were still there.

How different it was from Apple Street where there was only her mother. Often, Daphne seemed to be a weight across her shoulders. Her mother knew her every movement. Interminably, she wanted to know where Inga had been, where she was going, and what she was doing. Her mother fed on it. She also talked incessantly of Ralphie and all her dreams for his future. She never bothered at all about Inga's future, thought Inga wistfully.

Her childhood at The Turrets, with so much activity geared to her own musical parades with Grandma, was in a different drawer. Suddenly it all became clear to her. It was a part of her life her mother had no proper idea of.

As she neared the familiar road in Sale, graced by its ancient leafy trees, Inga still chuntered on in her mind about the contrast between being with her mother in Apple Street and living at The Turrets. Working at Vinny Swanson's was their only real bit of life. Nowadays, the only time they even spoke to their neighbour, Mrs Collywood, was when they happened to pass her in the street. Then she would regale them with snippets of gossip she had picked up from her jobs, cleaning in a bank and charring for a well-off local family. What a difference, thought Inga, from her past life of being treated like a special young lady who went round with her illustrious grandmother, singing for people in very respectable places.

'Inga! What a nice surprise.'

All her meanderings disappeared as Mrs Dawn opened The Turrets' front door to greet her. Inga's heart flooded with happiness. What pleasure to be standing here again, close to the shining rain-washed, ivy-covered walls, with the sun beaming down peacefully. She turned towards the smooth lawn and sighed in bliss. She turned back to Mrs Dawn and stood transfixed for a second, smiling and glorying in the welcoming gleam from the brass letter box in the front door. Everything was the same – still here to reassure her.

Not far from the house was Albert's oak wheelbarrow. The familiar scars on it were like old friends. She drank in this fresh, damp, woody air; she looked up to the sky and heard the sound of distant crows.

'Come in, lass.' Mrs Dawn stood back for her to enter. The house was warm and quiet, the carpets soft and spotless on the polished floors. Sounds of music were coming from a distant radio set.

She was home at last . . .

11

THE GRAND PASSION

'We'll just test you out with your old childhood song, "Rose Among The Heather",' said Grandma smoothly, 'and by then your Aunt Petsy and Ronalda should have arrived.'

They were in the drawing room. Margot was already sitting on the piano stool, gently toying with the ivory keys and fussily readjusting the music on the piano stand.

Inga braced herself. She was still in a state of euphoria from being back at The Turrets and completely out of Daphne's domain. Her grandmother didn't seem to hold any fears for her any more. She didn't care if she sang badly – now that she had given up music for ever. She began to bellow the words with soulless enthusiasm, but with perfect tune and timing, to Margot's accompaniment.

Margot peered at the music carefully and smiled slightly. 'Not quite so *loud*, dear.'

When it was over, Margot said, 'You certainly haven't lost your voice and that's for sure.'

They were interrupted by sounds of arrivals at the front door. Margot put the sheets of music away and closed the lid of the piano. 'We'll do some more tomorrow.'

Inga ignored her. All she was interested in now was to see what her cousin Ronalda was like.

The palaver when they arrived in the taxi was unbelievable. The skinny little cabby dragged their heavy leather pig-skin suitcases into the hallway of The Turrets, followed by a full set of golf clubs and a wire-haired puppy dog called Roly-Poly.

There was the flashing of wallets with crisp white five pound notes accidently fluttering to the pavement and respectful touching of forelock by the washed-out cab driver as he helped them gather the notes from the floor again. He stood waiting silently as they hastily tucked the notes away and tried to find coins to pay him.

Then, all of a sudden, everybody, except the driver, was talking at once and getting kissed. No one was listening to anyone else but they were all smiling. The driver was gone.

Inga watched with joy. She stood in the background near some laurel bushes. Margot turned and beckoned to her sharply. 'Why on earth are you standing there, Inga? Come and be introduced.' Margot looked across to her daughter Petunia and said with dry bluntness, 'Inga's the grandchild I've spent my last, lone years on – our young family star. I haven't given up hope of her yet.'

Petunia and Ronalda smiled with sudden frozen dignity. What an insult to the rest of them, thought Petsy. Especially when she and Ronalda had decided to come all this way just to see how Mother was getting on. Then she said briskly, 'You always did have that missionary zeal for producing a star, didn't you Mother? Thank goodness the rest of us all escaped!'

Inga felt herself going scarlet. Surely there wasn't going to be a family slanging match about the singing? Surely she had suffered enough from it? 'I've given it up, anyway.' Inga tried to joke as she said it, but Margot hung on like a fox terrier.

'Oh no you haven't, my girl. You'll never give it up. Just you see.'

Inga turned and hurried into the house, and Ronalda hurried after her. 'Don't worry,' breathed Ronalda. 'Mummy warned me about what to expect.'

They looked at each other comfortingly.

Ronalda and Inga were staying in the same bedroom. It had single divan beds, with pale blue fitted covers, each with a deep flounced frill at the floor line.

Most of the bedrooms, except those in the attics, had their own washbasins. Each room had a fireplace with a gas fire in it, which had a row of open latticed columns of pinky cream firebrick that almost resembled pale, fancy meringue until the gas jets were lit. Then it would glow with a warm, magic heat from the small blue and gold gas flames.

Oh, Apple Street, thought Inga. You with your open fires with their minute grates fit only for one or two jagged pieces of good-quality coal, or else some dusty scrapings of slack, smoking away, with damp tea leaves on top. What a different sort of world.

In this particular guest room, the wallpaper was patterned with sprigs of cherry blossom. Every small detail filled Inga with an inner pride. It was so good to be back and see it all. Even the pair of pictures on the wall was a fresh remembered delight: one was of a beautiful lady in grey, with a bustle, standing next to a piano on which stood a bowl of roses with petals falling. And the other was the same woman again, sitting in a garden with her parasol, and a dovecot behind her covered with fluttering doves.

'Which bed do you want?' said Inga shyly to Ronalda. She'd noticed that Ronalda was as tall as she was, even though Ronalda was two years younger. Ronalda was more modern, too. She wore a bright blue silk knee-length costume which had very short sleeves, a V-shaped neck and a white sailor scarf decorated with wavy, gold braid.

'Anywhere . . .' said Ronalda with a fluttering giggle of nervousness. Instinctively, she glanced towards the dressing-table mirror and smoothed her pencil-thin eyebrows as if to reassure herself, then she said, 'And please call me Nally from now on. No one ever calls me Ronalda except people I don't know very well, or when Mummy's feeling very official.'

Inga put Nally in the bed which was closest to the door and nearest to all the mirrors. It was strange to see another of Grandma's grandchildren in this very house; a girl so entirely different from herself. And as for Aunt

Petunia, with all that red hair and that penetrating voice which carried all over the place, she was amazing!

The relief to find that Grandma was no longer the main boss – even if it was only for a week – was like a gasp of freedom. Aunty Petsy was clearly the complete and impervious leader. She was another of those people with a one-track mind, but clearly had no interest in complete power when she was on holiday.

Inga had never seen Grandma so meek and mild, as Aunt Petsy's briskly booming tones filled the air. Her main topic of conversation was golf. 'Did you say your friend's daughter plays, Mother? See if you can get me fixed up to have a few rounds with her, will you? What's the course like? Not full of rabbit holes and bare patches, I hope. Are the men there all right? I hope to God they aren't all apoplectic woman-haters who go purple every time they see a female . . . Ours are a mixed bunch round *us*, but my friend Veronica and I usually flatten them pretty easily.'

'It's perfect peace when mother's out of the way, playing golf,' whispered Nally to Inga.

'It's perfect peace when Grandma's out of the way – *anywhere*,' smiled Inga.

'Do you think it'll be all right if Roly-Poly sleeps with us in our bedroom?' said Nally. 'He's only a puppy and he'll be ever so lonely if he's left somewhere else on his own.'

Inga nodded her head enthusiastically, remembering that muddled-up time, years ago, when Daphne had left The Turrets, taking the dog Rainbow with her. Nobody had guessed how sad Inga had been. She remembered

Grandma saying that Rainbow had gone to a dog's heaven in the sky. Grandma had seemed quite pleased about it. It had been an eerie surprise to find Rainbow still alive but very old at Apple Street, and to see a photograph of him with baby Ralphie.

The long spring evening when they all set off to see *Madam Butterfly* at Whittleshaw Hall was perfect. The place was packed. Every type of vehicle, from Daimlers to tricycles, stood outside in the courtyard. There was even an ancient Benz Victoria there, which resembled a large self-propelled pram with lamps on the front and a brass hunting horn tied on with twine. There were vast striped canvas awnings across the whole of the courtyard to protect the cars.

Everyone was in evening dress; both the girls wore velvet cloaks. Nally looked particularly wide-eyed and fluttery; she wore pearls and had pencilled in her eyebrows to perfection. Inga could hardly get over her constant use of the eyebrow tweezers and pencil. 'Don't they say anything at school about your make-up?'

Nally smiled good-naturedly. 'At Frithley Ladies' College, where I'm a day girl, I went to see the headmistress specially to explain about my eyebrows. I said it was for medical reasons, and told her about having them singed off once and about them never growing again and how the eyebrow pencil is a very special one which feeds them back to life.'

'And did she believe it?' Inga stared at her incredulously.

'She seemed to. Anyway, it was *almost* true except that

when I singed them it was with some coloured matches
on bonfire night when I was about six. Plus the fact that
Mummy doesn't mind if I pluck them, and she'd create
a fuss if the head got stroppy. Mummy says it's my own
business if I'm stupid enough to want to have a bald
forehead later on in life but, even so, it's nothing to do
with the school.'

Nally's mother wore a long, copper-coloured tailored
satin coat with an ornate emerald fastening, and Margot
wore a long silk moire skirt in deep blue-green, with a
short, squirrel jacket.

The first person they bumped into was Mabel, with
her great-nephew, Leroy Spinks. 'I'm ever so glad it all
worked out with the tickets, Margot,' beamed Mabel.
'You're at an advantage really – sitting at the back
of the baronial hall on those gigantic, regal-looking,
leather-seated chairs from the barn. It's like another
small stage at that end. You'll have a wonderful view:
it's where they keep their extra, raised dais when it's not
in use for anything else, and you're on it.'

She glanced at her watch. Leroy Spinks had already
vanished. 'I must dash. I was a bit late setting off. Leroy
has to get himself all dressed up as one of Butterfly's
relatives. The orchestra will soon be tuning up.'

Leroy Spinks had only been there for a moment. He
had seen Inga the minute they all walked in, but his
eyes weren't on her. His fleeting, perceptive glance was
towards the girl who was with Inga; the peach with the
smooth enamelled-looking face and beautifully waved
hair who was giggling. She was holding a wicker picnic
hamper with a ribbon on it.

Nally's wasn't the only picnic basket there. People with small food hampers drifted away during the intervals to the gardens, where they would sit around in subdued lighting from fairy lights set in the trees, polishing off their own home-prepared refreshments. Others preferred to pay noble sums for the Whittleshaw Hall special which consisted mainly of champagne and caviare.

'Let's find our seats then,' said Petunia, leading the way.

Margot followed her, happily waving and nodding to all the people she knew.

Inga and Nally followed behind more slowly. 'Who was that boy with the woman we met?' said Nally, as she followed after Inga.

Inga turned her head sideways as they drifted in single file amongst the crowds. 'Leroy Spinks. We've known him for years. I used to go to the same parties when we were tiny tots. I never imagined he would become a singer too.' She noticed her own mistake as soon as she'd said it – she was no longer there in all the jostling musical fray of those past years. She changed the subject. 'Shall I take a turn with the picnic basket?'

'Oh no.' Nally's voice became anxious. 'Whatever happens, we mustn't disturb him. He's behaving beautifully. That's because he knows I'm the one who's carrying him. He has a very strong sense of smell. He'd be able to tell instantly if we changed over. I'll just take one peep at him before the opera begins, stroke him with my finger and push in a few more dog biscuits, then I'll pop the hamper under my chair.'

Inga stared at her. 'I'd no idea the *dog* was in it.'

Nally smiled contentedly. 'Oh yes. How could I possibly have left the poor little thing all on his own in that vast house?'

'He would have been quite all right. He's not such a baby as all that.' Inga was slightly annoyed. Fancy her bringing the dog and never saying a word!

So did this mean there wouldn't be any refreshments for them, after all? Inga clearly remembered Mrs Dawn going to all the trouble of packing the hamper with goodies.

'What happened to all the bridge rolls and those cakes then? And the home-made lemonade?' She glanced at Nally with rising severity.

Nally's face crumpled into a slightly quivering laugh which she tried to hide. 'I left them in the bedroom drawer. We shan't need them really. People can walk for miles on one small bar of chocolate and if poor people exist on a bit of porridge and bread and dripping, I'm quite sure it won't harm us to be kind to Roly-Poly and get a drink of water somewhere for ourselves if we're thirsty. Which reminds me . . .' Unexpectedly, she began to fumble inside her dark blue velvet cloak, and from a large pocket inside the satin lining she produced a flat, leather-coated flask. 'It's water for my little precious one. In the interval I'll find him a saucer and he can get out to have a drink . . .'

Her plans misfired the moment they sat on the baronial chairs. It was just when the lights had dimmed and there was absolute silence for the start of the opera. The whole place was regal and hushed. Diamonds glittered in sparkling, perfumed expectation as profiles of autocratic dowagers tilted their shadowy noses slightly to the ceilings. Spectacles, lorgnettes, and monocles gleamed as middle-aged men in black and white evening suits sat in placid, expectant sobriety.

The stillness was suddenly broken by muffled yapping and whining. There was clearly a most unwelcome visitor. Excited scrabbling began, like some small mad demon wanting to be free. It shocked the pin-dropping silence. People froze; the yapping got louder; no one moved. Whittleshaw Hall was now a temple of doom filled with unbending statues all glued to their seats and staring ahead. Then one man snorted, 'It's a bloody dog!' in sheer disgust as he sat there in an over-tight satin cummerbund.

'I'll just get him out,' hissed Nally to Inga. 'I'll need to hold him and soothe him. I think he can smell something strange and exciting.'

Sweating with growing embarrassment, Inga held the basket whilst Nally opened the lid and tried with trembling fingers to grab at Roly-Poly's small, gold-rimmed dog collar and fat body. It was disaster. In a flash he had jumped from her powerless grasp and was under the chair barking loudly and tearing at the padding of it, like a terrier at a rabbit hole. Except that this time it wasn't rabbits; it wasn't even another animal at all. It was the lavishly inviting aroma of a large, abandoned mouse's nest.

Roly-Poly went mad, his paws clawed and boxed at the mound which was appearing as the chair gave birth. His jaws chewed and tugged as he growled with triumph. Scraps of newspaper dated 1788 shredded their way to the floor. Huge amounts of rough grey flock, mouse droppings, lumps of leather and threads of horsehair, sheep's wool, scarlet flannel and hen feathers, which had lain undisturbed since the eighteenth century, flew everywhere in a haze of foul-smelling dust.

People began to stand up all around and wave their kid gloves about, as they outdid each other in coughing. Cough, cough, cough, like cattle outside on a cold wet night. People were beginning to leave.

'Ladies and Gentlemen, I implore you, if you would only be so good as to remain seated . . . It is only a small mishap. We shall have the problem sorted out shortly.' Sidney Storell stood there in his softly tailored grey suit and flame-coloured silk cravat. His appearance was completely at odds with the rest of them. He looked about twenty, and was a handsome cross between a millionaire gypsy and a tall, rather thin, overgrown schoolboy. His hair was a mass of tight black curls above angular cheekbones; his nose was large and strong; and his eyes were perpetually narrowed, as if he was always looking across vast lands or seas with the sun ahead of him, but close-up they were a sharp, rain-washed, slate grey or a dreamy green, according to the light and his mood.

Inga fell in love with him immediately. It was as if he had been hidden all her life and had been waiting for the right moment to surprise her. He had a quiet, clear voice. Most people began to calm down again and return to their seats. Some of them were slightly ashamed, now that the fuss had abated.

Inga, who had been following Nally outside to hunt

for the vanished Roly-Poly, returned too, but not to her own seat. She noticed now that there were two seats still empty six rows from the front. She was drawn to them with magnetic compulsion. She went and sat on one of them and prayed that the people who had paid to sit there had gone forever. Grandma, Aunt Petunia and Nally had probably gone too, and she didn't care.

The lights were gently lowered and as the music began she was swept away by it. She never even saw the two people standing by the side of the row, staring towards the place where she was sitting, the woman having to move elsewhere and the man deciding to take the empty place beside her.

The story of *Madam Butterfly* had lifted her into another world. The singing was superb. Inga hardly even noticed Leroy Spinks, but she envied him. Oh, how she wished she was part of it all – up there on the stage, singing and singing, in Puccini's beautiful opera.

The first act took place at a house on a hill near Nagasaki. Oh, to be Madam Butterfly – Pinkerton's Japanese bride-to-be, Cho-Cho-San; or her maid Suzuki.

At the end of the first act Inga sat there lost in thought. Maybe Grandma was right; maybe she should continue with her own singing . . . She gazed up at the heavy blue plush curtains which were now drawn across the stage for an interval.

'Excuse me, I think there's someone trying to attract your attention.'

She blinked slightly and turned to the person next to her. She was staring straight into the eyes of Sidney Storell. He gestured towards the side of the hall where

Nally was waving her hand towards Inga with miserable desperation.

Inga got up to go to her, and Sidney Storell followed. He murmured in a low voice, 'I'm Jack-of-all-trades tonight; I must just check the refreshments.'

He hesitated as they reached Nally. She was distraught and trembling. 'You'll never guess what's happened, Inga. Some absolute brute has fired a catapult at Roly-Poly and he's lying there in agony. I only let him off his lead for a few seconds near the trees. It happened about a quarter of an hour ago. I've no idea where Mother and Gran went. I think they came back inside. Have you seen them? It was pure chance that I've just caught sight of you.'

'Perhaps they went back to entirely different seats, like me,' said Inga, looking alarmed at the news. What an awful shambles it was turning out to be. All she wanted now was to get back to the second act of *Madam Butterfly*.

'What was that you said – *catapult*?' Sidney Storell stared at them both with rising rage. 'Are you two the owners of that dog that caused all the trouble?'

Tears gathered in Nally's eyes. 'He's only a puppy and he's lying there in agony. I've found the catapult. I need help for him immediately. He could be dead by now.'

Sidney hurried outside and they followed him. 'Show me where the animal is.' His voice was tight with displeasure. He had a shrewd idea who was the irresponsible owner of the weapon that had injured the dog. And his annoyance at the dog's presence in the first place was almost outweighed by his distaste for a person who could deliberately attempt to cause the animal suffering.

They hurried to the spot where Roly-Poly lay whimpering beside some holly bushes. Sidney took one look at the dog. 'I'll find a vet as soon as I can. Paul Merritt is here with his wife. I'll fetch him.' He was off like a shot.

Five minutes later he returned with the vet and Roly-Poly was removed to a small stone outhouse at the back of the courtyard. He was suitably dealt with, and left to sleep in some hay with Nally sitting on a stool beside him drinking a cup of tea.

'We'll have another look at him at the end of the performance,' said Sidney hurriedly.

Inga had already vanished back to her seat. She was longing for Sidney to come back and sit beside her, but it was not to be. Instead, it was a rather beautiful and snooty-looking girl of about twenty, wearing around her forehead a silk bandeau that was beaded with small pearls. She completely ignored Inga in a very obvious sort of way until the next interval. Then, in icy tones, she drawled, 'Are you one of those two idiots who caused havoc with that dog, then moved your seat? No doubt you know that you took *my* seat next to Sidney and I had to move elsewhere?' She didn't wait for a reply as she got up and pushed her way out again.

During the second interval Sidney Storell went back to see how the dog was getting on. He looked at Nally sympathetically. He rather liked both of the girls and took them to be sisters. 'Did you say you actually found the catapult that did all the damage?'

Nally nodded. She took it from the empty hamper

basket which she was still carrying around and which now lay beside her. Roly-Poly had perked up a bit and tried to wag his tail. 'Mr Merritt called back to see Roly-Poly again just before you arrived, Mr Storell. I'm most awfully sorry for what happened, but he's only a puppy and I just couldn't leave him behind at Gran's when he's so far away from home. He's really an *Oxford* puppy. It's a big change for him to be in the north of England.'

Sidney looked at her solemnly. 'Is that so?' He had cooled down now. *Madam Butterfly* was going along perfectly at last, and was being acclaimed by hundreds of voices amidst champagne and caviare. 'I wonder if I could borrow the catapult and try to find its rightful owner?' A slight ironic grimness entered his tone.

'Please do, Mr Storell. I never want to see it again.'

Colonel Brawnshaw (Retired) wasn't particularly interested in *Madam Butterfly*. For one thing, he was bored by the complications of Pinkerton being fool enough to marry Butterfly in the first place. And having a child to think about in it was, to say the least, very tedious. Children were always a pain in the neck, wherever they were, so why get het up about them? However, he did sneakingly admire the tenor, Prince Yamadori. It was the umpteenth time Tubby Brawnshaw had been to see the opera. His wife, Madeleine, loved it and always wept copiously.

In Act Three, whilst his wife was in tears at the tragedy of it all, he sat back comfortably in a brandy-induced haze and contemplated his direct shot at the damned little dog who'd been mucking things up before Act One. At least, he thought, he'd done one good deed for everyone. It had settled the little blighter and had taught it a damned good lesson. He smiled to himself as the final tear-soaked end of the opera arrived and he patted the spot over his inner waistcoat pocket. His reveries suddenly ceased, and he began to scowl. Where in hell's name was his bloody catapult? Damn. He'd have to slip out and try to find it.

'Is that you, Colonel?'

Colonel Brawnshaw turned. He was prowling about in the grassy spot where that dratted little perisher had dropped down like a dead bird, but it was getting too dark to see much and his wife was already waiting in her fur coat by the car in the courtyard.

Suddenly a torch shone in his face. He blinked and put his leathery hand across his forehead. 'What the devil's going on?'

The torch shone on the other hand of the person who was carrying it. The hand held his catapult. 'Is this yours, by any chance?' Sidney Storell's voice was quiet and even.

Brawnshaw lunged towards it. 'It damned well is! Where ja find it?'

'Next to that dog with the granite chip stuck in its body.' Storell kept his distance.

'I don't know what you're talking about.' Tubby Brawnshaw peered at Sidney. 'Oh, it's you, Storell. Well, give it me back and let's be gone.'

'Not so fast, Colonel. There's the small item of the vet's

bill, and I'd like the money now so that it's all settled up. Five quid should settle everything all round, and then I'll give you back the catapult.'

'You'll *what*? Are you trying to blackmail me Storell? Give me that bloody catapult this instant. Don't try those bargaining tricks with me, me lad. I never heard such rubbish in all me life! Bloody *vet*? I did everyone a damned service, flooring the yapping little blighter. There's dogs, and *dogs*, Storell, and that little runt got what was due. Come on now. Give me back my property, or it'll be the worse for you. My wife's already waiting.'

'Five pounds please, Colonel, for a straight return of the catapult. Or an I.O.U. until you pay the vet's bill.'

Colonel Brawnshaw was a hefty man gone slightly to seed. What he lacked in activity he usually made up for in bellowing when confronted by an adversary. Tame civilian life was a curse to him. He was also extremely mean. The thought of parting with a five-pound note in these demeaning circumstances was abhorrent. 'If you don't give me back that catapult, Storell, I'll be forced to take it from you. Don't say you haven't been warned.' He lowered his head slightly, like a bull ready to charge.

Storell turned away in disgust. He had better things to do than waste any more time. He went back briskly towards the hall. He had just reached a rather large beech tree which was about a hundred years old when he heard the thundering of heavy footsteps and the heavy breathing of Brawnshaw at his back. He turned, and had just stepped neatly aside to let Brawnshaw past, marvelling a little at the man's sudden spate of energy, when Brawnshaw ran straight into the beech tree and knocked himself out.

Sidney sighed. What a complicated evening it had been. First the vet needed, and now the doctor . . .

Some time later, with the dazed Brawnshaw treated and driven home with his wife, Sidney returned to the hall. There he discovered that the injured dog had gone home with the girls. Seconds later he caught a last glimpse of the girls that evening, in the moonlight with the wicker hamper. The one who had been sitting next to him for a short time turned and waved. They were a good-looking pair, he thought ruefully. Who would have guessed they'd create so much chaos?

Two hours later the whole place was completely silent and serene in its silhouette of trees.

Inga and Nally sat in subdued, silent disgrace all the way back to The Turrets. Both Grandma and Aunt Petsy were almost speechless with anger over the havoc that had been caused.

'I shall never be able to show my face at Whittleshaw Hall again,' said Margot. 'And as for poor old Mabel Spinks going to the trouble of getting me those extra tickets, and us being the cause of that chair being ruined, it will live with me for ever.'

'In other words, Mother,' said her daughter bitterly when they arrived home, 'you're blaming poor little Nally and me for it all. So the sooner we get back to Oxford the better if you ask me . . .'

'Oh no, Mummy, not *yet*. I'm beginning to enjoy it all . . .' Nally lowered her eyelids coyly, and perked up amazingly, 'Roly-Poly's fine now. I met Leroy Spinks just before we were coming back. Leroy stroked Roly-Poly's ears very gently, and asked how he was . . .' She hesitated. 'He wants me to go round for tea the day after tomorrow. His Aunty Mabel will be there with his mother, so I'm sure they can't possibly be really cross about what happened.'

Margot and Petunia looked at her very hard.

'You needn't both stare at me like that. He's going to ring me up tomorrow, and then if everything's all right he says he'll call for me . . . and his mother plays golf too, Mummy, and tennis.' Nally's voice was soft and coaxing.

Petunia began to relax at last. It was obvious that Leroy Spinks was up-and-coming . . . Yes, they would stay the full week after all . . .

Inga listened with secret amusement. Leroy Spinks! Just imagine if he married Cousin Nally and they had loads of little baby bullies, just like him when he was little . . .

She began to think of *Madam Butterfly* again. Yes, perhaps one of these days, when she was twenty-one and could please herself, she would take up singing again as a sort of hobby. She would join an operatic society. Perhaps Sidney Storell would come to it in his grey suit and his flame-coloured cravat. He would fall in love with her and they would have a grand passion that lasted for ever . . .

'Whatever are you smiling at, Inga?' Margot glanced at her testily.

'Nothing, Grandma. Just thinking about something rather nice.'

That night, when the girls went to bed and Roly-Poly was there in the room beside them, they fell swiftly to sleep. Yes, in spite of certain upsets, it had turned out to be one of the best days they'd ever had.

Daphne was missing Inga dreadfully. Every day of that week she dreaded that Margot would cling on, and get Inga back into her clutches for ever.

Then, one calm, ordinary afternoon at Holly House, when she and Vinny were in the office quietly sorting out a few textile patterns, the most terrible thing happened: Ralphie and Billy had been smoking cigarettes in secret and had accidentally set a can of petrol alight.

The moment Billy had flashed open an old cigarette lighter close to a petrol can it all happened. But quick as the devil itself, they had leapt away with little damage to themselves and had shouted for help.

Upstairs in the house, sounds of a sudden muffled explosion coming from the yard were followed by a few seconds of silence, then Ralphie and Billy were heard.

'A petrol can's alight. Fire! Fire!'

'Oh my God . . .' Sick with fright and foreboding, Daphne and Vinny sprang from their seats and dashed downstairs towards the boiler house and coal store outside.

Briefly, when passing a large window on her way downstairs, Vinny saw the shapes of the boys. At least they were safe.

'You get outside to the yard, Daphne. Warn people. I'll phone for the fire engine first.'

In seconds Daphne was in the back yard near the boiler

house. Next to it was a small outhouse and already acrid smoke with lickings of yellow flame was filling the air.

'The boys, the boys!' gasped Daphne, weak with fear and panic as she tried to call Ralphie's name in the choking, heat-filled mist.

Then she heard Ralphie's voice strumming in her ears, 'It's *all right*, Mother.'

In a nightmare instant, she had plunged towards the outhouse door. 'I'm here, Ralphie, I'm coming.' Desperately she pushed forward to the flames and immediately her artificial-silk dress melted against her skin as she stepped back trying to beat out the fire.

'I'm here behind you, Mother. We're safe!' Ralphie dragged at her from behind. He put his hand towards the flames on her dress.

Billy found an old mat to try and damp the flames from Daphne's frock as she collapsed unconscious in the yard.

The clanging red fire engine arrived, followed by the ambulance, and Daphne and the boys were rushed to hospital.

A crowd began to gather in the street outside.

Two hours later the yard at Holly House was peaceful again. Blackened, charred, strong-smelling remains deadened the outhouse, and pools of water were everywhere in the silent unperturbed sunshine.

Billy and Ralphie had escaped lightly. But for Daphne it was not to be . . .

12

DESOLATION

Mrs Dawn was getting a bit tired of having two bosses instead of just Margot, especially after all the turmoil that had developed that week in the past spring, when Petunia Shoreditch and Ronalda had first arrived on the scene from Oxford.

That in itself had been bad enough. But at the time it had seemed to be the sort of short holiday stay one had to put up with, knowing that it would probably never happen again. But now, alas, it was happening all over again with a vengeance, even though Mrs Dawn put a brave face on it. 'Ah well, better the devils you know than them as you don't, Albert.'

As usual Albert said nothing and sipped his mug of tea. He had liked having the two young ones about, and had even managed to put up with the dog. But for Margot's daughter Mrs Shoreditch to come bounding back on her own – he took that with a pinch of salt, and began to think about winter Brussels sprouts.

Unfortunately, Mrs Dawn's comforting saying about
'better the devils' had not stood her in good stead. She
had underestimated Petunia's ability to take control
at The Turrets. There had been some awful turns of
events and now, at the end of November, Cissie Dawn
was heavily saddled with two dreadful devils, one she
knew well, and one she didn't.

Oh yes, at first – at the end of that holiday here,
when they'd all traipsed off to see *Madam Butterfly* it
had seemed to be straight sailing. Even the sad news,
later, from Apple Street hadn't really affected them.
What happened in Apple Street was only a passing news
item these days; something that only poor little Inga
might have to face.

The two Shoreditches had carted away their belongings by taxi at the end of the week, waving and dabbing
their cheeks with hankies and saying they hoped it
wouldn't be too long before they managed to come up
north again. Perhaps next summer?

So it was a real shock when Petunia arrived back after
only three months, with two sets of golf clubs and a
cabin trunk, announcing to the world in loud tones that
she and her husband had separated.

Her voice was so loud that Mrs Dawn heard the
whole story when she was buffing up some parquet
flooring close to the small sitting room where the door
was ajar . . .

Apparently, Petunia's husband had been having an
affair with a fellow academic – an American woman
he had met on a lecture tour. It had finally come to

Petunia's notice when the affair had become the talking point of the golf club.

'It was just after that,' explained Petunia, 'when we had it out with each other and decided to have an amicable parting.'

'It sounds absolutely scandalous, Petsy.' Margot's voice rang out like a trumpet. 'I've never heard anything quite so disgraceful in all my life.' Then she cooled down and said swiftly, 'But do you think coming back here was your best way of tackling it?'

'Unquestionably, Mother. *Unquestionably*. How could I ever face the Ladies' Section of the golf club down there again? I thank my lucky stars that this year's captain managed to get me an immediate introduction to the golf club at this end. It's been an absolute Godsend. It means I can rest here for as long as I want, assessing my whole situation.'

Margot's temper began to rise again. 'And what about Ronalda?'

'Oh, she's *quite* all right. She's being a college boarder for the time being and she can come here during her holidays . . .'

So that was the plan, was it? Mrs Dawn's buffer slithered with a tremendous thud against an innocent piece of skirting board, before she dragged it back to the broom cupboard.

Inga wasn't even aware of what had happened at Grandma's. Life had suddenly taken a truly terrible turn due to Ralphie and the fire which had been caused when the petrol can exploded.

Her *Madam Butterfly* experience with Nally was now hardly more than a happy and amazing memory. She was back in Apple Street, entirely on her own now. And worse still, Daphne, her own darling mother, was lying in the Royal Westhall Hospital with the most terrible burns from the fire.

In this gloomy, fog-ridden month of November, Inga's life at present consisted of going to Holly House every day, to do typing and general office work, and visiting her mother, daily, in hospital.

She had no real friends of her own age. Her only outside acquaintances at present were the people of Apple Street. They frequently took the time to speak to her, to give a speck of comfort, because they'd seen news of the petrol can explosion in the evening paper.

Mrs Collywood from next door popped round regularly with bulging paper bags full of butter mint humbugs, and often invited her to come in for a cup of tea. 'Though I does realise that you're a young lady now, Inga. Even so, if you need any help, love, you know I'm always here.'

Luckily for Ralphie and Billy, they had escaped with only minor injuries compared to Daphne whose dress had caught fire.

Vinny Swanson had blamed Ralphie for the whole affair and had refused ever to have him in Holly House again. He was forthwith dispatched to board out with his old child-minder Annie Murdoch, until Daphne was fit enough to leave hospital.

Annie Murdoch's beautiful daughter Florrie was now aged twenty-one and worked in a domestic science college as a technical assistant. She was going out with a chef.

Her twenty-year-old brother Dennis had long since left the clothing factory because of the dust and fluff affecting his lungs. He was fancy free and now worked as a park keeper in the municipal parks department, and as a pianist in pubs and clubs at night.

Inga hardly knew any of them, but called each week with money to pay for Ralphie's board and lodgings, to see that he was all right, and was attending his prep school regularly.

One day when she called, Annie Murdoch said, 'I hope you won't be offended or anything, Miss Abbott. But whilst the place is quiet and everyone is out of the way, I'd like to have a word with you about Ralphie. You are the only person I can turn to with Mrs Trent still being so ill in hospital.'

Inga's heart sank. She was well aware of Daphne's fears of Ralphie straying from the straight and narrow and getting mixed up with unsavoury people.

'Is it all right if I call you Inga? I feel that "Miss Abbott" is a bit too distant, now that we're getting to know each other more.' Annie Murdoch looked at her with a fair, freckled face full of solemn honesty, as Inga nodded.

'The fact is, he seems to be going round with some of the old Ragbottle gang who came from Back Gunners Street. Bulky Lobsworth is out of Borstal now and has Ralphie running messages for him. It was our Florrie who found out because she knows one of Bulky Lobsworth's sisters, Adeline.' Annie hesitated. 'Of course, I know I shouldn't be saying all this. Bulky has a completely clean slate these days, but on the other hand – if there's any sort of gang, he's always the leader. Young boys wanting a bit of adventure, like your Ralphie, are just what Bulky thrives on.'

Inga didn't know what to do or say as she thought of her mother lying in hospital ill. She had no experience whatsoever of gangs or any other part of male-dominated life.

'How old is Bulky Lobsworth?'

'Going on sixteen. He works as a parcel carrier in a small hut behind the back of Market Street. The whole family of them live just round this corner. Their mother died five years ago. There's five sons, four daughters, and an invalid father.

'It was just that I thought I'd better mention it. Especially with Ralphie supposed to be bettering himself at that posh school. Not that he's the least bit of trouble to us, mind. He certainly seems to get his homework done, and he's always very polite and well spoken. Such a handsome boy, too. I expect he'll go far – in the end . . . It's just this middle patch that's the worst, especially with his own poor father dying.'

On the way back from Annie's, Inga tried to think what to do for the best. Should she have a word with Ralphie herself? They hardly saw each other at the moment. He was often out when she went round with the money and although he visited their mother regularly at the hospital, their visiting times did not coincide.

Inga dreaded going to see Daphne herself these days. Daphne never seemed to get any better, and just lay there, so quiet and ill – speaking in whispers as if every effort at conversation was an agony. Sometimes she would put out a thin bandaged hand to touch her daughter's arm – and often her eyes were filled with desperate silent misery. Inga could hardly bear it.

Then one day, when she went to see her mother, she found an envelope waiting for her on the locker with just the word 'Inga' written on it unsteadily in faint pencil, in her mother's hand. The words inside had been written by one of the nurses for Daphne.

> My one and only darling daughter,
> This note is just to say that if anything should happen to me, I want you to look after Ralphie for me and to see that he comes to no harm. Please forgive me for the terrible wrong I did you by running off and leaving you all those years ago. But at the time it all seemed to be for the best. Maybe in years to come you will see how life ties us in its threads like helpless prisoners. Please forgive this sad letter and hope that things will get better in the end.
> Your ever caring mother,
> Daphne.

Inga stood alone in the small living room at Apple Street, sobbing quietly as she read the words of the letter yet again, then she went upstairs and put it slowly into her dressing-table drawer.

She lay on her bed in lonely desperation, her head buried against her arms and her fists clenched. Supposing her mother never recovered properly and just faded away in that terrible place, with its rows of hollow-eyed, ailing people in those black-painted tubular iron beds? Supposing she and Ralphie were left here in Apple Street alone to fend for themselves?

In vain she tried to blot out all the depressing thoughts that now crowded in, but they kept haunting her. So much so that when she went each day to work in the office at Vinny's her work became uneven and haphazard. Stupid mistakes began to appear in the letters she'd typed and often she forgot to carry out tasks that Vinny had set her to do.

Vinny was changing too. She was no longer the generous, party-giving hostess of the past. She had become more and more irritable and sharp as the pressures of business took their toll and with no Daphne close by to bolster her morale.

Then, one day at the end of November, Vinny broke the news that she would no longer require either Daphne's or Inga's services again.

'I think you must agree, Inga, that I've been a very, very fair employer. I've waited patiently over these past months for Daphne to show even the slightest signs of recovery and absolutely nothing has happened.' Inga saw Vinny's face gradually transforming itself into a hard expressionless mask. 'Forthwith, I'm afraid that both your mother and yourself are no longer in my employ.'

Inga stood there, sick with disbelief. Was this the wonderful Vinny that Daphne had always thought the sun shone out of?

'I shall have to settle up with Daphne personally in due

course,' said Vinny, in hard, clipped tones. 'Fortunately, although your mother always regarded herself as a partner in Swanson's Silks and Satins it was in words only and there was never ever a binding contract nor the complications of her being a proper shareholder. I am therefore giving you a month's notice from today, and your mother a month's notice starting a week on Monday. That will be all.'

Inga's face was ashen. She stood frozen to the spot, hardly able to believe what she was hearing. Holly House had become part of Daphne's whole existence, and even she and Ralphie had regarded it as a second home.

Silently, Vinny ushered Inga from the house with the smart speed of a steadily moving escalator as Inga found herself completely dazed, standing outside in the busy road with signs of morning snow chilling the damp air. The sky was grey and leaden. The whole world was full of foreboding.

'I'm afraid she's become a chronic case,' said Dr Fellows to Sister Boulting. 'Between you and me, if Mrs Trent stays in here much longer, her days are numbered. Her burns have never healed properly and there's a lot of ulceration. A mixed bag of a place like this just isn't right for her. Most of the others are here because they are completely bereft of relatives or have no one to take care of them. She would have been better with some sort of private, more individual care. Doesn't she have anyone close who would take her on?' Dr Fellows shook his head wearily. 'I don't think that recent news she received, about her former business partner deserting her, did much good for the situation. It could be the final nail in her coffin.'

As the general news of Dr Fellows' gloomy prognosis seeped through to Inga on her visits to see Daphne, she became even more stricken with grief. What on earth was she going to do?

Then at last, in sheer desperation, she went back to The Turrets one day to seek her grandmother's advice. 'God help me,' she thought to herself, 'that I'm going back to her for help. Especially with it being to do with Mother.'

It was a clear, sunny day, a week before Christmas, as she set off to catch the bus to Sale. She had bought Margot a small Christmas present of a leather-bound address book, and carried a little bunch of pink and purple anemones; their stout green stalks and dark poppy-like centres were carefully guarded by shiny white tissue paper. She hadn't let Margot know she was going; she was taking a chance on her being there.

When Inga arrived she was startled to hear people arguing with each other. The voices were coming from the stone terrace overlooking the back gardens. Inga frowned slightly. One voice was Grandma's. But that other voice? It sounded a bit like Petunia's.

'No, Mother. I do not agree with you at all. My mind is totally made up. She's coming here for good to stay with me and that's all there is to it. Nally hates the college and always has done. The headmistress accused her of drinking, and she was entirely innocent. Added to that she was pining for Roly-Poly. The poor little creature's getting an awfully bleak time at home, with Ronald. Yes, Mother. Nally *will* be bringing the dog with her again; they're arriving tomorrow evening.' Inga heard a loud, dramatic sigh. 'It will be the end of her schooling for the time being. We can have a long think about her future during the Christmas holidays, once she's up here.'

'Surely you don't expect to stay here for *ever*, Petsy? I'm not just an open house for all my wayward children.' Margot's voice was crackling with fury.

'Mother, what a thing to say! You should be glad we're coming to you. Especially now you're completely on your own. Nally will help to fill the gap in your life that Inga left when she went.'

'But I don't *want* the gap filling, Petunia. All I want at this very moment is for you to go back to where you belong and get on with sorting out your own life!' Margot's voice was rising to a hysterical shriek.

'You really are the absolute *limit*, Mother! Why must you always be so stubborn? Nally and I will be such a *help* to you. You should be *glad* we've chosen *you* to come to, in our hour of need . . .' There was a sudden silence as they went inside via the large french windows.

Inga tried to pretend she hadn't heard them. She rang the bell and Mrs Dawn came to answer it.

'I thought I'd just call and see Grandma, Mrs Dawn.'

'Bless you. Yes, love. And thank you for the lovely Christmas cards. Albert liked his with the robin and the holly. He said it was the best one he'd got. I don't suppose you knew that your Aunt Petunia was back?'

Inga followed Cissie inside to the cloakroom. Cissie Dawn followed her to the coat hooks then peered out again and closed the door carefully. Then she said, in sepulchral undertones, 'Yes, the Oxford ones are back, for Christmas, and your grandmother's none too pleased.'

Inga nodded. 'I had a feeling I heard Aunt Petsy's voice just now.'

'I'm sure you did, dear. Your grandmother and her go on and on at each other the whole time and never care who's listening. It gets very wearing.'

'The trouble is, Mrs Dawn, I'm awfully worried about Mummy. She's still terribly ill, and just never seems to get any better. Deep down I was wondering if Grandma would let her come back here and recuperate for a while. Especially if I came with her and promised Grandma I would go back to my singing and work hard at it.'

'But what about your own life, Inga? I thought you were involved in the silks and satins. To be honest, I don't think you could have chosen a worse time to suggest coming back here. But it's not for me to say . . .' Mrs Dawn began to look fidgety and glanced at her watch. 'Anyway, I'd best get on or I'll have the pair of them nagging at me. I'll just pop along and tell your grandma you've arrived. I suggest you just go and sit quietly in the drawing room with your present and those flowers and I'll get her on her own for you before she goes rushing off somewhere. I'll try to steer Petunia well away – towards Albert in the greenhouse, to ask him about some mistletoe.'

Inga sat timorously in the drawing room, clutching the

small bunch of flowers and the present. She had never dreamed of her aunt and Nally returning so soon. Her hopes began to fade.

Grandma came hurrying into the room, obviously dressed to go out. She wore a tweed costume with a fur collar and carried a basket. 'Whatever's brought this on, Inga? Why on earth didn't you phone before-hand? Christmas is about the busiest time there is, and your Aunt Petsy is here. Nally will be coming back tomorrow, too. Mrs Dawn said you wanted to see me about something special – but you'd better be quick.'

Inga shut her eyes slightly. It was like having to plunge into an icy pool of unknown depth. Breathlessly, she began to blurt out the whole problem. '. . . the situation is desperate, Grandma. The doctor seems to think that Mother might *die*.' Repeating the tale gradually reduced her to a hopeless welter of tears. '. . . And what with Ralphie and all *that* trouble – and me stuck there on my own in Apple Street – I'm at my wits' end as to know what to do for the best. You are my only hope, Grandma.' Inga looked at her beseechingly.

With a sigh Margot put her basket on the floor. It was full of little holly bunches with red berries, all done up with gold ribbon and tinsel. It now lay beside her as she sat down in a floral, linen-covered armchair. She took off her bottle-green felt hat and peeled off her gloves. At this rate, she could see there would be no dashing off to do good works or even Christmas shopping. This weeping suggestion that Daphne – now an ailing invalid – should come to stay here was the last thing in the world she would consider – especially now, with Petunia here and Ronalda due to arrive any day.

'Inga, dear. I do feel very, very sorry for you. I can see just what you're going through. But, dearest . . .' Margot's voice was calm and level and her face was cool and bland as she touched Inga's hand with a fleeting wisp of consolation. 'You see, it isn't really anything to do with me these days. Granted, I'm always delighted to see you when you come to visit. But, after all, it was your own decision to leave here and go to live with your mother, wasn't it? You were the one, dear, who decided to abandon all the life I'd made for you throughout your childhood. It was you who turned your back on all that training and striving to find you a proper place in the world as a singer.' Her grandmother sank back against the cushions and looked at her soulfully with raised, well-shaped eyebrows. Her eyelids lowered a little. 'What more can one say?'

Inga could hear the marble clock ticking on the mantelpiece and the wheels of a horse-drawn van outside grinding on the gravel drive. Then everything went as quiet as the tomb. She gulped, and said pleadingly, 'I could come back again, Grandma. I could start my music again. I think I would like it more now that I'm older. And you said yourself when I was staying here with Ronalda that my voice was still as good as ever. I'd be able to look after Mummy as well. We'd be no trouble.'

A faintly exasperated smile crossed Margot's face. 'Nothing is quite as easy as that, Inga. It isn't just a question of your coming here with Daphne and a magic wand being waved so that we all live happily ever after.'

Margot stood up suddenly and gave a short gasp of pain. 'I think I've got a stitch. It sometimes catches me' if I sit in the wrong position. Get me my indigestion tablets from the bureau, there's a good girl. I think I might have to go and have a lie down.'

Inga brought her the small bottle of white tablets and went to get a glass of water.

Margot sat down again. Her heart was beginning to race. All she wanted now was to be rid of all of them – Petsy, Nally, Inga, the lot. And as for the thought of Daphne on the premises as a permanent invalid, she just couldn't imagine a worse situation.

But by the time she'd swallowed her tablet and sipped some water she had perked up, back to normal. She glanced towards the piano. How little it was used these days. What a terrible gap Inga had left at The Turrets when she went to live with Daphne. To Margot it was like a young tree about to bloom suddenly being cut down, and left to wither. There was no hope now unless the tree grew again from fresh shoots . . . Which was quite possible if the stem and roots were there.

'I've been having some more thoughts about the situation, Inga. I think it was a good idea for you to suggest taking up your music again.' ·

Another idea had just struck Margot. If she took Daphne in for a week or two until Inga got back into her musical pattern it might well nip in the bud Petunia's plan to stay here for what seemed like ever, with Ronalda. It was obvious that they should go back home and sort things out with Ronald as soon as possible then stay in their own territory. It was stupid to take Nally away from her school.

Maybe just a couple of weeks of Daphne would be accceptable and by then Inga would have got back into her stride. Then, if Daphne was still no better she would just have to be transferred back to hospital.

'Perhaps we *could* try it then . . .' Margot ventured.

Inga's face lit up at last. 'Oh yes, yes, Grandma. The thought of doing just that has been with me ever since we all went to see *Madam Butterfly* at Whittleshaw Hall.' Inga began to babble with excitement. 'I swear I would look after poor Mother, and Ralphie is quite settled in lodgings and going to Erudine. Mummy and I would only need to take up one bedroom between us . . .' She saw her grandmother's face change and her heart fell again.

Margot shook her head sadly. 'No, on second thoughts, not your mother, dear. I just couldn't cope with that. The idea did cross my mind momentarily. It would have to be just you.' Margot's eyes looked towards hers. 'Your mother needs to stay where she is. She is getting the special attention she requires there. The Turrets would be of no help to her at all unless a private nurse was employed. It would be an added financial burden.'

Inga was desperate. 'But, Grandma, supposing Mother died? Surely you realise she is the person who means most to me in all the world?' Inga never noticed her grandmother flinch. She just thought Margot was looking for something in her shopping basket. But Margot heard the words with a sudden shock of realisation:

Daphne meant more to Inga than she did and always would. It cut deep.

'How could I ever forgive myself, Grandma, if I came back to live here with you and just abandoned Mummy to fade away so horribly in that dreadful place? Surely we must both help her all we can?'

Margot had become outwardly very calm, but inside she felt her heart was breaking. All the work, all that care, all the hope of those past years – bringing up her granddaughter to be something special, something worthwhile – and now Inga rejected her as if Daphne had been the best mother in the world. What a cruel life it was. Why was it that all the ones she loved most left her in the end?

'You are in no position to help her at all, Inga. You aren't even twenty-one. And your mother is not my responsibility either. Oh child – you are so innocent of how things really were and really are . . .'

Inga didn't wait another second. She hated to be called a child. She saw now exactly how things were. She just couldn't bear any more. Couldn't suffer the pain of the way her grandmother was only interested in her because of her voice and wasn't going to accept Daphne under her roof after all. What a terrible showdown. All Grandma had ever cared about was her own schemes and plans. She was hard and cruel, and always had been.

On the way home, Inga hardly realised she was travelling back to Apple Street. She was in a terrible trance – all her hopes, her dreams destroyed.

Whatever would she do now?

* * *

'Was that Inga who called in, Mother?' said Petunia to Margot ten minutes later when Margot was all set to rush off out at last, with Inga's visit still resting uneasily in her mind.

Margot tried to ignore Petsy. She nodded brusquely. 'Tell Mrs Dawn I shan't be in for lunch.'

'What did she want, Mother?'

Margot pretended not to have heard.

'What did Inga *want*?' persisted Petunia, as her voice nagged on and on. 'I hope she won't be wanting to stay here again when Nally arrives. I think she was a bad influence on Nally the last time. I don't think Nally would ever have taken Roly-Poly to that wretched do at Whittleshaw if Inga hadn't been with her the whole time, encouraging her. Nally needs to be kept in check these days. She needs to find a nice young man of her own style, and she'll never find that with Inga there. Anyway, now we're here for longer I shall be able to get everything organised my way for a change . . .'

Margot hurried along the drive of The Turrets at last, towards the gates with her laden Christmas basket. Mrs Dawn was talking to Albert by the side of a laurel bush in the sunshine and they saw her going. 'Gone at last,' breathed Cissie Dawn. 'Thank God to have a couple of hours with only one devil to cope with.'

Margot vanished round the final bend of the drive. Suddenly she dropped her basket. All the small bunches of holly with their glitter of gold and tinsel tipped lightly to earth and spread out as she collapsed on the floor to meet them. She lay there gasping slightly, dazed by an attack of excruciating pain. She heard bells ringing in her ears and saw violent flashes of brilliant light.

Fifteen minutes later Mrs Dawn was sending for the ambulance and Margot was taken to the cottage hospital on the very verge of death.

13

CHRISTMAS

Inga was in the depths of depression when she got back from The Turrets after talking to her grandmother, but she was entirely unaware of Margot's ultimate fate. It wasn't until the morning of Christmas Eve that anyone got in touch with her about it. At nine o'clock that day, just as she was stoking up the fire in the living room and staring miserably at two small Christmas cards which had arrived for Daphne, there was a knock at the door – and standing there was Nally.

Nally was beautifully dressed in a fur hat and camel-hair coat, and she had Roly-Poly on a lead. She was carrying a small parcel in fancy paper. 'Inga! Thank goodness I've found you at last. I've been lost for ages in this maze of streets. I was sent by Mother to tell you what's happened.'

Inga's face lit up with relief, then she looked puzzled. 'What *has* happened then, Nally?'

'Oh, by the way, I've brought you a small Christmas present,' smiled Nally, trying to put off the evil moment when she would have to break the news to Inga.

Inga opened the gift excitedly. It was a cut-glass scent spray with a rubber squeezer netted in purple silk strands and a real silver top to the spray.

Nally stood there bracing herself to start on the bad news, as Inga thanked her and placed the scent spray on the table. A slight sparkle from the glass was caught in a sudden shafting spurt of firelight from a lump of tarry coal in the small grate.

Nally's face had coloured up feverishly. 'I don't know whether you knew, but I'm a boarder at my college now. Mother and Father have been having a bit of trouble over a woman that father's been a bit too friendly with, and Mummy's come up here to stay at The Turrets until it's all sorted out. I shall only be here until the day after Boxing Day, and quite frankly I doubt if we shall see each other during Christmas. This was my only chance.' Nally glanced away as if she was slightly ashamed. 'The fact is, Inga, I'm the bearer of bad tidings . . .' Nally began to speak quickly to get it all over and done with. 'Apparently, the day before I arrived at The Turrets, and just after you'd been to see Grandma and she was on her way out to do Good Works, she collapsed in the drive and was taken to hospital. She almost died. She's still very ill.'

Inga clutched at the chair she was sitting in. It seemed unbelievable. Grandma was one of those women who she thought would go on for ever. Inga couldn't imagine Grandma being ill – let alone dying.

'It's caused a dreadful furore,' said Nally. 'All our other aunties are due to come to The Turrets immediately after Christmas. To be perfectly frank, Inga, I'm pleased to be getting back to the safety of boarding school. But at least I've warned you, so that's a good thing.' She looked at Inga anxiously.

Inga sat there in complete silence. What an awful state of affairs. She just couldn't imagine The Turrets taken over by a horde of strange, unknown relatives.

'Which hospital is Grandma in, Nally? I must go and visit her immediately.'

Nally's face clouded over in desperation. 'That's just the trouble . . . I've no idea. I can get neither rhyme nor reason from Mother as to where Grandma actually is. At first she was taken straight to the local cottage hospital and Mother went with her. Then she was quickly transferred to a private one somewhere in Cheshire. Mother hasn't breathed a solitary word about its whereabouts. She says Grandma has to have complete and utter rest, and when I said you would need to know, she jumped down my throat and said that would be the worst thing possible.'

Tears came to Inga's eyes. She began to weep and weep. Nally came and put her arm round her. 'It's my fault, Inga. I should never have been so blunt. Please forgive me. I feel awful about it all. Even Mrs Dawn doesn't know where the place is. It would mean going through Mother's handbag and all her private papers to find it out. And I would never do that.'

They both nodded towards each other sadly.

When Nally had gone, Inga sat in lonely solitude

thinking over it all. Surely it was her right to know where Grandma was? The Turrets had been her one and only home right through her childhood. Grandma had been her mainstay, along with Mrs Dawn and Albert. Granted it had been a hard life in some ways, because of Grandma's passion to make her into a singer, but even so, to be cast aside like this and not even to be given the address of the hospital was really cruel.

She began to brood even more. She stared round the dark little room, brightened only by its glowing fire, and the gift that Nally had brought. It was the darkest, bleakest time of the year now, and she desperately needed to find paid work. She realised now that there would never be a life for her at The Turrets.

Mrs Collywood had told her she knew of a job going for a clerk at Pearlways Insurance Company in town but it was a gamble as to whether Inga even had a chance for it, with all the unemployment about. Usually men were employed as clerks, and girls like her were just 'office girls'. Clerking covered a broad range of jobs. The only chance for a girl was to be a very good typist. Inga knew she was well below the standard of a secretarial college graduate.

At midday, after Nally had gone back to Sale, Mrs Collywood popped in. 'I've got a bit of good news for you, love. It's from Pearlways again. My friend Mildred, who's a supervisor there, says they've got some girls off with influenza, and they're desperate for temporary help in the filing section to do with fire insurance, as soon as Christmas Day and Boxing Day are over. I'm sure you'd be able to do that sort of work standing on your head, love. My friend Mildred says it's a 'Yes sir, no sir' job. You just have to be nimble-fingered, quick-witted and do what you're told. You'd soon pick it up.

'There's some interviews at two o'clock this afternoon. If you're still interested I could take you along and Mildred will fit you in to see Mr Tomkins. All you'll need is your birth certificate and your school leaving certificate. Mr Tomkins sets everyone a small arithmetic, spelling, and filing test to do before they go in to see him. Mildred says he's quite nice and he also needs someone to take round with him to use a tape measure when he's assessing fire damage.'

At two o'clock prompt, Inga arrived at the huge red-brick ornate Victorian building of P.I.C. It had multitudes of windows on four floors which were all lit up brightly in the city gloom. Some rooms were decorated with coloured Christmas paper chains.

Hurriedly, Mrs Collywood introduced her to Mildred Shaw who was a thin, elderly woman with grey waved hair, each brilliantined wave kept carefully in place with a large brown kirby grip. She wore a navy blue velveteen dress with a high white muslin collar. Mildred was an unmarried, motherly type of woman who had worked at Pearlways for the past thirty years, and was meticulous. 'I'll inform Mr Tomkins he's got an extra one to see,' she said to Inga. 'He won't mind in the least.' Then she took Inga to a small room next to the waiting room near Mr Tomkins' office and handed her the written test to do.

The room had polished brown cork lino on the floor. Two single wooden desks with inkwells and pens were set out at either end of the small room. The drab green-painted walls were bare except for a large notice which said SILENCE, in black capital letters, and had a piece of holly with two small red berries stuck across the top of it.

'Keep your test paper to take in with you when you go to see Mr Tomkins,' said Mildred. 'It'll be about three-quarters of a hour before it's your turn, Miss Abbott.'

There was one other girl, Donna O'Dee, already sitting at one of the desks, chewing her fingernails and mumbling. Inga went to the other desk and tried to sit down as quietly as possible. She managed to do the test without a single blot but just at the end her pen nib broke and she had to finish with an eyebrow pencil she had in her handbag.

She and Donna wished each other luck and went to sit with six others who were waiting outside Mr Tomkins's office to be interviewed for the three temporary vacancies.

The wait turned out to be much longer than three-quarters of an hour. Inga watched with more and more foreboding as, one after the other, the women went in to be interviewed. She was sure they must all be better qualified for the job than she was.

Eventually, she was the last one left on the chairs. Everyone else had gone. Mr Tomkins came and opened the door to her himself. He was a fresh-complexioned man in a dark pin-striped suit. He wore a very old-fashioned stiff white collar and a black tie. To Inga he looked ancient; he must have been almost fifty. There was a thin piece of silvery tinsel arranged round his inkwell, next to one solitary Christmas card. He looked at her test paper, checking it swiftly.

'Top marks, Miss Abbott. You and one other lady have been the only two to be perfectly correct.' Rapidly, he glanced at her birth certificate and her school leaving certificate, then he said, 'Are you good at doing measurements?'

Inga nodded vigorously. So near and yet so far. Please God don't let me make a mess of this interview.

'I need a trainee young lady to take with me when I'm going out assessing fire damage. You might fit the bill. Would it interest you?'

'Yes, sir.' She felt as if she was back at school again. She hardly dared to breathe.

'That's settled then, Miss Abbott. Would you be able to start the day after Boxing Day, on a temporary basis, with a view to more permanent work later?'

'Yes, sir.'

'The hours are from eight a.m. until five-thirty p.m. with Saturday afternoons and Sundays free.'

'Yes, sir.

'You will, of course, have unpaid leave for Christmas Day, Boxing Day, and New Year's Day.' Quickly he began to write out a short billet to say she was permitted to start work as arranged, on his instructions.

'Thank you, sir.'

They stood up and shook hands. Just as she was going he said, 'I see you live in Apple Street?'

'Yes, sir.'

'Am I right in thinking you are all on your own at present? I think Miss Shaw mentioned it. Mother in hospital? Well, a Merry Christmas anyway.'

Inga nodded.

Mr Tomkins said no more but on the way home Inga frowned to herself. For some reason she thought of her job at the wool shop all that time ago – and Mr Dermot Farthingale. She shivered slightly. Surely Mr Tomkins wasn't like that? Not at his age? She hurried into the empty house, thanking God it was warm and the fire was still in. Then later, after a hot drink of Oxo, she went to thank Mrs Collywood and tell her the good news.

On Christmas Day morning she went to visit her mother. She had been invited to have her Christmas dinner at Annie Murdoch's, along with Ralphie. She felt more cheerful today. At least there would be some good news to tell mother, about getting the temporary job. She decided not to mention anything about Margot also being in hospital.

The wards were full of festivity. A Salvation Army band was playing some Christmas carols and there was a huge Christmas tree in the entrance hall to the hospital corridors.

The ward Daphne was on was quiet and peaceful with subdued laughter, and mistletoe over the kitchen door. The doctors were due round – one of them dressed as Father Christmas – to give out presents to the patients.

When Inga arrived, Sister Kitson beckoned her into the Duty Room and closed the door. At first Inga could hardly take in the sister's words. '. . . and so the plain truth is, my dear, that this coma your mother has been in for the past night and is still in at present may well be the peaceful end to all her suffering, although there is always the chance that it could be a turn for the better and she could start to recover. All we can do is pray and hope. Hope is everything. We must never ever give up hope of a single soul. Miracles often happen . . .'

Inga walked slowly into the ward, with its heavy smell of pine disinfectant, towards her mother's bed. She gazed fearfully at Daphne and tried to blink back the tears which smarted her eyes. Then she bent down and whispered in Daphne's ear, 'Mother, I've got a job. I start it on the day after Boxing Day. Ralphie and I will both be here to see you again this afternoon . . .'

Her mother lay there, pale and lifeless, but at the sound of Inga's voice she gave a sudden shuddering gasp and her hand moved. Inga took her mother's hand and held it. How grey Daphne's hair was now, how marble-like her features as she lay against the hospital pillow.

As Inga left Daphne's bedside Sister Kitson, in her high white starched cap, her navy and white uniform, and her black shoes and stockings, stood there in silent sympathy as Inga walked slowly from the ward with her head tilted away in grief.

On the evening of Christmas Day, The Turrets was alive with people but one person would be forever absent from the house that had been her home for so many years. Margot had never recovered consciousness and had died peacefully in her sleep.

Mrs Dawn and Albert had been informed of the sad news by Petunia, and had been given a full week's unpaid leave to keep them at a distance whilst all the rest of the family arrived.

Nobody bothered to inform Inga that her grandmother

had died. They were all far too busy organising, planning and arranging, as they sifted through every item in the house with ruthless efficiency.

To Inga's relief, along with most other businesses, Pearlways Insurance Company worked on during the days between Christmas 1930 and New Year 1931. For Inga it was the difference between lingering, miserable and alone, in Apple Street, haunted with helplessness about Daphne who was still in a coma, and having a path to some paid independence.

'How's the job going, love?' Mrs Collywood was just opening her front door. The weather was atrocious.

The streetlamps which lit the morning blackness with morbid yellow light caught waves of blusterous sleeting rain. It was barely half-past seven but people, including Inga, were hurrying to work on foot. Many others travelled by pedal bike, or on motorbikes. Others were queuing up at bus stops for special early works buses.

Inga called back briefly to Mrs Collywood and waved. She was forever thankful to Mrs Collywood for helping her to find this job. She hoped and prayed it would lead to real permanence. Perhaps she would be able to work up to be a proper secretary and take evening classes in Pitman's shorthand and typing . . . She dashed along, thinking briefly of her wasted days being taught to become a singing star . . . How much better if she had been trained into something more practical. And as for her Grandma Abbott, Inga just hoped that wherever she was – in the mystery private nursing home – she would finally recover and come back safely to The Turrets.

Today was one of the days she was going out with Mr Tomkins to measure up and assess fire damage. She didn't know where it would be except that it was a few miles away, out of the city. She was getting on quite well with Mr Tomkins and had found that silence really was a virtue. 'Yes sir, no sir' was always the order of the day, as well as being able to hold the tape measure properly, repeat the measurements he called out from time to time, and stand next to him silently and respectfully when he was talking to anyone. And she had struck up a friendship with Donna O'Dee, the Irish girl who had been taken on at the same time as her.

Yes, she was quite enjoying it all. This was going to be the third time she had been out with Mr Tomkins away from the insurance office, and she now prayed that Miss Westfield, his regular assistant who was off work, would stay off work for ever.

Mr Tomkins had a brown and fawn four-seater saloon car. Inga sat beside him, absorbing its luxury thankfully as they roared out of town to Washway Road, through Sale, along towards Altrincham, and quickly branched off into the countryside.

She didn't pay much attention to the exact details of the journey. She began to think of her mother in hospital, and her grandmother in the private nursing home. It wasn't until Mr Tomkins had driven halfway along a winding avenue of beeches and oak trees leading to a large country house that she realised with quite a shock where she was . . .

'Nearly there, Miss Abbott.' Mr Tomkins had slowed down reverently to five miles an hour, as they wound their way round to the back cobbled courtyard where the stables were. There was an extra wing of buildings here which incorporated an ancient barn. One of the rooms near the stables was lit by electric lights. It was clear it was an office. Inga's eyes grew wide; with a shock she realised that they were at the back of Whittleshaw Hall.

Silently, in her neat navy blue serge costume and creamy white blouse with its frill down the front, and her navy blue French wool beret perched on top of her fair hair, she followed meekly behind Mr Tomkins as he strode forward with his briefcase and rang the small brass doorbell of the office building. Immediately, it was opened by Sidney Storell.

Inga stared at him as if she were in a dream. How different he looked today. Gone was the grey suit with that flame-coloured silk cravat. Today he wore a soft-collared, loose white twill shirt with the sleeves rolled up. It was unbuttoned at the neck and a loosely knotted navy blue tie was slung round his neck like an afterthought beneath an unbuttoned dark blue waistcoat. He wore dark blue striped trousers, tied at his waist with a neck tie, and fine leather boots.

He looked different in broad daylight. There were dark rings round his eyes. He was rather pale, and the shaved patches of his face were grey.

Unknown to Inga, Sidney Storell had, like herself, recently been through a deeply upsetting period. On his twenty-first birthday, only weeks ago, he had been cheerfully celebrating his engagement to the rich and beautiful Lady Lydia Clucksly who, apart from anything else, was very anxious to change her name to his. At that time he had been sluggishly pursuing his studies at Durham. Only two days after the announcement of Sidney's engagement, his father died suddenly of a heart attack. His mother, Katrin, was still in deep mourning, and the whole household was at sixes and sevens. Sidney's two younger sisters were abroad at the time at finishing schools, and he had cancelled any further studies at Durham and taken over as the rightful head of Whittleshaw Hall.

He didn't seem to recognise Inga at all. His attention was turned towards Mr Tomkins as they shook hands. 'I'm here in a temporary capacity,' explained Storell. 'My steward, Mr Renshaw, is away and many of the staff are off with flu. This fire damage couldn't have been at a worse time. It was damned bad luck: a briar pipe left burning by some unknown person on the edge of one of the library shelves. I'm afraid we've lost some valuable first editions, as well as half the oak panels and part of an ornate plaster ceiling. Anyway – come and see for yourself.'

Inga followed behind the two men at a slight distance.

'Have you any very tall stepladders, sir? I'll need to do a bit of measuring up,' said Mr Tomkins later, after he had taken copious notes of all the damage, made some small detailed drawings in a special notebook and taken two or three careful photographs with his Kodak camera.

By now Sidney Storell was getting rather impatient. He was pacing the pale pink Aubusson carpet, which was half covered with white dustsheets, and to Inga his grey-green eyes seemed to be glinting rather angrily. All at once she was glad he hadn't recognised her.

'I'm afraid I'll have to leave you now, Tomkins,' he said in disciplined, even tones. 'But I'll send my man Smithers along straight away to give you a hand – and I'll get the ladders sorted out. Don't fail to let me know if there's anything else you need.'

Sadly, Inga watched him vanish. Oh if only he could have stayed with her for ever – even though he had hardly looked at her once.

A few minutes later two men in brown aprons brought them some ladders. It was just when she was perched on the top of one of the ladders, holding the end of the linen measuring tape by its brass ring, when Sidney Storell re-entered the room. Mr Tomkins was standing halfway up the other ladder, at the far end of the room, holding the starting end to the leather-cased wheel of tape.

Sidney Storell stared up at them. 'Oh, by the way, Tomkins, I meant to say that if you wanted to see the remains of the tobacco pipe itself that caused all the damage, it's in a sealed manilla envelope in my office.' Storell stayed at the scene for a few silent seconds, then suddenly he walked across to the ladder Inga was on and said, 'Pardon me, but I feel I've seen you somewhere before. Are you a friend of one of the family?'

Inga felt herself blushing. How on earth could she admit she was one of the girls who had caused all the trouble with the dog at *Madam Butterfly*? On the other hand, to deny they'd ever met before might mean she'd be blotted out of his mind for ever.

She looked down at him and smiled reticently. 'I think I did once sit next to you at an opera . . .'

He smiled back as slowly, the truth began to dawn. 'I remember now. It was *Madam Butterfly* and you were with your sister or someone whose dog discovered the mouse's nest in one of our old leather chairs from the barn. And the wretched animal got hit by a fool with a catapult. Did it recover all right?'

Inga couldn't reply. Her mind was suddenly flooded by all the awful things that had happened since that evening: Her ailing grandmother and her exclusion from the goings-on at The Turrets, her mother still at death's door in a coma. She began to feel dizzy with it all. Then suddenly she lost her balance and both she and the ladder, which she had suddenly gripped for protection, came toppling down straight on to Sidney Storell.

When she opened her eyes she was lying on a sofa at the far end of the room. Sidney and Mr Tomkins were standing there and Sidney was holding half a glass of water for her. He passed it to her as she sat up.

'I was just going to send for the doctor,' he said.

She looked at him anxiously. 'Oh, please don't do that! I feel perfectly all right now, honestly . . .' I just can't think how it happened.'

'It happened because you weren't holding on to the ladder sufficiently,' said Mr Tomkins in cold, reproving tones. 'If Mr Storell hadn't broken your fall for you by thrusting himself forward you might have been badly hurt. As soon as you feel fit enough, Miss Abbott, we'll get back to the office.' He turned to Storell. 'Thankfully, I managed to complete the measuring, sir. But if it's convenient for you, I'd like to call back again tomorrow, alone. Just to check everything once more.'

Thirty minutes later, after a cup of tea and a digestive biscuit, Inga was being driven swiftly back to Apple Street by Mr Tomkins, who sat there inwardly fuming for the whole journey. He never even got out of his car to see her safely into the house. He was gone the moment both her feet were standing on the pavement, with the words, 'Don't come back until you are quite well, Miss Abbott. I think you are more cut out for a permanent filing occupation.'

Filing clerk . . . demoted to one of those! His cruel, dismissive hint was drumming through her aching head as she made herself a cup of tea, took two aspirins and lit the fire in the cold little living room. What an end to what had at first seemed to be a perfect working day – with that added bonus of actually seeing Sidney Storell again.

The following morning, apart from a few minor bruises, she felt all right as she set off as usual for work, praying that Mr Tomkins would have forgotten his mean suggestion. But alas she was due for a shock . . .

As soon as she set foot in the office she was met by Donna O'Dee with the news that yesterday Mr Tomkins's regular assistant Miss Westfield had returned and had been furious to discover that he had taken out a temporary assistant to help with the measuring.

All Inga's hope faded, especially when Mr Tomkins arrived in the office late, in a seething temper, proclaiming that one of his front car tyres had punctured. This was followed by a meeting between him and Miss Westfield, in which the name Miss Abbott rebounded again and again against the glass partition window panes that separated Mr Tomkins's inner sanctum from the main office.

That afternoon, when Mr Tomkins had gone out at last to Whittleshaw Hall to check up on yesterday's turmoil, and Miss Westfield was sitting in her own little niche in his office, typing, Inga received a note in an envelope. She suspected Miss Westfield might even have typed it. It was on blue headed P.I.C. notepaper.

Dear Miss Abbott,
    We thank you for your help to us as a temporary assistant. Unfortunately, at present, there are no permanent vacancies. Your wages, made up to the end of the week, are enclosed and you are free to leave at your own convenience.
    Yours faithfully

Inga read the words in despair. Donna tried to comfort her but she knew it was no use. 'Sure, an' I'm only here by the skin of me teeth meself. But we'll keep in touch . . .'

It was only now that the bruises and shock of yesterday began to make themselves felt, as Inga left the building in the depths of gloom, wanting only to get home to the now lonely Apple Street as quickly as possible, and to shrink into bed with a hot water bottle and sleep away the hours that would obliterate forever the memories of this demeaning day.

14

AN UNEXPECTED VISITOR

Inga lay on her bed. She had slept solidly for over four hours and the daylight was already fading into the murky greyness of a winter evening. As she gazed up at the ceiling, she suddenly realised that sleep had done her the world of good and she felt much better. It was as if Pearlways Insurance Company had never even existed.

She got up and had a wash. She had lain there under her eiderdown still in her office clothes, but now she changed into something more cheerful: her cherry-coloured, long-sleeved, velvet frock with silk collar and cuffs. It was on a wooden hanger with her other best clothes in the small alcove, behind a flowered curtain. She swept the curtain away with a sudden flood of energy, and held the frock up for inspection. What did it matter that she was going nowhere special or even seeing anyone? At least looking pretty would make her feel more optimistic and positive.

The frock was one Daphne had bought for her over a year ago. She had hardly ever worn it but it still fitted her perfectly. Its slim-fitting bodice had an unusually flared skirt which was a perfect fit for a frilly lace petticoat.

She wondered, with a streak of defiant abandon, whether to wear her only pair of pure silk stockings. Yet deep down she still felt secret grief. She knew it was make-believe, dressing up to go nowhere. But the defiant side of her persisted. Why on earth shouldn't she dress up in her glad rags? What was there to stop her? It was almost like those special childhood days with Grandma Abbott: Inga Abbott with the very loud voice, all arrayed in her party finery – going out to sing . . .

She stood in front of the small bedroom mirror and put a touch of make-up on her face. Her eyes were sparkling. She would put the gramophone on too, and waltz round to something nice like Sigmund Romberg's 'New Moon'.

Seconds later, before she had even fixed the gramophone needle into the pick-up head, there was an urgent knocking at the door. For an instant her heart fluttered with hope, then she heard Mrs Collywood's voice: 'Inga, come quickly. I need help.' She heard Mrs Collywood crashing back to her own door and slamming it.

Inga followed hurriedly along the pavement to the house next door. It was terribly windy. Mrs Collywood was already standing there to let her in, and as Inga plunged inside, Mrs Collywood quickly shut her front door again. A shower of choking smoke and black floating soot met them both like a torrent and they began to cough.

'What with the gale going on outside, I daren't open the door too much,' gasped Mrs Collywood, 'or the house'd burn down. It's that damned chimney; I reckon it's blocked by a fallen brick inside and it's sent down all this flaming tarry mess. There's real fire coming from the chimney top. It's getting quite frightening. Fetch me another bowl of water from t' kitchen then go out the back for me and phone for the fire brigade.'

Quaking like a jelly, Inga did as she was bid. Anything to do with fires put her in a panic after what had happened to her mother.

In five minutes she was back, and minutes later a fire engine had arrived and the chimney blaze was soon out. The two women groaned with heartfelt relief and thanked the firemen profusely. All of them stood there in a welter of hosepipes, water, soot and dying smoke.

When the red engine with its shining brass fire bell and its folded ladders had departed, Inga and Mrs Collywood stood there staring at each other. They looked a terrible sight. Mrs Collywood's cotton, blue-flowered overall was now mottled to black and her face was smeared in soot. She began to apologise to Inga.

'You poor, poor lass. Tha' looks awful. How could I have let you in for all that? And you in all your finery. That frock'll never be the same again, it's completely ruined. You've even got a hole in the skirt all tarred from burning cinders. And your face! If it wasn't so tragic, you'd look quite comical! It's just as if you're wearing black and white stripes of war paint. What can I do to make up for it all?' Mrs Collywood looked quite desolate and there was a hint of tears in her eyes.

Inga herself was so relieved that it was all over, with no one actually hurt, that she just smiled weakly and shook her head. 'The best thing, Mrs Collywood, will be for us both to go into my place and I'll put the kettle on. Then I'll get cleaned up properly, come back here in proper work clothes and help you get sorted out a bit. Are you insured?'

Mrs Collywood nodded. 'Yes, thank God. And not just to pay for me funeral, neither. Thank heavens it's for fire and theft an' all. The insurance man won't half get a shock when he comes round and there's a claim in. I'll fight like a tiger to get full compensation and the whole of the house redecorated.'

Mrs Collywood insisted on putting newspapers on Inga's chairs before they sat down to drink the tea, and a newspaper on the table for the tea pot. 'Soot carries itself everywhere, love. And you don't need to worry about coming back after your bath and clean-up to give me a hand again. I shall just go back, have a wash and clean-up, meself, then skedaddle to my sister's for the night, at Chorlton.'

They sat there in silence for a while drinking tea and eating biscuits, then Inga got up and put the gramophone on. 'It's "New Moon". I was just going to have a dance round to it, all on my own, when you called. We might as well both soothe ourselves with it. It's one of my favourites.' They smiled at each other, and sat there humming to the music. 'I know this much, now,' said Inga jokingly, with all the black, burnt coal dust still on her face, 'I wouldn't like to have to be a coalman or a miner.'

'Me neither,' agreed Mrs Collywood, swaying slightly to the music, 'though I wouldn't mind waltzing round with one at this moment.'

Inga went into the kitchen to top up the teapot with more hot water, and while she was gone there was a knock at the door. Mrs Collywood went to answer it.

A tall young man was standing there in a pale grey suit and a trilby – a real toff. He seemed slightly taken aback by the grimy dishevelled state of Mrs Collywood. 'Excuse me. I wonder if you could help? I'm looking for a Miss Inga Abbott. I was directed to this address.' He looked puzzled.

'Inga . . .' Mrs Collywood's calling voice had a slightly warning note in it, as she turned towards the back kitchen.

Inga hurried in at once, trying to wipe away all the grime from her face with the back of her hand. She was looking straight into the face of Sidney Storell. Her whole body flooded with a terrible panic. All she wanted was to vanish.

Sidney Storell took one startled look at her, then with hastily mumbled apologies he turned swiftly on his heel and walked briskly away.

'Who in heaven's name was that?' gasped Mrs Collywood with eyes popping.

Inga stood dumbstruck. Was she dreaming? 'I . . . I'm not quite sure,' she stammered.

When Mrs Collywood had gone Inga lit the gaslight, locked all the doors, and drew the curtains. Then she went into the kitchen and boiled two extra kettles of hot water to put in the old zinc clothes bath. Brooding sadly, she stripped off all her ruined clothes. They were only fit for the dustbin. Why did nothing ever work out properly? Oh to have met him in all her glory when she had been filled with romantic longings. Instead, the old saying 'All dressed up and nowhere to go' had been only too true.

Shivering slightly, she stood there like a fair water sprite, slowly pouring water over herself from an old tin jug, then scrubbing away at all the aftermath of Mrs Collywoood's chimney disaster, and washing her hair with pink carbolic soap.

Hastily she dried herself on a skimpy towel and dressed quickly again in some old cotton interlock knickers, a Chilprufe woollen vest, and a pale green, thick Celanese petticoat, topped by a rather shrunken woollen jumper and tweed skirt. Finally, she put on some old fawn lisle stockings, which had been carefully darned at the heels many times in the past by Daphne. She took her pale blue garters, stretched them with her hands and drew them up to her thighs to keep her stockings up then put on her carpet slippers. It was back to mundane normality.

She switched on the wireless set, walked over to the fire grate and began to toast a thick slice of white bread on a toasting fork against the hot glowing red embers of coal, whilst an egg boiled in the kitchen.

She smiled to herself ruefully. She felt as if she had grown up completely. And at this particular moment she felt like a real old maid. She would probably never marry. She had never ever been really close to any man except that awful vampire in the wool shop years ago.

And as for that first glimpse of Sidney Storell – on the day of the visit to Whittleshaw Hall – it was all past history. It had been a schoolgirlish grand passion.

Goodness alone knew why he had presented himself in Apple Street at the worst possible moment. And why had she let him go without explaining her ridiculous appearance? At any rate, one small thing was certain: she would never be bumping into *him* again. They always seamed to meet in the most humiliating circumstances. All she could hope was that she was blotted from his mind for ever. She and Mr Storell were both from entirely different worlds, and her world at present was about as rotten as it could be.

She wiped some toast crumbs from her mouth and finished off her boiled . egg. Then she went to the old cake tin on the shelf in the kitchen and cut herself a piece of some Christmas cake that Mrs Collywood had given her. Yes, she was really on her own now. But as she munched the fruity cake her spirits began to rise again. The fire was glowing; music was on the radio; by now, she was busily removing a luscious piece of marzipan from the cake to revel in it separately. Maybe life wasn't *all* bad.

Then, like a gale-swept weathercock, her mood of misery swept round again and soon she was biting her lips with grief once more. If *only* . . . if only mother could really start to recover. If only . . . if only . . . Complete sadness filled her.

The following day, she hurried off to the hospital in a sudden strange panic to visit Daphne, without even stopping to open a letter that had just arrived. She had taken the letter from the mat and put it hurriedly on the table, to read when she returned.

Just as she was going through the hospital gates she experienced a sudden feeling of grief, followed by absolute calm, and before she had climbed the stone steps to the ward, she knew that her mother had already died.

'It was a happy release, dear,' said Sister Kitson.

Slowly, Inga returned home to Apple Street in a bemused state. Her brain tried to list all the things she would need to do – including getting in touch with Ralphie immediately.

It wasn't until late that night that she took the unopened letter from that morning's post and read it. It was brief and impersonal. Petunia Shoreditch apologised for not getting in touch immediately to say that Grandma Abbott had passed away. She said that the funeral had already taken place. It had all been rather complicated with everything happening so suddenly at Christmas and all the rest of the family arriving. There had been a lot of arrangements to make . . . At the end of the letter there was a postscript. 'Our mother has left you £250 and the grand piano in her will. Please do call any time to see us.'

Inga read and re-read the letter in a disbelieving daze. First her poor dearest mother, and now this, all on the same day. At first she could hardly take in the sheer callousness of the letter. She would never have dreamed that she could have been deliberately blotted out of her grandmother's final days on earth. It was as if none of them wanted Inga herself even to exist. Her only true friend from that almost unknown side of the family seemed to be her kind-hearted cousin Nally. She began to wonder as well what would happen now to Albert and Mrs Dawn.

She locked the awful letter away carefully in a small wooden casket which she kept in a suitcase under her bed, and began once more to think of her own direct plight. She had already hurried round to the Murdochs earlier in the day to break the sad news about Mother, only to find that Ralphie was away.

'He's got a new pal now,' said Florrie, 'but you don't need to worry over much. He's not one of Bulky Lobsworth's lot. It's someone from school who lives at Wilmslow and has very wealthy parents who run a nightclub in a basement in Manchester called The Cat's Paw.'

Inga's state of depression went even lower. A nightclub in a basement in Manchester sounded to her to be no better than a more grown-up version of the Ragbottle Gang.

'I'll send Ralphie round to see you as soon as possible,' promised Florrie.

Daphne's funeral was a small, bleak affair. She had no close relatives apart from her children. In the past, after her husband had died in the war, her life had narrowed down to Margot and The Turrets, almost as if she were a prisoner there.

Vinny Swanson sent a wreath of lilies; Petunia sent

a white flowered floral cross, with the message, 'With sympathy from all the Abbott family', as if Daphne and Inga had always been complete outsiders.

All Daphne's money had been left to Ralphie when he reached the age of twenty-one. All she left to Inga were her personal belongings, including some jewellery. Daphne had somehow always assumed that Margot would leave Inga a huge amount.

Ralphie seemed stunned by his mother's death, but he kept his feelings to himself, appearing dazed and silent in the days before the funeral. Inga felt for him, sure that, deep in his heart, he blamed himself for the fate that had befallen her.

The only people actually there to see the small, plain coffin lowered into the damp, frosty earth at the cemetery were Inga, Ralphie, Annie Murdoch and her daughter Florrie, Sister Kitson from the hospital and Mrs Collywood from Apple Street.

'What a miserable month January is,' sighed Sidney 'Lotto' Storell gloomily.

He and his betrothed, Lady Lydia Clucksly, were in the library at Whittleshaw Hall, prowling around, surveying the fire damage again. It was several days since he had called round to see Inga Abbott at Apple Street and rushed off in that odd way. He still felt a little embarrassed at having blundered in on her just after what had obviously been a very distressing experience.

Lydia glanced at him sharply, wondering what had brought on this observation. She was tall and slim-legged with long, fine, dark hair arranged in a neat bun at the nape of her neck. She had fought hard to get herself engaged to Lotto Storell, the good-natured, popular darling of all the rich girls – even though he himself often seemed more interested in cars than women. Motor racing was his real passion. Lydia had known him since childhood. They had grown up together and now she was determined that they would eventually grow old together.

'You know,' went on Sidney thoughtfully, 'when Tomkins visited us again the other day, there was some mention of that young Miss Abbott who came with him the first time to help him do the measuring. Apparently, she was asked to leave her job simply because of all the kerfuffle when that ladder fell over . . . It seems she was only at Pearlways in a temporary capacity. All the same, I think it was a bit thick – sacking her.'

Lydia became extra alert and gave Lotto a shrewd sweeping gaze. Why on earth was he telling her all this in such detail about that little chit of a nobody? It was unlike him to show such interest in a girl of that sort. 'I don't,' she said firmly, her thin lips setting in a hard line. 'I remember her clearly from that catastrophic *Butterfly* night. She and that other girl caused all that upset with that wretched little dog. She even had the temerity to pinch my seat. She's a brass-faced little cow.' Lydia stared at Lotto with cool blandness.

Sidney Storell said no more. He didn't mention to Lydia or anyone else that he had telephoned one of the managing directors at P.I.C. to protest at the company's unfairness in sacking Miss Abbott.

'I can assure you that Miss Abbott's conduct at Whittleshaw Hall was exemplary,' he had said. 'The whole episode was a pure accident. It could have happened to anyone. The girl has been unjustly victimised. I feel so upset by it that I may well look elsewhere for insurance in the future.'

There had been a sudden cough at the other end of the phone as the director nervously cleared his throat. 'I can assure you, Mr Storell, that I knew nothing whatsoever of the incident. Mr Tomkins has no right to sack anyone without higher authority. It is not the policy of our company. I shall interview him immediately and see about Miss Abbott's temporary reinstatement . . .'

Now, Storell thought about his brief visit to Apple Street and how unfortunate it was that he had called at such a bad time. He had seen the fire engine leaving the area when he was approaching Apple Street and neighbours had been at pains to regale him with details of the incident when he had asked which house she lived in. He could have kicked himself for calling when she and her next-door neighbour hadn't even had the time to recover from it all properly.

'Sidney . . .' Lydia's voice had taken on a cooing softness. 'I've been having more thoughts about the wedding . . . I think it should be sooner rather than later. I even think we could try a register office and have a very, very quiet affair, out of respect for your dead father. It would look less blasé than a full religious ceremony. I'm sure your poor mother would welcome something less fussy when she gets back from recuperating in France. We can't wait for ever for all this mourning period to be over. We both know what big family weddings can be like – they cost a fortune, and simply provide an opportunity for the most distant of relatives to have a wonderful spree and then start a family row. Once you start making those sort of plans the whole thing snowballs. Not to mention the time factor – it would completely muck up your motor racing plans . . .'

Sidney looked at her with a bland expression, then said rather evasively, 'Anyway, old thing – there's no *real* hurry, surely? Perhaps we should make it later, rather than sooner. But I do agree about the wedding fuss. We don't need all that.'

Lydia's jaws clamped together firmly. He was never exactly easy to manoeuvre, but she let the subject settle for the time being.

After Margot's funeral, her children squabbled endlessly about the contents of the will and what to do with The Turrets. Margot had left it in a sort of trust 'so that it is available to all my relatives, including my grandchildren, when I have gone'.

'What a stupid thing to do. It should have been left to me outright,' grumbled Petunia Shoreditch in private to Nally. 'Here I am, the eldest living daughter, who was here to help her through all those last weeks of her life, and I have faithfully organised this whole household.' Petunia sounded as if the whole experience had been a great sacrifice for her when really she had been having a pleasant time, playing golf every day and planning to win back her husband and rebuild her marriage, using

The Turrets as a second home where they could go to relax.

She had also visited Margot in hospital just before she had died and bluntly described her plans for the future of The Turrets even as Margot lay helpless. She had left the hospital feeling almost cheerful.

'Yes, I can truthfully say in confidence, Nally, that I am the only one in the family who has kept things going here in the north amidst all this turmoil and shock. And now we're being chivvied by all the rest of them to sell the house and divide the proceeds. That's because your aunts are totally ruled by their husbands.

'Naturally, I shall be more than happy to make arrangements for all the grandchildren to come for holidays from time to time, and I may well keep Mrs Dawn and Albert on as retainers when we're not in residence. I thought it most generous of Mother to leave Albert that lovely set of chisels and some garden shears in her will. Though they would have come in very handy for us . . . And her gift to Mrs Dawn of that Singer sewing machine was quite unbelievable. That would have been better to have stayed here – with us, too.'

Nally could hear her mother getting more and more grandiose every second. 'What about Inga, Mother? She knows the house better than any of us. It was her childhood home.'

'Inga is no different from any other grandchild, Ronalda. I shall make up a schedule and she will be allowed the same amount of time here as all the other grandchildren. It will be for two weeks in the summer.' Petunia frowned. 'I expect we'll have to see about that wretched grand piano though. I always thought Mother would leave that to me . . . Where on earth will Inga put it? Perhaps I should drop her a note and offer to keep it here . . .'

It was on the same day – shortly after this private conversation – that Albert and Mrs Dawn both gave in their notice.

'The end of an era,' said Cissie to Albert. 'It will never be the same without Mrs Abbott. I quite envy you and Lotty having a paid holiday to sail to Canada to see your daughter.'

'And what'll *you* do then, Cissie – with all *your* spare time?' Albert winked at her, filled the bowl of his pipe with tobacco and pressed it down with his heavy, work-scarred thumb.

'A bit of dressmaking most likely. Seeing as I've now got two sewing machines to go at. Our Avril will be able to help me. I got that Singer machine from Mrs Abbott in the first place. She wanted me to run up a few pinafores for Inga when she was little, and repair some sheets and pillowcases. It was a very old second-hand one. She said it was mine. It'll be nice to see a bit more of my own home from now on . . .'

Inga was absolutely amazed to receive a letter from Pearlways Insurance apologising for a gross misunderstanding and offering her some further temporary employment in their counting house – counting out money under the supervision of Miss Mildred Shaw.

Her position as Mr Tomkins's assistant was now to be taken permanently by Miss Donna O'Dee. Miss

Westfield, much to her chagrin, was promoted to be permanent assistant to fussy Mr Robins who was a terrible hypochondriac, with a different illness for every day of the week.

It was a wonderful relief for Inga to be back at work again. It helped to lessen the strain and loneliness of her double bereavement. And although the counting house was boring work, at least she was getting a small regular weekly wage and had Donna there to make her laugh when she related her own experiences when out with Mr Tomkins. 'Sure an' didn't I read the measurements out back to front? An' wasn't he blazin' mad? How long will I last – can y' tell me that?'

But she did last. Mr Tomkins did not dare to utter a word of complaint.

Then, one Sunday in February, just when Inga was becoming more used to her solitary life, she was confronted at the front door in Apple Street by a well-dressed elderly woman who wore a black coat with a huge creamy fur collar and a deep black felt hat. She looked about Margot's age.

Inga had no idea who she was, but to Maud Beardsley it was almost a re-enactment of that time years ago when she had turned up on the doorstep at Apple Street to inform Daphne that Osmond was going back home with her – his proper wife.

Her white hair was still carefully tinted but less strongly. She was thin and healthy and sharp eyed.

'I'm glad I've found you in.' Maud gave a small, rather clipped smile. 'I know you don't recognise me, Inga, but I am Maud Beardsley. I'm Osmond's widow, and I knew your grandmother very well. Could I come in for a few minutes? There's something I'd like to discuss and it's quite important.'

Inga nodded silently, her brain in a bit of a whirl as she tried to guess what it could be about. She smoothed her hair nervously with her hand and wished that it was neater, and that she didn't have holes in the elbows of her old heliotrope woollen cardigan. But she put a brave face on her situation, opened the door wide and ushered Maud in. 'Will you have a cup of tea?'

Maud nodded. She sat down immediately in the best chair and before Inga even had time to go and put the kettle on, Maud was talking continuously. It was almost like receiving instruction from a headmistress, as Maud related the whole history of herself and Osmond, including the time he left her to run off with Daphne, and the subsequent birth of Ralphie. 'So you can see what a dance he led me. And not only me – but your own mother.

'At one time I only thought of it all in relation to myself. But as the years have gone by I now see it in a more rounded way. That's why I've come here today to offer Ralph board and lodgings at my home. I think Osmond owed that much to your dead mother. You may or may not know, but the monthly allowance he left for Ralph will cease when the boy is fourteen.'

Inga flopped down on the small sofa and took a deep breath. 'I'm afraid all this news is rather sudden, Mrs Beardsley. Ralphie is settled at his school at Erudine College and already boards out with some friends we have known for years called the Murdochs. I'm sure my mother would never have wanted him moved if she'd still been alive . . .'

The conversation came to an *impasse*. Inga escaped to attend to the tea and biscuits. Maud's offer was a proposition she would never have dreamed she'd be saddled with. To be quite candid, there had been so many other things on her mind that she had never given any proper thought to the forthcoming financial situation of herself and Ralphie.

When they were sipping their tea, Maud said, 'And of course there's the problem of this house in Apple Street too . . .'

'What do you mean?' Inga felt herself going bright scarlet.

'It was owned by Osmond but now belongs to me. Did Daphne never mention it?'

'No.' Inga began to shiver slightly. She well remembered her mother saying quite often in rather urgent tones that as soon as she had enough money they would all move from Apple Street to somewhere like Timperley. It was a constant dream. Inga hadn't taken much notice. It wasn't for her to pry into her mother's affairs.

'Anyway – give some thought to what I've said, won't you?' said Maud severely. 'I feel that both of us have become the victims of Osmond's past misdemeanours, and I want to make amends. It's all a lot of sudden responsibility for a young girl like you. After all, you have your own life to lead, haven't you? Whereas I have already lived most of mine . . .'

Inga was in a turmoil, not knowing what to do.

She felt the whole problem of Ralphie was beyond her. Hastily she decided to do what Maud had suggested and accept her offer to have Ralphie to stay with her.

'I expect you're right, Mrs Beardsley . . .'

'I *know* I'm right, Inga.' A slight flicker of triumph rose in Maud's eyes.

'I'll see Ralphie as soon as possible and explain what's happened and that he will be going to his father's own orginal home . . .'

'Quite . . . You're a very sensible girl, Inga. Let me know when he'll be coming to me – the sooner, the better.'

A few minutes later Maud had gone, leaving Inga with a sudden sense of impending doom. She tried to comfort herself; after all, she was Ralphie's nearest relative even though she was only his half-sister. He would be going to much pleasanter, even luxurious, surroundings belonging to his father's own background. Surely her mother would have approved of it?

'No, no. I will *not* go there!' said Ralphie angrily a few days later. Inga saw his eyes flashing. He stared at her stubbornly. He was ten now, and growing fast into a handsome youth. Inga could see a likeness to Daphne in his features. There was already a streak of languid elegance about him.

Inga was in a quandary. She knew he was beyond forcing. She tried to reason with him. 'Can't you see what a chance it would be to be living in your own father's house in really comfortable, gentlemanly surroundings? Some boys would absolutely jump at the chance. You would be on a par with all your friends at Erudine. You've no idea how much a background like that can hold you in good stead for the future, even if you are only a lodger. I'm sure Mother would have approved.'

He went slightly pale, and his young face seemed to age. 'She wouldn't. Mother would never like me to go there, never. Mother was an orphan, and I'm an orphan too. I never even had my father's true name. I have our mother's maiden name of Trent. And Trent my name will always be: Ralphie Trent.' He stared at her hard and the look spoke volumes. It was as if he knew he had to face the world, and that everything he did from now on would be entirely up to his own judgement.

Inga said no more. Instead, when Ralphie had gone back to Blossom Street to the Murdochs' house which he now regarded as his home, she sat down and wrote to Maud.

'. . . I'm afraid that Ralphie is adamant. He prefers to stay where he is. I am powerless to change his mind. Yours sincerely, Inga Abbott.'

The month of February passed without any reply. Then, early in a rainy March, she received a letter. It was from Halstead and Ferryman, solicitors on behalf of Mrs Maud Beardsley. Maud was issuing her with a month's notice and selling the house in Apple Street.

There was also a second paragraph saying that further money had been put aside for Ralph from his dead father's estate, should he continue with his education beyond the age of fourteen. Inga reread the letter again and again.

All *she* would have in four weeks' time was £250 and an unclaimed grand piano.

15

ONE FRIEND

Inga was sitting in the living room at Blossom Street on a Sunday afternoon talking to the Murdochs about looking for somewhere to live now that Maud was selling the house in Apple Street.

'Talk about *swiftness* . . . She's already found a buyer. She wants me out by the end of March.'

They all stared at her in consternation.

These days, Annie Murdoch had a part-time job as a hairdressing assistant in town. Florrie, who was now twenty-two, was still in the catering trade as a supervisor. Dennis had just got married and now lived round the corner with his wife whose father, Algy Foreman, ran the Ball and Chain (men only) pub in Ardour Street where Dennis was now working.

'Well, at least there's one thing,' said Inga. 'At least I don't have to worry about Ralphie being well cared for here with you in Blossom Street. The longer he can stay on at his education the better, because he will get the finance for it from his father's estate.'

'What will *you* do about work?' said Annie.

'I shall just keep my fingers crossed that the temporary job at P.I.C. spins out,' said Inga ruefully.

But two days later her hopes were dashed. She was 'given her cards' along with six other girls there – a week's notice, with gracious thanks for their faithful temporary service.

Inga was desolate. She went back home to Apple Street and stared round dolefully. She knew she was a great deal better off than most, for at least she had the £250 pounds her grandmother had left her. To some people that was the equivalent of being a millionaire: it was enough to buy a small modern house outright, in countrified surroundings on the outskirts of Manchester.

Yet she knew deep down she must hang on to the money – just in case of emergency. She would leave it in the savings bank, in the care of Donkins and Drury, Grandma Abbott's solicitors. Ideally, at present it was best to pretend she hadn't got it and to concentrate on finding work, and a rented unfurnished flat, as soon as possible.

A cheap small place . . . She became gloomy again. How on earth would Grandma's grand piano fit in somewhere like that? Or was it doomed to stay either at The Turrets, becoming more and more theirs every day, or to be expensively stored away in some huge tatty storehouse?

When the final day of her week's notice arrived, Inga had begun to cheer up and try to make the best of it. She and Donna O'Dee had sworn eternal friendship. There was a goodbye office get-together, with ginger beer and cake, for all six departing girls. Inga had also had an offer of work from an unexpected quarter. Knowing her background and present circumstances, Dennis Murdoch had approached her and asked if she would like to sing a few old favourites in the evenings in his father-in-law's pub in Ardour Street. With no alternative on the horizon, Inga had accepted gratefully.

'I'll keep a look out for you for a place to live,' promised Donna, 'and good luck with your singin' in that men only pub. Who can tell but it might be the start of your childhood singin' career all over again?'

Inga shook her head doubtfully, not confident that she had been right to accept the hurried offer from Florrie's brother.

'You'll do marvels, Inga,' said Donna comfortingly. 'Haven't I heard you sing meself and haven't you got a voice straight from heaven even without a piano?'

On the night she had accepted Dennis's suggestion Inga had gone back to Apple Street in a very unsettled, panicky state. What on earth had induced her to agree to go and sing at the Ball and Chain? The very name of the place was enough to put anyone off, added to the fact that it was men only and she was going to be paid a mere pittance.

But there was still some deep down longing . . . She felt she had to accept the challenge, to find out if all the training she had gained when she had lived at The Turrets with her grandmother would bear any fruit. For she was totally alone now in a harsh, ruthless world. Her trained voice and a working knowledge of piano playing were the only important basic skills she had. All the same, it was a far cry from the Cheshire Masonic dinners, the *conversazioni*, and afternoon tea parties of the past. She had led a very sheltered life when she came to think of it – she had never been in a city or street pub in Manchester in her life.

When she mentioned her new job to Mrs Collywood, she saw the colour rise in her neighbour's face and a guarded look appear.

'Are you *quite* sure you know what you're doing, love? I don't want to say anything I shouldn't – especially with you knowing those Murdochs so well, but the Ball and Chain has a bit of a reputation . . . There's been some very funny goings-on there, in the past. I can still remember a terrible scandal that happend there when I was a toddler which is best forgotten.'

'It won't be like that now, surely?' said Inga, trying to be cheerful. 'Dennis would never have got himself involved there if it had been a really seedy place.'

Mrs Collywood shrugged her hefty shoulders, and shuddered slightly. 'You can just never be too careful, Inga. But the best of luck, all the same.'

On the day she was due to sing at the pub, Inga was still wondering what to wear. She was becoming almost scraggy. Her buxom young bosom had practically disappeared. In some ways she was glad; it meant she could wear anything.

She had kept many of Daphne's clothes, never having had the heart to get rid of them, and Daphne had always been very thin, even thinner than Inga was at present.

In the end she decided to wear an ankle-length frock that Daphne had once made by hand from a remnant of heavy silvery grey satin but, for some reason, had put to one side. Inga tried it on. It fitted her like a glove, stretching across her youthful flat belly, as smooth and shining as ice.

Dennis had told her to sing old-fashioned songs that everyone knew, like 'Lily of Laguna', 'Down at the Old Bull and Bush' and 'In the Shade of the Old Apple Tree'. 'Bert on t' piana knows 'em off by heart and it'll be best for you to have summat easy for a first try-out. You'll need to go through 'em a bit before the pub opens.'

Inga felt her heart thumping as the time came to leave Apple Street for the Ball and Chain. She had packed the frock in a small travelling bag, interlaid with tissue paper, and had taken a small pochette with her which had also belonged to Daphne. It contained some bloom for her cheeks, a lipstick and a powder compact which was inlaid on top with deep blue butterfly wings in an oblong narrow band of gold.

She gave thanks to the Almighty that the evening was clear and dry as she took the tram towards central Manchester. Ardour Street was on the southern fringes of the city – tucked away behind the six-storeyed, ornate Watts Warehouse in Portland Street, between Oxford Road and Piccadilly.

It was when she was hurrying past the Midland Hotel that she literally bumped into Sidney Storell and Lydia. Lydia was swathed in a huge fur coat and tiny shell-like hat. The two of them were strolling along in the yellow dusky lamplight, taking up the whole of the pavement.

They were having a casual conversation dominated by Lydia's penetrating voice.

There wasn't room for her on the pavement, so she gave way and walked in the gutter, as they hadn't noticed her. As they passed, Inga's small suitcase knocked against them and, as she raised her head, she realised she was staring straight up at Storell.

He glanced back at her for a second then smiled and said genially, 'Miss Abbott, fancy us crashing into each other like this. How's life at the Insurance Company?'

'I'm not there any more. It was only temporary, and—'

Lydia interrupted them hurriedly with a meaning edge to her tone. 'If you don't mind, Lotto, I'll go and join the others – they'll be waiting . . . Right?'

He nodded absent-mindedly as she went into the hotel, and looked towards Inga again as he recalled the trouble he'd gone to in order to get her reinstated at work. 'Short and sweet, eh? I thought you'd last there even longer than Mr Tomkins. Have you found something better?'

'No. As a matter of fact – I have no work at present except . . .' she hesitated. Should she mention where she was going? 'Well, it's rather a long story . . .' She began to gabble it all out. '. . . and what with them both dying and the house going – and this offer to go and sing at the Ball and Chain – I—'

'The Ball and Chain?' His amazed reaction was exactly the same as Mrs Collywood's. 'Have you ever actually been there before?'

'Well no, but—' Suddenly she stopped and looked him up and down. 'Why, have you?'

He nodded and his mouth spread to a half-ashamed quirky smile. 'Look, I've got to dash. But why don't we meet again for a meal some time? Where can I get hold of you? Are you still in Apple Street? Shall I call tomorrow evening?'

She nodded silently, like someone in a dream, and he was gone. She began to hurry in a panic towards Ardour Street, hoping she wouldn't be late. The meeting with Sidney Storell was tumbling round her brain.

Even though she had so much else to think about, a random thought suddenly struck her: might it be possible that if she saw him again he could arrange to store her grand piano in one of the numerous out-houses at Whittleshaw Hall?

'You've been an absolute age, Lotto.' Lydia looked at him balefully from behind a gin and It in the hotel.

She was sitting on a wide leather sofa with Tiggy Lemster who had just refused her pleas for him to remove his tweed deerstalker hat. His girlfriend Dorita was smoking a Turkish cigarette from a long jade holder and was trying to take no notice, except to cough slightly and speak in a hoarse voluptuous voice about one of the waiters, who had a curvaceous black moustache with a small diamond in the centre of its two wings on his upper lip.

He prowled across to them and Sidney ordered a brandy, glancing at everyone apologetically. 'Lydia and I met Miss Abbott. She bumped into us.'

'Accidentally on purpose,' drawled Lydia with cool maliciousness. 'I think she's got a sort of schoolgirl pash on Lotto. She fell from a ladder into his arms, just after Christmas, and she's obviously never got over it.'

'I wouldn't put it quite like that, Lydia.' Storell was slightly rattled.

'I would,' said Lydia.

Sidney sipped his drink in silence as the others gossiped away. His mind was still on Inga. He just couldn't believe that she was going to stand up and sing in the Ball and Chain. In fact, the whole idea of it niggled him so much that when more friends arrived, Sydney began to get extremely restless. He declined another brandy and slipped away, glad to escape the conversation which covered such diverse topics as Jacob Epstein, Salvador Dali, Mickey Mouse films, George Gershwin, Gracie Fields, The Lord Mayor of Manchester, and Oswald Mosley and the Labour Party.

Deliberately ignoring Lydia's questioning look, he escaped into the cold night air, and hastened towards the Ball and Chain, like a man drawn by a magnet.

Inga had squashed into the silvery grey satin gown. She began to feel uneasy. She was struggling to get herself ready for the evening's entertainment down stairs in a small, badly lit cellar. In the bar upstairs was a chalked-up board: 'A MUSICAL NIGHT FOR YOUR DELIGHT – Sonia and her Patriotic Flags, Miss Flavia Dickinson and her Magic Moments, Ronny Redfern the Nightingale Referee.' Then, in small letters at the end: 'Miss Inga Abbott singing Old Favourites'.

With trembling fingers, Inga opened the pochette and took out her make-up compact. She didn't put much on because the light was so bad. There was no full-length mirror. Anxiously she sensed that she had swollen up a bit since she'd tried the long dress on in the peacefulness of Apple Street earlier in the day.

Her face was burning with nervousness. She began to wonder if her bottom would be sticking out too much, like a figure S, and if her nipples would poke up against the smooth satin and shake when she sang. Daphne's home-made gown left no space for heavy underwear with its narrow shoulder straps and a V neck at both back and front.

Her rehearsal had been a great success. Bert Hadley, the middle-aged pianist in a plum coloured velvet jacket and hands like bunches of bananas, had rehearsed the numbers with her when she'd first arrived and was most impressed.

'You're real class, love, real class. What I advise you to do is to stay in t' cellar whilst the other acts is on. Put your coat back on to keep warm and I'll whistle you when we need you. Sit near the boiler where it's warmest.' He patted her shoulder consolingly. 'The first time's allus the worst. And don't take any notice of cat calls or owt. I'll take care of all that.'

In the gloom of the cellar Inga sat there fearfully, wondering rather too late whether she had done the right thing in the first place coming here. She had already noticed some rather suggestive garments hanging behind the crude wooden door in the far corner. There were huge, well-worn pale orange interlock women's bloomers and some heavy pink cotton stays suspended by their long laces. On top of the rickety hook perched a moth-eaten wig of coarse brown hair. Everything stank of tobacco and beer. For some reason it all sent a shiver down her spine.

She comforted herself with the thought that, obviously, they were part of a Dame's pantomime clothes. She thought of the other people who were chalked up on the board upstairs. Where would they change into their clothes or did they arrive as they were?

Suddenly she heard roaring and heavy thumping and stamping going on upstairs and men laughing and shouting. Pinpricks of perspiration surfaced on her forehead, but her hands were cold and stiff. She was terrified.

Sidney Storell was sitting far back in a corner of the pub on a high-backed heavy oak bench, slowly supping a pint of black and tan.

Sonia and her Patriotic Flags had just been on. 'Sonia' turned out to be a six-footer, and the final flag, placed on his private parts, had risen, seemingly of its own volition, and fallen to the floor with the triumphant crash of piano chords.

The row died down as Miss Flavia Dickinson, a genuine woman well past her prime in a drooping georgette dress and a flat, working-man's cap sang 'Buddy, Can You Spare a Dime?' very badly. She was clapped heartily as the drinkers waited impatiently for Ronny Redfern, the man of a thousand vulgar swear words set to music, who was dressed as a football referee. Then, at last, Inga heard the cellar door open and Mr Hadley whistled her from upstairs.

Filled with dread, she climbed the cellar steps carefully, tightly cocooned in the grey satin. But in spite of her care and her cold hands she was immediately aware that the seams of her dress were giving way.

She put her fingers along the left hand side and felt small gaps appearing and broken stitching. Defensively, she held her arms close to her sides to cover the seams as thoughts from the past invaded her brain. Fleetingly, she remembered how Daphne had once complained about the poor quality of some silk cotton which was a disaster when she'd used it on a home-made blouse. She had blamed mice or rotting dampness. The thread had broken off the whole time in short lengths.

Mr Hadley greeted her at the open door of the cellar with a wide smile. 'This is your big chance, sweetheart,' he muttered. He turned and faced the packed, hot, sweating audience amidst the talking, shouting, boozy bonhomie of clattering mugs and clinking glasses.

'And now, gentlemen, our final treat: the beautiful and talented Miss Inga Abbott singing a few old favourites. She wants you to join in the choruses. Remember to use the right words please for this lovely little newcomer.'

There was loud applause as Bert sat at the piano and began to play. Then there was complete hush . . .

The moment Inga began to sing she was swept into a world she thought had gone forever. She was thrust into the excitement of doing something for herself at last.

She had never seen or sensed such concentration in an audience. She had never imagined that an all-male gathering would be so attentive. They were fixing her with amazed and glowing eyes. So much so that she went from one musical chorus to the next with more and more confident exuberance as her arms stretched towards them in passionate expression.

The applause at the end was rapturous. She turned and bowed slightly this way and that and then, like a dream princess, turned away in complete euphoria and almost flew through the cellar door which Mr Hadley had opened. Like a multi-winged angel she flitted down the steps, her face ablaze with triumphant joy.

It wasn't until she got back into the drab little whitewashed cell where her outdoor clothes were that she began to come to. It wasn't until she flopped into the old wicker armchair that she realised, with growing horror, that both the seams of her dress were completely apart with slits from top to bottom.

Hastily, she tore the dress from her body and pushed it into her bag. What a castastrophe! No wonder they had all gawped at her with such intent. She felt so awful now that she dreaded leaving the cellar again, wanting only to vanish into obscurity.

Sidney Storell, sitting in the semi-darkness amongst the crowd, had been transfixed like the rest as they had heard the beautiful voice. Despite Inga's fears, all they had seen was a slip of a girl in a long flowing tunic which swayed and fluttered with her body when she moved her arms.

'A real treat,' said one of them reverently.

'It's nice to get a bit of proper class,' said another.

Some of them were so lulled with happiness that she could have stood there naked and they would hardly have noticed. She had been the perfect ending for a 'reet good night'.

Full of shame, Inga crept out of the cellar again. Everywhere was quiet now. There was only one gaslight on and all the seats were dark and empty. Only the pub owner, Algy Foreman, was there with Bert the pianist and, to Inga's intense shock, Sidney Storell standing in the background.

Dennis Murdoch had already gone and Inga was thankful. She felt she would never be able to face the Murdochs again. What a fool she was to have worn that ill-fated gown of Daphne's! What ruination!

Mr Foreman stepped forward to greet her and shook her hand enthusiastically. 'What a terrific performance, Miss Abbott.' He thrust a small envelope towards her from the bar counter; it contained her meagre payment. 'I hope we shall see more of you.' She gazed at him silently with a slight smile of thanks for at least being so gentlemanly and kind. Fancy wanting to see more of her – when they had all seen the ultimate.

Sidney Storell came over to greet her. 'I came to see how you were going on and I wondered how you were going to get home. I didn't realise you had such a wonderful voice. Have you had it trained?'

She looked away in a complete fluster. 'Only when I was a child . . . my grandmother—' She stopped hastily. It was all gone for ever now.

'Shall I see you back to Apple Street?'

She nodded and tears began to form in her eyes. She was completely exhausted.

He took hold of her small travel bag as she followed him meekly from the Ball and Chain – never to visit it again.

16

DESTRUCTION

'So what happened to you then?' Lydia glared at Sidney. She was following him around, nagging at him as he strode from barn to out-house to empty stable, weighing up where he might store a grand piano. The Hall itself was out of the question; it was stuffed full of enough furniture and artifacts to start a fair-sized museum.

Lydia's life at present – while Lotto's ma was still away in the South of France – was completely geared to hanging on to Lotto's every movement like dear life. Her own home at Belhurst House was a hive of activity. Her mother and father were a thriving pair, with loud authoritive voices whose tones rang through the whole local community, and her three brothers and four sisters were forever bouncing about from educational establishments and places of work with healthy pink faces and alert eyes. As for her own actual work, Lydia managed to organise her days quite satisfactorily. Her great uncle was away for another month at present doing business in the wine trade. When he was in town she worked three days a week doing clerical work for him. The rest of her time she helped her mother.

Her father had managed to provide all his children with a quarterly allowance higher than any ordinary working factory employee's total annual wage. Yes, her own existence was entirely different from Lotto's rather lonely regime at home supplemented by his horrifically expensive motor racing escapades.

His sudden disappearance from the Midland Hotel last night had been rather disturbing, thought Lydia. It showed he wasn't entirely bound to her in spite of the fact that she would have a substantial marriage dowry to bolster his finances. First thing this morning, she had galloped all the way from Belhurst to Whittleshaw on Sunflower, her roan mare, to find out what exactly Lotto had been up to.

Sidney Storell wished Lydia wasn't here. He didn't feel like having to explain. He gave an exasperated groan. 'If you *must* know I toddled off to see the proverbial man about a dog, and eventually landed up in a small alehouse . . .'

She looked at him knowingly. 'It wouldn't surprise me in the least if you'd sloped off to find that gooey-eyed young pest we bumped into outside the hotel.'

Sidney turned and stared at her challengingly, but his mind was on other things. He had just found the perfect spot for the piano in a room behind the estate offices which was dry and weatherproof. There were three ancient filing cabinets in it. The stone-flagged floor was even and uncluttered. The room was mostly empty.

'How right you are, Lydia. In actual fact I went to a pub called the Ball and Chain to watch some boozy entertainment. Miss Abbott was there singing. She has a wonderful voice. I took her home and deposited her safely through her own front door.' His eyes narrowed with cool enjoyment as he saw Lydia's startled face.

The following Sunday was a sunny day.

During the previous week Sidney Storell had sent a postcard to Apple Street:

Dear Miss Abbott,

Just to say I have found the very place for your piano. Please advise me about when you will be moving it.

Yours sincerely,

S. Storell

Inga decided to go round to see her piano at The Turrets. These days there was never a peep from any of them. In some ways she was glad. She preferred to try and wipe that past life from her memory. She knew that to see Aunt Petsy there – ruling the roost with mercenary delight – would be like a dagger in her heart, but all the same she was determined not to let go of what was rightfully hers.

She wondered what had happened to Albert and Mrs Dawn. How would they be surviving without Grandma? In the past they had always been there for some part of

Sunday, keeping the place on an even keel, and forfeiting their own weekend comforts.

She set off early with blue skies, and glossy starlings strutting across walls and backyards, filling the quiet Sunday air with chatter. She was dressed in her best clothes, and wore a turquoise brooch of Daphne's on the lapel of her tweed jacket. Her fair hair shone from beneath the edges of a small neat hat, and she wore gloves.

As she walked along the road towards The Turrets, she was surprised at how exactly the same it was. It hadn't changed one jot from when she had lived there as a child. Deep in her imagination she had feared it might all have altered or vanished now that Grandma had gone, even though Grandma had died so recently.

Two young girls cantered by on horses, from a wide tree-lined avenue. It was the same Sunday morning ritual. As she started to walk up the drive, she glanced about expecting to see Albert's wheelbarrow, or movement from the side of the house where Mrs Dawn was usually to be found, but today it was as quiet as a tomb.

Petunia Shoreditch was upstairs in one of the attics and she saw Inga coming along the drive. At first she didn't recognise her. Petunia's mind was on other matters. She was entirely alone in the house now. Her sisters had all returned to their respective homes and families and Nally was back at college.

She was still sifting through the place, listing every item in every cupboard and drawer with determined satisfaction. Already she felt that the house and all its remaining contents, after her sisters had finished their raid, were hers for ever. After all, hadn't she been the one to be caring enough to visit her mother in the first place? Wasn't it she who came here and stayed on to be Margot's stalwart helper; ever present in times of need and emergency until the very end? Yes, this place and all its contents were virtually her property. She was the chosen custodian.

She was enjoying her golf, too. The ladies' section at Baguely Side Golf Club was a godsend. She played on every ladies' day, and had even managed to procure herself a male partner for other times: a widower called Mr Aleson, who was a perfect gentleman. Without all that going on she knew she would have felt a bit isolated, after her busy Oxford days. Her own idea of fulfilment was completely different from the Good Works of Margot.

Already she felt as if she had been here for years instead of a couple of months. But there was one snag. She hated being alone in the house at night. Sometimes in bed she thought about her husband Ronald. Was he resting at this very moment in the arms of his female engineer? She suspected that the younger woman might well tire of him . . .

Petunia frowned to herself as she hurried downstairs to answer the front door. Would Ronald come back to her if that happened? Would she return to Oxford again and pick up the threads? Or would she stay here in her rightful place and guard The Turrets, just as she was doing now, and play golf with her newly found friends?

'Good morning,' said Inga with a hesitant look as the door opened.

Petunia stared at her as if Inga were trying to sell her something. Then she forced a smile and said, 'Come in. What can I do for you? Isn't it a lovely day?'

She led Inga into the drawing room. The whole place almost echoed with emptiness. Most of the best pictures and ornaments had vanished; one big carpet had gone, and some of the rugs; two armchairs had vanished along with a glass-fronted bureau and a bookcase.

Inga looked with relief towards the grand piano. The stool had gone. Petsy saw the look.

'I really came to see how my piano was going on,' said Inga bravely. 'I think I've found a suitable home for it.'

Petunia stiffened. 'A suitable home?' she said defensively. 'Whatever do you mean? Surely you are joking, Inga? What could be more suitable than this home, where it has always been?' Petunia tried to keep the conversation in a lighter vein; she tried to be civil.

Inga looked at the red hair and the half-smiling steely mouth set in the substantial jaw and felt herself wilting slightly. She knew now it was going to be a battle. 'But it's mine, Aunt Petsy. Grandma left it to me in her will.'

'I *know* that, dear. All I'm trying to say is that with a valuable and delicate item like a grand piano one has to be very, very careful. You have to think of the *temperature* of a place, and the atmosphere, not to mention the moving of it from its permanent position in this room. Terrible damage could be incurred which we would both regret if it ever had to be moved. There's such a thing as tempting fate, you know . . .' Petsy's eyes fixed Inga's with such piercing precision that Inga began to think she was looking into her grandmother's eyes again. She began to feel quite weak.

She looked away deliberately. 'Even so, I want to take it somewhere else if you don't mind,' she said in a low voice. 'I want to do it as soon as possible – within these next few days. By the end of the week at the very latest.'

She could see a stubborn anger rising in Aunt Petsy's face. 'You just do not know what you're about, you silly girl! How can *you* – living in that small rabbit hutch of a place in the city – ever hope to keep it in better conditions than at The Turrets? It would be absolute sacrilege to put it in store in some warehouse – which I'm sure you'd never be able to afford for long. Have you really thought it through? I suggest you go straight back home and think again. It won't run away in the night, you know. It's quite happy staying here in this house for ever.'

Petunia became triumphant; she felt she had won. 'You can come here any time you want, to play it. I shall always keep it well tuned and polished. And of course, if you choose to spend a fortnight here in the summer, it will be yours to do what you like with for the whole of that time.' She glanced down at her gold watch.

Inga had glimpsed Petunia's watch so often in the past, gleaming softly from beneath a neatly folded cuff on Margot's wrist. Morbidly, it occurred to her that they were both wearing tokens of death: she with her mother Daphne's brooch and Petunia with her mother Margot's watch.

'Now, if you'll forgive me,' said Petunia with brisk

dismissal, 'I have to go out myself. I have an appointment at the golf club, for Sunday lunch with a friend.'

Inga stood there uncertainly then, without a word, she hurried from the drawing room towards the front door with Petunia following her. In seconds she had been ushered out and the door firmly closed again. She stood there on the gravel gazing towards the drive, her brain in a whirl. What should she do now? Did this mean that Petunia was going to hang on to the piano for ever? She was overwhelmed by sudden depression.

When she got home to Apple Street she re-read the note that Sidney Storell had sent her. Her only option was to write to him and explain what had happened. With a heavy heart she found a notepad and setttled down to write.

> Apple Street
> Sunday.

Dear Mr Storell,

Thank you for your note about the piano and your kind offer to store it for me. I have just been to my grandmother's house but did not manage to come to any arrangement with my aunt about moving it. I am wondering what to do. I fear I shall never manage to get it away from The Turrets.

Yours in thanks and sincerity,

Inga Abbott

She addressed the envelope with a feeling of doom, and, as she walked to the letter box with the letter, she almost wondered whether to rip it up – after all, what could he do about it? It wasn't really his problem and he had done enough for her already – what with getting her reinstated at the insurance company and coming to listen to her sing at the Ball and Chain.

She became so morose that she wished she had never even been to Whittleshaw Hall in the first place to see *Madam Butterfly*. But what was the use of wishing when life had already set its pattern? Nothing could ever be undone.

On Tuesday, Sidney Storell was sitting there alone in his study reading her letter and wondering what to do. He put it to one side in a small cubbyhole in the top of his desk. Then he unfolded some plans for a new Bentley racer at Brooklands. But his sights were already further than that even, as he thought about Le Mans, and maybe a motor racing challenge to Tripoli in North Africa in a year or two . . .

'My half-sister, Inga Abbott, has a very loud voice if you're interested,' said Ralphie, casually, to his pal Lister Maddingly. He was staying the weekend with Lister in Wilmslow. 'She had her voice trained for years and years. You should just hear her imitating Gracie Fields. She can get top notes as easy as wink.'

Ever since Ralphie had heard of Inga's success at the Ball and Chain, he had become quite proud of her. He realised she was the nearest thing he had to a proper relative even though he was vaguely aware that some-where in the far beyond there was an ancient half-brother on his late father's side who was probably old enough to be his grandfather and had lots of children. He knew that most people had something like that threading through their lives.

He wished he was as rich as Lister. Lister was a good pal. Ralphie was quite confident that he would be rich too, some day – but when?

Lister stared back at him idly, as they chewed caramels. He wished he was as handsome as Ralphie, instead of being just the opposite with his horn-rimmed glasses. Other boys at Erudine called him goofy and he hated it. But Ralphie never stooped to that sort of thing. They were looking at some stamp albums in Lister's bedroom. Lister's much older brothers both lived away. Ralphie was his very best friend now.

The Maddinglys owned a rambling, ivy-covered house with stables and vast gardens where small ornamental streams trickled and gurgled amongst the trees, not far from Mobberly Lane. It was a far cry from the Cat's Paw nightclub which Lister's father, 'Champion', owned and ran with his partner, Gilbert Smith.

'Do you think your father could find my sister a job?' said Ralphie nonchalantly. He chewed slowly at the jaw-sticking toffee, helping it off his firm, even teeth every so often with his tongue. 'You did say he was looking for someone good . . .'

'Mmm . . .' said Lister cautiously. 'The trouble is they all say they're good, and most times they're awful. One of them came round here once after Father had given her the push for screeching in people's eardrums. She arrived here one day all dressed in furs with a brick under each arm. Father said she would have broken the windows if the dog hadn't been there. There was a terrible to-do. The second brick hit our poor old bulldog Bonzo and he died. Father called the woman a bitch, sued her, and lost the case. So you can see he has to be very, very, careful.'

'My sister would never throw a brick at anything,' said Ralphie. 'Deep down she wants to be an opera singer.'

'They're the worst types for throwing bricks – according to my father,' said Lister gloomily.

'Anyway, I thought I'd just tell you,' said Ralphie, 'in case you're ever short of anyone. She uses her own name, Miss Inga Abbott. I'll bet your dad'd really think she's wonderful.'

Lydia had been as good as her word, getting Lotto Storell to marry her. It had been a quick register office affair in April and had caused a furore of anger on all sides. Lydia's parents worried about his passion for motor racing. Sidney's mother, Katrin, felt he had chosen too hastily. She had hurried back from the South of France in a bit of a panic. The only good point was that the wedding hadn't cost a lot of money and that Sidney was marrying a wealthy woman. On the other hand, she had hoped he would have waited a few more years, particuarly with his father dying. She had expected him to take over his father's place in a more leisurely manner and settle into running the estate without the complications of Lady Lydia Clucksly by his side. She would have welcomed someone less domineering as a daughter-in-law. She knew her own dominant position was over. She would have to fade into the background. Their marriage was a polite way for them to kick her out. Perhaps in a few years when her daughters were settled into decent marriages, she would go back to southern France and live amongst her friends.

Although no one knew it, Lydia and Lotto hadn't had a very good honeymoon. They had flown to Switzerland for three days, and on their first night there had been a blazing row over the grand piano now resting in one of the outhouses at Whittleshaw Hall.

It had all started quite casually when they were drinking cocktails in the hotel lounge lulled by a background of soothing piano music. They had drifted to a verandah and were gazing at a moonlit Lake Lucerne. Nothing could have been more perfect until Sidney said, with tactless innocence, 'That grand in the lounge is exactly the same as Miss Abbott's.'

Lydia stiffened. What a time to say a thing like that! she thought. She glanced away and sipped her drink with restrained fury. Her slim manicured fingertips pressed dangerously hard against the stem of her glass.

Sidney was completely impervious to her anger. 'As soon as we get back we must get that awful scratch on the lid repaired . . .' He sighed to himself. 'It might have to have the whole surface replaced. I wouldn't like her to see it – after all the trust she's put in me.'

Lydia placed her glass on the small carved table. She took a gold cigarette holder and some cigarettes from her handbag. Inwardly she was beginning to seethe. On their *honeymoon* . . . On what was to have been a perfect first night. The sooner he got that little weevil out of his brain the better. Lydia quivered with suppressed hatred.

Sidney saw her quiver and smiled. He glanced at his

watch. 'I think we should be turning in, old thing. What say you?'

Lydia nodded. Anything was better than this.

But when they got to their room she found it wasn't better. For although Lotto was now enraptured by removing her transparent silk voile nightdress, adorned with satin appliquéd ivy leaves, she had hardened into a shop window dummy, hardly moving a muscle.

'Is something wrong darling?' He began to look genuinely concerned as he stood there in his silk pyjama trousers ready for the first night of their honeymoon.

Lydia turned away and marched bitterly towards the luxurious double bed with its sky-blue satin eiderdown and the two gilded cherubs carved so wonderfully at the centre of the headboard. 'I know this much, Lotto,' she said coldly, 'if you so much as mention that bloody piano ever again or the name of its smarmy little owner, you can sleep on that ottoman for the rest of our stay.'

There was a frosty silence. Sidney was completely shocked. What was wrong with her? What had he said? The more he tried to protest his innocence, the worse it got.

It became so bad between them that Lydia was almost tempted to tell him outright that she was the one who had destroyed the surface of the wretched grand piano in the first place. She bit back the words just in time. Better that he shouldn't know who'd done it. Her temper never did her any favours in the end.

One day, just before their wedding, she had come into the outhouse and found the grand piano resting in all its glory, like some massive usurper of her position.

Lotto was sitting there playing a refrain by Schubert and Miss Meddlesome Matty Inga Abbott was blithely trilling away at the top of her voice.

Later, Lydia had found a chisel and had put the weight of her whole body against it as she dug a deep dragging cut across the grand piano's shimmering veneer. She could almost have destroyed Sidney and the girl as well. She had even had to put up with later romantic suggestions that his horrible protégée (for that was what the awful Abbott girl was fast becoming in Lydia's mind) should seriously consider the idea of training to be an opera singer.

Even so, she was not stupid enough to banish her chosen one on that first honeymoon night, so in spite of her threat, Sidney Storell did not sleep on the ottoman. He got into bed beside her and they both slept with their backs to each other. It wasn't until the second night that things improved. By then they were lulled by the bliss of their surroundings, and they behaved like a happy honeymoon couple should. There was a truce between them, and Inga Abbott was not mentioned again . . .

By April, Inga had found herself a cheap flat in Sale. It was in a small square close of Victorian houses. They all shared a pink shale tennis court in the centre, which had high wire netting around it.

The flat was found for her by none other than her childhood friend Mary Mullins whom she hadn't seen for years. They had run into each other by accident and vowed to keep in touch this time.

'It could be ideal, Inga. The flats are the whole of the

second floor of Lindale House,' said Mary happily. 'I'm sure there'll be more than enough room for all your furniture. Mrs Bond has only just decided to split the house up and live on the ground floor. She is most anxious to have only one or two young women who can look after themselves, and who won't be any trouble. The rent she was quoting seemed to be most reasonable.'

By the end of April, Inga had moved in. She sighed with relief as she arranged the last of her furniture in the rooms and wandered around in the spaciousness of it all. She revelled in the large sash windows which faced south on to views of trees and market gardens in the distance. She was glad to have left Apple Street at last. It now harboured far too many unhappy memories.

'I'll be sorry to lose you as a neighbour, Inga,' said Mrs Collywood sadly, 'but I'll know where to come for a nice cup of tea if I'm ever in Sale. And good luck to you, with your job hunting.'

On a sunny day at the beginning of May, shortly after she had settled in at Lindale Inga took a walk past The Turrets which was about a mile away but she did not stop or go along the drive for a glimpse of the house. Even that seemed to hold more bad memories than good, right up to the very day when Sidney Storell had come with her to see to the safe removal of her piano. The atmosphere had been like ice and Petunia had stood there in total silence.

Idly, as Inga walked along on this spring day, she cast her mind to more cheerful affairs. She planned to take her courage in both hands and call in at a soft furnishings shop which had just opened in School Road, to see if they might need any assistants.

She began to think of Sidney Storell again but this time in a more cheerful setting – when she had sung the song for him at Whittleshaw and he had played the refrain. He had suggested she should start having proper lessons again as soon as possible and train for singing in opera.

'Your voice is wonderful, Miss Abbott. You must not let all that early talent and training be lost. Just think of this grand piano, and how much it all meant to your grandmother. So much so that she left it to you when she died. She wouldn't have wanted it to lie unused . . .' He looked at her thoughtfully. 'I don't want to pry into your personal affairs but if ever you think of taking up your singing again I can recommend a first-rate man who might consider you as a pupil. And it wouldn't be too dear; I'd make sure of that.'

She had nodded politely at this last remark. There was a vast difference between what Sidney Storell might regard as cheap and what a girl with no proper job could afford.

But as she neared the shop in School Road, another thing suddenly occurred to her . . . What about the idea that Ralphie had mentioned to her one day? He had said that his friend's father, who owned the Cat's Paw nightclub in Manchester, might be interested in giving her an unpaid try-out as a singer, and that, if it was successful, there could be an offer of some regular paid work . . .

If that happened she would be able to afford singing lessons. Joy flooded to her heart. Her enthusiasm became so great that when she walked into Fairweather's Family Soft Furnishings she was walking on air.

'I've come to speak to the manager about a job vacancy.'
She did not pause for breath, 'I've had a great deal of
experience with soft furnishings. I worked for some time
for the well-known firm of Swanson's Silks and Satins,
who have recently re-upholstered all the chairs in the
mayoral chamber of Manchester Town Hall and—'

'I *am* both the manager and owner of this emporium,'
said Mr Fairweather, peering at her regally over the top
of his rimless glasses. 'I wasn't aware that we had any
job vacancies. What did you say your name was – Miss,
er, Miss . . .'

'Miss Abbott. Miss Inga Abbott from Lindale House,
Hollybush Close, Sale.'

Mr Fairweather's eyes narrowed with latent curiosity.
Hollybush Close was a posh area. 'Do you happen to
know a Mrs Bond?'

Inga nodded confidently. 'She's my landlady. Her husband died and she only lives in part of the house now.'

'Well I never! I never knew that had happened. I
replaced all those top-quality Regency pattern curtains
for them just over a year ago. Mr Bond was in good
health then so it must have been quite sudden . . . What
did 'e die of? 'E was a year younger than me.' Then he
added quickly, 'Can you do typing an' all? And mebbees
a bit of book keeping?'

Before she had left the shop he had presented her with a
tape measure and a small pair of Fairweather's Souvenir
Fancy Scissors fashioned to celebrate twenty-five years
of Family Soft Furnishings and faithful service to the
customer.

In five more minutes Inga had become a full-time

employee of Fairweather's Family Soft Furnishings, starting the following Monday morning, with a very humble wage, and long hours.

She thanked her lucky stars.

17

TALK OF THE TOWN

Sidney Storell was glad to hear Inga was settled in Sale. She'd sent him a note to thank him for his past help. He hadn't breathed a word about her piano having to be repaired. It was back in perfect condition now, still waiting at Whittleshaw.

In fact everything that August seemed good. His mother was back from France; Lydia was expecting a baby; and his motor racing was going from strength to strength. Pictures of Lotto Storell's racing triumphs were in the *London Illustrated News*: wreaths of laurels round his neck; racing goggles on his head; champagne, beautiful women and the Union Jack prominently displayed. And all the time his mind dwelt on designing bigger supercharged engines for his never ending track adventures.

Even in the ordinary world Inga was doing well. Her job at Fairweather's was happy and uneventful, selling yards and yards of material to be made up on family sewing machines into summer frocks, flowery curtains, and men's cotton sports shirts in every home in Sale.

She was singing at the Cat's Paw nightclub now, on Friday and Saturday evenings. Champion Maddingly and Gilbert Smith paid her well, and she was able to save up for singing lessons.

There was only one small snag in her life at present, for even though she had her own keys to her flat and could come and go as she pleased, Mrs Bond was getting a bit pernickety.

'Miss Abbott, do you mean to say you'll be coming back *regularly* in a taxi, two nights *every* week, at well after midnight?'

'I'm afraid so, Mrs Bond. I would much sooner it didn't have to be like this, but it's the sort of employment that means a great deal to me. Naturally I shall be as quiet as possible in order not to disturb you.'

'But from all accounts you already have a suitable situation during the *day*. It seems extremely strange—'

'I can assure you it's all perfectly respectable, Mrs Bond. I am committed to keep the appointments at a very select club which plays music. I am a trained singer . . .' Inga chose her words carefully. She knew that if she'd said she sang at a nightclub in a basement in Manchester, Mrs Bond would probably collapse!

'But surely you weren't trained to go out and sing so late at night and on top of the job you've already got at the shop? If you ask me, nothing good can come of a double-edged life like that. Greed never got anyone anywhere.' Mrs Bond shook her head, her lips set to a fine thin line as she walked away.

The following day, when Mrs Bond was having elevenses with her friend Mrs Clarice Rogers from across the road, Clarice enquired how Mrs Bond's new flat-dweller was going on.

'To be perfectly frank, Clarice, I'm finding her a teeny-weeny bit worrying . . .'

Clarice's eyes widened with anticipation. She had been extremely jealous when Mrs Bond decided to convert part of her house into the flat. She, Clarice, was the one who had the idea first. She wanted to convert *her* house, but her husband had kicked up a fuss as soon as she mentioned it. Then, to add insult to injury, when she had suggested that her own niece would like to rent Mrs Bond's flat she found it had already been let to this Miss Abbott.

'What a pity it went so quickly to someone else when my niece Dora would have jumped at it,' said Clarice, pointedly.

'Yes,' said Mrs Bond dolefully. 'I must admit I'm starting to rue the day I let her have it if this pattern of late nights is to continue. It's well past midnight every Friday and Saturday when she arrives back in a taxi . . .'

'Do you think she goes to see her young man?' suggested Clarice in sly, slightly purring tones.

'I'm sure I don't know, but it's beginning to get a bit unsettling. She says that she sings at a very select club and that she is a trained singer. I am curious to find out exactly where this "select" club is. As you know yourself, Clarice, this road of ours has always been a very quiet place.'

Clarice nodded solemnly and leaned forward to hear more.

'In all our married lives my Bondy and I never got to bed later than ten-forty-five, unless it was a very, very special occasion. If Bondy had been alive today he would have thought far worse of Miss Abbott than I do. He would probably have thought she was a streetwalker.'

'Never!'

'Yes – I'm afraid he would, Clarice. So there you are.' They stared at each other. 'God forbid if I have let out my flat to someone like that . . .' They both sipped their tea and nibbled their pink wafer biscuits in thoughtful silence.

The Cat's Paw Club was packed out.

'You certainly draw the crowds, kid,' said Gilbert Smith to Inga with a cheeky glint in his eyes. He began to murmur the words to a jazz refrain under his breath as he continued to look at her. 'My woman . . . She has a heart of stone . . . My woman . . .' He gave Inga a playful wink and wandered away towards a group of well-dressed men who were drinking together.

Inga laughed and walked off in the opposite direction. He was always flirting with her but she knew it was harmless. She was glad the place was popular. The success meant that her bank book would go from strength to strength, just when she needed money the most.

In a couple of months – perhaps October – she planned to get in touch with Sidney Storell again, and ask him to help her with the singing lessons. He was the only true friend she had in the background these days. She had lost touch with most of her childhood playmates, who were either engaged, married or had left Sale altogether. Even her very best friend, Mary Mullins, was entangled in a passionate love affair and had thoughts of nothing else.

As Inga got ready to leave the Cat's Paw and go back to her flat, she felt slightly downcast. As usual some of the loving couples were leaving the place reasonably early. The club itself stayed open almost all night. Oh, how she longed for some romance to spread to her own life. Or did drinks and heady music at the nightclub leave many lonely, lovesick hearts one solitary memory? Here she was, she thought, as she waited for the taxi to take her back to Sale, moving swiftly towards her twenties with never a steady boyfriend in sight. To the customers at the Cat's Paw she was like a picture on the celluloid screen; in spite of all the rapturous applause, she was nothing but an image. She was a bit of passing spice – a small contribution to someone's good night out.

The rain poured as she stood in the side street in her plain outdoor clothes with no umbrella. It was almost one-thirty a.m.

She shivered. She hated waiting in this drenching darkness for a taxi. Where was it? She began to pace the pavement edgily. She always had the same cab driver. Bert Stanton was usually prompt. It was a regular arrangement made by Champion Maddingly himself.

Out of the corner of her eye, she caught sight of one of the Cat's Paw's most valued shareholders moving unsteadily from the club. Toby Lord was sozzled. By his side was his latest pick-up, an unknown young girl in a beaver lamb coat, court shoes, and dangling rhinestone earrings.

Inga stood well back in the shadow of a wall and watched them cautiously. Lord had a terrible reputation. She could see he was out for only one thing, and he was in such a state he didn't care when or how he got it. Every so often he started to paw the girl, dragging her against him with such a powerful grip that she could not escape.

From where she was standing, Inga heard his voice wafted towards her as the girl struggled a bit then gave up.

'What's up with you, ya little bitch?' sneered Lord. 'You don't want to pay your side of the bargain, eh?'

His hoarse slurred tones sent a shiver of horror through Inga, as she watched them half fight their way to where his green Lagonda was parked, then get in it.

Seconds later, both the passenger's and the driver's door of the car were opened again.

The girl got out of her side and shouted in a piercing voice, 'You sadist! I'm not going with you. I want my own cab this instant – or I'll report you to the club!'

Inga's heart seemed to lurch.

The girl had lit a cigarette and the tip suddenly glowed red then went out as she stood there. But Toby Lord was heading straight towards where Inga was standing.

Then, not a moment too soon, like a gift from God, Bert's taxi arrrived. 'Sorry I was held up, love . . .'

Inga almost threw her arms around him. 'Thank goodness you're here, Bert.'

But before she had hardly opened the taxi door, Toby

Lord was already there arguing with Bert. 'I want your taxi for that girl standing over there next to my Lagonda, Stanton.' He pointed towards the girl aggressively, then fixed Bert with a hard challenging stare.

Inga watched helplessly.

'Look *Mister* Lord,' said Bert with steely firmmness, 'My job is to deliver Miss Abbott here back safely to Hollybush Close in Sale. I do so every night at this time, at this spot on the instructions of Champion Maddingly himself – and you bloody well know it! All I can suggest is that you find another cab for your . . . your . . .' Bert checked himself. He knew Lord was a dangerous customer. And, alas, he was right, for as he tried to start off in his cab with Inga, Lord parked his own body a yard or two in front of Bert's cab bonnet. He was standing in the middle of the road swearing drunkenly and waving his arms, leaving Bert no option than to reverse into what was virtually a local cul-de-sac next to the club.

'You need teaching a bloody good lesson,' bawled Lord, staggering back to his own car just in time to see his young girlfriend escaping from him and driving away in another cab. He turned back angrily towards Bert and his cab again. 'I've not done with you yet, Stanton. I'm out to get ya . . . Make no mishtake, *an' the shooner the better*.'

'I was a fool to mention the address in Sale, earlier on. It just slipped out,' groaned Bert to Inga as they drove along. 'I know Toby Lord only too well. In his present state I wouldn't put it past him to follow me for a final punch-up. He knows this side of town like the back of his hand. He's pretty groggy but his memory may not be as pickled as I first thought.'

The taxi had just branched off towards Stretford Road when Bert said gloomily, 'Just as I feared . . . The devil's on our trail.'

They drove in tense silence through the quiet lamp-lit roads towards Sale. Usually they talked, but tonight it was ruined as both of them wondered silently what the outcome would be, from Toby Lord.

In vain Bert tried to shake him off but the green Lagonda reappeared behind them again and again, until finally they reached the road leading to Hollybush Close and Inga's flat at Lindale House.

Lord's car drew up only a few yards behind them.

The close was dead to the world with not a lighted window to be seen. Inga was beginning to tremble with fear. What on earth would happen? The rain had stopped now, and windswept dark clouds scurried across the moon.

'Get out quickly, love, and go straight for the house,' ordered Bert. 'Ignore Lord and don't turn back or try to help if you hear a row going on. Right?'

She nodded.

'Now!' He almost pushed her from the cab as she hurried to the front door of Lindale and with thumping heart and trembling fingers let herself in – closing the door swiftly.

No sooner was she in her flat than she heard fighting and loud thuds outside and someone's voice screaming for help. Then there was thumping on the front door, and the bell rang without stopping.

Inga hurried downstairs. She was consumed with guilt. She could hardly expect Mrs Bond to cope with it all. She hovered uneasily in the hall, but did not open the front door. Instead, she crept into an unoccupied front living room and peered between the drawn, heavy, brown plush curtains.

Outside was an uproar. Police had arrived and an ambulance. Bert was slumped in the driving seat of his taxi – semi-conscious, and the man from the Lagonda was spread-eagled across the road. Lights were on in all the windows in the square and some people were standing outside in the distance in their dressing gowns.

She saw that the police were taking particulars. Please God, Inga prayed, don't let them come here . . .

Suddenly she realised that Mrs Bond was downstairs too. She was standing to one side of the door. Her straggling hair was in a pink net boudoir-cap bulging with rag curlers and her nightie was covered by a heavy check dressing gown which matched her carpet slippers. Mrs Bond was livid with rage as she shuffled slowly towards Inga and said, 'This is all your doing, Miss Abbott. I knew all along you were trouble.'

Bert was taken away from his taxi to the local police station. By now Mrs Bond was also peering through the curtains. 'What in heaven's name has been going on, Miss Abbott? It's absolutely disgraceful. I shall never live it down!'

In vain, Inga protested her innocence and apologised profusely. 'It was absolutely nothing to do with me, Mrs Bond. I swear it. It was just a normal night of work for me. And Bert, my taxi driver, was absolutely blameless. It just happened that—'

'Just *happened*?' Mrs Bond's voice rang out with a

threatening shrillness. 'It just happens too that you can pack your bags and get out of here first thing tomorrow!' A loud and long tirade continued as Mrs Bond decorated Inga's lifestyle into one of total debauchery until, gasping for breath and pressing her hand to her heart, she tottered off to bed, clutching at the mahogany banister as if her last moment had arrived.

In vain, during the rest of the night, Inga tried to get to sleep as she lay in her flat in total misery. Why, oh why did so many bad things happen to her? And where was she going to live now?

According to the terms of their contract, Mrs Bond had to give Inga a week's notice, so she had seven days to find somewhere else to live. Thanks to Clarice Rogers, the news of Inga's 'disreputable behaviour' spread like wildfire and there was even a small piece in the local paper. 'Commotion at Respectable Hollybush Close' the headline read.

When Mr Fairweather heard about it, he wasn't pleased. 'I'm sorry, Miss Abbott, I'd like to keep you on,' he said, 'but my customers are respectable people who don't take kindly to scandal. Any hint of a connection between my shop and a place like the Cat's Paw nightclub – well, Miss Abbott, it wouldn't do my business any good at all. I shall write you a *very* good reference though.' He pulled out his handkerchief and blew his nose very loudly. Then he fiddled in one of the drawers and drew out a box of chocolates tied in pale blue ribbon. 'Please accept these with the compliments of Fairweather's Family Soft Furnishings.'

The final straw came when she arrived for work at the Cat's Paw a couple of days later. She found her way barred by Champion Maddingly, who avoided looking her directly in the eye.

'Sorry, Miss Abbott but, in view of recent events, I think it would be best if we found another singer for the club. Thank you for all you've done, and good luck in your singing career.'

Three catastrophes in only a week! Inga began to panic inside – no work, no place to live, and due out of Mrs Bond's as soon as possible.

Every time she walked to and fro in Hollybush Close she felt the hidden hostility. People looked the other way as she passed, or stopped their conversations as she drew near. No one met her eyes any more. Now she longed to escape from Sale for ever. No longer could she face going anywhere near School Road where so many of the shops were, including Mr Fairweather's.

She could see that her only option was to move further into the centre of Manchester again to some place near Moss Side where there were rows and rows of older houses, many containing cheap lodgings and bedsitters to rent. At least she wouldn't be the talk of the town there, in the bustle of the city.

Within days, she found herself a set of cheap and seedy rooms in a stinking, noisy place overlooking a meat market and abattoir. It was a case of getting somewhere very quickly, then hopefully looking for somewhere better later.

With grim reluctance, she removed her belongings and bits of furniture to her new home, and the following day was fortunate to find part-time casual work as a cleaner in a small, scruffy hotel called Boatman's Halt, which fifty years ago might still have been a pleasant, rural location. Now, it had back views of warehouses and the murky Bridgewater canal. All of a sudden, it seemed that her past life had counted for nothing.

Her rented rooms in Baxley Street were on the ground floor, and the landlord lived six doors away. As soon as Inga had arranged her furniture, she realised even more what a hole it was. The haste of finding somewhere cheap so quickly had blinded her to its overall defects and now she soaked up the horror of filthy, mildewed wallpaper which hung in swollen lumps of damp and was peeling away from corners of the rooms. She shuddered at the frothy white fungus exuding from the surface of bricks in the backyard lavatory. The more she hunted, the more she found: soot-encrusted cobwebs, mouldy mouse droppings, scurrying black beetles, and slow grey woodlice beneath the cold sweating broken lino in the kitchen.

A mental picture of her only real treasure, her grand piano, rose up in her mind. Never could she bring it here! She would have to leave it even longer at Whittleshaw Hall. She prayed it would be safe. Meanwhile she would have to get out of this awful place by hook or by crook.

Then, on a sunny day towards the end of August, something stupendous happened . . .

18
THE GARDEN PARTY

For Inga, August dragged along until out of the blue an invitation to a garden party arrived. It was from Nally and Leroy Spinks. It came in a bulky letter in Nally's large sprawling writing and had been forwarded on from Sale.

'Dear Inga,' it began, 'I've had a terrible job tracing you, and only hope you eventually receive this invitation to celebrate my engagement. It so happened that Leroy met Mary Mullins one day and she said she had found you a flat in Hollybush Close . . .'

Inga blinked quickly. Nally, *engaged* to Leroy Spinks? What a combination!

The letter continued: '. . . We shall be announcing it officially at this garden party his mother is giving, in early September.

'I have finally left college. It just didn't work out. I am now at The Turrets again with Mother. As you can imagine, everybody thinks Leroy and I are far too young to be engaged, but it has finally been agreed on all sides.

'Leroy's mother, Tessy, has got it into her brain to invite all his childhood friends to the do. I feel at a real disadvantage. I only have three people coming: two who were at college with me and our cousin Sybil from Denham who's coming to stay at The Turrets with Uncle Dennis and Aunt Yvonne for a few days.

'It's not a bit like it was when you were here. We have two awful daily cleaners, and a man who never does any proper gardening but sits about in secret, smoking and reading newspapers. Oh, how I wish Mrs Dawn and Albert were still around . . .'

Rapidly Inga soaked up each page of the exuberant letter. Her heart sank a little when she realised that, of course, Petunia would be there in full force. The thought of her Aunt Petsy gave her half a mind to turn down the invitation, but she knew deep down she wouldn't because Nally was such a darling. And Mary Mullins would be there, and they'd be able to catch up on each other's lives since that awful episode at Mrs Bond's . . .

She read on and on as familiar names from her early days loomed up: Ruby Selwyn, whose great-uncle was Mr Protheroe the famous music teacher; Brenda Frogmorton, who had been in the clutches of nannies all her life; Robin Stubbs and Little Angel Janey Jackson . . .

For a few minutes, Inga's mind was happily and wonderously engrossed with that past world of small, flat dancing slippers with their crisscross bands of corded elastic, and that one terrible time when she had been in trouble for singing the wrong sort of party song in a very loud voice. She smiled now as she thought of herself and that little horror Leroy, and how he pinched her arm really deep and they had a fight. It was amazing how people turned out so different when they were grown up. She wondered what all the rest of them would be like. As for herself, she seemed to have slipped from being a very loud voice to being a very small mouse.

Smiling to herself, cheered by the letter, she found a pen and began to write back to Nally. '. . . Congratulations . . . I shall be delighted to accept . . . Yours affectionately, Inga.'

'What a tragedy it was when Margot passed away.' The day of the garden party was calm and glorious. Leroy's elderly Aunt Mabel seemed, to Inga, to have hardly changed. She was sprightly but frail with pure white hair set in a bun, and wore an elegant, wide-brimmed hat in an interwoven pattern of inky blue and natural straw.

'Of course,' Mabel sighed with secret pleasure, 'I'm seven years younger than your grandmother was. But all the same it was a terrible shock when she went. She was devoted to you and your music. I hope you haven't let it slip . . .'

Inga didn't reply. She looked across at the broad sweeps of green, carefully tended lawns. She and Mabel were standing close to some sycamore trees near the refreshments marquee where champagne was flowing freely. People were strolling about in warm drifts of idle conversation, looking for chairs to sit on.

Then Mabel said, 'We miss Margot, and we've missed you too, dear. Everyone in our little music world always hoped you would be a shining star.' She shook her head in bewilderment. 'But there you are, God moves in the most mysterious ways, and it looks as if Leroy was the real "chosen one". He has turned out to be quite a heartthrob as far as the ladies are concerned. I'm glad he's going to settle down with someone who will surely help him go from strength to strength.'

Inga nodded. He wouldn't need much help on that score, she thought.

'By the way, I hope you'll manage to have a word with Ruby's uncle Protheroe whilst you're here. I'll keep my eyes open for him. He's always so delighted to link up with past times.' She pointed out two empty seats and began to walk towards them. 'Do you remember that pianist called Phoebe Strangeways from Blackpool days?'

Inga nodded politely, but she couldn't remember the woman. She had been a child with quite different memories of Blackpool.

'She married that Mr Forwardly, the Director of Education for Stanton-on-Medlock,' continued Mabel. 'He's still in the education, and she runs a small private music academy.'

After an extravagant sit-down meal in the tent and some toasts drunk to the future happiness of the newly engaged couple, Inga was amazed to see a young woman standing by the piano, ready to sing to them.

She knew the accompanist well. He was still as agile

and lively as ever. It was ancient Mr Protheroe – Ruby Selwyn's great-uncle and famous music teacher. He was wearing ordinary grey flannels and a white open-neck shirt. Before he sat down to play, he wiped some sweat from his forehead with a bright saffron-coloured handkerchief and peered at the music carefully through half-moon spectacles, nodding to himself.

Inga stared at the girl who was singing. She was about twenty-one, thought Inga. She had a beautiful voice. Inga felt a sudden streak of sad envy as she stared at the girl's tall thin figure with the large bust and the 'Jean Harlow' bottle blonde hair.

Surely it wasn't . . . ? Yes, it *was*. It was Mimi Garter who, as a child, must have attended every known singing competition in the whole country.

Inga soaked up Mimi's glorious, over-dressed brilliance. She was in an emerald water-marked taffeta two-piece with a flounced peplum at her waist. Diamond and jade costume jewellery gleamed; the sort that Margot would have described as very common.

Mr Protheroe nodded towards her proudly when she'd finished. He waited for the applause to die down then he said, 'And now I should like to introduce you to Mr Scott Ivorson. He and Miss Garter will sing that popular duet from the old music hall days which we all know and love so well, "Tell me, pretty maiden".'

Scott Ivorson seemed to Inga to emerge from nowhere. He was an entirely new face. Tall, lean and confident with a rich versatile voice and a humorous mouth, he had dark eyebrows as thick as thatch over his sparkling eyes.

'Tell me, pretty maiden, are there any more at home like you?'

'There are a few, kind sir . . .'

He and Mimi Garter were perfect together as they melted into the decorous melody. Finally they brought their repertoire up to date by finishing with two further songs, 'Tea For Two' and 'Lady Be Good', in a deluge of approval, with Mr Protheroe standing up from his piano seat and bowing to both them and the audience.

Inga was quite overcome. Whatever had Mabel Spinks been thinking of to suggest she should meet Mr Protheroe? She was just a nonentity compared to all this. She could never, *never* be as good as those two!

She turned away to look for some of her childhood friends but within minutes was forstalled by Leroy's Aunt Mabel again, waving to her and beckoning. 'Come over here, dear. I've managed to catch Mr Protheroe.'

Reluctantly, and feeling almost like a fraud where singing was concerned, Inga went over to Mabel as Mr Protheroe stood up from one of the chairs to greet her.

'I remember you quite clearly when you were only a little tot,' he smiled. 'Your grandmother was a great one for boosting your talent.'

Inga went scarlet. The same old feelings of fear and a need to escape from Margot's clutches welled within her. It was as if her grandmother were still here, as if she would suddenly come striding towards them, smartly dressed and overpoweringly confident, holding a sheet of music.

'I – I . . . Well, the truth is I haven't been in the position to do much singing lately, Mr Protheroe. Although I did spend a short time performing in a night club.'

From the corner of her eye she saw Mabel's expression drop a mile. But it had quite the opposite effect on Mr Protheroe. His face lit up with pleasure. 'So you are still singing, after all?' Then slowly he stood up from his chair again, touched her arm and said, 'Let's go for a little walk. I'd like to talk to you. I'm sure Mabel won't mind.'

'Not at all,' said Mabel scurrying away to gossip to someone else.

They walked across the grass until they were safely away from the crowds. Mr Protheroe chose a small woodland path which opened up towards some fields. 'I wonder if you'd do me one small favour, for old time's sake, Inga? I'd like you to sing to me.'

She was slightly taken aback. 'Sing to you? Well, of course . . . but—'

'How about "The Bluebells of Scotland"?' he said. 'It goes well without any accompaniment. I'll join in with you towards the end of the refrain.'

Inga took some deep, steadying breaths then, turning towards the open fields and standing there squarely as if to face the whole world, she began to sing.

In seconds, as the tune took over, she felt as free as the air itself. 'Oh where, and oh where has my highland laddie gone . . .'

Quietly Mr Protheroe joined her.

When the melody was finished he smiled and said, 'You have a good voice. It just needs a bit of refining in certain places. I expect you heard Mimi and Scott singing together? Have you ever thought of singing duets with a partner?'

She looked at him in amazement. 'No, never.'

As they walked back towards the garden party he said, 'Mimi Garter is getting married and going to America in the spring. Scott will have to work with someone else.'

Inga nodded politely. Never for a second did she see what he was suggesting.

'I was wondering if you would like to consider replacing Mimi? It would, of course, depend on whether you and Scott got on together. But in any case I would be quite willing to train you for the next six months.'

Inga was stunned. 'I can't quite take it in, Mr Protheroe. I never even *dreamed* . . . And besides there's the question of the fees: it's just not posssible. I, well, at the moment – I . . .' She felt a wave of hopeless gloom descend as she thought of her true circumstances, away from all this luxury.

He patted her shoulder. 'It's an invitation, my dear. There will be no fees involved. These days in my old age I have no need of them. It's just the eternal pleasure of being able to recognise talent and nurture it.' He took a silver propelling pencil and diary from one of his shirt pockets, and wrote down her address.

Inga hardly spoke as they walked back to the marquee. She was still unable to take it all in. And when Mr Protheroe introduced her to Scott Ivorson she could hardly say a word as they shook hands.

'I'll arrange a meeeting for the three of us at my home next week,' said Mr Protheroe.

Meanwhile, Leroy's mother, Tessy Spinks, was having

a few polite words with her future daughter-in-law's mother, Petunia Shoreditch. They were sitting in the drawing room of the impressive timber-beamed black and white mansion which overlooked the lawns.

'We couldn't have hoped for a more successful day,' sighed Tessa thankfully. 'I just don't know what we'd do without Aunt Mabel always at the helm. She's a born organiser. She and your mother were like twin souls.' They both sipped their coffee in polite unison.

'I only hope our children will have as happy a married life as ourselves,' said Tessy Spinks impulsively. Then suddenly realising – from what she'd heard in the past on the grape vine – that she was on thin ice, she hastily passed the chocolate fingers across to Petunia and asked her to have another one, followed by quite a long screed on chocolate biscuits in general.

Petunia didn't have much to say. She just kept nodding and smiling. It was a matter of allowing Tessy to be the star, on this one occasion. This morning she had received a letter from Ronald in Oxford suggesting they should get back together again.

'I can assure you, dear,' he had written, 'that your fears about Lena were always much exaggerated. She has now gone to work in Australia and our relationship is completely over. All I want is for you to come back to your proper home . . .'

Petunia had read the letter very carefully and thought deeply about it. Secretly, she was getting a bit restless at The Turrets. She told herself she was being used by the rest of the family as a sort of unpaid housekeeper for their northern property. This was entirely her own interpretation. The fact was that now her daughter Nally was engaged to Leroy Spinks she felt a bit isolated. Nally was hardly at home, treating the place like a railway station waiting room as she dashed hither and thither with her beloved, leaving Petunia with no one of any worth to boss about. Nally almost lived at the Spinkses and was due to live around there when she married.

These days Leroy Spinks's heart revolved more and more around motor cars. His singing took second place to being a travelling salesman for motor accessories. He owned a Mercedes-Benz and took Nally with him, when he was working.

And as if this wasn't enough, there had been rumblings from Petunia's other sisters who did *not* regard her as a northern housekeeper – far from it. In her absence there had been family consultations at a get-together in Brown's Hotel in London and they had decided that they all wanted a share of being so-called 'caretakers' themselves, on a grand scale.

Petunia had purposely avoided Inga at the garden party. She had been annoyed when she realised Nally had sent her an invitation, and even more annoyed when Nally had once suggested that perhaps Inga should be invited to come back to The Turrets as a flat-dweller.

'There's so much space going to waste, Mother, and with her own flat you'd both be entirely independent from one another, yet the whole place would still be in the hands of the family.'

Petunia had dismissed the idea with shocked anger.

As the garden party came to its happy ending Petunia caught a glimpse of Inga. She was talking to the elderly music teacher who had played the piano for the duettists. The young man who had been singing the duets was standing there talking to them. Then she saw them all shake hands.

What on earth was all that in aid of? she thought.

It was hard to believe that, only two months after that gloriously sunny September, November was here with all its murkiness, as Inga set off to Bowden for her weekly singing lesson with Mr Protheroe.

Inga's lessons were going very well. She had already had some duet practice with Scott Ivorson, and Mr Protheroe was delighted. He said they matched each other perfectly.

At the end of their duet practices, Scott invited Inga out for afternoon tea in the Copper Kettle teashop in Hale, not far away from his lodgings.

'I'm glad I've got fixed up with you well before Mimi goes,' he said as they munched toasted teacakes oozing with butter.

'I'm glad, too,' smiled Inga. She just couldn't believe how well they were both getting on with the duets, and with each other. He never had very much to say but he was always polite and patient if she made any mistakes.

The more lessons she took the more she was intrigued by him. He was handsome, too, and so decisive. The woman who eventually married him would be the luckiest person on earth, thought Inga almost ruefully.

At the same time as Inga was innocently enjoying

afternoon tea with Scott, Petunia Shoreditch was having afternoon tea with buttered crumpets at The Turrets with her sister Yvonne and Yvonne's daughter Sybil. Their visit was totally unexpected. They had just appeared one darkening afternoon, at the front door with a couple of Harrods suitcases.

'Dennis has gone away on business,' explained Yvonne, 'so I thought it would be nice for Sibs and me to come for another break and keep you company. It must get very lonely for you, and we're all determined to do our share. It's quite possible that Dennis could be coming up here himself in a few weeks' time, to a conference in Manchester, so perhaps we'll stay on and wait for him, then all return together.

'Where's Nally then?' said Yvonne helping herself to the last crumpet.

'She's staying at the Spinkses,' said Petsy off-handedly. 'As a matter of fact, you've arrived at rather a bad time. I'm travelling to Oxford tomorrow to see Ronald. We're thinking of getting back together again permanently.'

Yvonne's well-preserved face lit up with hope. 'Does that mean that Sibs and I will have to hold the fort whilst you're away?'

'I'm afraid so. But you'll know the routine from when you were here for the garden party . . .'

'But of course, Petsy. We'll be absolutely *delighted*.' Then Yvonne said, 'Have you heard any more about Inga? I believe Nally said she was living in some perfectly dreadful place at present.'

'No,' said Petunia, 'all I know is she is taking extra lessons to get her voice up to scratch but I doubt if it'll come to much. She was always a very spoilt child. Always very troublesome and restive. A leopard never changes its spots. She is totally unreliable, and very self-centred.'

'Sibs never got round to meeting Inga at the garden party,' said Yvonne casually, as she looked across at Sybil. 'But Nally was telling Sibs that she thought it might be a good idea to offer Inga a flat of her own here at The Turrets.'

Petsy flared up. 'It's a ridiculous idea! And completely unfair. Just because she was fortunate to have all that luxury wasted on her when she was a child doesn't mean we've got to mollycoddle her for ever. And look at the way Daphne treated her own child and our own poor mother when she ran off with that man? The whole sordid affair was an absolute disgrace.'

'I wasn't looking at it quite like that,' said Yvonne pouring herself another cup of tea. 'Time has moved on. I was thinking of it being a sensible thing to do for the only one of the younger end of our family who needs a decent roof over her head just at a time when there's one going spare. I think I shall at least invite her round when you're away in Oxford.'

Petunia stood up angrily. 'Do what the devil you like, Yvonne,' she muttered through clenched teeth, 'but don't come moaning to me if it all goes wrong.' Then she stamped out of the room.

'I'll come and help you to wash up shortly if you want,' called Yvonne, completely unperturbed. Then she said to Sybil, 'I'm sure you'd like to meet Inga wouldn't you, Sibs?'

Sybil nodded and smiled. 'I think Nally's idea of the flat was good. She thinks Inga's lovely. Aunty Petsy's far too bossy and you mark my words, Mother, she only pleases herself the whole time. She could well go off to Oxford tomorrow, settle down in her own home again and ditch everything here, including all of us. She's like that.'

Yvonne nodded knowingly. Then they put the wireless on and relaxed in unconcerned comfort. 'We'll wait till she finally disappears tomorrow,' smiled Yvonne.

19

APRIL LOVE

Inga looked around her attic flat at The Turrets. It was a glorious morning and Scott was due to arrive any minute.

Mimi Garter had sailed for America three weeks ago.

It was Inga's BBC day. She and Scott were going to sing on their weekly Wednesday programme, *Rainbows of Song with Scott Ivorson and Inga Abbott*, accompanied by Miss Rowena Dorelli on the piano.

She had been back here for almost six months now. It was like being home again without the worst bits. The attic windows no longer held memories of the day Margot had locked her in this room and she'd fallen through the window. All her meagre belongings and bits of furniture had fitted easily into The Turrets except her grand piano. She hadn't dared to uproot it again. She paid no rent but acted as a sort of house minder.

The same unenthusiastic gardener was still employed by the rest of the Abbott women and there was a vague part-time cleaning service for the house.

According to Nally, who was expecting a baby in October, Petunia had rushed back to Oxford in a huff after an argument with Yvonne about Inga.

'I doubt if she'll ever come back once she's got things patched up with Daddy,' said Nally one day, 'although I know for certain she'll be popping over occasionally to see me – especially with the Spinkses finding us that little cottage to rent so close to them.'

Inga smiled. She was glad it had all worked out so well for Nally. Cautiously she was hoping things would work out well for herself and Scott, too. They were lovers now, but she never told anyone. It had happened almost two months ago in her small bed in the attic. Afterwards there had been slight traces of blood on the pale satin quilt. She was glad it had happened, but it was the first and last time that passion was allowed to reign without restriction. Ever afterwards Scott took precautions. She knew he didn't want to. 'It's like washing your hands with your gloves on,' he said, 'but it has to be. Perhaps if we were married it would be different.'

His words puzzled her slightly. He was a good companion and almost obsessive about their duet work. But it suddenly struck her that he had very little true imagination, and even had a slightly crude streak. Were all men like that at heart? she wondered. Had her innocence led her to expect a fairy-tale romance that could never be?

She had become quite matter-of-fact now about her intimacy with Scott. It wasn't exactly romantic but the sex was getting more important to both of them as they gloried in the warmth and comfort of each other's bodies. For Inga it was gradually becoming more exciting and relaxed. She knew she would have been devastated if he had stopped this secret side. It was a private strength between them now, balancing their whole working relationship.

The front doorbell rang. He was here. She rushed downstairs and opened the door. His two-seater MG sports car with its folded down roof was waiting.

He smiled and looked at his watch in the sunshine. 'Are you ready? Got your change of clothes?'

She nodded. The studio where they did the broadcasts was very formal. Everyone wore evening dress whatever time of the day it was – although their audience could not see them.

When they arrived Scott changed into a white dinner shirt, bow tie, black suit with tails and patent leather shoes. And she wore a sleeveless, ankle-length lemon silk voile party frock. Her fair hair was parted in the middle and combed back flat and tight against her skull. Her eyebrows were two finely plucked arches filled in with eyebrow pencil. It was a complete transformation.

Ashley Watkins, the producer of the programme, was a giant of a man, full of professional bonhomie, with innocent-looking blue eyes, as hard as flint. He always fussed about at the beginning, making sure they had a carafe of water and two glasses close by. Today was just the same. There was nervousness in the air. The programme went out live; there were no second chances.

'Unfasten your collar a bit, old chap,' he said to Scott. 'Quite candidly, I don't care a damn if you both perform completely in the buff just so long as you are comfortable. I always tell the older ladies to loosen their corsets. It annoys them intensely but the rise of blood pressure increases the strength in their top notes wonderfully.'

It was just as they were reaching some top notes themselves in a passionate duet that catastrophe struck. They were halfway through the programme. She and Scott were singing 'Some day I'll find you', in unison, when Inga began to feel sick. Panic-stricken, she started to heave. Someone rushed forward with a wastepaper basket but it was too late. The programme was switched off immediately, officially due to a 'technical hitch'.

Ashley Watkins tried to remain civil as Scott led Inga hastily from the studio. He stared at the sour-smelling mess through gritted teeth as the live programme was replaced with gramophone records of sea shanties. Underneath his urbane exterior, Ashley was livid. Never, as far as he was concerned, would Miss Inga Abbott ever grace or disgrace the portals of the British Broacasting Company again. Queues of other musical people were quite willing to step into her place. From now on the *Radio Times* would print: 'Rainbows of Song with Scott Ivorson and others'.

On the way back to The Turrets that day, Inga was overcome with grief and shame. Everyone had been very nice at the BBC – telling her not to worry, it could have happened to anyone. The exception to this show of sympathy was Mr Watkins. He had remained totally silent with a glazed smile on his broad face.

'Mr Watkins never mentioned anything about next week's programme,' ventured Inga to Scott who was grim and silent as they drove back to The Turrets.

As they neared Sale, Scott said, 'You made a real hash of our chances. But fortunately I wasn't involved so if you don't mind I'll go on my own next week unless we hear otherwise. I can't chance another episode like today's.'

Inga's confidence sank to rock bottom. 'I just can't think what came over me. I only had a cup of tea for breakfast and banana sandwich for lunch plus a piece of Madeira cake.'

The car slowed down at The Turrets. Scott got out and, shrugging his shoulders, opened her side of the car and said, 'I won't stop if you don't mind.' Quickly he handed Inga her valise. 'I'd sooner be at my digs. I feel a bit upset.'

'What about me?' said Inga, with tears in her eyes.

He got back into his car without another word and drove off.

With heavy heart she unlocked the front door and went upstairs to her flat. Then she flopped down on the bed. Her breasts felt swollen from the heat and trouble of the day. And no sooner was she lying down than she had to get up again to go for a wee. Her period was very late but that couldn't mean anything surely? Scott had always taken care of things except for that very first time which was over two months ago and she'd had a period as usual last month – though it had been scantier than usual.

After a while she got up from her bed and began

to walk restlessly around the house. Surely she wasn't really *pregnant*? She had heard of morning sickness but it normally took place the moment one got up in the mornings and she'd never had any of that.

She wandered into the drawing room. The space was still there where the grand piano had once been. The piano was still at Whittleshaw. She had almost given up hope of ever seeing it again. Sidney Storell was nothing but a glamorous photograph in motor racing news these days.

Nally and Leroy had once been to see Lotto – as he was always called – performing down south at Brooklands. Leroy was becoming a fanatic spectator of the sport.

Sidney Storell's other claim to newspaper fame had been the birth of his son, Richard Stephen, which Inga had seen in a *Country Life* magazine.

For the whole of the following week Inga had two things niggling her brain. The first was would Scott get in touch with her about the BBC? And secondly, should she go to the doctor about her fears of pregnancy?

She decided to wait, as far as the doctor was concerned. She had never felt sick or been sick again. She had stared at herself nude, both sideways and frontward, in a large wardrobe mirror in one of the bedrooms and looked entirely normal. She began to think she had blown her sickness problem out of all proportion.

Then, two days before she was normally due to go and sing with Scott in their programme at the BBC, she received a typed letter.

Dear Miss Abbott,

It is with great sadness that I must inform you we are changing the format of our Wednesday programme.

Due to unforeseen circumstances the programme has been changed from *Rainbows of Song with Mr Scott Ivorson and Miss Inga Abbott*, and will now be known as *Rainbows of Song with Mr Scott Ivorson and Others*, accompanied by The Jazz Band Three.

Thanking you for your wonderful performances in the past and wishing you well for a new and exciting future. We are sure you will do well whatever field you choose.

The signature was large, flourishing, and unknown. It was someone called G.R.F.Trotworthy, Senior Producer.

Inga sat there completely stunned. 'Some other field' – like a horse being put out to grass. Her whole present musical life which had only just started and was gaining a modicum of success had been effectively blotted out. Automatically she had assumed that she and Scott would go from strength to strength with their singing duets. Sometimes recently she had even dreamed that she and Scott might marry. But now it had been snuffed out as easily as a candle, by this one letter.

After a few minutes she decided she had better get in touch with Scott straight away and take the letter with her. He wasn't on the phone. She knew where he lodged in Hale but had never actually been inside his rooms. There had always been excuses about his eccentric landlady and with Inga being so constantly alone at The Turrets, they had spent their spare time together there instead, still visiting Mr Protheroe's studio each week for piano accompaniment and singing practice.

It was a day of sunshine and showers as she set off to see Scott. She had written him a letter to take with her explaining what had happened in case he wasn't in and had said that she would be at Mr Protheroe's studio as usual the following day.

The Victorian house where he lodged was close to the church and had a long front garden with some daffodils blooming. It was well kept. Her heart began to thud as she pressed the bell in its circle of polished brass. She was treading into entirely unknown territory.

'Yes?' The woman's tone was sharp and suspicious as she stared at Inga from the narrowly opened door.

'I've called to see Mr Ivorson. I believe he has digs here?'

The woman shook her head. Already two young children had crept forward and were peering from behind the woman's grimy-looking overall. Their faces were smeared with jam and one was sucking a dummy. 'There's no Mr Ivorson here, and I certainly don't take lodgers.' She began to shut the door, but Inga persisted.

'I'm absolutely certain this is the address. Mr Ivorson once showed me the house.'

'Well, he showed you wrong then – didn't he? He's got you muddled up with Mrs Shearing next door but two.' The door closed with a sudden slam.

Inga walked away in puzzled silence. She was absolutely sure this was the place. She sighed. Maybe she *had* made a mistake, after all. She began to walk to next-door-but-two. It was a house with a large yew tree in the garden. The wrought-iron gate said 'Danefield' and in the window there was a neat card saying 'Mrs Shearing: Corsetière'.

Inga rang the bell disconsolately. She saw the net curtains in the front room move slightly and suddenly the front door opened. A plump lady in a well-tailored flowery frock with white collar and cuffs beamed towards her.

'Can I help you?'

'I'm trying to find where Mr Scott Ivorson lodges,' said Inga with growing hopelessness. 'I was sent here from number thirty-four. The lady there said you took lodgers. Yet I could swear it was number thirty-four Mr Ivorson showed me as the place where he was in digs.'

'It would be Mrs Cragstone you spoke to, deary,' said Mrs Shearing knowingly. 'She's never taken lodgers and neither do I. In fact there's no one round here who does. Are you quite sure you've got the right road? They wind round a lot. What does Mr Ivorson look like?'

Inga was slightly taken aback. 'Well . . . He's tall, he's a bit older than me and quite good-looking.' She hesitated, then added, '. . . and he has rather dark bushy eyebrows.'

Mrs Shearing's expression suddenly changed. She said slowly, 'The only person I know round here that might look in the least like that is Mrs Cragstone's husband.' Then she looked hard at Inga and said, 'Would you like to come inside for a cup of tea, dear?'

By now her eyes were bright with curiosity. 'You must have been trailing round for ages.'

Inga nodded and followed her into the peaceful, comfortably furnished sitting room with its buff and brown plush three-piece suite and the cream linen antimacassars. Mrs Shearing lifted a sheaf of papers with diagrams of corsets on them from a well-polished oak gate-leg table, placed them in a nearby box file and closed the lid. Then she rang a small brass crinoline-lady bell.

A young girl arrived in a pink cotton uniform and white apron. Mrs Shearing ordered tea and biscuits.

When the girl had gone she turned to Inga and said, 'Now, dear. Tell me all . . .'

'. . . And that's about it,' said Inga, two cups of tea and three chocolate biscuits later. 'Scott Ivorson is my duet partner for professional singing.' She had been careful not to mention the BBC. The conversation had been somewhat interspersed by mentions of the various people Mrs Shearing had as clientele, one of them being an opera singer whom she had fitted with the most perfect corslet guaranteed to expand threefold with every movement and breath of the body then spring back to sylph-like shape.

'And as light as swansdown, dear. None of that nasty jabbing or red, raw rucking; or one bosom bouncing out, without the other one. Before you go I'll give you all the fitting and price particulars.' Then, glancing at her gold wristlet watch, she said, 'Good gracious, is that the time? I'm expecting a brassiere consultation in another ten minutes.' She began to rush around, hunting for some corset information leaflets which she finally presented to Inga as she ushered her from room to hall. 'And as for that wearisome Cragstone family, my dear – perhaps it was just a coincidence that both she and Trevor used to be in the local choir before they got married. I always understood he was just a commercial traveller these days, but then I don't have very much to do with them.'

Mrs Shearing closed the door swiftly and as Inga walked to the front gate she felt it had all been a complete waste of her time.

No sooner had she reached the pavement than to her amazement and relief she actually saw Scott himself. He was walking along quite briskly and disappeared quite openly into next-door-but two: the Cragstones' house.

So she was right! He *was* lodging there and his landlady *was* eccentric or why would she have denied all knowledge of him?

Yet why had Mrs Shearing told Inga that no one kept lodgers round there? Perhaps Scott was in secret digs at number thirty-four and just kept very quiet about it. And perhaps he was a relative of the family, but felt too ashamed of it to say anything to Inga . . . It was all very odd.

Inga took out the letter which she had planned to leave at his digs in case he was out. At least she would be able to drop it through the letter box knowing it was the right address after all.

She retraced her steps past the daffodils in the long

front garden of thirty-four again. Quickly she put her note to him through the letter box and hurried away.

The following day she could hardly wait to get to her singing practice at Mr Protheroe's studio. She took with her the terrible letter about getting the sack from her programme with Scott.

Mr Protheroe was annoyed and perplexed. 'And what did you say happened? So you were sick? Not a very good thing, but surely not enough to warrant your removal from the programme? Incidentally, I have received a message from Scott only this morning saying he won't be here for our practice today. We shall just have to do the best we can without him.' Then Mr Protheroe muttered to himself, 'Perhaps one of his children is ill . . . they seem to suffer a lot from adenoids.'

Inga could not believe her ears. In all the time she had been attending the studio, Mr Protheroe had never mentioned anything about Scott having any children, or indeed anything at all about Scott's personal life.

'I think we'll have a rest from the singing,' said Mr Protheroe a bit later. 'I can see your heart isn't in it.' He patted her shoulder consolingly. 'Whatever you do, you must not be put off by this letter you've shown to me. Nor must you be upset over Scott still remaining with the programme – whatever the new form takes. Your own talent is far too good to let slip and I will do all in my power to keep on helping you to find suitable work.'

Just as she was going home Inga said, 'I took a note round to where Scott lives yesterday to tell him about the letter I've shown you.' She hesitated, then seeing the kind fatherly look on Mr Protheroe's face she said, 'It was all rather strange really. I always thought Scott was in digs, but when I first went to the house the person who opened the door said no one of that name lived there and she had no lodgers.'

'Didn't Scott ever tell you anything about himself?' Mr Protheroe gave a slight gasp of surprise and took his glasses off to polish them. He seemed embarrassed. 'You mean to say he never revealed that his real name is Trevor Cragstone?'

Inga shook her head in a flood of horrified bewilderment.

'His wife Valetta has a beautiful voice but it all came to nothing when she started having the children,' said Mr Protheroe sadly. 'She used to be one of my pupils too at one time. She and Trevor sang in the choir together.'

Inga felt herself going faint and sat down.

'He changed his name to Scott Ivorson on my advice, for his professional work,' said Mr Protheroe, 'but I assure you I had no idea he had kept you in the dark about it.'

By the time Inga left the studio that day, she felt that her adult singing career had met the same fate as Valetta's – in spite of Mr Protheroe sternly insisting that she should turn up again for her practice without fail next week.

'I can see how it is now for you with regard to Scott. I will arrange for you to come to me on your own on Wednesdays. We shall concentrate on opera. In that way you will still be singing on the day of your programme but in *my* studio, and with different aims.' A slight twinkle came to his eyes. 'In the long run, I think it will prove more useful and I promise I shall never ban you if you are sick.'

At first Mr Protheroe's words had cheered her, but on the way back to The Turrets she suddenly thought of Valetta again and the small children with faces covered in jam. What a traitor Scott had been – both to her and to his wife.

She felt quite ill when she was back in the large empty house alone. Never again would there be the regular sessions of love; never the innocent anticipation of marriage; no longer were there confident hopes of their singing duets bringing joy to themselves and others; no longer his quiet silence and his cheerful handsome face. It had all become a marred unwelcome, selfish trick, and she never wanted to see him again.

The only thing she refused to think of at all was whether or not she could be pregnant . . .

20

SECOND BEST

In the summer of 1935 Sidney Storell was away receiving yet another motor racing accolade abroad. Champagne and beautiful women were the story of his life for millions of newspaper readers.

His mother, Katrin, had read of him only this morning. She had passed quickly from his photograph to another page. Already his racing obsession had caused deep clefts in family fortunes. Money had dwindled away from the Whittleshaw estates to feed his desires to invent better and better prototypes of racing car, and each one cost the earth. As a result, hundreds of acres from the Whittleshaw estate had already been sold to shore up the rushing drain.

It was almost the end of July.

Inga's grand piano was resting diagonally in the knot gardens on the terraces of Whittleshaw Hall for all the world to see. It had been placed there yesterday by the servants – instructed by Lydia. Its legs were digging into all the small formal beds of rosemary and thrift.

Another month passed and, as a sort of protest, Katrin placed a thick doormat on top of the piano surmounted by a shallow wooden tub of violet and pink bellflowers. Her small grandson Richard was by her side.

'Nan-ma' lifted him up, kissed him and sat him next to the bellflowers. 'Sit very, very still my little sugarbuttikins whilst Nan-ma takes your photograph . . .'

Katrin had just lifted him back to the ground again when Lydia arrived to find out what he was doing. She glared at the flowers. 'That doormat will take away all the surface from the lid,' she said icily. 'So if Lotto wants to preserve the wretched thing he'd better get it away from here as soon as possible before I either attack it with an axe or send the owner a demand for two years' back rent for storage.'

She gave Katrin a tight, bitter smile. 'You know full well why I put it outside in the first place, Katrin. It's because I'm tired of being second best in Sidney's life. This place has become no more than an expendable source of finance for him alone and all his foibles. Sometimes it terrifies me.'

'It terrifies me, too,' said Katrin quietly.

'The papers are full of him again,' said Lydia grimly. 'Another sordid tale about him and Dolores Zeig the fashion model.' She looked across at the piano. 'And as for *that*! It has haunted me since I got married. I'm telling you right now, Katrin, that as soon as he comes home I shall be asking for a divorce.'

Katrin went pale. 'There'll be a terrible lot involved,

Lydia. It's never easy, even with evidence of adultery. You're not just divorcing a man – you'll be divorcing all this . . .' She spread out her arms to the house and its land. 'But worst of all, you'll be denying yourself and your own son your rightful places.'

'Denying myself and my son?' Lydia shook her head. 'Whatever the law says, Katrin, wherever I go, my son will go. I'm a rich woman in my own right, and I'll see it stays that way for the sake of myself and Richard.'

They both looked across to the child. He was standing out of earshot with his chubby arm resting playfully against the fur of one of the family's clumber spaniels.

'If Sidney goes on in the way he's doing now, there'll be no Whittleshaw Hall left for any of us. It's been his fault all along.'

Katrin became agitated. 'You're quite wrong, Lydia. The situation will never reach that state.' Her voice quivered with fear. Her prime position was gone, she thought miserably. She counted for nothing. What on earth was this younger generation coming to? Her only son and his wife – intelligent, well-educated, cultured. Two people with everything before them, including a healthy, male heir for the family heritage. All to be ignored and cast aside for the turmoil of divorce which would be a disruption of so many lives – including her grandchild's.

'Surely you could come to some other agreement rather than the finality of divorce?' Katrin stared at her in anguish. 'Even if you no longer love each other, you could come to some private settlement?'

'Looking back, I don't think we ever did love each other,' said Lydia bleakly. 'Marrying Lotto was the stupidest thing I ever did. But it didn't seem like that at the time.'

Katrin looked at her pleadingly. 'And divorcing him might become the stupidest thing you ever did – if you ever look back later.'

Lydia turned away. Her mother-in-law was so naïve, she thought. One might even call her *stupid* . . . Lydia took hold of Richard's hand and hurried away with him. As she went she called, 'There could be ashes of a bonfire still glowing in that knot garden tomorrow.'

Katrin knew she meant it. In a panic she began to try and recall exactly who the piano belonged to. Her only vague hope was to get in touch with Mabel Spinks who had always supported their musical evenings which Katrin still did her best to persist with.

She hurried back to the house in a fever of quickening panic to find Mabel's telephone number. As she did so she was surprised to see a telegraph boy arriving with a telegram which he gave to her. She opened the envelope nervously and read it quickly. The boy stood there in his dark blue uniform, waiting to see if a reply was required. She shook her head.

The telegram was from Sidney. Katrin was filled with a mixture of shock and disbelief. He would be home in three hours' time. BACK IN AMBULANCE. EVERYTHING FINE. SIDNEY.' it said.

The misery in her heart rose even further.

Sidney hadn't mentioned in the telegram that the fashion model Dolores Zeig was accompanying him home in the private ambulance.

His car had crashed on a racing circuit and one of his legs was in plaster and completely done for, but he had demanded to be brought back home almost immediately. He thanked God it was only his leg. The hazards of motor racing had produced terrible injuries to many drivers he'd known.

Dolores had insisted on looking after him for the journey back. 'But once we're safely at your place, Lotto, I'll go back to London.' She had assured him she would return to London the following day. Her diary was packed with work, and she couldn't afford to have her own career disrupted.

Her pencil-thin good looks and her mass of short dark curls, together with her huge green eyes with their curled eyelashes were her fortune. Her exercise was obtained by wriggling in and out of awkward clothes and twisting her limbs into unusual poses. She was already married to a photographer who was away in Africa. She and Lotto were just good friends.

'Thank goodness you're all in one piece,' exclaimed Katrin when he arrived. Katrin shook her head in wonder and smiled with relief. The car he had been driving was a complete write-off. He'd been very lucky . . .

'Lydia and Richard have gone over to Belhurst.' She glanced surreptitiously towards Dolores who was standing by the side of Sidney's wheelchair. She recognised her straight away from magazine photographs, and wondered what the effect would be on Lydia when she returned. One thing was certain: this other woman was just another nail in her son's coffin.

'Dolores has to get back tomorrow,' said Sidney.

Katrin nodded and smiled at her. 'I'll show you up to your room.'

Whilst Dolores was upstairs Katrin purposely wheeled Sidney towards the terrace. 'I'll get a bed made up for you downstairs in the summer room, and I'll tell Dr Frobisher you've arrived back.'

A slightly ashamed expression swept over her face. 'I also want to show you what Lydia's done with that grand piano – so that you'll be forewarned. She's threatening to set it on fire if it isn't removed very quickly. I think she means it.'

There was an uneasy silence as they both stared towards it. A picture of Inga suddenly welled up in Sidney's mind. What would she be up to now? Yes, he would most certainly have to return it – but where to? He knew the piano had always been a thorn in Lydia's flesh. It would be a tragedy if anything serious happened to it.

He frowned and looked at Katrin. 'Is there any hope that the Spinkses might know where to send it? Didn't you once say they were somehow linked up with Miss Abbott who owns it?' His voice was vague and tired. 'I think Miss Abbott's cousin is married to Mabel Spinks's great-nephew or something.'

His mother brightened. 'Of course, Nally and Leroy! Nally is becoming quite a treasure these days, helping with tickets for our music.'

Sidney nodded. The ramifications of all that were only of passing interest. The network of local gossip was lost on him these days. In the past, before he was married, he'd always enjoyed helping to organise

Katrin's occasional musical interludes at Whittleshaw Hall.

When Lydia got back from her parents' home at Belhurst and saw both Sidney and Dolores it was the final straw. They all stared at each other dumbly. There was absolutely no communication. Lydia turned her back on them.

She retired to an entirely different part of the house with Richard, telling Katrin she would stay there until Dolores had gone. But she didn't mean exactly that . . .

Already her rage was so formidable that another plan had already formed in her mind.

When she put Richard to bed that night she dressed him in his socks, a thick vest and his dressing gown. She explained to him that when he'd had a bit of sleep they would be going to see Gran and Grandad at Belhurst. Then she read him a story and lay down with him until he fell asleep.

She willed herself to wake at three a.m., helped by the distant chimes of a church clock. She didn't set an alarm clock; she wanted Richard to stay asleep for as long as possible. Then, dressed in cotton twill trousers, canvas deck shoes and an old high-necked dark sweater, she carried a basket of straw and paraffin-soaked rags to the piano on the terrace. She placed the wicker basket underneath the piano, lit a match, threw it into the basket, and vanished into the darkness.

It was a calm, beautiful night. She didn't need to turn back. She was already aware of the lightening sky behind her and the smell of the paraffin as the straw and basket burnt. Flames began to lick the piano; sparks began to fly in a welter of crackles and burning veneer. The grand piano fell sadly and reluctantly to its knees, one leg at a time.

By the time the blaze was at full force and the whole of Whittleshaw was out of bed, Lydia was in her small Austin Seven and had driven almost back to Belhurst with Richard.

It was now past four in the morning and in her own family home some of the servants were already up as she settled herself and her son back to sleep in one of the spare bedrooms.

She slept like a log.

'Obviously I can't go back and leave you with all this mess to cope with,' said Dolores the next day to Sidney, as a photographer and a local journalist arrived. 'I'll just have to let them know in London that I'm staying for another few days.'

Sidney Storell nodded with relief and smiled. 'You're a brick, Dolly. What would I have done without you?' He stared at her wondrously for a few seconds. Even early in the mornings she was beautiful. She would brighten any man's life . . .

The first Inga knew of any of it was an urgent call on the phone from Nally. 'Do you mean to say you haven't seen the local papers?' exclaimed Nally. 'It was burnt to a cinder in the knot gardens on the terrace. Police are regarding it as suspicious. Someone said it was an attempt to burn down the Hall but it was denied. Sidney Storell says it's all been blown up out of all proportion.

Katrin Storell rang up Mabel today to find out your address.'

Inga was stunned.

'Are you still there?'

'Yes. It's just that I can't believe my own bad luck. All the time for nearly two years now I've been hoping and hoping I'd eventually find somewhere of my own to keep it. And now it's fit for nothing but an urn full of ashes on a mantelpiece.'

'Oh, Inga . . .' Nally's voice overflowed with genuine grief. 'Whatever can I say? Whatever can I do? Ever since you had that awful—' Nally didn't dare to mention the actual word 'miscarrriage' in case by some terrible mischance it was heard by someone else on the telephone wires. '—upset, I've kept worrying about you. To think you suffered with all *that* completely alone and in secret. Forever by yourself in that huge rambling house, and now to have all this trouble.'

'It was better like that,' said Inga, thinking about her miscarriage. 'It's just something I want to forget. I never expected it to happen. But at least it was early on, and no one knew – except you, later on.'

She sighed heavily as she replaced the receiver. Having the miscarriage had been the most awful time of her life, she thought. There had been no dignity, no love, no friends. She had suffered the gruesome agony entirely alone – thankful at the time that it had happened here at home, in private.

When it was all over, she had felt heavy and dead as she walked back to her bed to lie down. Nothing more had happened or ever did happen. After a week she started to feel normal again, and her next period arrived on time. For a while she brooded on what it would have been like with her own baby to look after, and she wept for it. But when she thought of the true circumstances of Scott Ivorson and his double life she felt relieved that fate had made it this way instead. A few weeks later, when she felt she could come to terms with it all, she mentioned it to Nally.

Later in the day Inga was surprised to receive a phone call from Sidney Storell. She recognised his voice immediately.

'I expect you will know why I'm ringing?'

'Is it the piano?' She spoke the words timorously, wondering what fate would deal out next.

She heard him hesitate, then he said, 'Can I come round and see you this afternoon? I shan't stay long . . .'

She was tongue-tied, then she took a deep gloom-ridden breath. 'Yes.'

'About two-thirty?'

'Yes.' She put down the receiver and placed her hands to her face desolately.

What other answer was there? Nothing now could ever bring back that one true thread from her childhood – Margot's piano. That one real token of her grandmother's hopes and her only personal possession of any true worth.

These days, although she was still continuing with her opera lessons with Mr Protheroe, her professional engagements were few and far between. And as if that wasn't enough there had been ominous hints about changes for The Turrets.

Only yesterday she had received a letter from her cousin Sybil warning her that Aunt Yvonne and Aunt Petunia were now united with the rest of the family in wanting to sell The Turrets altogether and divide the money between them all.

'. . . They seem to think they may get thousands for it,' Sybil had explained.

Inga had screwed the letter up, then uscrewed it again and smoothed it out to put in the desk drawer.

These days there was a lot of larger, empty property for sale. Some of it, hidden away behind unkempt drives and overgrown laurels, was completely derelict. Almost forgotten. People could no longer afford the upkeep of the houses and the cost of servants. Everyone with a bank balance wanted smaller, easily run, cheap modern places.

But Inga herself wasn't in the running for either. If by some chance The Turrets was sold, it would just mean she'd be worse off than ever and back to the story of her life: hunting for rented accommodation.

Slightly before two-thirty that afternoon, Inga looked from one of the bedroom windows and saw a huge black Bentley purring along the crackling gravel and pulling up at the front door. Then she saw a wonderfully slim, smart, attractive girl get out and start to bring out a wheelchair. Whatever was happening?

Inga almost flew downstairs to open the door. She was just in time to see Sidney Storell, with his leg in plaster, easing himself into the chair. His leg was resting on a special raised extension to the chair.

Deftly, the girl manoeuvred the wheelchair into the hall. She turned and smiled at Inga. 'That's the first hurdle done. Where do we go next?'

Inga led them to the drawing room.

'That space'll be fine,' said Dolores moving the chair to where the grand piano had once been. Then she said, 'I daresay you'll have quite a lot to discuss so I'll leave you to it for a bit and call back later.'

Sidney nodded gratefully and smiled at them both. 'Thanks, Dolly. Give us about an hour?'

Inga began to cheer up. He looked towards her and she nodded politely. But although she was glad to see him she was now in a panic. How on earth would she be able to talk to a man confined to a wheelchair for a whole hour? It was a situation she had never come across before.

'I'm afraid I can't offer you anything to drink except ginger pop or milk or tea.'

The choice seemed to amuse him. 'How about the ginger beer? I haven't had any of that for years.' They both began to smile at each other as she hurried away to get some.

She came back with a large greenish glass bottle of local brew. He stretched forward from his wheelchair to help her unfasten the top with its glass ball stopper. He watched as she poured it into the glasses on a small table next to them. She handed him his glass. Unintentionally and almost imperceptibly their fingers touched. His were long and sunburned, and

310

properly manicured. Her own were small and rather uncared for.

'I expect I'd better get down to the real reason for coming here to see you,' he said. 'I expect you'll know the worst already?'

She nodded. 'My cousin Nally told me. It was quite a shock. I expect it must have been some terrible accident?' She tried to make a joke of it and said nervously, 'Unless you'd got so fed up of storing it for me that you decided to get rid of it for good . . .'

He ignored the remark. 'The fact is there's been a bit of a general upheaval and your piano was only part of it. My coming home in this state hasn't helped matters. The least I can do at present is to offer you the cost of your piano. I realise that it can't in any way compensate for what the loss must really mean to you – but at least it might help towards getting another one.'

She didn't know what to say. Even if she accepted his offer in order to get another one, where on earth would she keep it? It was the same old problem going round and round. There was one sure answer: there would never be a temporary home for another one at Whittleshaw Hall again.

Then, as if he'd read her mind, he said, 'I gather from your cousin you are still hoping to find a permanent place of your own?'

She nodded. She began to wish his lady friend would come back for him. They just seemed to have nothing to say to each other.

'Are you still doing your singing?'

'Yes, I am, but I've changed to opera. I practise every

week at Mr Protheroe's studio, but there hasn't been much work up to now.'

'Have you ever thought of coming to sing at Whittleshaw?'

His words astounded her.

'Never . . .' she felt herself becoming flustered. 'Not because I wouldn't like to. I just thought that it was . . . well . . . Out of my plane. Perhaps a bit too high-flown for my experience.'

'Surely not? You have a wonderful voice and if you are training in opera singing it could be an ideal start. At least you'd be amongst friends.' Then he added with a streak of ironic humour, 'Well – one friend anyway. One totally incapacitated cripple.'

The hour flew until Dolores was due to return. They had totally warmed to each other, as he described his racing life, pinpointing all the funniest and most exciting episodes.

'And now,' he said calmly, 'I've been assured by the medics that it will all have to end. You need full use of all your limbs to be a top racing man. He looked at his leg. 'It's going to take some time to repair this old peg properly, and time waits for no one in the motor racing world.'

'Whatever will you do?' She stared at him thoughtfully.

'No need to look so worried.' His hand grasped hers gently. 'I shall keep on designing. In fact, strangely enough, just before this happened an old pal of mine had asked me if I'd ever considered switching to designing aeroplanes. There seems to be a need developing. I shan't fade away too much. My mother will bless me for being back at home and not dribbling away all the family estate funds.' He spoke lightly, but his eyes were serious.

Inga noticed that he never mentioned his wife Lydia nor his child at all.

When they had gone at last, Inga sat on her own in the drawing room, going over it all. Would Miss Zeig go back to London or stay longer at Whittleshaw? And if she did, Inga wondered, how would she get on with Lydia?

It was good to know the Whittleshaw concerts were still continuing, and that she might even have a chance to take part in them.

In vain, for weeks and weeks after that, Inga waited to hear from Sidney Storell again. But there was a complete blank. Then, in November, shortly after her twenty-second birthday, she received a cheque for a hundred pounds signed by Katrin Storell. Inside its crested envelope was a small white visiting card with the words 'Towards a new piano'.

The other letter in the same post was written in neat, firm writing on pale buff notepaper. It informed her that The Turrets was in the process of being successfully sold and advised her to seek new accommodation immediately.

21

MOONLIGHT AND ROSES

'Why don't you come and live here for a while?' said Annie Murdoch to Inga.

Inga had called in for news of Ralphie. These days, at just fifteen, he was a law unto himself. He had fulfilled his dead mother's dreams and had done well educationally. But his mind wasn't set on staying in college too long. Already he was planning to leave after his matriculation exams and was hoping to try and get a job in a local newspaper office, training to be a journalist.

'I'm completely alone these days,' said Annie. 'Florrie has just gone to live at Chorlton-cum-Hardy. She's been married three months. Our Dennis is now a cinema manager in Stretford and lives there. It's all working out quite well.'

Annie beamed at Inga. She hadn't aged much. She had one of those fresh, fair, rather delicate faces and was eternally thin. 'Hasn't it been an awful February though?' she said, suddenly becoming serious. 'Everything seems to be bad news, except those Olympic Games in Germany. I hope we win something. But when you read in the papers what's going on over there it sounds dreadful.' She looked at Inga helplessly. 'I've never got over reading about a film of ours being banned over there because its star and director were Jewish.' She frowned doubtfully. 'There's all sorts of war trouble going on abroad, isn't there? P'raps poor old King George the Fifth just died at the right time. He had his share in nineteen-fourteen. That dictator Hitler is goose-stepping everywhere. I hope we never gets involved in any of it in this country.'

Over two months afterwards, in early May, the sale of The Turrets was complete and the Abbott women were relishing the proceeds. Inga and the other grandchildren received nothing, but Nally had arranged to store all Inga's dwindling bits of furniture.

Every time Inga moved she decided to throw away something. 'Each time I weigh up all my worldly scraps, Nally, and I see them getting more faded and useless. All I ever dream of is getting a place of my own and starting to furnish it completely from scratch.'

Nally nodded sympathetically then she said, 'I wonder if that's how Sidney Storell will feel when they sell Whittleshaw Hall? I heard about it through the grapevine only yesterday. They're supposed to be selling it lock stock and barrel to an aviation manufacturing company. But for goodness sake don't say anything or let on that I told you. Rumour has it that it's going to be turned into an aeroplane design place and that Lotto is going to work for them and find himself somewhere else to live. I was told the Storells are getting a fortune for it which is being divided between himself and Lydia, with a special settlement for Richard when he comes of age.'

Inga was amazed. She hadn't seen or heard anything of Sidney Storell since the day he came round to The Turrets in his wheelchair.

Then, only a couple of weeks later, when she was well settled in at Annie's and was just coming away from her usual weekly singing practice with Mr Protheroe in Bowden, she bumped into him. He was walking fairly slowly with a stick. The weather was so hot and sunny that they almost peered at each other through its dazzle, then they both smiled.

He looked thinner and his hair was slightly longer and more loosely curling. He was wearing grey flannels, a faded striped merino blazer with a button missing, and an open-necked cream silk shirt.

'Hello there.'

'Hello.' Hastily, so as not to leave a shy gap, she said, 'You'll be pleased to know I'm still practising my opera . . .' She put her hand up towards her small straw hat. She was stuck for anything else to say.

To him, at that moment, she looked a picture of sunlit radiance, with her slim blue and white crepe polka-dot frock with a taffeta bow on its draped collar; her sun-kissed bare arms and her short white cotton gloves, and her high-heeled glossy white sandals. The sight of her had suddenly brightened his complicated life. So much so that in the next breath he said, 'I'm just doing a casual bit of house hunting. We'll be holding our final musical evening at Whittleshaw in June. Do you think you'll be there?'

She shook her head slowly. 'It's nice of you to ask – but—'

'As a singer, I mean. As a performer. We're having a programme of favourite well-known arias. Do you fancy coming to sing "One Fine Day" from *Madam Butterfly*?' She gasped, but he went on, 'Are you doing much this minute? Would you like to come back with me to Whittleshaw to discuss it? I'll drive you back home afterwards?' His eyes fixed her with passionate intensity.

'I just don't know what to say except yes. I never do much these days except hunt eternally for some sort of permanent job to keep me going.'

'We're both hunters by the sound of it.' He said it as if he was glad. 'Shall we have a snack before I fetch the car?'

She nodded her head. She was curious to see inside Whittleshaw again, especially after what Nally had told her.

On the way back there Sidney Storell described the situation just as Nally had. 'There've been great changes recently. I'm no longer motor racing. In March I was down at Eastleigh Aerodrome in Southampton to look at the new Vickers "Spitfire 1". It has a Rolls-Royce "Merlin" engine. It's going to be the Royal Air Force's most powerful weapon.'

Then he said quietly, 'I expect someone will have already told you that my wife and I have parted? Our child Richard is with her. The divorce will soon be finalised. After this last concert Whittleshaw will be a completely different place, geared to aircraft design, but I shall still be working there. My mother has just gone back to live permanently in France – even though it seems rather foolish in today's unsettled political climate. And my two younger sisters have already settled down in London to work in publishing.'

She was quite embarrassed by his sudden revealing of personal details.

Inside the house, there were large packing cases about, and much of the furniture was hidden under huge white dustsheets. Most of the paintings had been removed from the walls.

Whilst they were there arranging her placing in the final concert programme at Whittleshaw, he said, 'Would you like to come with me to Glyndebourne next year? To John Christie's place near Lewes in Sussex. He arranges an opera festival there every year now. There's plenty of Mozart.'

She didn't know how to answer but he seemed unaware of it.

By the time he had returned her to Annie's in Blossom Street Inga's whole being was in a whirl. What was happening? It was almost as if Sidney Storell were trying to woo her, and yet in all honesty she had no experience of being properly wooed – so how could she really know? Her sad affair with Scott Ivorson had never caused such strong and immediate feelings within her.

That night, before she fell asleep, all the events of that day were still in her mind and had become strangely soothing.

'You were absolutely marvellous at the Whittleshaw concert,' exclaimed Nally excitedly the day after it had all taken place. 'Within a few seconds of your opening solo an intangible thread was there between you and the audience. Everyone remarked on it. Quite frankly, Inga, according to Lotto it was the best rendering of that song they've ever had, including that first *Madam Butterfly* we were at all those years ago.'

They smiled at each other affectionately. Inga was overwhelmed with shy embarrassment at the welter of praise.

The following week Sidney Storell sent her a bunch of deep red, wonderfully scented roses to Blossom Street, and a letter suggesting they should meet again. '. . . I have found myself a decent flat at last in Bowdon, not far from Mr Protheroe's place. Would you like to come round one day after one of your opera sessions?' He had written his telephone number on the note for her to ring him and signed it 'Sidney'.

The following week he met her and she went back to his flat with him. They walked in the sunshine in the direction of Dunham Park. The red brick mansion along the tree-lined road was divided into two private flats. It had a resident married couple who acted as caretakers and the house was larger by far than The

Turrets. There were well-kept gardens which included a miniature lake.

Sidney's flat was very modern inside. There was a small library with light oak-panelled walls. Scale models of racing cars rested in mirrored alcoves. The main living room was furnished with emerald green leather upholstery and stainless-steel tubular chairs. There were motor racing trophies on the walls and on one wall adjacent to the large windows was a poster-like photograph of the old Brooklands racing circuit. In a corner of the room was an impressive light oak Pye radiogram and close to it were some photographs, including some of his son Richard.

He had prepared a salad meal with a platter of cold meat already waiting on the table in the dining room. With a strange solemn nervousness, Sidney asked Inga if she would care for some champagne and she accepted.

As they sipped it he said, 'I was wondering if you would like me to help you at all with your singing engagements? I know from talking to others in opera that it helps a lot to have an official representative to work behind the scenes. I expect you'll know all that really – from your own childhood and how your grandmother virtually acted as your manager.'

He refilled her champagne glass. She looked at his earnest face dreamily and nodded. She could hardly believe she was actually here with him. It was all such an entire change from Whittleshaw and all its old-fashioned tradition.

When they had finished their meal she helped him to wash up. And then something awful happened. Perhaps it was carelessness, or perhaps it was the wine, but a beautiful gold-edged plate decorated with fruit fell from her linen tea towel and crashed on to the tiled floor in the kitchen. Tears of remorse came to her eyes as she hastily blinked to try and hide them.

He rushed to get a dustpan and brush. 'It's nothing, really. Please don't be upset.' Hastily he tipped the remnants in the kitchen bin. 'Come and sit down and listen to some music.'

But now she was even more upset as the floodgates opened. It was as if years of pent-up, lonely strain and tension had formed a waterfall, as tears cascaded down her cheeks. 'I'm not *really* upset,' she protested. 'I think it was just the shock of it dropping, and the noise it made, and the shame of such a beautiful plate being broken.'

They sat down on the green leather couch and he put his arm round her. 'If you're not *really* upset, you're a damned good actress.'

She began to laugh. Then suddenly she relaxed and he relaxed and he kissed her.

'I never really finished the bit about helping the famous new opera singer,' he said. 'I was going to end up asking her to marry me.'

By the end of the evening she had accepted his proposal to marry when his divorce came through.

Just as he was kissing her goodnight in Blossom Street that evening he said longingly, 'Why not come and live with me now? What is there to stop us?'

By now she had regained her composure completely. She felt more confident than she could ever remember.

'I will be your wife and your mistress in marriage, but never the mistress first, Sidney Storell. Never, never that.'

He nodded slowly. 'Perhaps you're right,' he said.

As she lay in bed that night, alone in Annie's house in Blossom Street, oh how she longed to have fallen into his arms and agreed to going back to Bowdon with him and live in unmarried bliss. But deep down she knew it would never work. They were both too formal when it came to true love; they were too steeped in their hearts with how it should really be. And for both of them, it was to be their second chance.

She lay there wondering if they would have a baby when they married. If they did, her child would have a 'hearth-brother', just as she had Ralphie. She smiled.

It was a warm night and she decided to get up and open the window. There was a full moon and in the distance there was a man singing 'Moonlight and Roses' along the street at the top of his voice. Someone else crashed open their window and told him to shut his bloody row but he took no notice.

Inga lay back between the sheets. She closed her eyes blissfully and hummed the music after him, falling into complete, peaceful sleep.

EPILOGUE

1951

It was Festival of Britain year. The Festival was in May in London – a gesture of hope to a brighter future. Nearly thirty acres of derelict bomb-damaged London had been transformed into fantasy and fun as thousands wandered around it good naturedly from all parts of Britain.

Inga and Sidney Storell had been to the festival with their thirteen-year-old daughter, and now they were back in Manchester again, where much bomb damage mixed with slum clearance still remained. They were now living in Prestbury.

Sidney was in his forties now, and Inga was thirty-seven and blooming.

It was now autumn and the red gold of fallen leaves against a clear turquoise blue sky imbued perfect peace.

Inga and Daphne had just come from Dr Meldrum's

music studio in Bowdon. It was the same one used in the past, before the war, when it had belonged to Mr Protheroe.

Mother and daughter were very much alike in build. Both hatless, Inga wore a calf-length two-piece pink and grey wool woven suit with satin edging and Daphne – with distinct looks of Great-Grandmother Abbott intermixed with a touch of Storell – wore a long black coat with a velvet collar.

A few minutes previously Inga had looked expectantly towards Dr Meldrum at the end of her interview with him. She had been waiting in his studio for his verdict whilst Daphne sat meekly outside in his small office.

At first he had turned away from Inga a trifle sadly. Then he said in undertones, 'Your daughter's voice is charming, but it's very slight at present. I doubt if she will ever become an opera singer like you.'

Inga was silent when she came from the room.

'What did he say?' pressed Daphne as they got in the car.

'Nothing much. Come on, let's go into Manchester and I'll treat you.'

All the way into town Daphne stared at her pleadingly with soulful eyes. 'But did you actually *tell* him I want to be an opera singer like you? Did you make it *quite plain*?'

Inga nodded.

'What did he *say*?' The nagging continued all the way to St Anne's Square.

'There's a long way to go in a singing life, my darling,' said Inga evasively.

'But I *want* to be one!'

'It's a case of the type of voice you have,' said Inga quietly. 'A question of what sort of vocal cords you were given. Some have rather strong voices and others are soft and quiet. On the other hand, a loud voice means nothing on its own and neither does a very quiet little voice.'

Daphne bristled. 'Surely he didn't say I'd got a quiet *little* voice, Mother? Surely he never said that? You know it's not true. You know it isn't.' Daphne's tones grew louder and louder.

Inga could hear the harsh, unleashed chords trembling in her own brain. 'Sh . . . sh . . . For goodness' sake. Of course he didn't *quite* say that. It was just my way of putting it. Just to keep you from plunging into something you might regret . . .'

'Have *you* regretted it, Mother?' Daphne glanced towards her truculently. .

'No, but . . .' Inga sighed with controlled impatience. 'I was compelled into it in a way by my Grandmother Abbott when I was very, very young. But I don't believe in forcing people. Your voice is sweeter than mine, it's gentler.' Inga began to drive the car extra slowly.'

'*Sweeeter*? *Gentler*?!' bellowed Daphne.

The car window was open and passers by stared towards them.

'What a hellish loud voice!' said a young man in a posh bowler hat. 'It sounded like an animal in pain.'

His pal, who was hatless and wearing a fawn, belted Burberry raincoat with a reporter's notebook in his pocket, smiled. Ralphie Trent had recognised the small red MG immediately. He stared ahead towards the town hall. 'They probably think they're both opera singers,' he murmured with a rather proud, humorous sigh.

PILLGWENLLY 21/2/7